EverQuest®

The Blood Red Harp

Other titles in the exciting series

EverQuest: The Rogue's Hour

EverQuest: Ocean of Tears

EverQuest: Truth and Steel

EverQuest®

The Blood Red Harp

Elaine Cunningham

SOE®
Sony Online Entertainment

cds
Books
New York

Printed in the United States of America.

For information and inquiries, please contact:
CDS Books, 387 Park Avenue South
12th floor
New York, NY 10016
1-800-343-4499

Library of Congress Cataloging-in-Publication Data

Cunningham, Elaine, 1957-
EverQuest : The blood red harp / Elaine Cunningham.
p. cm.
This novel is a spinoff of the EverQuest multiplayer role playing game.
ISBN-13: 978-1-59315-224-6 (pbk.)
ISBN-10: 1-59315-224-8 (pbk.)
I. Title. II. Title: Blood red harp.

PS3553.U472E94 2007
813'.54—dc22

2006019033

Designed by Holly Johnson

DEDICATION

ANY STORY SET IN A SHARED WORLD OWES AN enormous debt to that which has come before. The world of Norrath is an incredibly large, well detailed setting, and the list of people who have made it what it is would probably be as long as the story that follows. In my experience with EverQuest, however, several people stood above the throng. R. A. Salvatore suggested the idea of writing EverQuest fiction, encouraged me to write about an elven bard, and was exceptionally encouraging and supportive throughout the writing process. Thanks again, Bob. Thanks also to Veronica Chapman for her keen editorial eye and extraordinary patience during the early stages, to the folks at Sony who did the continuity reviews, and to the copyeditors and proofreaders at Perseus who batted clean-up. The game design team at Sword & Sorcery did a terrific job converting the online game to a pen and paper RPG, and these products were, collectively, my main resource outside of the game itself. Another important source was the expertise of EQ gamers, as shared on fan-created Web sites. I owe a particular debt of appreciation to EQ Diva, who has put together what I consider to be the best cyberspace collection of information about EverQuest bards.

But without a certain talented gamer, best known in cyberspace as Don Signo, I couldn't have written this book. Without (stealing) his high-level characters, I wouldn't have been able to walk with impunity across so much of Faydwer. He spent a considerable amount of time doing in-game research and answering questions. Thanks for all your help, Sean. This one's for you.

This book is also dedicated to the memory and magic of Keith Parkinson, whose vibrant artwork first drew me to EverQuest.

EverQuest®

The Blood Red Harp

PRELUDE

THE NECROMANCER STALKED FROM THE SILENT chamber, his black and scarlet robes swirling around him. Frustration twisted his face, and his pale blue eyes, though deeply shadowed by the cowl of his cloak, burned like azure flame. Behind him, one of the finest bards in all of Faydwer knelt in a pool of her own blood. Tears of pain and despair coursed down her cheeks as she stared at the twisted, broken things her hands had become.

"Is this the best you could find?" the necromancer snarled at the man waiting in the main hall.

His visitor, a tall, swaggering fellow whose face had probably been considered boyishly handsome a few years back, shrugged off the reproof and glanced toward the weeping bard. Still lovely despite her many hurts, she was both slender and curvy in the lithesome manner common to half elves. Her fair skin and golden hair suggested a high elf parent, rather than one of forest folk. She was, in short, an unusual and elegant ruin. The rogue's gaze lingered for a moment, more in admiration than regret.

"She came highly recommended. They say the strings of any instrument she touches turn to gold."

"Only if the instrument is a lute. A *lute!* That is of no use to me."

A crooked grin touched the older man's face, recalling the roguish charm that was still his stock in trade. "Well, imagine *my* disappointment. I was counting on the wench to perform that bit of alchemy with the strings, as I find myself rather coin-short at the moment."

"You'll be paid," the necromancer said coldly, "when you bring me what I need."

The man folded his arms and leaned back against the wall, taking care to avoid the grinning skulls set into small alcoves around the hall. He had recently learned, much to his sorrow, to take no chances where necromancers were concerned.

"We would both stand a better chance of success if you told me what you wanted, and why."

A nasty leer twisted the necromancer's lips. "Still trying to pick my pockets, are you?"

For just a moment, the rogue's easy smile changed into something ugly and bitter. He quickly covered his reaction and lifted one shoulder in an insouciant shrug.

"A necromancer's secrets aren't every man's idea of treasure, but yes, I know a few people who'd pay for them. Believe me, I'd sell you out in a heartbeat, if only I could. If there's anything I hate more than being coin-short, it's being so . . . *trustworthy.*" His shudder was only half feigned.

"Ah, yes," the necromancer said blandly. He lifted one long-fingered hand to toy with the silver medallion pinned to his tunic. "Loyalty charms are useful little spells, if somewhat outside my specialty."

"Then *use* it and be done!" the rogue snapped. "Tell me why you need a bard, and I'll find one tailor-made to the purpose. But I want your oath that once this job is finished, so are we."

The necromancer settled down on a padded bench and draped one arm over its high back. The movement caused the hood of his short cloak to drop away, revealing long black locks that had been gathered into numerous small braids, each fastened at the end with what appeared to be a finger bone.

"I will release you from the charm spell upon the bard's *success,*" the necromancer countered. "That should spur you to greater efforts and a more discerning choice. In addition, you shall have twice your usual fee."

"Twice the money, eh? What befalls me if this bard fails?"

"Let's not contemplate that possibility. It is too fine a day for such unpleasantness." The necromancer glanced toward the torture chamber he had just quitted, and his cool smile promised that this morning's work did not *begin* to define his concept of "unpleasantness."

The rogue stroked his chin as if he were thinking this over. Not that he had much say in the matter, but maintaining the illusion of choice eased his bruised pride somewhat. Never before had he served any man; he himself was a leader of men, and the freedom to determine his own path held more value for him than the treasures he stole or the women he charmed.

He tipped his head toward the music room. "Before I agree, tell me why yon pretty songbird failed to please you."

"Simply put, she can't play the harp."

The man's eyes widened. "Well, of course not. She's a bard. They don't bother with harps."

"Why not?"

"Because—" He stopped short, frowning. "How should I know? They just don't."

"I need someone who does. Not some village musician," the necromancer cautioned as he rose and walked back into the room he'd just vacated, "or a midwife who plays to ease the pain of childbirth, or the idle son of a rich merchant twanging away as he warbles odes to his lady's eyes. I need a *bard* who can play the harp exceedingly well."

After a moment, the necromancer returned to the hall, brandishing a bright red object. "*This* harp."

Lips pursed, the rogue studied the small instrument. A pretty thing, with graceful curves and a smooth, flawless finish, but it boasted no intricate carvings or gemstone inlays or magic-promising runes. And the wire strings were not, sad to say, made of gold.

"Anything special about it, other than the color?"

"Mayong Mistmoore seems to think so."

Several moments passed as the older man absorbed this. "*The* Mayong Mistmoore? The dark elf vampire, lord of Castle Mistmoore? What does *he* want with a harp?"

"That's what I'm trying to ascertain. The harp is ancient, and its provenance is, to say the least, obscure. I've located four previous owners, but none could shed light on this interesting question. Of course, two of them were mad, and all of them are dead."

"Death does tend to put a damper on conversation."

The necromancer smirked. "I'm sure you'd like to think so, but I seldom find it an inconvenience."

He made a languid gesture with one hand. Dozens of thin beams of blue light shot across the room, forming a tangle of glowing magic.

The rogue's gaze traced one beam back to its source, and he swallowed hard when he realized the azure light poured from the empty eye sockets of one of the skulls.

A soft, hollow hum began to emanate from that skull, a single high, unwavering note. Around the room, other ghostly voices joined in, some echoing the note or repeating it at octaves, others adding harmony. Then, suddenly, the weird choir broke into wordless song. Skulls floated out of their alcoves, bobbing somberly as the dead bards performed a well-known dirge to the accompaniment of clicking teeth.

After what seemed an eternity, the eerie melody faded away and the singers returned to their interrupted repose. The rogue had to clear his throat twice before it relaxed enough to allow sound to pass.

"You've made your po—"

He broke off abruptly when he heard another voice lifted in song—a once-sweet soprano now ragged from screaming and still hitching with tears. At first little more than a whisper, the defeated bard's voice grew stronger and clearer with each note, and so bewitching was the melody that both men instinctively paused to listen:

A cold spill of moonlight awakens me.
As star-song drifts on the midnight winds
You'll dance to the rhythm of my bloodless heart.

The rogue shook off the enchantment cast by the dual forces of the song's sheer beauty and his own slack-jawed astonishment. He would have bet his last coin that the half elf hadn't enough strength left to whimper, much less cast singing magic.

"You'd best put a stop to this," he warned the necromancer in a low, urgent tone. "I'm no expert on bardspell, but no tale told from a vampire's point of view is likely to have what you and I might call a happy ending."

If the necromancer heard this warning, he gave it no heed. His head nodded in time to the song, and innocent enjoyment glazed his pale blue eyes—an expression that sat oddly on so cruel and aristocratic a face. He rose slowly and began to glide toward the far wall, where a collection of swords was displayed, fanned out in a half-circle like the petals of a deadly flower.

Understanding smote the rogue with the force of an ogre's fist. The bard sang a charm spell of some sort, and she'd cast her soprano net over the necromancer. Most likely she intended her tormenter to die by his own hand—*after* killing the man who'd betrayed her to him.

That betrayer's first impulse was to flee the room and leave the necromancer to his well-deserved fate. But his feet wouldn't obey this sensible command, and his scalp began to tingle and itch—the first warning of pain to come.

Hissing a sigh through clenched teeth, he drew his dagger and strode into the music chamber. Thanks to the spell of compulsion that bound his will and ruled his actions, the only way to save himself was to save the necromancer. A moment later, the bard fell forever silent.

Killing was not a task the rogue relished, and he bitterly resented the man who'd forced it upon him. He stalked back into the hall and snatched the harp from the necromancer's hands before the ensorcelled spell-caster had time to blink away the last remnants of the bard's charm spell.

"Let's finish this," the rogue said, clutching the harp as he backed out of reach. "I might know someone who could play well enough for your purposes, but I'll not bring her here to have her hands stomped into jelly or to join your bone choir. She'll do the job, given the needed time and space, but some birds won't sing when they're caged."

The necromancer thought this over and conceded with a single curt nod. "Very well. We will let this bird flit free until she finds the answers I seek."

That would give her a fighting chance, the rogue reasoned; not bad for someone who usually made do with less. "Now, about the harp . . . "

"There is remarkably little to tell. The harp yields its secrets to neither research nor magic. It needs to be played with proficiency by someone who also wields a bard's spell-casting ability. In such hands, the legend will reveal itself over time." An unpleasant smile lifted the corners of the necromancer's lips. "I daresay this will not be a wholly pleasant experience."

"Then what's to keep her from tossing the harp down the nearest midden hole when things get unpleasant?"

The necromancer considered. "She must not recognize the harp as the source of her troubles. Some sort of misdirection is needed to divert her attention to another focus."

This time the rogue's smile was genuine and slightly wistful.

"That shouldn't be too difficult," he said. "She's easily distracted, like a child who needs to stop every five paces to catch an insect or study an interesting leaf. Everyone she meets is a new friend, and she can't resist any situation that might yield a new story or song."

The necromancer's black eyebrows rose. "It sounds as if you know this bard very well."

"I ought to," his unwilling servant said softly. "After all, she *is* my wife."

1

A New Song

MORNING CREPT SLOWLY INTO THE FORESTS OF Faydark. The chirruping music of the insect chorus began to change as nocturnal creatures stopped singing to burrow deep into the mossy forest floor or take refuge in hollow logs. Bats left off their shrill cries, settling down to groom the blood from their talons and let the morning-birds' song lull them into slumber. Soon the morning dew would disappear into the warm, mist-heavy air, and the first rays of sunlight would filter down through the dense forest canopy, fading the blackness of night to a deep green gloom. Under the trees of Faydark, darkness and dawn were no farther apart than two sides of an old coin.

The caravan road gave forest dwellers an occasional glimpse of sky. A large log cabin just off the road served as a ranger station, and at certain times and seasons, when the day was fine and the sun high overhead, the gleam of sunlight on that honey-colored wood seemed brighter than fairy gold.

At this hour, however, the only light came from the

glimmer of hearth embers inside the ranger station. The faint glow spilled into the forest as the door swung open, silhouetting the small, slim form of a wood elf female.

Moving through the darkness with the ease of a nocturnal hunter, she circled around to the back of the building and nimbly climbed the ladder leading to the roof. She raised one hand in greeting to the fair-haired elf who'd stood night watch and walked toward him with a wide smile and a dancer's light-footed step.

"Hail, Anlar! Hiding from me again, are you?"

The ranger turned to face her, and she stopped in mid-stride. Her teasing smile froze, then faltered. "Oh! I mistook you for Anlar Oakwind. He used to take this watch."

"He still does, most nights, but he's gone off scouting."

She lifted one high-arching brow and regarded him with mild curiosity. "The orcs are out and about again?"

In the young ranger's opinion, her tone was better suited for asking a shopkeeper if he kept barley beer in stock than for ascertaining the dangers of the road ahead.

"No, Anlar is not hunting orcs," he said coolly. "A southbound caravan came through four days bypast, and the drover complained of giant wasps gathering near the road. Anlar thought there might be a nest. He has been out these past few nights searching for it."

"Then I suppose I'll meet him on the road," she said lightly, dismissing a swarm of hound-sized wasps as a matter of little consequence.

The ranger's gaze skimmed over her, seeking some clue to her easy confidence. Her slight, almost girlishly thin frame made her an unlikely warrior, and few wizards dressed as simply: breeches and tunic in forest hues of green and brown, well-worn boots cuffed below her

knees. No rings graced her slender fingers, and the dry, cracked leather of her weapons belt and scabbard suggested great age or coin-short quality.

He noted the crest of the Songweavers' Guild sewn onto her tunic: a bard, then. The small hand drum hanging from her belt marked her as rather new to her chosen path. Among the elven people she would not be accounted a great beauty, but she fell easily upon the eyes—brown as a meadow bird, with an abundance of dark hair that held the rich gloss of polished chestnuts. A ready smile lurked at the corners of her full, expressive lips, and her large amber eyes brimmed with good-natured fun. The ranger thought her face well suited to the voice he'd heard laughing and singing far into the night.

"You'd be the bard everyone kept calling for last night. Elizerain, isn't it? Like the queen of legend?"

That seemed to amuse her. "Not yet a queen, legendary or otherwise, but the day is young!"

A faint alarm sounded in the back of the young ranger's mind. "For a bard, you seem unusually ambitious."

She shrugged. "Only in pursuit of a good story and a bit of a tune to help it along. As for the name, well, I've never been sure whether my parents were afflicted with high hopes or an unseemly fondness for irony."

He recalled the noisy revelry and observed, "Judging from what I heard last night, you're in hard pursuit of your own legend."

The bard's lips twitched—a fleeting grin, quickly replaced by an expression of meek contrition. "We went on a bit too long for courtesy," she apologized. "I do hope the singing didn't keep you awake."

"Of course I was awake," he said stiffly. "No ranger falls asleep during his wa—"

He broke off, suddenly realizing that she'd been teasing him. Gathering his dignity about him like a cloak, he inquired, "How may I serve you, Songmistress?"

"Oh, please—save the formality for the Koada'Dal!" She tipped her head to one side and considered. "Though come to think of it, I've been called some fairly informal things by high elves. Why don't you call me Elizerain? Or Rain, if you prefer."

Before he could respond, she shrugged off the shoulder strap that slung a large water skin over her back. She uncorked the vessel with her teeth and handed it over. His watch had been long, and his water flask was empty, so he accepted it gratefully and took a hearty swallow.

Potent sweetness filled his mouth, swiftly followed by a kick like that of a bee-stung pack mule. The ranger's eyes widened in pleasure as the complex flavors of fruit and flowers and spice unfolded on his tongue.

"Excellent mead," he said appreciatively as he handed back the skin. "You've just come from Felwithe, I suppose? They say the wineries there are incomparable."

"Aye, 'they' would," she said lightly. She sipped from the wineskin and replaced the cork. "So, my friend, what are you called?"

He inclined his head in a small, formal bow. "My name is Rimvi Straightarrow."

For no reason he could fathom, the bard's lips quirked again, and mischief flared bright in her eyes. She quickly arranged her face in more somber lines. "Straightarrow. You seem well named."

"It is my father's name." The very thought of that famed ranger made him stand a little taller. "Like you, I have much to answer for."

That comment chased the laughter from her eyes and brought a wry smile to her lips. "For your sake, I hope our cases are not too similar."

His brow furrowed as he sought some polite way to respond to so strange a comment. Elizerain did not notice his puzzlement, for she was busily rummaging through the bag attached to her belt. From it she took a small flagon of oil and a pair of small rags. She anointed both rags and tossed one to the ranger.

Rimvi deftly caught it and nodded his thanks. He pulled his dagger from his belt and began to smooth the rag over the steel. Oiling weapons was a frequent necessity, for the warm, moist air of the forests could reduce the finest blade to rust and ruin. He glanced over at Elizerain, who carefully tended a short sword, a beautifully crafted weapon with a cross-guard fashioned to resemble a pair of feathered wings. Between these silvery wings was a large red gem cut in a diamond shape.

Rimvi's eyes widened, and his estimation of the bard climbed several notches. Such swords held potent magic, and they marked their wielders as bards of considerable skill and experience.

She noticed his scrutiny and sent him a saucy wink. Smiling, she stepped back and spun into a brief, fluid practice routine—a graceful dance of dips and turns and slow sweeps of the blade. A faint dusting of luminous blue notes followed the sword, leaving softly glowing ribbons of silent music to mark its passage.

"A fine weapon," he said in sincere admiration, "and a fitting reward for hard effort and brave adventure. I would like to hear you sing that story!"

A rosy flush suffused her cheeks, which Rimvi took as

a becoming sign of modesty. "Maybe next time," she murmured. "I'm still working out the rhyme."

"I look forward to it." He recalled something she'd said earlier, and his eyes lit up. "You expect to meet Anlar on the road, so I take it you're northbound. You'll be singing at the Songweavers' Feast in Kelethin?"

A shadow passed over her face, quickly banished by a smile. "Not this season. I'm not familiar with the new festival ballads, since I haven't been to Kelethin for years."

He nodded knowingly. "You've been off adventuring. Such swords aren't easily acquired."

Elizerain responded with a modest shrug before slinging her wineskin over her shoulder. "It's been a pleasure, Rimvi Straightarrow, but it's time I was off."

"Safe journey to you. And speaking of which," he added as a new thought struck him, "is it wise to walk past a giant wasp nest carrying a large skin of honey wine? Perhaps you should leave it here."

She shot him a quick grin. "Nice try."

The young ranger looked mortified. "That's not what I meant—"

She silenced him with a teasing wink. When a rueful smile of understanding dawned on his face, she blew him a kiss and scampered down the ladder, her mind already on the northbound road.

Elizerain set off at a run, an easy pace she could sustain for hours without tiring. She hummed softly as she ran, fitting new rhymes to a bawdy tavern song a new-met friend had sung last night. The original ballad would scandalize any proper bard, but she saw no reason why the tune couldn't be dressed up in more demure garb and presented in polite society. Knowing the song's origins would give her a bit of private amusement.

So intent was she on a troublesome bit of verse that her first hint of danger was the telltale *twang* of a loosed arrow. Startled, she looked up into the multifaceted eyes of the largest wasp she'd ever seen. Big as a sow and every bit as ugly, it plunged straight toward her.

An arrow glanced off the wasp's hard shell, shaking loose a small cloud of yellow pollen. The giant insect did not seem inconvenienced in the slightest, but Elizerain's nose began to itch.

She dived toward a massive tree trunk and hit the ground rolling, forcing the giant creature to pull up and veer away sharply to avoid plowing into the tree.

As she scrambled to her feet, she heard the high-pitched whine of an approaching swarm. At a glance, she estimated at least two- or three-score wasps, all headed her way. A small storm of arrows rose from various places in the underbrush to hold them at bay.

Elizerain smirked. She'd sensed her unseen protector for several days now but had seen no real evidence of his presence. Now that he'd been forced to play his hand, perhaps they could conclude the game that had gone on overlong.

But first, she had to deal with the wasp circling back for another attack. Elizerain drew her new short sword and raised it to high guard position.

The loud, meaty thud of a fired crossbow resounded through the forest. A large barbed arrow soared toward the wasp, trailing a thin line of spidersilk rope. The wasp was almost upon Elizerain when the arrow struck, plowing deep into the furred body.

The wasp screamed—a high-pitched chittering that reverberated in Elizerain's bones and sent an echoing stab of pain through her clenched teeth. The eerie sound cut off abruptly when the wasp came to the end of its tether and jerked to a stop. Its four translucent wings swung forward and slapped sharply against its body.

Momentarily deprived of flight, the wasp described a quick downward arc and hit the ground hard. Pollen flew from the giant body like spores from a dried puffball mushroom.

Elizerain darted into the pollen cloud and finished off the insect with a single quick stroke. She backed away, sneezing violently and repeatedly, until she was certain the next sneeze would expel her liver through her nostrils.

When at last the spell passed, she heard a soft splashing sound behind her. She whirled around and beheld a small amber puddle, rapidly disappearing into the hard-packed soil under the tree.

Clearly, Tunare's smile wasn't aimed in her general direction today! Just when Elizerain really needed a drink, her wineskin decided to spring a leak.

She snatched it off her shoulder and held it high overhead with both hands, letting the mead drizzle into her mouth. After taking a couple of hearty swallows, she upended the bag and sprinted over to a nearby spicegum sapling.

One slender limb had been torn away during the wasp's final flight, and a drop of thick amber fluid leaked from the tree's wound like a single tear.

Elizerain scooped up the sap with her forefinger and popped it into her mouth, chewing vigorously until the sweetness was nearly gone and the sap had thickened to the consistency of half-melted wax. She pressed the wad into the wineskin's hole, then pinched the soft leather to flatten the sap on both sides. That accomplished, she gave the wineskin an experimental shake and nodded in satisfaction.

"That ought to hold," she murmured.

The whine of the wasp swarm grew louder and decidedly more agitated. Elizerain slung the wineskin over her shoulder and set off toward the unseen archers, intent on lending a hand. Sooner or later they would run out of arrows, and they could no doubt use another sword against the persistent insects.

Branches rustled overhead, and a heavy thud sounded right behind her. Even as Elizerain whirled toward the sound, she realized what it meant: someone had dropped from a hidden perch amid the branches.

A rough sack came down over her head. Her startled intake of breath drew an acrid herbal scent deep into her lungs. Immediately her thoughts began to whirl in the sort of giddy, fuzzy patterns usually found at the bottom of a large flagon of dwarven spirits.

Now who, she asked herself, *would pull a bag of sleeping powders over my head in the middle of the forest?*

Who, indeed . . .

Elizerain's last thought before the darkness claimed her was an epiphany of sorts. She'd often wondered why her divorce had been so expensive. The answer was amazingly straightforward: because it was worth it.

2

THE GALLOWS TREE

CHANZOON NEXIS GLUMLY REGARDED THE ATtractive corpse laid out on his worktable. Even for a necromancer as talented as he, animating the dead was never an easy task. Creating an illusion of life was nearly impossible.

But he needed a female bard, one who would serve as a compliant tool. His experience with females in general and female bards in particular suggested that death was a necessary precursor to compliance. This particular corpse was in reasonably good shape; a little creative spell-casting would keep it fresh and viable long enough for the legendary Manarla Willowmere to win accolades at the Songweavers' Feast.

Getting the half elf to Kelethin was one thing; enabling her to perform, quite another. In his anger at her inability to coax magic from the harp, Chanzoon had damaged the woman's hands so severely that they would never again hold a lute, much less play one. And Davin, that fool, had cut her throat. A thousand ways to end a life, and that dim-witted thief had to pick the one most likely to cause inconvenience.

The necromancer studied the corpse with a critical eye. A pair of gloves might mold her hands back into something resembling their original shape, and perhaps the throat wound wasn't as bad as it looked. As long as the vocal chords were still intact, all would be well. A velvet ribbon or a triple strand of pearls should hide the damage.

He probed the gaping cut, and his thin lips grew a smile. "Alisar! To me, and hurry."

His apprentice, a gnome wench who was entirely too cheerful for Chanzoon's liking, swept into the room like a summer breeze. Today she wore a white ruffled apron over a gown the color of spring bluebells, which, combined with her curly brown hair, apple cheeks, and upturned nose, made her resemble a miniature dairy maid. Chanzoon supposed she was a fetching little thing, but he was far more interested in her nimble fingers and utter lack of maidenly squeamishness.

At least, her utter lack of squeamishness during the *day*. Alisar had offered twice the usual apprentice's fee to induce Chanzoon to take her on, but she was very clear about her desire to quit Chanzoon's lair well before nightfall. A gnomish superstition, she'd said. The necromancer had harbored doubts about this arrangement, but Alisar made herself so useful during the daylight hours that her nocturnal absences were, at worst, only a minor inconvenience.

"Fair morning to you, master," she chirped. "I see you've acquired a new bard skull for the great hall, and a fine one it is! Shall I fetch you the hacksaw?"

"Get your sewing things. This one we're putting back together and taking for a walk."

Alisar dimpled happily. "Can I make some alterations? I've always wanted to try—"

"Some other time. Unless, of course," he said facetiously, "you'd like to stitch on a new pair of hands."

The gnome leaned in for a closer look. "I can do that," she announced, "as long as they're just for show. Muscles have memories, you know, and none of the hands I have at present knew how to play an instrument."

Chanzoon stared at his apprentice. "*None* of the hands?" he demanded, surprised to learn of what sounded to be a rather large collection of spare body parts.

She looked vaguely offended. "I do my best, but the graveyards to be found hereabouts don't provide a ready supply of freshly interred bards."

He was about to correct her misunderstanding of his words when a stab of alarm set him back on his heels. Grave robbing was risky work for a strong man. The image of pretty little Alisar going about this business, shovel in hand, was so incongruous that he wasn't sure whether to be amused or appalled.

"Have you ever been seen at this work?" he demanded.

Her head bobbed affirmation. "But if I hear someone coming, I just fall to my knees, cover my face with my hands, and pretend to cry. Few people want to trouble what they suppose is a grieving child, but if someone comes over to 'comfort me,' I point to the pile of dirt and send them running off in pursuit of the bad man who defiled my daddy's grave."

Chanzoon chuckled, admiring both the mental image and the worthy ploy. It occurred to him that a disarmingly clever gnome apprentice might be just what he needed for the trip to Kelethin. Suspicion and fear greeted necromancers whithersoever they went, and rightly so, but Alisar appeared to be about as threatening as a fluffy white kitten.

"Give her whatever hands you like, then pack your things."

Her blue eyes widened with dismay. "I'm being dismissed?"

"You're being promoted. As far as the good folk of Kelethin are concerned, you will be the orphaned child adopted by the kind-hearted Manarla Willowmere."

The gnome's gaze shifted to the lovely corpse, betraying the first hint of revulsion Chanzoon had ever seen on her face. She *looked*, he realized, precisely the way he *felt* whenever he ate something cloyingly sweet.

At that moment, he realized that he had become rather fond of his apprentice.

"With respect, master," she said hesitantly, "it is difficult to pass as a human child for any length of time."

"A lady's maid, then," he suggested.

"One who gossips shamelessly with the other servants," she added, "learning and imparting all manner of scandalous secrets."

They exchanged a smile of perfect understanding, then set to work tidying up the dead.

THE RICH SCENT OF VENISON AND MUSHROOM STEW insinuated itself into Elizerain's dreams. Her stomach rumbled, and she inhaled deeply, feeling herself being drawn toward the scent and away from the jumble of images and half-formed thoughts that filled her enforced slumber. Gradually she became aware of other things—

the hard wooden floor beneath her, the murmur of male voices.

She sat up, a bit too fast for her still-spinning head, and flopped back down, groaning.

The footsteps of a large but light-footed man moved closer, and a familiar voice said, "Glad you finally decided to join us."

Elizerain blew a lock of hair off her face and gazed up at her captor—a tall man whose dark, curly hair was liberally sprinkled with gray. His hairline was migrating north, and the laugh lines around his eyes had deepened into wrinkles. Once-taut cheeks were starting to sag; they were not quite jowls, but only a well-fed winter or two away. Ah well, it *had* been a matter of years.

"Davin the Dark," she said flatly. "You're holding up well, considering."

"Aye, considering," he agreed cheerfully. "Long years gone by, and there you are, still as fresh as a spring morning. They treated you well, did they?"

She sat up slowly, touching experimental fingertips to her temples. "I've no complaints. Say what you will about Freeport, but those people run a mighty fine city dungeon."

Davin grimaced. "About that—"

"No complaints," Elizerain repeated firmly. Her gaze skimmed the room, lingering on three familiar faces—longtime members of the bandit gang known as the Greenleaves, one of them distant kin to her. "You boys promised to show me the wonders of Antonica. We saw a few of them, heard some stories, had some fun. We just took a few too many chances along the way, that's all."

"And you got caught, while the rest of us got clean

away," Davin said softly. "The Freeport authorities would rather have had any one of us than you, but you said never a word against us. There's not a man here who doesn't owe you his life."

She shrugged. "Any of you would have done the same."

"Aye," agreed a rangy half elf who'd seen roughly 50 winters, "but only because Davin the Dark would hunt us down, otherwise."

The bandits joined in the sort of dark laughter that greets unpleasant, jest-clad truth.

"I've missed you, Viscor," Elizerain said with a grin. "You were always one to see the bright side, even as a boy. How fares your mother?"

The half elf's smile faded. "I haven't been back to the lake country for some years. The Greenleaves aren't welcome there anymore."

Silence filled the room, thick as wood smoke. Before it could get too uncomfortable, Davin extended a hand and helped Elizerain to her feet.

Her gaze swept the room, studying a rounded chamber about 20 feet across. It seemed to be roughly carved into the heart of a single, enormous block of wood. There were no windows, but air rose from grated vents in the floor to similar vents in the ceiling, some 40 feet above. A pot of stew simmered over a low brass brazier, filling the room with fragrance and just enough warmth. Niches were carved into the walls for storage, and cloaks and weapons belts hung on wooden pegs. A tall ladder led to a wooden hatch on the ceiling that suggested another floor above.

"What is this place?" she marveled.

Davin bowed. "Welcome to Gallows Tree, so named

because they'd hang the lot of us from its branches—*if* they knew where to find us."

"Which explains the sort of invitation you chose to extend," the bard said dryly. "You never were the most trusting of souls."

A grizzled veteran wearing a leaf-shaped patch over his left eye removed the pipe from his mouth. "We didn't live this long by taking foolish chances, girlie. Not that you could find us again if you wanted to. We're well off the path and too high up to see from the forest floor. Door's a good 60 feet off the ground, so don't you be dashing out in a hurry."

Elizerain studied the old man. "You make it sound as if I'm a prisoner, Grib."

He shrugged. "I hear Davin's got no hold on you. Fickle wench," he added under his breath, loud enough for everyone in the room to hear.

"Davin and I wedded the old way, for a year and a day," Elizerain reminded him. "It's what we both chose. The marriage is long over. But so there'd be no question, I got this from the priests of Felwithe."

She took a small, tightly rolled scroll from her bag and handed it to the bandit leader. Davin unrolled it, scanned the tiny runes, and raised an eyebrow.

"A cleric-blessed divorce doesn't come easy," he observed. "Or cheap, for that matter."

"Consider it a gift," she said. "Now you can charm every woman who crosses your path with a clear conscience."

The notion of Davin possessing any sort of conscience, clear or otherwise, prompted another chuckle from the Greenleaves.

Still smiling, Davin went to a curtained alcove and removed a bright red object. "Since we're exchanging gifts, I've a little something that might strike your fancy."

A small, glad cry burst from Elizerain, and she rushed forward to snatch the red harp from his hands. Immediately she sank down onto a wooden stool, her cheek pressed lovingly against the harp's smooth wood. She ran her fingers lightly over the strings and looked up, startled.

"It's perfectly in tune. How? None of you hoof-fingered clods could have done it. No man here could carry a tune in a bucket if his life depended on it."

"There's a small enchantment on it," Davin said smoothly. "Sing us a story, Rain."

Her hands paused over the strings. "Before I fall in love, is there anything I should know about this harp? Let's start with the basics: is it stolen?"

"No more so than that winged short sword you're carrying these days," Davin said with a grin.

Elizerain slapped one hand to her scabbard and swore when she found it empty. "Give it back!"

"Oh, I will, but it seemed prudent to leave you unarmed until I knew how much of a grudge you held."

She nodded, accepting his excuse. "The sword isn't stolen. I found it. The owner was long dead."

"Same with the harp."

"I didn't kill the owner, mind you."

"Nor did I."

Elizerain considered. "Well, then."

"My thoughts precisely."

A brilliant smile broke over her face. Her fingers began to dance over the strings, and a merry jig filled the room—the sort of music that farm folk danced to when the harvest moon was full and the crops gathered in. The men listened with pleasure, toes tapping the wooden floor. One tune flowed into another, sometimes dancing alone, sometimes entwining artfully with some second melody to form music both familiar and new.

Finally Elizerain lowered her hands from the strings and heaved a sigh of soul-deep contentment.

"Your folks would be proud," the half elf said softly. "Many's the time I heard them play those very tunes, though never so well."

Elizerain shook her head. "It's kind of you to say so, cousin, but my parents were the best harpers in the lake country."

"They took it hard, you deciding to go bard," he recalled. "Though I never saw why you couldn't be both."

Her only answer was a shrug.

"You should take the harp to Kelethin and play it at the Songweavers' Feast," Davin suggested. "Who knows? Harping might become the fashionable thing."

"Harps are considered too informal—a folk instrument, nothing a proper bard would bother with," Elizerain said wistfully. "The Songweavers would never let me play one in a guild-sponsored competition."

"But you *could* join the singing competition," he pointed out. "And if you sang an ancient ballad about a harp, maybe they'd think playing along on a 'folk instrument' was quaint and charming—or better yet, scholarly."

"Tell the story of why bards don't play harps," Viscor suggested. "I'd like to hear that, myself."

"As would I!" she agreed avidly. "But I've asked a dozen bards about such a tale, and none had ever heard it told."

The bandit leader treated her to one of his crooked grins. "About time then, wouldn't you think? If no one knows the real tale, what's the harm? Make up a story and sing it to that melody you were humming when the wasps attacked. I've seldom heard so catchy a tune."

Elizerain nodded slowly. Already the story was taking shape in her mind, and the melody from the bawdy tavern ballad made a good fit.

"What'd those wasps want with you, anyway?" asked the old man Grib. "They moved off after a while, but they needed more persuading than per usual."

She dragged her attention back to the Greenleaves. "There's mead in my water skin. I suppose I shouldn't have carried it through the forest. The guard at the ranger station warned me that wasps might be a problem."

A wide grin split Davin's face. "You knew about the swarm, and still you strolled past with a wineskin of honey wine?"

"It's very good mead," she explained.

"Ah. Well, then."

Davin glanced at the youngest bandit, who promptly rose and hurried over to a shelf holding a row of tankards. He put several of them on a tray and brought them over to the bandit leader.

"Think again," Elizerain warned Davin. "This isn't your usual honey wine. It's rare, potent stuff, made with the fey folk in mind and far stronger than humans are likely to handle well."

"I've no pressing business for a day or so." He uncorked the wineskin and started to pour out tankards. "Consider it payment for the harp."

"Payment? You gave me the harp as a gift."

"And gifts never carry a hidden price?"

Elizerain acknowledged this philosophy with a

pragmatic shrug as she accepted a brimming tankard. She lifted it in a mock toast. "At least you're including me in this party."

For no reason that she could ascertain, Davin's cocky grin suddenly seemed to go brittle around the edges.

"Trust me," he murmured, "I couldn't possibly leave you out of this."

3

THE CITY IN THE TREES

NIOLA IMPHOLDER PULLED HER WHITE MARE TO a stop and gazed at the massive wooden platform that slowly descended from the trees above, thanks to some clever and typically gnomish contraption of pulleys and levers. Except for the platform—and the merry throng awaiting its descent—the elven city in the treetops would be invisible from the ground.

Odd, she mused, that so many considered Kelethin to represent the spirit of the elven people. Everyone, Koada'Dal and Feir'Dal alike, echoed Niola's opinion that her beloved Felwithe more closely duplicated the grandeur and beauty of Takish-Hiz, the legendary, long-lost city of their ancestors.

"My lady?"

She glanced down at the tall elf who stood ready to help her dismount and recoiled in surprise to recognize an old friend.

Regren Steelforger served Kelethin as captain of the Emerald Warriors, the city's elite guard. Clad in the green scale armor and embossed bracers and greaves of his order, he wore nothing to set him apart from the elves and half elves he commanded.

Niola supposed that it made sense to have Kelethin's best defenders ready at hand, with so many people pouring into the city for the Songweavers' Feast. She let Regren lift her down from her horse and thanked him with a smile.

But the warrior was scanning the crowd with growing consternation. "Where is your guard, Lady Impholder? Surely you don't travel alone!"

"On this road?" she said dryly, letting her gaze sweep the festive scene.

The road to Kelethin was a procession of cart and carriage, horse and rider, and many who came on foot. Scattered among the largely elven throng were humans, a race that ranged from the heavily muscled and lightly clad barbarians to the more esthetic-looking Erudites, who appeared to be uncomfortably warm in their scholarly robes. Niola was no expert on human customs, but the varied garb and speech of Kelethin's human visitors suggested that not a few had traveled from distant lands. There were also half elves in lamentable plenty, as well as a few members of races less commonly seen in the forests of Faydark: gnomes, halflings, even a dwarf or two. Almost everyone was clad in some version of festive garb, and the young girls of all races wore wreaths of leaves or flowers in their hair. Many people were already singing or passing around flasks in anticipation of the revels to come.

"You should have escorts," Regren Steelforger said firmly.

Niola's blue eyes cooled. "I have been known to cast a spell or two in defense of myself and others."

He inclined his head in a bow of apology to one of the

three rulings masters of Felwithe's famous Arcane School, perhaps the greatest high elf magician in the land.

"Even so, I would be remiss in my duty if I did not assign a guard to you during your stay in Kelethin. In fact, your position demands it."

No stranger to protocol, the mage yielded with a sigh. "Very well, but I would prefer discretion to an obvious presence." A new thought occurred to her, and her eyes brightened. "In fact, I would be in your debt if you could assign a discreet protector to my son, Nyson."

A bemused smile touched the warrior's face. "Little Nyson is traveling with you?"

In response, she tipped her head toward a band of approaching riders.

Regren turned to regard the leader, a tall, fair-haired youth seated on a high-stepping charger. The lad was Niola's son, no doubt about that. He had the same blond beauty, the sharp aristocratic features, the proud tilt to his head. His long, lean form was clad in rich sky-blue garments, and an impractical white cloak snapped and fluttered behind him. Three young blades accompanied him, all wearing similar garments and riding near-identical golden stallions tricked out in matching blue-and-white barding. If their goal was to proclaim some joint and lofty purpose, they lacked only a banner showing four enjoined swords and a jaunty motto. Young elves of high position and higher spirits, the warrior concluded, out to seize the fame and fortune they considered their due.

"That's little Nyson?" he marveled. "He must be half a head taller than me! When did this happen?"

"If you feed them, they grow," Niola said dryly.

"Eventually, they may also mature—provided they live so long."

The quartet of would-be adventurers clattered up and pulled to a halt. Nyson leaped from his horse and strode forward. He inclined his head to his mother and then to the warrior.

"Hail, Captain Steelforger," he said politely. His voice was unexpectedly deep and resonant, years older than his face and frame.

"You remember me?" Regren said, feeling absurdly flattered. "Last time I set eyes on you, you were knee-high to a house cat."

The youth's handsome visage took on the pained resignation of one all too familiar with variations on "My, how you've grown!"

This expression made Regren aware of how he must appear to the young elf: a doddering ancient, making what passed for conversation among those grown too feebleminded to avoid annoying cliché. It was a strange and unfamiliar experience. His own children were still young; he had yet to see unflattering images mirrored back to him from their eyes.

"You must both stay with me, of course," Regren said hastily, sparing Nyson any need to respond to the inane comment. "My family would be honored."

"I thank you for your kind offer, but my friends and I have rooms reserved at the Larksong Inn," Nyson said. "I will be happy to escort Lady Impholder to your home, however, if that will free you to tend to your other duties."

"As you will," Regren said politely. He escorted Niola onto the platform and bowed to them both, then turned back to the crowd. Nyson's friends stayed behind to give precise instructions to the forest hostler concerning the care of their horses.

The platform swiftly filled with revelers. When it could hold no more, one of the guards sang out a warning and pulled a lever. The lift jolted slightly and then began a smooth upward ride.

"That was unnecessarily rude," Niola said softly, as soon as she thought the creak of rope and gear sufficient to privacy.

Her son regarded her with a faintly puzzled expression. "To refuse the captain's invitation?"

"To refer to it as a 'duty.'"

"And so it is, according to the wood elves," he replied. "The folk of Kelethin regard hospitality as a virtue of the highest order."

"And it *is* a virtue," she said. "Regren and his wife will sleep in hammocks tonight so that I might have the best bed, but not because of my high position. They would do as much for any chance-met visitor to Kelethin who found himself without a place to sleep. One does not belittle so generous an offer with talk of duty."

Nyson's fair brows rose. "I never thought to hear you speak lightly of duty, Mother."

"And I never thought to hear you speak of it at all," she replied. "You failed to attend your weapons training again, with never a word to your sword master. Only by chance did I hear you were headed to Kelethin."

"Ah. That would explain your burning desire to attend the festival this year."

"Why should I not? For all I know, you have bardic pretensions."

He sniffed. "Hardly. Bard's magic is fine for one who aspires only to support others."

"And what, precisely, are your aspirations? You refuse to attend the Arcane School, yet you do not apply yourself to a warrior's training."

His lips firmed into a straight line. "Why do you insist upon painting me with colors of your choosing?"

"I don't care what path you pick," she retorted, "so long as you chose one and pursue it with something approaching enthusiasm."

The platform slowed, and Nyson waited to speak until the gears ground noisily to a halt. "In that case, Mother," he said softly, "you should be exceedingly pleased to note the enthusiasm of my departure, as my current path takes me to a tavern."

He bowed to her and spun away, his white cape whirling about his shoulders as he stalked off.

Niola sighed. Her son was impossibly spoiled, and she could blame only herself. She'd doted on him, overindulged him, made his path too smooth and pleasant. Nyson was incredibly gifted in so many ways, and it broke her heart to see his talents lying fallow. She'd tried time and again to engage his interest in his own future, with no discernible success. Niola had run out of new ideas long ago and had resorted to repeating the old. Their mutual frustration with this tactic was growing by the day.

As she stepped off the platform, she noted several brown-haired girl children greeting guests with small gifts. The nearest elfling gave Niola a gap-toothed grin and handed her something from the basket at her feet.

Niola regarded the trinket dangling from her hand: a simple necklace fashioned from a bit of thin green ribbon, from which hung a small linen bag containing fragrant herbs.

"It's a songbird sachet," the child explained cheerfully. "Dried leaves and petals from plants the singing birds favor. We leave them the seeds, of course, but the leaves smell fine, do they not?"

"Indeed they do," the mage agreed. She noted the tiny, even stitches on the bag and added, "This is a pretty thing, and finely made."

"And useful!" the girl said. "The Songweavers say it brings inspiration."

Niola promptly draped the ribbon around her neck and held out a silver coin. The child's eyes widened in awe of the proffered riches, but she shook her head and put her hands behind her back.

"I can't. The sachet is a gift."

"And so is the coin," the magician said, gently taking one of the girl's hands and folding her small fingers over the silver. She glanced toward a nearby vendor who was selling small, fragrant hand pies. "You can treat the other girls and so pass the gift along."

This notion appealed mightily to the child, judging from the width of her smile and the sparkle in her brown eyes. She dipped a curtsy to Niola and darted off.

The mage lifted the sachet to her nose and breathed deeply of the spicy scent. If the herbs worked as they were said to, she would have to see about planting an entire garden of the forest songbirds' preferred plants in Felwithe. It would undoubtedly become a popular refuge for parents of talented sons who were no longer children, but not yet fully adult. After all, who needed inspiration more than they?

Now, if only she could find flowers that inspired serenity and patience, she might just survive Nyson's between-age years.

THE HEARTWOOD TAVERN WAS MUCH AS ELIZERAIN remembered it, from the wooden sign depicting a tipped foaming mug to the sweet, yeasty smell wafting from the open windows. It was more crowded than usual, but all the better; she and Uulianu, one of the female barkeepers, hadn't parted on the best of terms. It had something to do with an unpaid bill—apparently Davin had set up an account in Elizerain's name shortly after they'd started keeping company.

Elizerain had explained matters to Uulianu, but in the doing had blackened her reputation in the barkeep's eyes. The elves of Kelethin were tolerant of half elves and the relationships that produced them, but rumors were beginning to circulate that the man known as Davin the Dark might be one of the bandits who plagued the trade road. Uulianu's husband was a merchant, and she took the existence of bandits, and all those who consorted with them, as a personal affront.

Elizerain peeked through the open window. Luck was with her: Uulianu was nowhere in sight. She breezed in, smiling broadly at the tall male elf behind the bar.

"Hail, Malawen!" she said, raising her voice over the clamor of conversation and laughter. "I'll have my usual, if you please."

Without comment, the barkeep reached past a row of red pottery bottles and picked up a large, squat bottle of blue glass. He uncorked it and filled a small pewter cup to the depth of three fingers.

More than seven years gone by, and he still remembered her favorite libation! Elizerain had always been of the opinion that a good barkeep could teach bards a thing or two about the art of long memory.

She took a sip and heaved a heartfelt sigh. "Sweet

Tunare, but I've missed your liquid magic! No one in all of Faydwer brews a better fire-ale."

A wry smile lifted one corner of the barkeep's lips. "Flattery isn't accepted as currency hereabouts. Will you be paying for that in coin or barter?"

She tossed back the rest before asking, "What sort of barter goods did you have in mind?"

"A few songs, a story or two. Something to keep the patrons happy until a bard wanders in."

"I *am* a bard. Joined the Songweavers about eight years ago, then took off for Antonica. I learned some lessons there."

Malawen's gaze flicked to the small crest on her tunic, and his face fell. "My apologies, Songmistress."

"Mayhap you had in mind something a little less lofty than bard-song tonight?" she asked slyly. "Thinking a bard's arrival might signal an *end* to happiness, are you?"

The wry grin returned. "It's the crowd," the barkeep explained. "A merry lot, excited and pleased to be here, but too road-weary for weighty lore and magic-heavy songs. Come tomorrow, they'll listen to it for hours on end with pleasure, but tonight they want to sit easy and laugh or dance as it pleases them to do so."

"A bawdy ballad or two, then."

"That sounds about right," Malawen agreed. "Nothing too bawdy, mind you."

"I'm sure she'll be the model of discretion, as always," murmured a voice at Elizerain's elbow.

She turned to find herself face to face with a male elf, a ranger clad in leather garments dyed a shade-dappled pattern of greens and brown, of the sort designed to make the wearer disappear into forest shadows. Nor would he stand out among a crowd of wood elves, being only a hand-span taller than petite Elizerain, but he was somewhat stockier and more heavily muscled than most elves. His face, too, was broader and his features more rugged than most of his race. Elizerain had reason to know that when he scowled, prudent people tended to take a step back. Few would consider him handsome but for his thick, dark red hair, which, with typical lack of vanity, he'd pulled back and secured with a leather thong.

Elizerain met the ranger's cool stare with a wink and a cheerful leer. "Xander Fletcher! You're looking as tasty as ever."

Malawen's snort sounded suspiciously like laughter. Xander shot a glare at him, then took Elizerain by the elbow and led her a few paces away from the bar.

"I heard about your adventures in Freeport," he said somberly, "and have a fairly good idea what 'lessons' you encountered in Antonica. I hope you learned them well, for we'll have no thieving here in Kelethin."

Elizerain lifted her chin and met his gaze squarely. "I'm no thief."

"The authorities in Freeport say otherwise. You can hardly blame them, given the company you keep."

"I'm no longer married to Davin. In fact," she added slyly, "I'm thinking maybe *we* could pick up where we left off."

Xander dropped her arm abruptly. "Thank you, but no. I've a sensitive nose, and find that a skunk's scent lingers long after the vermin has passed on."

She met rejection with an easy shrug. "Your loss."

Yet her gaze followed him as he pushed through the crowd, and she held her smile only with effort. Xander had been a good friend, solid and steady. He'd ignored her cheerful innuendos, hearing only the teasing and never the very real interest that prompted it. Elizerain had started to think Xander might never take her seriously when Davin the Dark had swept into her life, dazzling her with the promise of high adventure in distant lands.

Her shoulders rose and fell in a sigh, and she firmly put the past behind her. She made her way back to the bar and climbed onto the polished wood counter.

The chorus of voices muted as the patrons lifted expectant faces to her.

Elizerain loosened the ties to her hand drum and began to tap out an intricate rhythm, a jaunty, syncopated beat that started toes to tapping in time with her own soft-booted feet. When she figured that most of the patrons were fully caught up, she started to sing:

In days of yore the dwarves kept score
On axes deeply notch-ed-ed.
They reigned supreme in Kaladim
Until some poor sod botch-ed it.

As her strong, clear alto and nonsense rhythms filled the room, many of the patrons began to grin in anticipation. The tune was a classic bardic lay celebrating the victory of some long-moldering dwarf king. The common folk knew a less lofty history of this event, and it appeared that the pretty girl with the red harp slung over her shoulder was about to celebrate in song and verse an embarrassing moment in dwarven history. To a tavernful of well-oiled elves, few prospects could be half so appealing.

Elizerain finished the song with a flourish—a risqué double entendre that had her audience clapping and hooting with laughter.

"That's not how it happened," announced a deep, resonant male voice.

The merriment faded as Elizerain turned to regard the speaker, a well dressed, high-nose Koada'Dal who didn't look old enough to be frequenting taverns.

But Elizerain was no stranger to hecklers. Her face furrowed in mock concern. "What's the matter, youngling? Need someone to explain the ending to you?"

That brought another burst of laughter, as well as several shouted requests for a private explanation. Before Elizerain could launch into another song, the elves seated closest to the door—all of them wearing the Songweavers' crest—rose to their feet to honor someone just entering the tavern.

Elizerain's gaze went to the newcomers: a tall man with long black hair and the palest blue eyes she'd ever seen, and a lovely half elf, her face deeply shadowed by the hood of her blue robe.

But Elizerain knew that face, as did most everyone in Kelethin who loved music. Her eyes widened in something approaching awe, and she promptly hopped down off the bar. She might not be much of a bard, but she knew enough to give way to her betters. Manarla Willowmere had entered the room, and they didn't come much better than that.

"The young elf lord is quite right, you know," the man with Manarla said. "A bard should have more regard for tradition. Perhaps we should hear the song as it was meant to be sung?"

A murmur of anticipation rippled through the tavern,

and chairs and tables scraped aside to clear a space in the center of the room. The traditional ballad might be heavy fare for such a night, but Manarla was an incomparable singer.

The half elf moved to the center of the makeshift stage and delivered the ballad flawlessly, in a high, clear tone that had often been compared to crystal bells.

But something about her performance struck Elizerain as odd. For one thing, Manarla did not put down her hood. For another, no thread of emotion connected song and singer. The skillful vocal ornamentation—little trills and turns meant to add color and commentary to the tale—seemed strangely divorced from the words, as devoid of meaning as the frills and ribbons on a party gown. And the magic that was a constant, almost audible undertone to bard-song was completely absent.

The applause was respectful but brief. Elizerain refused to climb the bar again after that, for it would be an insult to follow so renowned a bard with tavern tunes. Mindful of her deal with the barkeep, she made up the difference in the agreed-upon cost of her fire-ale with a small silver coin. No matter what Xander thought of her, she was no thief.

But the ranger's words stayed with her, and Elizerain found merriment elusive with his brown-eyed, somber gaze fixed steadfastly upon her. Shortly thereafter she left the tavern, deep in thought.

And *what* thoughts!

She, Elizerain Greenleaf, had engaged an audience more completely than had Manarla Willowmere, one of the greatest bards in the land!

Granted, her little song had been helped along by plentiful ale and a festive mood, but the listeners had been pulled into the tale and pleased with her singing. It wasn't bardic magic, but wasn't it an enchantment of another sort? Mayhap it would be enough to gain her a spot in the ballad competition tomorrow.

Mayhap she might actually *win* that competition.

This grandiose thought brought a grin to Elizerain's face and set butterflies aflight in her stomach. An unlikely scenario, and well that it was!

After all, it wouldn't do to have the Songweavers taking too close a look at her recent adventures.

A DARK FIGURE CREPT OUT OF THE SMALLFOLKS INN, glancing surreptitiously into the night. The midnight hour had come and gone, and though revelry continued in the guildhall and the taverns, most of the city's residents had long ago sought their beds. The Songweavers' Feast would last for days, and those who had experienced it knew better than to sprint at the start of a long race.

Drawing a dark cape more tightly around her shoulders, the small hunter slipped into the night. Her slippers made no sound on the broad planks of the city platform. When someone approached, she simply stood still—utterly still, with never a breath to betray her presence among the night shadows.

She moved with unerring instinct to the home of a village apothecary—an easy place to find, provided one could follow the scent of herbs and flowers. But the hunter followed a far more subtle trail: the scent of a dark lord's blood, and the call of his magic.

The soft sound of deep, even breathing came from the apothecary's hut. Doors and windows were flung open to catch the night breeze, revealing a simple two-room cottage, with one room equipped for cooking and general purposes, the other for sleeping. Just behind it stood an outbuilding, a fragrant shed filled with drying herbs and small bottles of tinctures and oils. Several hammocks stretched between the two buildings.

The hunter went to the first hammock, standing on tiptoe to peer in. She immediately rocked back, dashing a hand under her pert nose to dispel the scent of tainted blood. The same herbs that cured could also kill, and years of handling them had rendered the apothecary about as appealing to her as day-old fish.

Ah, but the next one! The scent of fresh, young blood rising from the next hammock filled the hunter's senses like fey wine and raised her burning thirst past the point of endurance. The hammock had been slung low to accommodate the short limbs of an elven child, which simplified matters greatly.

For a moment the hunter regarded the elfling, a pretty brown-haired girl who slept with a small thumb tucked into the place a pair of baby teeth had recently vacated—very recently, judging by the faint tang of blood riding on the child's sweet breath.

Moving softly, so softly, the predator leaned into the hammock and smoothed soft brown locks away from the elfling's neck. Small white fangs flashed down, drawing a gasp from the sleeping child. The creature stayed at the girl's throat as long as she dared, then moved on to the next hammock, where the mother slept. She took a bit of blood from each—enough to sustain her, but not enough to kill.

At last she eased away from the elf woman and crept into the cottage, moving more quickly now that she'd fed. Dawn would not be long in coming, and she had one other compelling need to tend.

The harp stood on a small bedside table. Even in the dark, its blood red hue gleamed invitingly. The hunter's small hands traced its crimson lines, lingered lovingly on the silent strings. She would steal it if she dared, play it if she could. The harp's voice was something the hunter craved more than blood.

Yet she knew it could not be. In such a place as Kelethin, too many ears would be tuned to such magic as might be cast with an artifact as powerful as this.

The elven bard stirred in her sleep. Hatred burned bright in the hunter's unbeating heart as she gazed at the undeserving wench. Her hands were reaching for that slim brown throat when the crow of a cockerel rose from behind a nearby hut.

When yard-fowl sang, dawn could not be far away.

The hunter hurried from the hut, almost running in her haste to get back to the Smallfolks Inn before morning overtook her. As she dashed around a corner, she plowed solidly into a tall figure clad in black and crimson. Her acute night senses were rapidly fading, but she caught the scent of old death amid those robes. Terror made her heart leap and skip a beat.

Her heart was beating.

This realization brought a measure of calm to the gnome. The night had passed, and with it the curse of the blood red harp. She was once again mortal, apprenticed to a necromancer of great and terrifying power. She took a long, calming breath and stepped away from the necromancer's steadying grasp.

"A fair morning to you, master," Alisar said brightly. "I trust you slept well?"

4

THE BAD LOSERS

LATE THE NEXT AFTERNOON, HER STOMACH RUMbling for lack of a midday meal, Elizerain stood beside the stage of the Songweavers' guildhall, her harp in her hands and her heart in her throat.

It had seemed like such a lark, passing off a newly made song as an ancient ballad. Her enthusiasm for this little jest had lasted through the long morning of trials and the selection of those deemed worthy to compete. But now, standing before an audience of bards—including living legends whose names had been spoken with awe for many years—Elizerain was ready to add this day's work to her collection of tales ending with, "But it sounded like a good idea at the time."

Last night she'd taken liberties with a traditional song and had been duly chastised by a bard she deeply admired. What greater humiliation awaited her today?

Her trepidation increased when Manarla Willowmere glided into the guildhall, still swathed in her blue cloak. Manarla had not competed in the morning trials—that was not necessary for a bard of her stature—but Elizerain had allowed herself to hope she would not face the half elf soprano again.

Manarla's human patron was with her, clad in robes of black and crimson. His long black hair had been plaited into many small braids, which were caught back into a knot at the nape of his neck. It was an elaborate, almost feminine style, but the man's sharp-featured face and broad shoulders conspired against this interpretation. Indeed, he was an exceptionally handsome man, of the sort that usually brought a smile to Elizerain's face and a pleasant heat to her imagination. For some reason, however, this man left her utterly cold.

She noted then how the bards at the judging bench drew back from him in mingled distaste and horror. Sylia Windlehands, the bard guildmaster in charge of the ballad competition, hurried over. A low, furious conversation ensued, which every person in the hall did his best to eavesdrop upon. The word *necromancer* drifted through the room on a soft murmur.

Elizerain shifted from foot to foot while the debate raged quietly on. Finally Sylia broke away, her face set with anger. Her bosom, most of which was displayed by her low-cut leather armor, rose and fell with her sharp, rapid breaths, and the emerald set into her gold belt buckle flared with banked magic.

The guildmaster strode back to the stage and curtly announced, "Elizerain Greenleaf, singing 'The Ballad of Harpers Past,' a folk song with novelty instrument accompaniment."

Novelty, was it?

An unaccustomed spark of anger flared in Elizerain's heart, and she used it to set her song alight.

She climbed onto the stage and poured into the made-up tale her lifelong love of the harp. She imbued the melody with the childhood comfort of falling asleep to the sound of silver strings. She celebrated the magic in the music her parents had played, music the simple, hardy people of the lake country loved. Her passion lent strength to her voice and a layer of irony to her song, written to be no more than a pseudo-folktale "explanation" of why the bards of yore had set aside their harps. Elizerain gave the song everything she had and more than she'd ever suspected she possessed.

Her audience listened politely and applauded with what sounded like genuine enthusiasm. Elizerain quit the stage gratefully and slumped into a seat near the back. She would have dearly loved to flee the guildhall altogether, but that would have been considered an egregious breach of etiquette.

The singing went on until twilight, each bard performing according to the ranking assigned at the morning trials. Elizerain had sung first, which told the listening world that she'd just barely squeaked into the competition.

Yet as the afternoon wore on, her embarrassment wore thin. In truth, Elizerain didn't think the other ballads were that much superior to the one she'd presented. Tradition was a fine thing, but apparently something could also be said for innovation!

At last Manarla Willowmere took the stage. Sylia Windlehands gave the name of her ballad as "The Blood Red Harp."

Elizerain sat bolt upright. Then, keenly aware of the eyes turning her way, she slumped back down in her seat and wished with all her heart she could disappear into the cushion.

Sweet Tunare, not again! She wasn't sure she could bear

two comparisons to Manarla Willowmere in as many days!

But the tale that unfolded in the half elf's crystalline soprano was nothing at all like Elizerain's. Instead of singing of bygone days when bards were harpers and proud of it, Manarla told of a crypt in the Hills of Shade, unearthed by the shifting landscape, and the strange treasures found there. She sang of a small band of dark elves who'd discovered the crypt and their fate at the hands of the powerful young spell-caster who outwitted and overcame them.

The ballad's elegant verse and perfect meter did little to disguise its purpose: a blatant paean to the magic-wielding "hero." Manarla sang his praises long enough to make an entire roomful of Feir'Dal and half elves wish they could in good conscience root for the vanquished Teir'Dal crypt robbers.

Manarla's ballad was the last in the competition. The judges did not require long debate. They put their heads together, consulted briefly, and quietly passed their decision to Sylia Windlehands. The guildmaster smirked and turned to face the room.

"By unanimous decision, the winner is Elizerain Greenleaf."

Elizerain sat in stunned silence, bracing herself for a general outcry against the judges' decision. But to her astonishment, people were applauding, and many actually smiled and nodded to her. For a moment it seemed to her that even the necromancer looked pleased.

She made her way to the front of the room and accepted her prize: a finely embroidered badge for her tunic and a scroll containing a new bard-spell. She stuffed both into her bag for future perusal. The only thing she wanted to see at present was the bottom of a tall tankard.

Someone pressed a goblet of green wine into her hand as she stepped off the stage. Close enough, she reasoned, lifting the elegant vessel in a gesture of thanks to the well-wishers who crowded around. They mirrored her salute with raised goblets and tankards of their own and then attempted, with varying degrees of sputtering success, to mimic her single-minded attention to emptying her goblet.

By the time Elizerain came up for air, the general mood of the gathering had changed from competition to revel. Servants wandered about carrying trays laden with refreshments. A quartet of string players struck up a quadrille. Normally Elizerain would have been fascinated by the theorbo one of the bards played, for the large, deep-voiced version of the lute was rarely seen in Kelethin. Tonight, however, she felt uncomfortably aware of measuring eyes upon her.

Thank Tunare she had thought to leave her singing sword back at the apothecary's hut! The fewer questions asked about *that*, the better.

For what seemed like hours, Elizerain accepted congratulations and parried questions about her training in Antonica. As soon as she decently could, she made her excuses and hurried out of the hall.

Her host family lived nearby. Elizerain hurried to the sleeping chamber and removed her sword belt from under the mattress of sweet-smelling leaves. She quickly belted it on and set off for the nearest tavern. An overabundance of green wine had left her feeling lightheaded, and the pretty tidbits served at the guild hall had about the same effect on her hunger as being poked with a stick had on a chained wolf. A bowl of thick stew, she thought longingly, and perhaps some bread and cheese to go with it.

She hadn't gone more than a few paces before a strong hand clamped down hard on her shoulder and yanked her to an abrupt halt. She pulled free and whirled to face her attacker, one hand on the hilt of her short sword.

To her surprise, she found herself face to face with the necromancer.

She must have been mistaken about the human's reaction to the outcome of the ballad competition. Far from smiling, he gazed down at her with purest hatred.

"You did not deserve to win," he declared.

Elizerain shrugged. "Take it up with the judges."

"They only chose you to shame Manarla Willowmere. Elevating the lowliest person in the room was the deepest insult they could deliver."

Since similar thoughts had flitted through Elizerain's mind, she didn't feel inclined to debate the matter—particularly not in Manarla's hearing. The legendary bard stood a few paces behind her patron, observing this exchange in silence.

"Would you like to know why the judges did this?" he persisted.

Irritation began to win out over fear. "Not especially, but I suppose you're going to tell me."

"Mind your manners, wench," he warned. "You might not know who I am, but you know *what* I am. For a wiser woman, that knowledge would suffice."

The necromancer motioned Manarla Willowmere to his side, then reached for the hood of her cloak and yanked it down.

Elizerain instinctively fell back a step.

The half elf, one of the most famous bards in Faydwer, was dead. Walking dead, even *singing* dead, but thoroughly deceased nonetheless. A milky film clouded her blue eyes, and no hint of emotion or thought enlivened her lovely face. The faint, sickly-sweet odor of decay lingered about her, despite the silver pomander attached to the ties of her cloak. From a distance Manarla could pass, but up close there was no mistaking her for a living woman.

Yet Elizerain had been almost this close to the half elf last night. She didn't know how she could have missed it, even considering the faint, flickering light of the tavern. An illusion spell, perhaps? No, such magic was the purview of an enchanter, not a necromancer.

Of course, sufficiently wealthy folk could *purchase* magic they could not *cast*. Judging from the abundance of rings bedecking Manarla's gloved hands and the wide collar of gold and gems encircling her slender throat, the necromancer had no shortage of coin to lavish on his new songbird. Any of the dead bard's ornaments might hold the magic needed to dull the perception of everyone in the tavern last night. No doubt the guildhall had been warded against spell-casting to keep the playing field level, but the Heartwood Tavern would have less need for such precautions.

Whatever the magical explanation, this legendary bard, through no choice of her own, trotted about Kelethin like a lapdog on a leash, or a prance-puppet in the hands of a particularly malevolent child.

Horror and pity battled for supremacy in Elizerain's heart as she stared at the animated corpse. She dragged her gaze to the necromancer and found that he wasn't much easier to behold.

"So that's what the judges' discussion was about,"

Elizerain said slowly. "Apparently no one thought to specify that bards have to be *alive* to participate in the Songweavers' Feast competitions."

"But apparently they *do* have to be alive to *win* them," the necromancer retorted, "and 'alive' is the best that can be said of you. The judges couldn't have chosen a competent bard from among the living. Oh, no! They had to pick a flighty wench who can't even get the simplest of stories straight."

Pique made Elizerain stand a little taller. "I do just fine."

"Oh? I've heard you sing two ballads, and in both performances you displayed a complete disregard for history and tradition."

Before she could respond, an oily smirk of inspiration oozed over the necromancer's face.

"I could change that," he said slowly. "With the right curse, you could be *forced* to sing a proper ballad. Of course, the effort of acting like a true bard would probably kill you . . ."

"There are worse ways to go," she shot back. "I've no doubt you *talked* poor Manarla to death."

He seized her arm when she turned to leave and spun her back. Anger flared in his pale eyes, and he muttered words in a language Elizerain had never heard. Spellcasting accomplished, he gazed at her expectantly.

Elizerain shook off his hand and stepped back. "I'm impressed, truly I am." She cocked her head and considered. "Oh, wait—your spell was supposed to make me tell the truth, so shouldn't I be unable to say things like that?"

The necromancer snarled and pulled back his arm to deliver a fisted blow. Strong, weather-bronzed hands seized his wrist before he was even close.

A tall wood elf guard, resplendent in the green scale armor of the Emerald Warriors, stepped between Elizerain and the necromancer, who stumbled back a pace or two, freeing his wrist from the elf's grasp. He tried to steady himself by seizing a handful of Manarla's cloak. The silver pomander came off in his hand. He thrust it absently into the coin bag on his belt and turned coldly malevolent eyes upon the elf guard.

"Don't lay hands on me again," he said softly.

"Come with me peaceably, and I will have no reason to do so."

The necromancer lifted an inquiring brow. "Why would I wish to do that, peaceably or otherwise?"

"Your wishes are of no consequence. There will be an inquiry into Manarla Willowmere's death, whether you *wish* it or not."

"Oh. That. I didn't kill her, if that's your concern."

"That's as may be," the warrior said sternly. "But you *did* lift a hand to this girl. You will find to your sorrow that in Kelethin, we protect the living and respect our dead."

A small crowd had gathered by now, and every person in it regarded the necromancer with unfriendly eyes. He measured his odds, then cast a final, furious look in Elizerain's direction before turning to the guard.

"Very well. Come along, Manarla," he said, as one might summon a dog.

"*No.*"

The ringing magic in that single word of command stopped the undead bard in mid-stride. Sylia Windlehands pushed her way to the front of the crowd and laid gentle hands on the half elf's shoulders.

"Manarla, old friend," she said softly. "Your name was entered on the competition rolls, and no elf in all Faydwer would deny you the right to be heard. But the time for singing is past. You will be laid to rest with the honor your life has earned."

Sylia gently turned Manarla into the hands of two green-robed clerics. A single tear spilled down her cheek as she watched them lead the bard's mortal shell away.

The guildmaster brushed the back of her hand across her face and glanced at the necromancer, fury and loathing in her green-eyed gaze. "Get that vermin out of my sight."

The Emerald Warrior inclined his head in a respectful bow. "At once, Songmistress. But as he is a spell-caster, it would be prudent to have an enchanter along."

"Of course," Sylia murmured. She lifted her gaze to the crowd. "Is there an enchanter among you who can meddle with this human's memory? Someone who can separate him from the ability to summon the undead, be they persons or beasts?"

A high elf female, an unusually tiny Koada'Dal whose golden head barely reached Elizerain's chin, stepped forward. "I can make him forget his own mother, if indeed he ever had one," she promised darkly.

"Well enough." Sylia waved the guards and their prisoner on their way and turned to Elizerain, who was scratching at a suddenly tingling scalp.

"Are you unharmed?"

Elizerain quickly lowered her hand. "I'm fine," she said hastily, though in truth she felt a bit odd.

Even as she spoke, the tingling in her scalp changed to a burning sensation, which gathered heat and strength with the speed of wildfire.

Suddenly she was aflame with pain. She staggered

away, only faintly hearing the indignant comments of the people she bumped into, only dimly aware of the guildmaster's voice lifted in concern.

Her knees gave way, and she fell to the hard wooden platform, rolling back and forth as if doing so could put out the flame. A new wave of white-hot agony struck, freezing her in place. For a moment she stared upward, seeing stars despite the thick leafy canopy that obscured the sky. Then came a second wave. Her back arched like a drawn bow, and a scream tore free of her throat.

Strong hands lifted her and carried her to a nearby building. Healing music surrounded her like incense, pushing back the attack. Elizerain felt somewhat eased: pain still pulsed through her with the force of a dragon's heartbeat, but her vision slowly cleared, and she thought that soon she would be able to draw enough breath to speak.

A high elf woman, flaxen-haired and richly dressed, moved into Elizerain's field of vision.

"What magic has done this to you?" she inquired, her blue eyes searching Elizerain's face. "Who cast this charm?"

"Necromancer," she managed. "He cursed me . . . must seek . . . the truth behind the songs I sing."

"Bards who place accuracy above accolades would have nothing to fear from such a curse," observed a musical female voice—but not so musical that the pedantic tone couldn't ring through clearly.

"This is hardly the time for that, Sarialiyn," declared Sylia Windlehands.

A moment of panic seized Elizerain. What was happening to her that could merit the attention of *two* Songweavers guildmasters?

The high elf took Elizerain's icy hands in both of hers. "I'm Niola Impholder, child, and no stranger to magic. I want you to keep your eyes on mine while I rid you of this charm. All right?"

Elizerain nodded, feeling better already. She knew that name: Niola Impholder was one of three masters of the Arcane School, an aristocrat who was near kin to royalty and said to be as wealthy as any three gods and, most importantly, a great magician. She also looked vaguely familiar. Possibly Elizerain had seen her from afar during a visit to Felwithe.

She kept her eyes steady on Niola's blue gaze as the magician cast spell after spell. The worst of the pain ebbed away, but the curse remained, like a pack of wolves lingering just beyond the circle of a campfire's light, crouched and ready for the attack.

Finally the mage fell silent and slumped back into a chair, her lovely face drawn and pale from the effort of so much spell-casting.

"I feel much better," Elizerain said tentatively.

This brought a wry smile to Niola's face. "You needn't humor me, child. The spells didn't work as they should have; I know that as well as you do. I'm afraid the necromancer who cursed you will have to be induced to lift the spell. Can he be found?"

Sylia Windlehands explained the circumstances of the necromancer's departure. A young half elf male wearing a Songweavers' crest offered to seek him out and fetch him back.

The rest of them settled down to wait, with the bards taking turns singing healing spells. None of them improved upon Niola's efforts, but bard-song kept Elizerain's burning agony at bay, even if it stopped short of dousing the fire.

At long last the half elf returned, a large sack slung over his shoulder. He was limping badly, and his bronzed face was strangely gray.

"Gone," he said in a dull, strange voice. "They're all gone."

Niola bolted to her feet. "The necromancer escaped? How is this possible?"

The half elf seemed not to hear the high elf's question or even note her presence. He stood as if caught in a sleepwalker's nightmare, swaying uncertainly on his feet.

Sylia Windlehands strode forward and backhanded the young bard across the face. "Collect yourself, Geminar! What befell?"

The youth lifted his gaze to hers. The dazed expression in his eyes gave way to dawning horror.

"I . . . I don't remember."

5

Chained Lightning

MEMORY, MUSED CHANZOON NEXIS, WAS A funny thing. Not as tangible as treasure, hardly more substantive than shadow, it was a complex marvel of spirit, flesh, and the peculiar alchemy of the brain. Enchanters put great store in their ability to separate a man from his memories, but in Chanzoon's opinion, they gave insufficient consideration to the question of precisely what memories were and, more importantly, where they *went*.

Any mind, even the primitive mind of orc or ogre, had many rooms, including hidden chambers that opened only to dreams or madness. And as his gnome apprentice had observed, even muscles had memory—else how could a master swordsman fight without pausing to consider strategy or a bard's fingers so knowingly traverse the lute strings? Indeed, the memories belonging to the body outlasted those of the mind, as anyone who had dealings with the undead well knew. Chanzoon knew the undead, and on the whole, he preferred them to the living, but that didn't keep him from remembering lessons learned before he found his true calling. He possessed wards and countermeasures far beyond the common defenses against an enchanter's intrusive magic.

In short, Chanzoon was no helpless captive, but he saw no reason to deprive his two elven guards of this comforting fiction. The necromancer let the two elves march him briskly away from the harp-playing wench he'd just placed under a curse, and, more importantly from his point of view, away from the powerful spellcasters who'd come to claim what was left of Manarla Willowmere.

The necromancer's guards were taking their charge seriously; the Emerald Warrior's hand clamped around Chanzoon's wrist like a band of iron, and the little enchanter regarded him steadily, her narrowed eyes all but daring him to attempt a spell.

The high elf had spirit, Chanzoon noted, and confidence in her magical prowess. Clearly, she thought herself more than his match. Under other circumstances, he might have enjoyed taking the time to explain her error to her at length.

Behind them, the latest wielder of the blood red harp let out a scream of pure agony. It would, the necromancer knew, be the first of many.

This prospect brought a smile to his face, which in turn earned him a shove from the elf warrior. The necromancer made note of this small indignity and vowed to deal with it anon. At the moment, however, he was more interested in the enchanter.

Chanzoon doubted the little high elf was powerful enough to breach his mental shields, much less ferret out the hidden pathways where memory had burrowed deep into mind and muscle. If perchance she managed this feat, she was not going to like what she found.

"This place will do for our purposes," the enchanter decreed. She pointed to a narrow walkway between two shops, deserted but for an elf child trying to coax a striped cat out from under a tumble of empty crates.

A gesture from the high elf brought the cat stalking out of its small fortress, its high-held tail and haughty mien proclaiming that this had been its intent all along. The child gathered up the cat and gave the enchanter a nod of thanks before scurrying off, fondly scolding her pet the while.

A frisson of unease ran down Chanzoon's spine. Cats were the most contrary creatures on four legs, and the mind of a cat was no easy thing to influence. He knew of only one other enchanter who'd even bothered to try.

He glanced at the high elf female, taking note of her narrowed eyes and small, knowing smile.

"Cyntharia Starflower spoke of you," the enchanter said casually, confirming Chanzoon's suspicions—and revealing the reason for her confident manner. "Nothing good, of course."

Her smile dropped off her face so suddenly Chanzoon expected to hear it shatter on the tree city's wooden platform. An expression of intense concentration furrowed her brow.

Chanzoon barely had time to ready his defenses before the first wave of her assault engulfed him. Magic bombarded his thoughts like rocks hurled by a siege catapult. Painful, to be sure, but hardly a subtle attack, and easily defended.

But as the necromancer shored up his outer mental defenses, he noted that the walls within had begun to fade into translucence. The enchanter had already passed through his first boundaries, as easily as if they'd been woven from smoke and shadow, so skillfully that he had not noticed her passage. She'd distracted him with simple magic to conceal her real purpose, and now the outer rooms of his memory lay bare to her, like a garden maze fashioned of glass.

Chanzoon swiftly gathered his thoughts, as a laundry maid might snatch up fallen linens, and retreated deeper into his mind. The enchanter followed, brushing easily past Chanzoon's memories of the day's events, past the journey to Kelethin, moving deeper, closing in on his hold of ready spells like a pack of hounds running a wolf to ground.

The necromancer made no move to defend. He could not stop the enchanter now or even slow her much. She was simply too powerful to deny.

And too proud to understand.

Her probing magic tripped a guardian spell, something Chanzoon had learned from his first master. The unleashed ward-spell skittered back along the enchanter's magical path, like lighting skimming across water toward the lone swimmer too foolish to come in out of the storm.

A flash of brilliant blue lit the outer corridors of Chanzoon's mind, which were now satisfyingly empty of magical intrusion.

The necromancer blinked away remnants of the spell and turned his focus outward. His attacker sat several paces away amid a tumble of crates. Her face was slack with astonishment, and her blond hair stood on end in a near-perfect globe, like the gossamer strands of a meadow flower about to cast its seed.

"Cyntharia spoke of me? How gratifying," Chanzoon

said, mimicking the mockingly casual tone of the enchanter's last comment. "Oddly, I'm not surprised that *your* name never came up in conversation."

A heavy blow to the back of the neck dropped Chanzoon to his knees, and a booted foot drove toe-first into his gut, driving the air from his lungs and leaving him gasping for breath.

Ah, yes: the wood elf guard. Chanzoon had almost forgotten about him. A foolish, proud oversight on his part—and ironic, too, considering his contemplation on memory, not to mention the importance of mind *and* muscle!

The wood elf dragged the necromancer roughly to his feet. "Can you rise unaided, Lady Mage? If need be, I can throw this human scum off the city platform to free up my hands."

"Nay, hold him fast," the enchanter said grimly. She hauled herself up and hobbled forward, one foot dragging slightly and every movement as jerky as a string puppet's.

But there was nothing wrong with her magic. Chanzoon could feel the building power of it even before she seized a handful of his tiny braids and dragged his head down to her eye level. Her slim fingers clasped his temples, and memory flowed away from Chanzoon like lamp oil rising through ten thirsty wicks.

Finally the high elf stepped back, her face as white as death and her eyes dark with the terrible knowledge she'd taken from the necromancer.

The guard studied the enchanter with concern. "Can you carry this burden long enough for us to take him from Kelethin? A place has been prepared in the forest beyond to contain the likes of him."

"Then to the lift platform, and quickly," she said in a

strained voice. "The sun has set, and some say a necromancer's power grows with the night. I've no desire to test the truth of that saying."

They did not speak again until they reached the platform that led down to the forest floor. The wood elf guard spoke a few low, urgent words to the lift keeper, who waved away a small band of approaching revelers and bid them seek the south lift. He motioned the necromancer's guard onto the empty platform.

Chanzoon allowed the elves to take him onto the lift, though he was fairly certain there was reason he should not. The lift keeper pulled a lever, and the gnome-built device began its descent. This troubled Chanzoon. He'd enjoyed the novelty of this transport when he arrived in Kelethin—was it just yesterday? But now he felt edgy, restless, and unable to shake the mental image of himself frantically rummaging through a dusty library to retrieve some forgotten but important information.

"Scrolls," he mumbled, reacting to the image of his own hands triumphantly dragging a handful of spell scrolls from an iron-bound chest. "But look—they're sealed, and the wax bears elven markings. No matter. Surely there's a small knife hereabouts . . ."

An expression closely akin to panic flicked in the high elf's eyes. She turned to the lift keeper. "Can't this thing move any faster?"

"Patience, Lady Mage. Your prisoner has nowhere to go. And he's a necromancer, is that not so? There is nothing dead here for him to command."

As if in response, the wooden platform under their feet buckled and groaned. A long fissure ran across one broad plank, and a shard of wood, long and sharp as a sword, peeled away from the wood with an eerie scream.

The platform jolted, obliging all four occupants to adjust their footing or fall.

Before they could regain their balance, a small figure dropped onto the platform, landing like a cat on all fours and then immediately springing, still catlike, to the Emerald Warrior's throat. Chanzoon had caught a glimpse of her bloodless face and slender white fangs just before she struck.

It was a small, pretty, and very familiar face.

"Alisar?" the necromancer said wonderingly.

Then his stolen spells flooded back into his mind, and with them the full memory of this evening's events.

Wrath came hard on the heels of memory. At his bidding, dark magic gathered in his outstretched hands, swiftly shaping into pulsing globes of malevolent purple light.

He hurled one globe at the lift keeper, who had thrown his weight against the lever in an attempt to change the platform's direction. The dark fire struck the elf full in the chest and burned right through. He went down like a felled tree, falling straight back, an expression of astonishment on his face and a charred hole where his heart had been.

Chanzoon turned to the enchanter, his next missile at the ready. But the high elf had flung herself at Alisar, burying her hands in the gnome's abundant brown curls as she tried to tear her away from the guard's throat.

The necromancer had no wish to harm his gnome apprentice, whatever else she might be. He dismissed the dark fire with a flick of his fingers and stooped to retrieve the dagger from the lift keeper's belt.

It was well for him that he did, for at that moment the lift shuddered and swayed as a new passenger joined them, leaping down from the city platform. The sudden jolt knocked the enchanter loose and sent her reeling away from the dying guard. He stumbled and fell, with Alisar riding him down.

The newcomer, a young half elf who made up in muscle what he lacked in elven agility, rose from an awkward crouch, his horrified gaze fixed on the fallen guard and his small, strange attacker. Like the enchanter, the half elf's first thought was to try to pull Alisar away. But he soon realized the futility of this: the guard had fallen onto the wooden spike. The point of it thrust up through his tunic, and the sluggish flow of blood around it declared that the elf was already dead, or near enough as made no difference.

A soft chanting drew Chanzoon's attention to the female elf. She had risen to her knees, and her hands gestured with deadly grace as she wove a spell.

The necromancer swiftly rose to his feet and closed on the enchanter in two quick strides. He silenced her with a single brutal kick, hard enough to knock the breath from her body. The interrupted spell lingered uncertainly, fragile as a soap bubble and glowing with faint azure light.

Chanzoon muttered a spell of his own that sent the enchanter's mind-numbing spell hurtling toward the half elf. The youth stopped dead, one hand on the hilt of his half-drawn sword. All emotion, all intelligence, drained away, leaving his face as vacant of life as the dying guard's.

Quite a spell, Chanzoon admitted. It was almost a shame to kill so talented a spell-caster.

Almost.

He dropped to one knee beside the enchanter and got a good grip on her head. A single sharp twist, and her neck gave way with a satisfying crack.

At the sound, Alisar lifted her head from the fallen guard's neck. She wiped an errant drop of blood from her lips with a delicate forefinger, which she touched to her tongue.

"What are you?" Chanzoon demanded.

The gnome sent him a dimpled smile, a familiar expression that nonetheless chilled him to the bone. "At the moment, I'm quite full, thank you."

For the life of him, the necromancer could think of no response. Fortunately, Alisar didn't seem to require one. She stepped over the fallen guard and pulled the lever easily. The lift creaked to a stop a few feet short of the forest floor and began to rise.

"Can you turn the female into the walking dead, Master? We need at least one of the guards if we're to escape, and this one—" She paused to toe the warrior's torn throat with a dainty blue slipper, then shrugged prettily. "Ah, well. My table manners are usually much tidier than this."

By now Chanzoon was becoming accustomed to Alisar's newly discovered talents. "The elf wench will be greatly improved by the transformation," he said grimly.

This comment earned him another flash of dimples. "I'm sure you have a plan, but may I tell you what I had in mind?"

"By all means."

"Just before we reach the forest floor, the lift will change direction again. You and I will jump out as if we are attempting to run. The enchanter will follow. Will she be able to talk?"

"I retrieved the enspelled pomander from Manarla Willowmere," the necromancer said. "She will repeat any words I give her."

He took the little silver orb from his coin purse and attached it to the stays of the enchanter's gown. An unusual magical item, it cast an illusion of life around any undead creature. Having secured it, he glanced up at the creature he knew as Alisar.

"Can you deal with the half elf while I cast the spells of animation? There's no telling how long the mind-numbing effects will last."

She nodded happily and traipsed over to the dazed half elf. Chanzoon bent his attention to the complicated spells needed to bring the dead back to a semblance of life. His concentration faltered once at the thick, wet sound of tearing flesh, but he got through the casting—and judging by the steady crescendo of sound from the forest below, with not a moment to spare.

Shouldn't they be changing direction? For what was Alisar waiting?

"Why aren't you—"

The necromancer's question froze in his throat as he took in the scene before him.

Alisar lay face down, sprawled across the guard's body. The tip of the wooden spike protruded from her back, and the half elf stood over her, his face still glazed with the remnants of the enchanter's spell.

Memory, the necromancer noted with a sort of numb detachment, was indeed a strange and complex thing.

Rage swept over him in a swift, red wave, but he dared not give way to it. The lift had nearly completed its ascent; there was no time to avenge Alisar, much less to retrieve her body.

Instead he gave the undead enchanter the words she should speak and sent her over to pull the lever. Alive, her strength was less than his own, but the dead spent themselves freely without care for torn sinews and strained joints. Again, the platform creaked to a halt and changed its course. When it had nearly completed its descent, Chanzoon leaped to the ground and began to run. He heard the lighter footfall as the undead elf woman followed, heard her call out the words he'd taught her. Playing his part, he faltered to a stop and turned toward her, his face carefully arranged in an imitation of the half elf's vacant stare.

Apparently the petite enchanter was well known and highly regarded, for the squadron of guards below Kelethin accepted her explanation of attempted escape and her intent to deliver the necromancer to the detainment area prepared for unruly, magically gifted guests. They stepped aside without argument, allowing the undead enchanter and her "prisoner" to disappear into the forest shadows.

SYLIA WINDLEHANDS GRIPPED THE HALF ELF'S shoulders with both hands, her green eyes searching his face.

"He's under some sort of enchantment. Lady Impholder?"

Niola Impholder rose wearily and came to the guildmaster's side. She spoke a few words of a dispersement spell.

Memory returned to the young bard's eyes in a sudden rush, and the blood drained from his face.

"Tell us," the mage said gently. She touched the sack slung over his shoulder. "Or show us, if that is easier."

The half elf swallowed hard, then dumped the contents of the sack onto the floor.

For a long moment the elves stared at the body of a small gnome maiden, a pretty little thing with curly brown hair and blue eyes—eyes that were open and staring in what appeared to be a poignant plea for her young life. A wooden stake, a makeshift weapon formed from what appeared to be a handful of arrows, had been driven through her heart.

"That's a gnome," Elizerain said at last, raising incredulous eyes to the young bard. "What were you intending to do—roast her on a spit?"

Anger brought some of the color back to the half elf's face. "Where is it written that only dark elves and humans can become vampires?"

"A gnome vampire?" Sylia said skeptically.

"I know what I saw," the youth asserted. "She had Michlar down and was clinging to his neck like a tick."

"So you killed her with a handful of arrows? Impossible!"

"That's not how it happened," Geminar said miserably. "We fought and fell. There was a long wooden spike, thrusting up from the lift platform. You'll see it."

"And you removed her from it, and put a handful of arrows in its place?" persisted the guildmaster.

"Good thinking," Elizerain put in. "I can think of risks worth taking, but none of them involve vampires."

"I suppose," Sylia allowed.

The half elf shot Elizerain a grateful look and a nod of thanks. "That was my reasoning. No—that's not quite true. I was ruled by instinct, not reason."

"Understandable," Niola said gently. "Where did this happen?"

"On the lift. It had not descended very far, so I jumped down, though not without injury. The necromancer must have escaped while I was subduing the vampire."

Sylia's eyes narrowed. "He escaped from the lift? From Zindra's enchantments?"

"I . . . I believe Zindra went with him," he faltered. "More, I don't know."

"I'll send word to the Emerald Warriors," Sylia said curtly. She and several of the other bards left. Two of them carried the gnome girl away.

Niola considered Elizerain. "Your best chance of ridding yourself of this curse would be to find the necromancer and induce him to lift it. In the meantime, however, I suggest you fix the ballad in question. Which one is troubling you?"

There was no doubt about that. Images of stone walls and brilliant mosaic floors flooded Elizerain's mind. She'd never seen the dwarven kingdom, but she'd heard enough about Kaladim to recognize it. Even if she had not, the tune she'd sung in Heartwood Tavern was running softly and insistently through her thoughts.

"It's 'The Prince of Kaladim.' I . . . don't know all the words to the original version," Elizerain admitted.

"Nor do I, but I know where it can be purchased," offered the half elf. "Serilia Whistlewind sells bard-song. If she's not in her shop at this hour, someone else should be. Such places never close during the Songweavers' Feast. If you like, I'll show you the way."

Elizerain nodded her thanks and fell into step with the young bard, who gave his name as Geminar Wolfsong. At first she leaned on his offered arm, but with each pace, the pain ebbed a little more. By the time they paused before a small, round, wooden shop, she felt more like her normal self and not inclined to part with hard-won silver for a set of moldy lyrics.

Her head immediately began to itch. She quickly

rededicated herself to this small quest and stepped into the shop.

An elf woman with brown hair dipping into a pronounced widow's peak glanced up when they entered. Her faint smile of welcome broadened.

"Elizerain Greenleaf, isn't it? The winner of the ballad competition?"

"Imagine my surprise," she said dully. "I'm in need of a new song. Or more accurately, a very old song."

The shopkeeper gestured to the neat rows of scrolls. "You've come to the right place. If I don't have it, chances are you'll have to compose it yourself."

That was clearly meant as a jest, and it had the well-worn feel of words frequently employed. Elizerain managed a wan smile and made her request. The dark-haired elf quickly located the scroll and handed it over with a flourish.

"Mind if I sing it here?"

The shopkeeper's eyes lit up. "Not at all. In fact, having someone sing in the shop might draw more customers. I can't think why that never occurred to me before."

Elizerain unrolled the scroll and regarded the long, long ballad. She took a deep breath, winced from the residual stab of pain the effort caused, and began to sing the words to the melody she'd pilfered for her performance the night before, albeit at a more sedate pace and without the rollicking percussion.

"Feeling better?" Geminar asked when at last she'd finished the ballad.

"Much. I'd feel better still after a tankard or two." She studied his face, which was still rather pale. "You look as if you could use a little fortifying, yourself. My treat, to thank you for your kindness."

The half elf's smile didn't reach his haunted eyes. "I would be pleased to have the company."

On impulse she took his hand, as she might comfort a child. They walked in silence to the Heartwood Tavern and settled down at a corner table to let the music and happy chatter wash away the experiences of the last few hours.

Several pair of eyes took note of their arrival. To Elizerain's surprise, Xander Fletcher was back at the tavern. He'd never been one for crowds. Like most rangers, he preferred his own company or that of a few comrades to merry gatherings such as the Songweavers' Feast.

Xander was leaning against the bar and sipping a mug of cider, his brown eyes looking at nothing in particular. Even so, Elizerain doubted he missed much.

The fair-haired heckler was there again, too, and with him were three friends who seemed cut from the same piece of cloth. Four golden heads leaned in close as the young conspirators devised some grand plot. Elizerain noted that this quartet of young Koada'Dal, all of them handsome and obviously wealthy, drew many admiring glances.

"You play very well."

Elizerain snapped her attention back to her companion. "Excuse me?"

"The harp," Geminar said, nodding to the instrument she kept slung over her shoulder. "Where did you learn to play?"

"In my cradle, and I mean that quite literally. My first harp was a tiny thing, only eight strings. It was carved from a single piece of wood so it would be durable enough to withstand childhood. It didn't come through unscathed, of course—there are bite marks on it from when I was teething. For years my father called me Rabbit, insisting I was part rodent."

Geminar sent her a fleeting smile to thank her for the tale. "The song Manarla Willowmere sang—surely it was about your harp? I've never seen another of that color."

A faint prickling sensation started at the back of Elizerain's neck. The blood drained from her face in a sudden dizzying rush.

"Sweet Tunare," she whispered. "*That's* what the necromancer wanted! He meant for me to acknowledge Manarla's song as the right and proper story!"

If only she could! In her embarrassment, she'd paid scant attention to the great bard's performance.

The half elf stared at her for a moment, then comprehension washed over his face. "It's happening again, isn't it? The curse?"

She nodded miserably. Geminar shot to his feet and cupped his hands to his mouth to amplify his words.

"Does anyone here know where to find Niola Impholder?"

The fair-haired youth looked over, and suddenly Elizerain realized why Niola had seemed so familiar to her. There was a strong family resemblance between the magician and the youngblood.

The Koada'Dal rose and strode over to the corner table. "I am Nyson Impholder," he announced in a deep, cultured voice. "What do you want with my lady mother?"

Well, this was just marvelous, Elizerain thought glumly. What better path to a long and prosperous career than insulting the scion of a prominent Felwithe family?

But she could spare scant concern for this misstep now, not with the curse rapidly closing in. Elizerain's temples pounded like kettle drums, drowning out the half elf's hurried explanation. The room began to swim around her, and the colors melted together and faded into darkness.

The next thing Elizerain heard was the chanting of healing magic. She forced her too-heavy eyelids open. Niola Impholder once again leaned over her, her beautiful face creased with fatigue and concern.

"Manarla Willowmere was laid to rest," she said softly, answering Elizerain's unspoken question. "It was done before we knew of the curse and cannot be undone."

Elizerain struggled to sit, glancing around to get her bearings. Judging from the neat rows of kegs and bottles lining the wall of the small room, someone had carried her into the tavern's storeroom. Malawen, the head barkeep, had laid in a good supply for the bard festival; there was barely room for the elves who loomed somberly over her.

And it was quite the gathering: Niola Impholder and her son, Geminar Wolfsong, and a trio of wood elves whose names Elizerain didn't know, all of whom wore the Songweavers' crest. Even Xander Fletcher stood over her, his rugged face set in gentler lines and his brown eyes warm with concern.

Elizerain dragged her attention back to the high elf mage. "What of the bards who heard Manarla sing?"

Manarla's ballad had been sung before a hall full of bards, all of whom had highly trained memories. Surely one of them would remember it.

Niola glanced at the wood elf bards, silently relaying the question.

"It would seem that no one was listening closely enough," one of them said hesitantly. "The ballad was exquisitely performed, but it was, well . . ."

"Boring," Elizerain concluded.

The bard nodded unhappily. "I'm sorry."

Geminar brightened. "Oddly enough, perhaps that is a blessing. The ballad was not of the quality one would expect from Manarla Willowmere. That suggests it was written by someone who was not a bard, and thus it may not tell the true tale. Perhaps your tales lie closer to the truth, Elizerain."

"Well said," Niola agreed. She turned to Elizerain. "It can be difficult to find the source of folktales, but you must continue the scholarly work you began and find the history that gave rise to the legend."

Panic began to well up, pushing aside the pain. For a long moment Elizerain stared at the circle of silent, expectant faces, dreading what she must say.

Understanding flooded Xander Fletcher's face, quickly chased by exasperation. "You *didn't*."

Elizerain nodded miserably. She had no choice but to confess that there was no legend behind her winning ballad, nothing but a vivid imagination and an overactive sense of mischief.

For the first time it occurred to her that some might consider her little jest to be fraud, a deliberate cheat. There was no doubt about it—this day's work would dog her steps more closely than her ill-fated romance with Davin the Dark.

But what else could be done?

She was about to confess all when the harp began to glow with a faint, azure light.

6

THE BARD'S APPRENTICE

THE SILENCE THAT FOLLOWED WAS BROKEN BY the soft sound of chanting—a deep, resonant voice that sounded years older than the elf from whence it came, and carrying a power no between-age elf should have been able to wield. Magic, powerful and unfamiliar, swirled through the sound, as tangible as the light that surrounded the red harp.

Niola Impholder stared at her son, stunned into silence by this unexpected feat. Nyson had never shown any interest in learning the art of magic: to the contrary. He had refused to attend the Arcane School and had tormented the succession of private tutors Niola had hired until each one quit in exasperation.

Questions flooded the magician's mind and danced on her tongue, but she held them back until her son's spell-casting faded into silence.

"What was that spell?" she demanded. "Where did you learn it?"

Nyson shrugged. "There's more magic in Felwithe

than Faydark has trees. Most everyone picks up a trifle or two."

His mother bit back a retort about evasive responses, for suddenly an answer came to her: Cyntharia Starflower, the youngest and certainly one of the comeliest instructors at the Arcane School, had left Felwithe shortly before the last new moon on a personal quest. She was an exceptionally powerful enchanter who had traveled widely in pursuit of her art, so her requests for occasional leaves of absence were to be expected. A few days before her last departure, she had confided to Niola that she'd been working with a gifted young student, someone who for personal reasons did not wish to enter the school.

Who but Nyson? Who among the elves of Felwithe had greater reason to avoid the Arcane School than a youth too proud and independent to walk in his mother's shadow?

Niola had been aware for some time that her son had been keeping company with some maiden. She'd assumed it was but a summer's fancy.

Apparently not. Whatever had passed between Nyson and the beautiful enchanter, it had been enough to spur him into action.

Nyson had not only bestirred himself, he had dedicated himself to a quest. His first.

The magician was not quite prepared for the twin waves of pride and worry that followed in the wake of that realization. She carefully banished all such thoughts from her face and set out to learn the nature of her son's ambitions.

"I assume that was some sort of inquiry spell. What answer did it yield?" she asked Nyson, using the respectful tone she would employ when addressing any fellow spell-caster.

He glanced at her warily, as if seeking mockery in her face or voice. Seeing none, he said slowly, "The answer came to me in riddle form:

Seek the lowest of the low, and then descend.
Seek those who can fall no further, and there begin."

Several moments passed as the small group pondered the riddle.

"The lowest of the low," Niola mused. "Some sort of burrowing creature? Or perhaps a scoundrel? Or a particularly vile monster?"

"Orcs," Xander Fletcher said decisively. "What else could it be?"

The other elves nodded, in complete agreement with this assessment of their ancient enemy.

"If orcs are the lowest—and you'll get no argument from me on that—how can you descend from there?" wondered Elizerain. She snapped her fingers. "The slave pits of Crushbone! The phrase 'and then descend' wasn't talking about being greener and nastier and worse-smelling than orcs but literally moving to a lower place."

Xander nodded approvingly. "That fits the riddle in other ways, as well. The slaves of Crushbone have fallen as low as is possible, for what fate could be worse than being slave to an orc?"

"But the next phrase instructs 'and there begin,'" one of the bards reminded Xander. "The slave pits are an end, not a beginning. There is nothing beyond, save death."

Nyson cleared his throat. "There is a legend of a hidden treasure trove under the slave pits of Crushbone. Perhaps that is what the Songmistress must seek. Perhaps the harp's origins could be learned in lore books or scrolls kept in that trove."

"I've heard that legend," Elizerain said, "but even the people who told me the tale didn't believe it. It's the sort of story people enjoy telling around a fire, and nothing more."

"You are an expert in matters of hidden treasure?" the young elf asked coolly.

"No, but I've known my share of treasure hunters," she told him. "Mind you, these are people who will devote years of their lives to chasing a rumor or following an old map. If *they* didn't take the legend seriously, why should I?"

Niola listened thoughtfully, then turned to Xander. "You are a ranger, are you not? You would know the forest's secrets better than most. What is your opinion on this matter?"

"I believe the rumors to be true."

Elizerain paused in mid-yawn and turned incredulous eyes to her old friend. "You're jesting."

The ranger shrugged. "I never have before."

"Well, that's certainly true," she murmured. "But when did you start telling tavern tales?"

"More can be learned from listening than speaking. Have you not heard of the dark elf ambassador D'Vinn? He is here in Faydark, sent by Cristanos Thex, Queen of Neriak, to make an alliance with the orcs."

"What do the Teir'Dal want with orcs?" she marveled.

"That's the question, isn't it?"

Throughout this exchange, Nyson had regarded Xander closely, his own expression carefully guarded. "This does give credence to the notion of a treasure trove beneath Crushbone," he said slowly. "I can see how rumors of ancient magic might draw some people to the orc citadel."

And there, Niola thought, was her answer. Cyntharia Starflower was just ambitious and arrogant enough to believe herself the equal of Crushbone's orcs. In such matters, it would seem that the young enchanter and Nyson had much in common.

As, apparently, did Nyson and his father.

The physical resemblance between father and son was slight, but Niola had seen just such a look on her late husband's face many a time, and she knew what it meant. Once he had decided upon a course of action, Tunare herself could not sway him from it.

"How are you feeling now, Elizerain?" she asked abruptly.

The bard considered that, and her eyes widened. "Better," she said wonderingly. "Talking about it seems to help."

"Which might mean you're headed in the right direction," put in Geminar Wolfsong. "I noticed that the closer we came to the bard-song shop, the stronger you got. Maybe this compulsion ebbs once you're on the right path."

"A valuable insight," Niola said gravely, in a tone that suggested the matter was resolved, the discussion at an end.

She thanked the bards for their help and sent them on their way, assuring them that Nyson and Xander would be sufficient to seeing Elizerain safely to her host family's home.

Niola closed the door to the storeroom behind the departing bards and leaned against it. For a long moment her gaze lingered on the ill-matched trio of elves: the stern and upright ranger; the bard who, though she flouted Songweavers convention with her red harp and Antonican training, had earned a winged sword at an impressively young age. And, of course, Niola's surprising son. Other than their elven blood, the only thing the trio had in common was the wary curiosity with which they regarded her.

The master magician took a long breath and prepared to do the most difficult thing she had ever done.

"It has long been our custom," she began slowly, "to send aspiring magic users on quests—not as adventurers pursuing their own ends, but as assistants whose sole purpose is to further the goals of their elders. Acting the part of servant teaches important lessons—lessons anyone who aspires to summon and command powerful creatures must learn."

"I am aware of this custom, as is everyone in Felwithe," Nyson said cautiously.

His mother's gaze shifted to Elizerain. "The Songmistress needs to learn the true story of the harp she carries. You, my son, will travel with her—as her apprentice."

The dumbfounded expression on the bard's face brought a faint smile to Niola's lips. "You don't particularly want an apprentice, I take it?"

Elizerain hesitated, no doubt trying to form some sort of diplomatic response. "How could I possibly refuse a request from Niola Impholder?"

There was a note of desperation in the girl's voice that suggested she would be grateful if a real answer to her seemingly rhetorical question presented itself. The mage suppressed a smile and turned to her son.

"Do you agree to this, Nyson?"

His hooded eyes held secrets, and his answering smile was wry. "How could I possibly refuse a request from Niola Impholder?"

"You do understand that on this quest Elizerain will be your master?" pressed Niola. "You will answer to her in all things."

Pride flared bright in the young elf's eyes, but the flame was swiftly banked. "I understand."

"You'll need more than two to make this work," Xander announced. "I'll go with you."

The bard threw up her hands in exasperation. "Oh, that will make all the difference in the world! Three elves should be more than enough to handle all the orcs of Crushbone."

Niola acknowledged the wood elf's words with an equally ironic smile. "In that case, I'll leave you to the task ahead."

She nodded to Elizerain, then exchanged a long glance with Xander. Finally she extended one hand to her son, who raised it to his heart in the traditional leave-taking between family or very close friends.

"May Tunare show her favor to this quest, and may her smile shine upon you all," Niola said softly.

She turned and left the tavern storeroom, walking serenely through the crowded taproom. She even managed to make her way to Regren Steelforger's home and exchange a few pleasant words with his wife before escaping to the best bedchamber. Only then, when the door was closed and there was none to see, did she allow the tears to fall.

"You said Xander was among your best," she whispered, addressing the words to her absent host. "You said he'd be equal to any mischief Nyson might get himself into. Would you have said that, my old friend, had you known my son was bound for the slave pits of Crushbone?"

MOONLIGHT FILTERED THROUGH ANCIENT TREES, casting dappled shadows on the pair of wood elves who sat at the very edge of the city platform, their legs dangling over the precipice and their hands gesturing sharply as they argued.

Xander was every bit as stubborn and opinionated as Elizerain remembered. Too bad Niola Impholder hadn't made *him* an apprentice, as well!

Elizerain had sent Nyson away hours ago, telling him to get some sleep and bid farewell to his friends. The young elf had argued this decision, pointing out that three more swords could only come in handy. Xander had ended the matter by reminding Nyson of his role in this particular excursion. Elizerain was grateful for the support. One high-nosed charge was quite enough. Her life had taken enough of a downhill turn of late without having to play nursemaid to a whole band of betweenage Koada'Dal.

That was the last point, however, on which she and Xander had agreed.

"There is a reason why Crushbone still stands," Xander explained with visibly fraying patience. "All the elves of Kelethin are not sufficient to destroy the orc citadel. The three of us can't fight them, and we certainly can't walk in unnoticed."

"Perhaps we could hire an enchanter—"

"The orcs have shamen," he broke in. "In their own citadel, the strength of their warding magic would likely go beyond any cloaking or illusion spells we might employ. I know you don't like it, but the only realistic way for an elf to get into the mines of Crushbone is as a slave."

"I spent nearly two years in a dungeon," she reminded him. "*Two years,* and another five to work my way back home. It was a rather nice dungeon, as such things go, but I'm not eager to go back underground."

"We won't be staying long."

"So you say," she retorted. "The orcs might have a different opinion on the matter."

"Would you feel better about the prospect if we had a guide? A former slave who knows the way into the orcs' citadel, and more importantly, a way *out*?"

Elizerain responded with an inelegant snort. "Well, of course. And naturally the forest is full of escaped slaves who are willing to dance back into the orcs' waiting arms."

"We only need one," he pointed out.

She regarded him for a long moment. "I don't suppose you'd happen to know anyone who fits that description?"

"As a matter of fact," he said calmly, "I just might."

7

On the Trail

CHANZOON NEXIS STALKED THROUGH THE DARK forest, following a path visible only to a necromancer's eyes.

Or so he'd thought.

The trail of necromantic magic that marked the way to his lair held some new and mysterious attraction for undead creatures. The skeleton of some long-dead elf shambled by, the mossy skull turning this way and that in apparent puzzlement as it stumbled toward the necromancer's hideaway. Chanzoon ducked as a skeletal creature winged past—a small, draconic beast with batlike wings of faintly glowing green membrane. At this rate, any fool with eyes in his head would soon be able to find Chanzoon's lair simply by following the trail of undead his magic had attracted!

Or perhaps, he mused, it was not *his* magic that attracted them.

His gnome apprentice had not advanced too far in the necromantic arts. Chanzoon had made certain of that, deliberately slowing Alisar's progress to ensure that the useful little gnome served a long apprenticeship. If someone had told him she was capable of laying a magical trail that any undead creature might follow, he would have laughed scornfully and wagered several of his favorite spells against this possibility.

Of course, he also would have bet heavily against the notion that little Alisar was a vampire.

A *vampire*!

Even now it seemed impossible. He wouldn't have believed it, had he not seen with his own eyes the speed and strength of her attack.

Alisar, a vampire. How was that possible? And how was it possible that he had never suspected?

Quite simply, because there had been nothing—*nothing!*—to raise his suspicions. Chanzoon was a necromancer of no small accomplishment. He knew the dead and the undead, and he was certain his apprentice was a mortal gnome.

Of course, he'd never before seen Alisar during the night . . .

Chanzoon stopped so abruptly that he nearly tripped over a tangle of exposed tree roots.

Mortal by day, vampire by night.

Was that possible?

If it was, the necromancer had a very good idea why the vampire lord of Mistmoore Castle so eagerly sought the blood red harp.

ELIZERAIN REGARDED HER YOUNG CHARGE WITH a critical eye. "You really don't plan to wear that, do you?"

Nyson Impholder flipped the folds of his cloak back and glanced down at his new garments. He had abandoned his fine silken wardrobe and was now outfitted quite practically in sturdy, well-cut clothing and stout walking boots.

"I don't see why not," he said at last.

The bard cast her eyes skyward. "Your cloak is *blue*. So is your tunic. If you wanted to stand out in the forest, you could hardly have chosen a better color."

"Why does it matter? It is not my custom to skulk in the shadows."

"It's not my first choice, either, but I do like to reserve skulking as an option. You never know when you might need to hunt or hide."

"If necessary, I could cast a small illusion about myself."

"And waste magic when a simple cloak would do? Save your spells to use for the good of the group. And while we're on the topic, I want a list of the spells you can cast."

Nyson considered this advice and decided that it was sound—up to a point. He peeled off his cloak and turned it around so the dull brown lining showed.

"Is this acceptable?"

The bard pursed her lips and examined him critically. Her sigh proclaimed louder than words her opinion of his sartorial judgment. "It'll have to do."

"I can purchase another cloak," he said stiffly.

Elizerain shook her head. "We've a long path ahead, and little time to waste in the shops. Xander's waiting for us at the north lift."

They walked in silence through the city to where the red-haired ranger awaited them. Like Elizerain, he was clad in forest hues of dull greens and browns, and he was armed with a sword, a pair of daggers, and a hunting bow. He returned Nyson's scrutiny with a searching gaze of his own.

"Let's see that sword."

Nyson unsheathed the slender weapon and presented it, hilt first. The ranger didn't spare even a glance at the rich jewels adorning the weapon. He hefted the sword to test the balance, then sliced the air with a trio of swift passes that traced a jagged lightning bolt. He raised it to eye level and sighted down the length. Morning light glinted off the keen double edge. The ranger gave a single nod.

"Well made, well maintained," Xander said as he returned the weapon. "Do you know how to use it?"

Nyson named his former sword master, noting with satisfaction the flicker of surprise in the ranger's dark eyes.

In truth, Nyson suspected that he had learned more from this exchange than had Xander. The great Koada'-Dal master had become reclusive in later life and had not accepted students for many years. His regard for Niola Impholder had led him to make an exception for her son, on the condition that no one in Felwithe learned of this arrangement. The old elf had carried another name during his adventurous youth, but only the most avid students of the fighting arts knew the master's true name, and Xander Fletcher did. That, in Nyson's opinion, boded well for the ranger's skills and, by extension, the success of their quest.

The sound of merry chatter grew ever louder as the lift carried the latest revelers high into the trees. When it came to a halt, a dozen or so Koada'Dal, richly dressed in festival silks and fine gems, swept past the waiting adventurers. None of them gave the brown-cloaked Nyson more than a passing glance.

A wry smile touched his lips. He knew these elves. Had they met in Felwithe, they would have greeted him with all due respect—that is, all the respect due a kinsman of Niola Impholder. Out of context and on his own, he was apparently much less impressive and far less visible.

No matter. Borrowed fame was of little use to him. The success of his quest was dependent not upon his noble Koada'Dal connections or even his own, not inconsiderable talents; it rested on the slight shoulders of a wood elf wench. That should have struck him as ironic. That it did not was . . . interesting.

His gaze dropped to the sword on Elizerain's hip. The red gem and winged hilt were clearly visible above the battered scabbard, a shining promise of her persuasive power. Nyson had seen her bewitch a tavern of elves with naught but a silly little song. Tunare only knew how many warriors she could sway with true bardic magic!

They rode the lift down in silence and began to make their way through the encampment under the city. With every step, Nyson's anticipation grew. Surely now the bard would gather the reinforcements they so desperately required!

But the wood elves wove their way through the tangle of wagons and horses and guards with no more than a nod to those they passed. When he could bear no more, Nyson prodded, "Shouldn't we discuss a plan?"

"We already have," Elizerain said, shooting a sidelong look at Xander. "Find some orcs. Get captured. Go to Crushbone."

"*That's* your plan?"

"It has some additional refinements," the bard said dryly. "First we're going to hire a guide who can help us find some orcs, get captured, and go to Crushbone."

"An escaped slave," Xander elaborated. "He knows a secret way out of the citadel. You may judge him a little rough around the edges, but he's our best chance of finding what we came for and getting out alive."

As much as Nyson hated to admit it, that thin strategy was superior to anything he and his friends had been able to devise. Upon consideration, it sounded vastly superior to the spur-of-the-moment plan he had set in motion last night.

Recruiting Elizerain Greenleaf to his cause had been an act of impulse. He'd seen how the crowd at the Heartwood Tavern had responded to her singing, and he'd noted the fine sword she carried. Nyson needed an army, and he knew that a powerful bard could sway crowds. When he beheld her in the throes of some mysterious and obviously painful curse, he saw opportunity. If she believed her salvation lay in Crushbone, perhaps she would rally Kelethin's wood elves to her cause in sufficient numbers to serve *his* cause.

But the ranger's notion had merit. Stealth, not strength, might well be the safer, surer route to success. Nyson mentally reworked his plans as he fell into step behind the wood elves.

They took a narrow northbound path and walked until the morning dew had lifted. Neither Elizerain nor Xander spoke, but the morning didn't pass in silence. Never having traveled on foot, without an armed escort or a band of merry companions, Nyson had never before realized how *noisy* a forest could be.

Insects clacked and hummed and chirped. The sheer variety of birdcall was staggering, a constant, ever-shifting chorus of song. Every now and then this music was punctuated by the snarl of a hunting cat or the howl of distant wolves.

Nyson was so busy listening to the forest that he didn't notice exactly when they left the path. The underbrush rustled just a few paces ahead, drawing his attention to the fact that there was no path at all.

A small armored creature burst from the bushes and scuttled toward a thick patch of briar berries. The two wood elves immediately stopped and averted their eyes until the creature had passed. Elizerain shifted her position, placing herself between Nyson and the little creature.

"What was that?" he demanded.

"A basilisk hatchling," said Xander. "You'll run into them from time to time."

Elizerain glanced back at the young elf. "They're mostly harmless, but I wouldn't look one in the eye. No one knows for certain when the creatures acquire the ability to turn you to stone with their gaze."

The two Feir'Dal began walking again. Nyson took a step—and found that his foot could not complete the stride. He came up short, lost his balance, and fell heavily to the ground. He caught himself with his hands, but most of his weight landed on his right knee. The sting of a scraped knee was a pain he hadn't felt since childhood.

Elizerain was at his side in a heartbeat, squatting down beside him. He expected impatience or even mockery, but her eyes went right to his boots. Nyson rolled over into a sitting position and followed the line of her gaze. His bootlaces had been pulled loose and then tied together.

"Pixies," the bard said. "They're fond of jests and like to play little pranks."

Nyson scowled and reached for the knot. "Very amusing."

"This is pretty mild, as pixies go. They don't particularly like outsiders in the forest."

He stopped retying his boots long enough to send her an incredulous look. "*Outsiders?* But we're elves."

The bard shrugged. "The fey lived in Faydark long before our ancestors came."

She rose and extended a hand to him. Nyson took it out of courtesy and was surprised by the strength in the little wood elf's grip. That, too, was good to know.

They walked until early twilight, stopping only to eat a bit of trail bread and refill their water flask from a small, swift-running stream. Xander finally called a halt at the base of a massive fallen tree.

The tree had been a venerable giant, as large as some of the mainstays of Kelethin. It was not the first fallen tree they'd come across; like every other living thing, trees were subject to the circle of life. Eventually even the grandest tree reached the end of its days. When this one fell, its dislodged roots had torn open the ground, forming a cave large enough for a tall human to stand erect in.

"Nice," Elizerain murmured, peering in among the tangle of roots. "Homey."

Xander suddenly leaped at the bard and took her down in a flying tackle. They rolled aside as a log, attached at either end to long ropes of braided vines, swung past the cave opening.

Before Nyson could react, a strong hand clamped down on his shoulder and a keen blade pressed lightly against his throat. He glanced down carefully, noting the blunt, stubby-fingered hand. His captor, apparently, was a dwarf.

On the whole, Nyson rather preferred dealing with pixies.

"State yer business," demanded a gruff bass voice. The dwarf gave the knife an encouraging little twitch.

Xander rose slowly to his feet, taking care to avoid the log, which still swung back and forth like a pendulum.

"The lad might find it easier to talk without a knife at his throat," he suggested.

"Suppose so. Most do."

The ranger took a step closer. "Trobe, it's me, Xander Fletcher. Let the lad go."

"Bah! Couldn't be! The Xander I knew wouldn't begrudge a dwarf a bit of fun."

Suddenly Nyson was reeling forward, propelled by a hard shove. He caught himself, then spun around and with narrowed eyes regarded the dwarf.

Trobe was not a particularly impressive example of his kind. Much thinner than most dwarves and as bald as an egg, he sported a short black beard, cut straight across just below his chin. His thick black mustache was also drawn into a straight line by the broad grin he currently wore, and his small eyes were shadowed by a single, continuous black brow. But for the bulbous nose, the dwarf's face was a study in dark, horizontal lines.

"If it's fun you're after, I've a proposal that might interest you," Xander said, taking a cautious step closer. "It involves legendary treasure and dead orcs."

Trobe folded his sinewy arms over his chest. "You have my attention."

The ranger quickly explained the quest as a desire to find valuable lore in the treasure trove under Crushbone. When he fell silent, the dwarf pursed his lips, considering.

"I'll do it, fer payment in advance."

"We'd hoped you'd take a share of the treasure as payment," Elizerain ventured.

"And so I will, girlie, but first we got to *get* the treasure, am I right? For that, I'll be needing my axe. You three help me fetch it back, and we'll get on with yer business."

"We don't plan to fight our way into Crushbone," Nyson pointed out.

"Yeah, but who's to say the first orcs you meet will have slaving in mind?" the dwarf retorted. "The ugly green buggers would rather kill elves than tote 'em along to Crushbone. If they've run short on slaves and are out hunting fresh ones, yer in luck. If not, I'd just as soon have my axe handy."

"Where's the weapon now?" asked Elizerain.

"Band of rogue orcs got it. They're not Crushbone orcs—just a pack of thieving mutts."

Xander's eyebrows rose. "And how is it that a dwarf got parted from his axe?"

An odd expression crossed Trobe's face, and for several moments his features twitched as if he was striving mightily to hold back a sneeze.

"A dwarf's got to bathe sometime!" he said, the words bursting out as if they'd been shot from a catapult. "Can't be taking an axe into the water, can you?"

Xander started to respond, but something in the forest beyond caught his attention. He held up one hand to indicate silence.

Nyson listened but heard nothing.

His eyes widened as he realized what this meant. He heard *nothing*. The constant birdsong had ceased, and the animals had gone silent. Only the drone of the flying insects and the distant murmur of the stream broke the stillness.

"Better'n a watchdog, those birds," the dwarf observed. He shot an unfriendly look at Xander. "Bringing me more company than these two elves, are you?"

"Not intentionally." Xander took his bow off his shoulder and nocked an arrow.

A rollicking song came drifting through the trees, sung in a pleasant but untrained baritone. The singer was too far away for them to distinguish the words, but judging from the expression on Elizerain's face, he was not unfamiliar.

She stepped between Xander and the unseen singer. "That's Davin. He's no threat to us."

The ranger slowly lowered his bow, but he looked far from pleased. "What is he doing here?"

She shrugged. "We could ask him."

Before anyone could protest, she cupped her hands to her mouth and let out a high, ringing call, a bit of melody that sounded very like one of the birdcalls Nyson had been hearing throughout the day.

Six figures stepped out into the open and began to approach the tree cave. Trobe watched the men the way a horse trader might study a filly's gait, his little eyes appraising the fighters and their weapons.

Nyson tried to see them as the dwarf might; after all, his own experience with human ruffians was not sufficient to provide a useful measure.

The tall man with curly brown hair and a sword on each hip seemed to be the leader. Behind him strode four men and a half elf, all of them well armed and battle-scarred. Their gear looked to be of good quality, and they were far from paupers. Rings glittered on the leader's hands, and all of the men were well dressed. The only faintly disreputable individual among them was an older fellow who wore a leaf-shaped patch over one eye.

Nyson found himself profoundly unimpressed by the band of humans, but Trobe nodded happily.

"A likely-looking bunch. Might be a good thing these boys happened along. We should keep them close to hand."

"They're bandits," Xander said flatly. "We want nothing to do with them."

"Don't know about that," the dwarf countered. "Many axes level the forest."

The three elves turned to stare at him.

He had the grace to look abashed. "It's a figger of speech, is all. What I meant was—"

"We understand your meaning," Xander broke in. "Yes, we could do with more fighters, but how do we know these men won't throw in with our enemies?"

By then the bandits were but a few paces away. The leader's eyes widened in mock pique, and he splayed one hand over his heart.

"The Greenleaves, siding with orcs? Now, that's just insulting."

"The Greenleaves, eh?" said Trobe. "That'd make you Davin the Dark, I suppose."

The bandit bowed. "I see our fame precedes us."

"If you keep going, you may catch up to it," Elizerain suggested.

Davin grinned. "Not quite the loving welcome I expected. Aren't you glad to see me, Rain?"

"I was glad enough to keep Xander from shooting you, but that doesn't mean I like being followed." She lifted her chin and met the bandit's eyes squarely. "We've had our day. It's over and done. Everything that needed saying was spoken back at the Gallows Tree."

"That doesn't mean the Greenleaves don't owe you, cousin," the half elf said quietly. "If you need our swords, they're yours."

"Well, now. That means you won't be wanting any of the booty?" the dwarf said slyly.

The bandit leader's smile broadened. "And here I thought you were familiar with our little band. What sort of booty might we be speaking of?"

"Whatever the orcs we're hunting could steal from travelers, I suppose. They got an axe I'm wanting."

"You get that; we take the rest," Davin suggested.

Trobe's snort expressed his opinion of that offer. "Greedy sort, aren't you? Those orcs have been in yer line of work for some while now. Could be they'll have quite a trove piled up."

"Enough for everyone, eh? Name your preference, then."

"First pickings on the weapons," the dwarf stated. "We take whatever we want. You boys get the rest of the weapons, and anything else of value."

"Done."

Dwarf and bandit spat in their palms and shook on the deal.

That settled, the half elf offered a brace of rabbits for the evening meal. Trobe countered with the offer of a night's lodging.

It seemed to Nyson that the evening passed pleasantly enough, despite the ranger's grim-faced silence. The young Koada'Dal approved Xander's values—he himself was not in favor of casting his lot in with human and half elf bandits—but on the other hand, he could see the dwarf's point of view. Nyson did not fear death, but despoiling a band of orcs of their ill-gotten hoard was not the glorious end he had in mind. Six extra fighters could mean the difference between a simple raid and a deadly struggle. To his surprise, Nyson found that he rather approved of the simple practicality of Trobe's thinking.

When the fire had burned to ash and the lantern bugs began to kindle their fey, flickering lights, Davin turned to the bard.

"How about a tune, Rain? Or better yet, sing us a story."

She shot a glance at their host. "I recently learned 'The Prince of Kaladim . . .'"

Trobe beamed with pleasure. "That's a good one. A mite short, though."

"Short? It has seventeen stanzas!"

"Like I said," he agreed.

The bard shrugged and reached for her harp. A soft chord rippled into the night, and she began to declaim the story—a ringing speech that was not quite song. As the story unfolded, her fingers wandered the harp strings, striking an occasional chord.

Then a melody began to emerge from the lower strings, like soft footsteps marching through the tale. She began to sing that melody, while her fingers danced over the strings, sometimes highlighting the drama of the tale with biting harmonies, sometimes playing a lilting little flourish to underscore the irony one often found in stern dwarven humor.

It seemed to Nyson that the music *told* the story, on a level that words could not begin to address. Small snatches of melody sang of terror and tragedy, of desperate courage. The chant of hard-won victory mingled with a dirge for the dearly loved dead. All of this the bard coaxed from the harp, blending it seamlessly with the traditional melody she sang.

Nyson had never heard anything quite like it. Nor, apparently, had Trobe. The dwarf listened intently, sometimes nodding, sometimes with a wry smile. Under the spell of the music, his visage, which had struck Nyson as coarse and even rather comic, seemed to take on a borrowed nobility.

When the ballad ended, Trobe regarded the bard as if seeing her for the first time. "You might have been there," he said wonderingly. "Makes me wish I'd been, too."

"Patience, dwarf," Davin said lightly. "You'll get plenty of fighting tomorrow."

The dwarf's small eyes lit up with anticipation. He turned to Elizerain. "And come tomorrow night, you'll sing the battle?" he said eagerly. "I'd surely like to hear what orc blood sounds like, put to music. And my axe! Can't wait to hear the song *it* sings."

"That's . . . an interesting challenge," Elizerain said carefully.

"A challenge for another day," Xander said, speaking for the first time that evening. "We should all get some rest."

The bard nodded, but her face was wistful as she ran her hands lightly over the harp's strings.

"Play us to sleep, Rain," the bandit leader suggested. "It's clear you're not ready to put the harp aside. What's a pleasure to you will be rare luxury to the rest of us."

A murmur of assent overrode the ranger's dubious

scowl. Xander shrugged and strode off to take first watch as the others settled down to listen.

Silvery music drifted into the night like threads of starlight. Nyson listened with ever-increasing pleasure. Never had he heard any music he liked so well. He suspected that once this quest was over, he would forevermore seek out the sound of silvery strings.

With a sigh of rare contentment, the young elf drifted toward slumber, letting the music follow him into his dreams.

MUCH LATER, NYSON SAT BOLT UPRIGHT, JOLTED out of a nightmare he could not recall. But the smothering sense of darkness remained, and with it a yearning he could not begin to understand. Whatever the dream, it had been as compelling as it was terrifying.

Nyson did not understand how that could be. He lay back down, listening to the frantic rhythm of his own heartbeat and waiting for the last echoes of beautiful, terrible music to fade from his ears. He would not have thought his dreams could fashion such sounds.

He glanced at the wood elf, but Elizerain's songs were over for the night. The bard slept sprawled on her back, with one out-flung hand resting on her red harp. The only sounds were the voices of the forest and the grating snores of the oldest bandit.

Many moments passed before Nyson could tame his shallow, rapid breathing. Even then, he lay awake for a long time, certain that sleep had fled for the night. But after a while the shadow of the forgotten nightmare faded away, and his eyes began to grow heavy again.

As he drifted toward slumber, he could have sworn he heard the sound of harp music riding the air, accompanied by the compelling rhythm of a swift-beating heart.

DAWN WAS STILL A HOPEFUL THOUGHT WHEN Elizerain and her odd band of allies reached the orc camp. As planned, they encircled the encampment and waited for Trobe's signal to attack. At Xander's insistence, the three elves would fight as a unit.

Elizerain wasn't sure what to think of that. She could see the sense of keeping young Nyson close, as he was unproven in battle. But she and Xander had been on the same side of more than one fight, and he knew she could hold up her end.

A soft, angry oath escaped the ranger as he gazed at the orc bandits' camp. Elizerain understood his reaction, for indignation flared bright in her own breast as she studied their foes' grim handiwork.

The orcs had left an ugly scar on the forest—a burned and barren clearing devoid of life. Piles of refuse had been tossed into the underbrush, and a shallow midden trough had been dug far too close to the stream. Pelts dried on rough wooden frames, and high-piled furs spoke of profitable carnage.

The camp was larger than she'd expected, with at least a dozen tents fashioned from slaughtered saplings and badly cured hides. Even if the orcs slept one to a tent, they were a formidable band. No wonder Trobe wasn't eager to attack them on his own!

Even as the thought formed, a war howl cut through the predawn stillness. With a thunder that was more suggestive of a team of horses than a single dwarf, Trobe stormed into the encampment, a spiked club held high overhead.

He took down one of the tents with a single swing, then leaped onto the squirming hide and began to stomp the orc beneath.

Xander quickly nocked an arrow and let fly at the nearest tent, even before the orc occupant emerged. His timing was perfect: the arrow took the orc in the throat and sent him staggering back into his tent. The structure collapsed, and sprawling tent posts tripped one of the orcs who was charging toward Trobe.

Meanwhile, the Greenleaves brought their bows into play, sending a storm of arrows into the camp. Several of the orcs howled and dove back into the tents. One enterprising soul pulled up stakes and ran, using the tent as a makeshift shield. Arrows bounced off the thick hide with soft, dull thumps.

The success of this strategy inspired imitation, and in moments the orcs were in full retreat. Trobe gave one final kick to the now-silent orc beneath him and hopped down from the fallen tent.

"This way," he said decisively, striding toward the midden.

The stench grew stronger with each step, and flies buzzed as thick as smoke around a greenwood fire. But as they got closer, Elizerain noted that a second pit had been dug beyond the first. A glint of silver showed through the cover of roughly woven sticks and reeds that obscured it.

"That's almost clever," she admitted. "Who would want to come this close if they didn't have to?"

"Not me," Trobe agreed. "Only reason I know it's here is I watched the buggers dig the pit. Them being downwind, of course."

He tossed off the cover and hopped into the hole,

busily tossing out small wooden boxes, bolts of fine cloth, armor, and weapons.

One of the boxes broke open, spilling a bright puddle of gems onto the hard-packed ground. From the corner of her eye, Elizerain saw Nyson stare, then stoop to pick up a pendant: a large, flat blue stone surrounded by a delicate filigree setting and hung from a silver chain.

"I'll be taking that," Davin announced cheerfully as he reached for the gem.

Nyson snatched it away. "I think not."

The dwarf tossed a well-notched axe out and climbed after it. He took in the scene at a glance, and his face hardened.

"Hand it over," he growled at Nyson. He picked up the axe and brandished it. "The only shiny thing worth having is a good weapon."

"You've taken your choice of the spoils," Nyson said coolly. "This is mine."

"I made a deal with the bandits!" howled Trobe.

The elf drew himself up to his full height. "You don't speak for me, dwarf."

"More's the pity."

Elizerain came over to join the argument. "The deal was made, Nyson, and it will be honored."

For a long moment the young elf regarded her in silence. Then he stripped two rings from his hand and offered them to the bandit leader.

"A new deal, then," he suggested. "These rings in exchange for the blue gem, which, according to the dwarf, is your rightful property."

Davin grinned and collected his prize. "Gold and emeralds. Very nice."

He took one of Elizerain's hands and slid the smaller of the two rings onto her middle finger, then he turned her hand over and dropped a kiss into her palm. "That's to remember me by, until we meet again."

He winked and sauntered off, beckoning his men to follow. The bandits flung well-filled sacks over their shoulders and headed off into the forest.

Elizerain resolutely turned her back on her unlamented past and sent an inquiring glance in Nyson's direction. "What was that about?"

The young elf shrugged. "I fancied the gem."

"It's pretty, but of no great value," she pointed out.

"A matter of opinion."

He walked off before Elizerain could respond. She went over to Xander, who was sorting through the cache of weapons.

"I notice you snatched up everything with an edge or a point," she said lightly. "Who's going to carry all that steel?"

"We'll take what we can and toss the rest into the midden," he said. "Better that than arming orcs and thieves."

"The Greenleaves did help us," Elizerain pointed out. "I expected a pitched battle. This way, it was quick and easy."

Xander rose, a dagger in one hand and a grim expression on his face.

"Has it not yet occurred to you," he said quietly, "that the battle was a bit *too* easy?"

8

THE TOWER

A DENSE GREEN TWILIGHT SETTLED OVER THE forest, deepening the shadows and intensifying the sense of gloom that permeated the small clearing. Three men crouched in the thick underbrush nearby, their faces grim and watchful. Two of these men studied their leader, Davin the Dark, who in turn contemplated the enormous tree stump some 100 paces into the heart of Faydark.

The hideaway of the necromancer Chanzoon Nexis blended into the forest, not unlike Davin's own beloved Gallows Tree. There the similarity ended. The Greenleaf bandits had made their home in a living tree; in fact, carving away the diseased and insect-ridden wood had probably saved the tree's life. Davin suspected that the necromancer had done quite the opposite, casting some sort of magical blight that had eaten the heart and the life from this forest giant.

The massive stump—all that remained of the grand tree—had a height and girth to rival any necromancer's tower, and it had the look of one, too: dark and foreboding, with twisted limbs providing spires and a thick maze of brambles serving as outer wall. Fetid mists seemed to linger around the blackened wood, and birds of prey perched on the blighted branches like living gargoyles.

Even so, forest travelers would likely pass this way without realizing what prompted the inexplicable urge to quicken their pace. Today, however, there was no mistaking the dead tree's uncanny nature.

A small host of undead creatures was converging on the necromancer's tower. Several skeletons shambled about, oblivious to the brittle crackle of the bramble hedge and far past caring about the thorns. The rhythmic flap of leathery wings drew the eye upward to the small, dragonlike skeleton endlessly circling the tower. This undead flyer seemed oblivious to the huge undead wasp that buzzed drunkenly about on tattered wings, mindlessly continuing the feud that had been the end of all participants.

The objects of the wasp's attacks were several giant spiders. These creatures, their empty carapaces dusty and crumbling, were crawling madly over the gigantic stump and leaping back and forth to nearby trees in a futile effort to weave an entrapping web. Each impact resulted in a small shower of spider fragments or the breaking off of a brittle leg joint.

One of the spiders had fallen to the ground, where it lay on its back, limb stumps twitching in an attempt to right itself. The heavy-boned skeleton of an ogre lumbered by, and one massive foot came down squarely on the delicate shell. The creature's unnatural existence ended in sickening crackle and a puff of foul-smelling dust.

The bandits crouched lower as three elven skeletons

rushed past their hiding place. The high-pitched clatter of their bones sounded eerily like a madman's giggle.

Davin lifted a hand to the back of his neck, where his hair rose like the hackles of a spooked hound. His half elf companion tugged at his sleeve, drawing his attention from the uncanny scene.

"Nothing in that stump could be worth the getting of it," Viscor said softly. "The way I see it, either we *leave* the dead, or we *join* them."

The bandit leader couldn't disagree with this assessment, but neither could he ignore the waves of compulsion radiating from the general direction of the dark tower.

"We attack," he said firmly.

Viscor shook his head, and the man behind him mirrored this denial. "I'm not dying for you, Davin, nor is Henzer. Not today, at least."

It was the first time the half elf had ever refused an order or turned away from a fight. Davin was too surprised to be angry. But he did not fault Viscor for speaking truth; the half elf was Davin's oldest friend, and no one had a better right to speak his mind. Still, Davin had to maintain some semblance of control, some façade of leadership.

Before the rogue could decide how to respond, a sudden stab of pain stole his breath.

No, on second thought it was not *quite* pain, but rather an intense sensation of heat near the center of his chest. The swift, hot surge swept through his body, setting his blood aboil and making him feel as if his bones had been newly forged of steel, his muscles rewoven from strands of unbreakable spider silk.

An explanation came to him readily enough. Obviously Chanzoon Nexis was near enough to cast a common spell, a handy bit of magic that lent a temporary surge of physical strength. Davin had experienced such magic before with no ill effects to any but his chosen foe. But he realized, with swiftly growing despair, that the enchantment was strengthening more than his body.

The compulsion binding Davin's will to the necromancer's was also growing. The bandit's sword arm throbbed with a desire bordering on lust, and he could taste his weapon's thirst for blood in the back of his own parched throat. Worse, his will—indeed, every quality of mind and spirit that enabled him to call himself his own master—was slipping away in a manner frighteningly akin to the sea's retreat just before the strike of a tidal wave.

That disturbing image filled his mind as the necromancer's will crashed over his.

Against instinct, contrary to anything approaching self-preservation or even sanity, Davin the Dark rose slowly to his feet.

Enough conscious thought remained to Davin to allow him to feel horror at the sound of his sword hissing free of his scabbard. Enough to recognize the shock of betrayal in Viscor's eyes.

Enough to feel sorrow at the sight of the half elf's head rolling clear of his shoulders, his body slumping lifeless to the forest floor.

It had been easy, so easy, to end the life of his oldest friend. Davin's sword had swung almost casually, had cut through sinew and bone with contemptuous ease.

But there was nothing casual about his next attack. Roaring in helpless fury, the bandit leader charged out of the underbrush, his bloody sword held aloft in both hands.

He caught up with the undead ogre and brought his

sword around in a vicious downward sweep that cut the shambling skeleton off at the knees. The ogre toppled, bony arms wind-milling in a doomed attempt at reclaiming its balance.

Davin leveled out his swing as he spun around in a full circle, and as he completed the turn, he muscled his sword into a sharp, upward arc. The rising blade met the falling ogre, slicing through one thick arm bone before parting the fist-sized bones of the creature's neck.

The skeleton fell into a lifeless tumble of bones; the ogre's skull, however, was not yet ready to concede to final death. Dull greenish light was rapidly fading from the empty eye sockets, but the massive jaws flung open, ready to snap at whatever came within reach.

Quicker than thought, Davin's sword dived down to hook one of the wicked, yellow-gray fangs. He flicked the skull into the air, drew back his sword, and used the flat of his blade to launch the grisly missile at the trio of elven skeletons.

Whether through random chance, the necromancer's aid, or some residual echo of the ogre's own inclinations, the great jaws managed to clamp down on the spine of one elven skeleton. Delicate neck bones gave way with a crackle reminiscent of broken glass as the undead elf pitched face-first into the brambles.

The ogre skull rolled away, bits of crushed elven bone spilling from the nose and eye sockets. It came to a stop against a particularly thick bramble cane. The uncanny light in its empty eyes flared as if in satisfaction, and then faded into darkness. In some corner of his mind—that small part he could still call his own—Davin noted that this was an end the evil creature might have appreciated.

Then a shrill keening had him spinning around, sword

leveled at the potential threat. But it was only Henzer, who ran toward the necromancer's tower in a shrieking, wild-eyed frenzy.

The cause for the bandit's wild charge was apparent, and it was not a sudden desire to do battle with the undead. Running close on Henzer's heels was the headless half elf Viscor, a long, slim dagger in one hand and his own recently detached head swinging from the other.

Henzer's screams drew the attention of the flying horror circling the tower. The steady flap of leathery wings abruptly silenced as the skeletal beast tucked into a dive, its bony jaws stretching into a dragon's deadly smile.

The animated corpse that had been Viscor skidded to a stop. Raising the decapitated head, the undead half elf abruptly thrust the dagger into one pointed ear and out the other. He adjusted his grip to the end of the long tail of brown hair and began to twirl the head like a bolo. Three quick turns, and he let fly.

Undead creatures have no fear of injury, and the sickening crack coming from the half elf's shoulder suggested the missile had been launched with a force greater than any Viscor might have managed in life. The head whirled toward the small dragon with remarkable speed and force, and the spinning dagger tore a ragged gash through the monster's wing. The dismembered head punched through the opening, completing the wing's ruin.

The dragon-beast listed hard to one side and described a tight, swift spiral into the brambles, which promptly ignited into a small fire—necromancer fire, judging from its azure hue. The creature's brief, final struggle had a certain grim beauty: black bone silhouetted against brilliant flame.

Meanwhile, Henzer's frantic flight had taken him into the midst of several elven skeletons. He fought them not out of design or choice, but with the frenzied instinct of a cornered beast intent upon survival.

The unnatural surge of strength was fading from Davin's limbs, and his mind was returning to his own control. But like Henzer, he could no longer choose whether or not to fight. The undead wasp swooped swiftly toward him.

Davin reversed his grip on the hilt of his sword so he held the weapon as he might a javelin. Steadying the sword with both hands, he lifted it high overhead to meet the creature's attack.

The sword sank easily into decaying flesh, and Davin's arm might well have followed had not the hilt of his sword caught on a still-solid section of the creature's shell. This impact sent a jolt of pain down the bandit's spine and forced him back a staggering step or two.

For several moments Davin struggled with the creature, which writhed and twisted as it attempted to stab him with its barbed stinger. It took all the rogue's considerable strength to hold the wasp at arm's length and all his agility to evade its attacks.

As Davin's mind continued to clear, it occurred to him that he need not hold the wasp aloft. He could thrust the sword into the deep, mossy soil and let the impaled creature struggle, safely out of his way—or for that matter, he could simply cast it away.

Of course, in so doing, he would also lose his sword.

A horrific stench rolled toward Davin, rapidly gaining in loathsome power. He glanced over his shoulder to see the half-rotten corpse of an orc, its body bristling with arrows, closing in fast.

With all his strength, the bandit swung his sword down and to his right, stabbing back toward the approaching orc. Luck was with him: the wasp slammed stinger-first into the orc's thigh. Davin released his sword and spun away, ducking under the swing of the orc's fist.

The two undead creatures began to grapple, their original quarry forgotten. Strong mandibles clacked on bone as the wasp bit deep into decaying orc flesh; wicked fangs and strong jaws snapped brittle wasp limbs and crunched through the great insect's shell as the orc returned the favor. For several moments Davin circled the rolling, biting combatants, looking for an opportunity to reclaim his sword. Finally he got the chance to seize the hilt and tug the blade free.

He stumbled away from the tangle of animated carrion and looked around for his men. Henzer had fallen, but not before he'd taken several skeletons down, as well as one of the spiders. The rest of the spiders had put themselves out of the fight through their self-destructive attempts at spinning a web. The only undead creature remaining was Viscor, who stood at the base of the wizened tree.

The headless half elf was daubing at the stump of his neck with one hand and using the blood to write on the rough bark.

A faint glow began to rise from the tree, revealing twisted blood red runes and the curving outline of a hidden door. As the portal swung open, Viscor, his usefulness at an end, slumped into a lifeless heap.

Nearby shadows parted, and Chanzoon Nexis stepped

into view. The smile he sent Davin would not have looked out of place on a well-fed shark.

"Nicely handled. You did far better than I might have expected from a trio of bandits. But your men *did* take some . . . persuading." The necromancer prodded Viscor's headless body with one foot.

Since every response that came to mind would almost certainly earn him a painful death, Davin held his tongue.

Chanzoon's smile collapsed when it became apparent that the bandit wasn't going to rise to the bait.

"Well, come along and give your report," he said curtly.

The rogue sheathed his sword, covered though it was with unspeakable gore, and stalked over crushed brambles to the door of the tower. He did not, however, follow the necromancer inside.

"I followed the bard," he said tersely. "I encouraged her to play the harp, as you instructed."

A strange gleam entered the necromancer's eyes. "Did the playing have any effect on her?"

"None that I could see." Davin's eyes narrowed. "Why? What effect were you expecting?"

The necromancer dismissed this question with an impatient wave of one hand. "Where is the bard headed?"

"North."

Chanzoon's lips thinned with annoyance. "Perhaps you could be a little more specific."

Davin folded his arms and stared the necromancer down. "As it turns out, no, I can't. The four of them were pretty tight-lipped about their plans."

"Four of them?"

"Elizerain picked up some traveling companions."

The bandit leader shrugged. "That's to be expected—she's a sociable sort."

"Name these companions."

"There's a wood elf ranger by the name of Xander Fletcher, a between-age high elf whose name was given only as Nyson, and a dwarf who goes by Trobe."

Davin noted the flicker in the necromancer's ice-blue eyes at the last name. "You know this dwarf?"

"I haven't had the pleasure," Chanzoon replied. "Tell me more."

"There isn't much to tell." The much-hated compulsion prompted him to add, "I can pick up their trail if I have to."

The necromancer slid a pointed glance at the headless half elf. "I don't doubt it for a moment. It's amazing what one can accomplish if properly motivated."

Rage and grief clenched twin fists around Davin's throat, making speech impossible. Just as well: his mute fury seemed to entertain the necromancer, whereas any words he might say would likely be his last.

When at last Davin could trust himself to speak, he drew a small pouch from his jerkin and held it out to the necromancer.

"This holds the finest gems from a thieves' hoard, as well as an elf-made ring of gold and emeralds. Yours, in exchange for my freedom."

The necromancer's only response was a derisive sniff.

"And of course, I'll get the harp back for you," Davin offered, hating the hint of desperation that had crept into his voice.

"Indeed you will," Chanzoon agreed, "but not just yet. The harp will do well enough where it is."

The bandit spilled the contents of the bag into one

hand and held out the small, glittering hoard. "Surely the harp can't be worth more than this, even when you throw in my services and those of an elven bard."

A slow, cruel smile curved the necromancer's lips. "Perhaps you should consider how much it might be worth to me to keep that harp at a safe distance."

Davin felt the blood drain from his face. "And what of the bard who carries it?"

"Whence this sudden concern?" mocked Chanzoon. "Belated qualms of conscience, perhaps? Or has the wench suddenly become less expendable?"

It occurred to Davin that, despite the obvious mockery, the necromancer's ice-blue eyes were searching Davin's face as if seeking a real response to that last question.

What did Chanzoon hope to see?

The bandit quickly replayed the conversation and seized on, if not quite an answer, at least a more telling question:

What change might the harp bring to Elizerain that would increase her value in the necromancer's eyes?

It was a grim thought, but Davin forced himself to shrug lightly. "The elf I once called wife is much the same as she ever was: always ready for a good story or a bit of mischief, quick to befriend others. A bit flighty, perhaps, and trusting to a fault, but a fine companion for all that."

"And yet you let this prize slip away," Chanzoon observed softly. "Some men might call you a fool for that."

Davin shrugged again and spoke with rare and total candor. "I might be inclined to agree with them."

"Keep that thought firmly in mind," the necromancer advised him. "You must not let this bard slip through your fingers again. She is far more valuable to me than ever she was to you. Not," he concluded coldly, "that that is any great measure of my regard."

And Davin, whose abandonment of Elizerain in Freeport now seemed a small thing in light of this new, greater betrayal, could not bring himself to disagree.

9

MISCHIEF

NIGHT WAS RAPIDLY DESCENDING UPON FAY-dark, but Xander kept a brisk pace northward, eager to put as much ground as possible between the Greenleaf bandits and the small band under his protection.

His three companions followed him, each in his or her fashion. Elizerain kept pace easily, her feet falling softly on the forest floor. Talkative though she might be, she knew enough woodcraft to keep silent during an off-trail march, and Xander had no doubt that her ear was tuned as keenly as his to the forest sounds.

She could have been a ranger, he thought wistfully. A good one. Certainly she could tread as softly and run as well as any elf he knew, and no one could want a better companion on the road. At such times as these, it was dangerously easy to forget some of the strange choices she had made.

Just then a soft birdcall sounded behind him, an echo of the melodic trill drifting down from some high-canopy singer. Again it sounded, and then a third time, as if the singer sought to affix the lilting tune-shard in memory.

A rueful smile touched Xander's lips. It was Elizerain's habit to sing along with any bird whose song caught her fancy. Xander knew rangers who could mimic birdcalls more precisely, but none who sang them with such obvious affection. At such times he allowed himself to think she might fit into his austere world.

But it was not to be; Elizerain was a bard to her very core. Though she savored the forest music when she found herself beneath Faydark's trees, Xander knew she would greet a human's tavern-told ballad with equal enthusiasm. That, he reminded himself, was something to keep in mind.

The ranger shifted his attention farther down their line. After a long day's march, many dwarves might be grumbling and huffing with exertion, but Trobe rolled along stoutly—not quite as quietly as the elves, but nearly so. Most of the sound behind Xander came from the unseasoned Nyson.

When they'd first left Kelethin, the young elf's boots had demonstrated an uncanny knack for finding and crushing every twig and dried leaf in his path. Finally Elizerain, who had demanded a list of Nyson's spells, bid him cast a silence charm over his own feet. That had improved matters considerably, but every now and then Xander heard the unmistakable sound of bent branches whipping free and striking the young elf. Some of them met Nyson's leggings or cloak with dull, hollow *thumps*; others rang with the stinging sound of branch meeting unprotected flesh.

Xander said nothing, giving the young elf time to drop back a step or so and thus evade injury from the dwarf-bent branches. Nyson readily learned this simple lesson, but it didn't seem to stick in memory for any length of time. For a while there would be silence, then two or three hits, then more silence.

After a dozen or so repetitions of this routine, Xander could no longer keep silent. He held up one hand to indicate a halt and turned back to explain to the high elf what any wood elfling knew from his first toddling steps.

But Nyson was not walking hard on the dwarf's heels. If anything, he could be a pace or two closer. Yet his face, which was set in grim determination, was marked with several thin red lines.

"More pixie mischief?" asked Xander, suddenly understanding what the welts meant.

Nyson answered with a curt nod. "It's of no consequence. I'll handle it myself," he told Elizerain when the bard tried to daub at his welts with a bit of fleshy leaf—a particularly soothing treatment most travelers carried in their herb-and-bandage bags.

The ranger didn't quite trust the sound of that. "You haven't tried to catch the pixie, have you? Or swatted at it?"

The young elf's visage darkened. "I might have, had I actually laid eyes upon the wretched bug."

"Don't," Xander cautioned. "Pixies can be quick to anger, and surprisingly inventive when taking vengeance. If tied boot laces and bent branches are the worst of it, we can consider ourselves lucky."

Nyson responded with an ironic smile as he shrugged his water skin off his shoulder. "In that case, perhaps I should drink to my own good fortune."

He regarded the skin first with puzzlement and then consternation. "It's empty! It was almost full when we stopped at midday, and I haven't touched it since."

Elizerain took the water skin from him and examined

it for a moment. "Here's the problem," she said, giving the sack a little squeeze. A bead of water formed near the bottom of the water skin. "The pixie poked a hole in it. Probably hours ago, judging by how long it would take a full water skin to drip itself dry through a hole this size."

"And you never once noticed?" demanded Trobe. "You should be as wet as a boiled rooster by now."

"My cloak is spell-woven," Nyson said coolly. "It would stay dry if I swam in it. In fact, it's probably the only thing in this mist-soaked forest that *is* dry."

Elizerain handed him her own water skin. "What's done is done, and it's just as well we stopped. You shouldn't walk so long without drinking."

Nyson thanked her with a nod. He uncorked the water skin and tipped it up for a sip. His face twisted with revulsion, and he spun away to lean and spit.

The ranger took the water skin from Nyson and poured a bit of the liquid within into his palm. He sniffed, and immediately upended the water skin, pouring out the contents.

"Silver mosswort," he explained in grim tones. "It wouldn't have killed you, but it would surely have slowed us down."

"Slowed us down?" Nyson repeated. "I'm not sure I understand."

"We'd have to stop frequently so you could dash into the bushes," Elizerain elaborated.

"Oh."

"Very frequently," put in Trobe. "Worse than tainted meat, is silver mosswort."

Elizerain took the empty water skin from Xander and rolled it into a tight cylinder. With a sigh, she tucked it into her travel pack. "We'll have to share. Nyson's skin can be repaired, but this one is past salvaging."

"But how—"

"Mosquito snout syringe," Xander broke in. "The pixies make a tea of mosswort and store it in a bladder with a hollow mosquito snout attached as a spout. A lot of work to prepare, but once ready, all the pixie needs to do is stab and squeeze."

He hesitated, then decided the others needed to know. "They have been known to add other, even less pleasant potions to a traveler's water supply. Fortunately Trobe carries his in a flask."

The notion of sharing the contents of that flask brought a scowl to the dwarf's face.

"These pixie pranks of yers are getting harder to swallow," he complained. "'Twas one thing to tie the elfling's bootlaces together, and what's a *thwap* in the face every now and again? But giving a traveler, any traveler, a case of the galloping gut grumbles? That's another story entirely."

"Fortunately, it will remain a tale untold," Xander said as he uncorked his water skin. He sniffed the contents and was relieved to discern nothing but water.

As he was handing the water skin to Nyson, a faint, distant crackling sound caught his ear. He held up one hand for silence.

"Fortunate indeed," he repeated, "as we'll soon have a larger problem to think about."

"Orc patrol," said Trobe flatly. "At least four of the buggers, by the sound of it, and they're headed this way. What say you, bard? I'm thinking an ambush is our best move."

"Agreed," Elizerain said softly. She looked to Xander and gave him a quick nod, ceding her place as party leader to the more experienced fighter.

Xander already had hiding places picked out, as he did at each step of the journey. With quick hand gestures, he directed the others into position. He paired Elizerain and Nyson and sent them scrambling up a vine-draped tree, where they'd be out of harm's way. A bard and a spell-caster could better aid him and Trobe with magic than steel. And Elizerain was handy with a bow. She'd be more effective from on high.

The ranger had other reasons for this decision, but now was not the time to contemplate them.

He crouched near the dwarf and took his bow off his shoulder, bending the supple wood and slipping the loose end of the string into the deep notch that would hold it in place. He took a handful of arrows from his quiver and thrust them point-down into the mossy ground, so they would be right at hand when needed.

Preparations made, he and Trobe waited in silence as the patrol crashed into view.

There were five orcs. All wore leather armor and carried reasonably well-maintained weapons. Crushbone orcs, beyond doubt, but any orcs who encountered elves this far from their citadel would probably be more inclined toward slaughter than slave-catching.

The elf fitted his first arrow to the string and began to draw it taut. At the lower edge of his vision, he caught a glimpse of swirling motion. He glanced down at a rapidly fraying bowstring.

Immediately he released the tension, but he was not quite fast enough. The bowstring snapped with an audible *twang,* and one of the flying ends drew a thin line of blood across his forearm.

One of the orcs looked up sharply at the sound.

"So much for ambush," Trobe said, not sounding particularly unhappy about this development.

He rose, hefted his axe, and ran straight toward the patrol, howling like a banshee's brother. Some bard-cast spell amplified the noise, making it sound as if dozens of stampeding dwarves were bearing down on the scouting party from various parts of the forest.

The orcs didn't linger for visual confirmation of their foe. All of them turned tail and fled, with Trobe hard after them. Xander noticed that the canny dwarf didn't try too hard to catch his quarry, but rather kept far enough back to allow the sound-spell's illusion to play to best effect.

One of the orcs tripped over an exposed tree root. He might have regained his balance, had not Trobe shoulder-slammed him and sent him plunging face-first into the tree trunk. The orc hit hard, rebounded, and fell straight back, his arms flung out wide.

Trobe sent a quick glance over his shoulder to measure the outcome; after all, *going* down wasn't the same as *staying* down, and the game would be over if the orc figured out the true size of the pursuing "army" and shouted this intelligence to his fleeing brothers. But the ranger was already at the fallen orc's side, and he waved the dwarf on.

Xander turned to the tree where Elizerain and Nyson perched. The pair of them looked highly pleased with the result of their spell-casting. Grinning like urchins, they clasped hands and shook them high overhead in a gesture of shared triumph.

This sudden burst of camaraderie made Xander's next task somewhat easier.

"You two go ahead and start camp. There's a small clearing some 500 paces to the north-northwest, beside a spring with potable water."

Xander gave Elizerain a more precise location in the simple code every wood elf knew. The two elves promptly shimmied down the tree and set off.

As soon as they were well out of sight, Xander kicked the orc awake. He waited until the orc's eyes focused, cleared, met his gaze—and went hard with hatred.

"I've got some questions," Xander said softly. "How we go about getting the answers depends entirely on you."

THE CLEARING XANDER HAD INDICATED WAS A pleasant place, well cushioned in moss and scented by the spicegum sapling that grew near a deep, sweet-water spring, leaning over the small pool of water as if admiring its reflection.

"This is good luck," Elizerain said, pointing toward the young tree. "Draw a bit of sap and chew it until you've worked the flavor out. It's good for patching, and should hold your water skin until we can get you a new one."

An expression of fastidious distaste crossed the young Koada'Dal's face, but he offered no comment. He pulled a dagger from his belt and nicked the tree. Elizerain noted with approval the small, careful cut, and the way Nyson patiently collected the golden sap, one slow drop at a time. He might be somewhat out of his element in the forest, but he had an elf's innate respect for living things.

She set about cutting and peeling back a section of the

moss to make a place for a fire. Once that task was accomplished, she gathered some deadfall wood and built a small fire on the bare soil. Soon water from the stream was simmering in a travel pot, to which Elizerain added a handful of plants.

"There's dried sobria in the mix," she said, naming the meaty paste made from a certain root, an elven delicacy as filling and nourishing as meat, "so we won't have to hunt tonight."

Nyson nodded approvingly and drew in a long, appreciative breath. "I prefer sobria. The dwarf, of course, might have other ideas."

"So he might, but he and Xander won't be back for some time," she said casually. "If they don't like the stew, they can hunt."

Fortunately Nyson didn't seem curious about his companions' whereabouts, for Elizerain wasn't sure what she would have told him, had he asked. She had a pretty good idea what might be keeping Xander, but there was no need to burden the youngling with such grim realities.

When Elizerain pronounced the stew ready, Nyson held out his travel bowl for filling. As he leaned forward, the bluestone pendant he'd claimed from the orc thieves' hoard swung free.

Elizerain caught the gem in one hand, noting well the scowl on the young elf's face and how near he'd come to swatting her hand away.

"A pretty thing," she said lightly as she turned it this way and that. "I've not seen many gems of this shade—a light, clear blue, like a glimpse of summer sky. You were wearing much the same color the first time I saw you."

"And you assume there's some significance to this?" Nyson said quickly, his tone rich with hauteur.

She'd suspected there was, and now she was certain of it. Nyson's three companions had been dressed in the same shade. At the time she'd thought it a little odd—not quite a uniform, but certainly suggestive of a common purpose. And judging by Nyson's reaction when he found the necklace, that purpose was somehow linked to the blue stone in Elizerain's hand.

"Of course I grasped the significance," she said, speaking in rounded tones that mimicked and mocked his own. "What fashionable Koada'Dal could resist a gem that matched his favorite tunic?"

A reluctant, almost sheepish grin tugged at the young elf's lips. "Do I really sound like that?"

"Of course you do," she repeated in the same tone.

They joined in a companionable chuckle. Still smiling, Nyson tugged the gem free and tucked it into his tunic. He took a spoonful of soup and nodded appreciatively. "Excellent. You must tell me what you put in that mix."

Elizerain swallowed a smile at this transparent attempt to change the subject. It would serve him right if she answered his question in boring detail!

She was about to do just that when a small deluge dropped from the trees, dousing their fire and splashing both of them with cold, none-too-fragrant water.

Nyson leaped to his feet, his face dark with anger. "I've. Had. Quite. Enough," he announced through clenched teeth.

With a few words and a sharp, rising sweep of one hand, he sent a spell soaring up into the trees.

A high-pitched squeak of protest shrilled, then broke off abruptly. After a moment, a small, faintly glimmering figure drifted down toward the smoking ruins of their campfire. It was the pixie—a miniature winged fey, a tiny fair-haired lass dressed in a short green gown that matched her iridescent wings. She was motionless, held captive by some sort of freeze-and-summon spell.

Elizerain watched the captured fey's descent, noting with interest that none of the spells Nyson had admitted to knowing could have produced this particular result.

The pixie came to a stop when she was at eye level with the young high elf. Nyson scowled in puzzlement. "That's odd. There's nothing in the spell to stop the wretched bug in midair. You'd think she'd simply drop to the ground, or fall into the fire."

To Elizerain's ear, he sounded a bit disappointed. She could work with that.

She took firm but gentle hold of the pixie's legs, taking care not to touch the gossamer wings. "All right, you can let her go now."

The young elf frowned, but he did as he was bid. As soon as the counter-spell was cast, tiny green wings began to beat furiously, and the pixie squirmed and twisted in Elizerain's grasp. Small though she might be, great indeed was her indignation, and her insults rang out with remarkable volume and clarity.

"You dare to touch me, you great walking tree stumps, you short-fanged orcs, you wingless dung beetles? Ugly as cave bears boiled until hairless, and twice as malodorous! Misbegotten ogre-spawn! No troll would condescend to eat you if you were garnished with onions and herbs, and not even the most wickedly randy barbarian would—"

"We grasp your point," Nyson broke in coldly, "subtle though it may be."

"Not to mention delivered without once coming up for air," Elizerain said with genuine admiration. "That was a truly excellent rant."

She sent the young Koada'Dal a sidelong glance. "The pixie's got remarkable lungs, hasn't she? She'd be a fine bard. Or better yet, a pearl diver! Why, I'd wager that she could stay underwater longer than you and I could, even with our times combined."

The glint in Nyson's blue eyes suggested that not only did he understand the role Elizerain wished him to play, he relished it.

"There's a stream not far away. Let's put your wager to the test."

The pixie's fluttering wings suddenly stopped, and her tiny face froze in alarm. "You would kill one of the fey in her own forest? Take care, two-legged vermin! None who commit such villainy could leave this place alive. The very trees would rise up against you!"

"No, no," Elizerain said soothingly. "I mean you no harm. I only wish to talk with you. The youngling, though. . ."

She let her words trail off, and her eye shifted meaningfully to the sword on Nyson's hip. The young elf obligingly narrowed his eyes in feigned menace and began to toy with the hilt of his weapon.

The pixie's wings resumed beating at a slower pace. "What do you wish to talk about?" she asked in sullen tones.

"You can start by telling us what we did to offend you."

Instantly the pixie's ire returned to the boiling point. "Other than breathing?" she said scornfully. "Other than defiling the forest with your tall-folk cities and your tree-killing roads?"

"Other than traveling with an axe-wielding dwarf?" Nyson suggested.

The pixie glanced at him, clearly surprised by this notion. "What do I care about such petty distinctions? Was it dwarven axes that leveled hundreds of trees to make a trade road? To my eyes, you tall folk are much the same."

"Yes, you made that very clear," Nyson said. "Seldom is a Koala'Dal of noble lineage mistaken for 'misbegotten ogre-spawn.'"

Elizerain sent him a quelling glance. The fewer people who knew of Nyson's family ties, the safer they were likely to remain.

"And a neat turn of phrase it was," she said quickly. "I'll have to add it to my quiver of insults—with your permission, of course."

That seemed to please the pixie. "Feel free. I have others."

"No doubt," Nyson murmured.

The bard inclined her head to the little fey in a gesture of respect. "Lady of the woods, would it ease your mind to know that we have nothing but love and respect for the forest? That we travel with a ranger who would fight to the death to protect Faydark?"

"And speaking of fighting," Nyson put in, "you may have noticed that we've been rather busy. We have troubles enough without adding your mischief into the mix."

A derisive smirk twisted the tiny face. "Silly elf boy, whining about a few harmless pranks."

"Cutting my friend's bowstring wasn't a harmless prank," the bard pointed out. "It could have put out an eye when it snapped. And what if our lives had depended upon his getting off that shot?"

The tiny woman shrugged. "And yet here you are. And here I stay," she added meaningfully.

Elizerain had dealt with enough merchants to recognize that tone. "Unless . . ."

The pixie eased herself down so that she was sitting on Elizerain's fist, then she smoothed her short, filmy green skirts primly over her thighs. "You saw a basilisk hatchling. It ran across your path, right under your big clomping feet."

"That's true," the bard said cautiously.

"But have you seen a full-grown basilisk in Greater Faydark? Not just on this particular trespassing excursion, but ever?"

Elizerain considered this question. "I haven't, no, but there are a lot of creatures in this forest I haven't actually laid eyes upon."

"But do you *know* of anyone who has seen a basilisk?" the pixie persisted.

"People who've seen one aren't likely to boast of it around a tavern table—or anywhere else, for that matter."

"That's because being turned to stone tends to put a damper on conversation," Nyson explained, with the exaggerated patience usually reserved for slow-witted children.

Tiny fists drummed Elizerain's hand in frustration. "You're missing the point! What if there *are* no basilisks in this forest, other than hatchlings?"

The elves exchanged puzzled glances. Elizerain cleared her throat and prepared to state the obvious.

"To my understanding, a 'hatchling' is a young creature, recently emerged from an egg. If there are no adult basilisks, how can there be hatchlings?"

"There you go," the pixie said approvingly. "Answer that question, and I'll trouble you no more."

"Why?" persisted Elizerain.

The pixie shrugged again. "Curiosity?"

"A trap, more likely," Nyson said. "Each of her little tricks has been more vicious than the last. I wouldn't be the least surprised if the bug intends us to come face to face with the biggest, most deadly basilisk this side of the Butcherblock Mountains."

Their tiny captive scoffed. "Not likely! If you were turned to stone, I'd have to look at your big ugly face every time I passed this way."

"Then what do you want of us?" Elizerain urged. "Is this a riddle test? Or perhaps you seek assistance?"

The bard knew that her last arrow had hit its mark when the agitated flutter of wings began anew. The pixie squirmed and bit her lip, obviously in turmoil over the notion of asking help from an elf.

After a moment the wings slowed and slumped in defeat, and she beckoned for Elizerain to come closer.

The wood elf leaned in and listened carefully to the whispered tale, her eyes widening first with astonishment, then with wonder.

"I'll do it," she said eagerly. "Most gladly will I do it! There's not a bard alive who wouldn't give the nose off her face to learn such a song."

The pinched, uneasy look faded from the pixie's face. "Aye, I thought you might see it that way," she said loftily, seizing upon the opportunity to turn the situation around. "Of course you'd be glad to do it, you being a bard and all. And not a bad one, for an elf," she added generously.

Elizerain smiled and opened her fist. The pixie leaped for freedom—and seized a tiny handful of Nyson's hair on the way past. The Koada'Dal yelped but managed to stay his hand just short of swatting his tiny tormenter.

The pixie flittered into the trees, followed by her tinkling, derisive laughter—not to mention several threads of golden hair.

10

The Centurion

TROBE STROKED HIS BEARD THOUGHTFULLY AS he considered the orc lying facedown and unconscious on the forest floor. The dwarf's small, shrewd eyes took in the battered form, reading the story told by livid bruises and shallow cuts.

"Grim work, elf."

"Aye," Xander said softly. "Still, it needed doing."

"Don't hear me arguing, do you? What did the ugly bugger have to say fer himself, once he started talking?"

"Very little."

Trobe folded his arms and glared up at the elf. "And here I thought orcs were hard to coax into a friendly chinwag. You got worries, I want to hear about them—preferably a good while *before* I need to take an axe to them."

"Fair enough," the elf conceded. "I've been troubled about the battle with the orc thieves. Something about that fight just didn't seem right to me."

"Too easy," the dwarf summarized.

"That's it exactly," Xander said, pleased that Trobe had come to the same conclusion. "At first I suspected the orcs had made common cause with the Greenleaf band, but I am satisfied this orc had no knowledge of any such alliance."

The dwarf snorted. "So? What an orc *don't* know could fill a root cellar. Maybe this one just wasn't in on the plan."

Xander shook his head and planted a foot on the orc's ribs. He shoved hard, rolling the creature over. The orc flopped over onto his back, revealing the insignia on his leather armor.

"A centurion," noted Trobe. The eyes he raised to the ranger's face held new respect. "Not bad, elf. Those buggers know their business, yet you tanned his green leather arse and handed it back to him, gift-wrapped in his own breechclout!"

The elf's brow furrowed, but he swiftly abandoned any literal contemplation of dwarven metaphor. "The point being, this orc was undoubtedly the patrol leader. Say what you will about the orcs, they have a knack for gathering information. If there had been any sort of an alliance between orc thieves and human bandits, there's an excellent chance a patrol leader in this part of the forest would have known about it."

"Most likely," Trobe agreed. "So, what do you plan to do with him?"

"If I let him go, he will seek revenge. As a centurion, he's in a position to get it."

"That's my thinking, too. Getting into Crushbone alive won't be easy. Getting *out* will be a wee bit trickier. But if this bugger sets eyes on you, I can guarantee we won't live long enough to worry about that."

Xander sighed. "I know. Yet killing him like this, insensible and unarmed, would be an action without honor."

Trobe smirked and toed the battered orc.

"The centurion was armed and able to fight back," the ranger said quietly. "It could just as well be me lying there, though I doubt the orc would have ended the fight by offering me my life in exchange for answers."

The dwarf shrugged and went back to stroking his short black beard. "There might be another way," he said slowly. "Lemme give it a go. Keep that sword of yers handy, just in case."

Trobe pulled his silver flask from his travel pack. He uncorked it, pinched open the orc's slack mouth, and dribbled a small amount of amber liquid over the fangs.

The orc snorted, sputtered, and jolted into sudden consciousness. He lunged up into a sitting position so abruptly that he sent Trobe tumbling backward. He would have leaped after the dwarf, but the sudden prick of Xander's sword against his throat persuaded him otherwise.

Trobe rolled to his feet and brushed the leaves from his tunic. "That was good dwarven gutrot," he said, sounding vastly surprised and slightly wounded by the orc's reaction. "Best I've had in . . . well, *ever*. If you've anything better on you, I'm all for breaking out the tankards."

"I don't drink wit' dwarf scum," the orc growled, his gruff tones thickened by his swollen lip.

"Well, an orc's got to have his rules, same as the rest of us," Trobe said mildly. "You hail from Crushbone?"

The orc's hate-filled gaze shifted to Xander. "Ask *that*."

"It's you I'm asking, and I got my reasons. Know you an ugly ogress, name of Mirdit Smallplague? Got a scar from here to here?"

The dwarf illustrated the question by sweeping a stubby forefinger in a crescent that started high on his bald head, swept across one cheek, and traced the lower curve of his bearded chin.

Disgust twisted the orc's battered face. "*Know* her? *Hates* her!"

"I'm guessing she gets a lot of that," the dwarf observed companionably. "It's a marvel to me why no one's opened her from gut to gizzard and served her up as main course at a rats' banquet. Alive."

A wistful look crossed the centurion's face as he contemplated this scenario. But his pleasure was short-lived; reality soon dropped a grim veil over his musings and his visage.

"Can't," he grunted. "Emperor Crushbone likes."

"No accounting for taste, is there? I suppose she's still in charge of the slaves?"

The orc's piggish eyes narrowed in suspicion. "How you know that? And why you ask?"

"I'm just thinking out loud, is all," Trobe said.

The brute sneered, then balled his fist and thumped it over the insignia on his chest. "Orc centurion think first, talk later."

Trobe's single eyebrow rose in the center. "Smart," he said admiringly. "A good plan, if you can follow it. But me, I'm a talker. That's how I do my best thinking. And right now, I'm thinking that a slave could get right up close to old Mirdit, no problem."

He raised his axe and ran a finger lightly along the keen edge. Blood welled up immediately. He regarded it thoughtfully for a moment before returning his gaze to the orc's face.

"No problem," he repeated meaningfully.

A slow grin stretched the orc's swollen lips. "You do this thing?"

"I'll need help, of course. Mirdit's meaner than a gut-shot sow, and twice that big and ugly. I'll want this elf with me, and the two more that came with us. And we'll need some of our weapons hidden in Crushbone, so's we can lay hand to them when the time comes."

The mention of Xander brought a scowl to the orc's face, and the final requirement added a layer of skepticism to his anger.

"How I know you kill ogress? Maybe you wanna kill emperor. Or maybe Ambassador Duh—"

He broke off suddenly, feigning a cough to cover his slip.

"That's a reasonable question," Trobe admitted. If he noticed that the orc had revealed more of Crushbone business than he'd intended to, the dwarf gave no sign of it. "Lemme think on it."

After a few moments of contemplative beard-stroking, he leaned in confidingly. "Know you a shaman? Someone you can trust?"

"Sort of," the orc said cautiously.

"There's a frog pond a short run from Crushbone, almost due east. Meet us there in two days' time, come twilight. I'll swear any oath yer shaman wants to hear that I won't kill anyone in Crushbone but Mirdit Smallplague, excepting if I need to protect myself and the three elves with me. In turn, I'll want *yer* oath you won't harm or betray me and mine."

He glanced pointedly at Xander, then returned his gaze to the orc and raised an inquiring brow. After a long moment, the orc gave a reluctant nod.

"I'll swear the oath," Trobe repeated, "and I'll stand

still for whatever magic your shaman wants to cast to make sure I'll keep it."

The orc's expression suggested that he was giving the offered merchandise serious consideration but wasn't quite ready to count out his coins. "I could maybe do that. Not sure why I'd want to."

"Slaves, for one thing," the dwarf reminded him. "You'll be bringing four slaves to work the mines of Crushbone. And treasure," he added. "We raided the Wolfskinner band a couple days back. Got us some good weapons, some of them with Crushbone markings.

"But of course," he added slyly, "the story don't have to be *told* quite that way. Those thieving curs have been a boil on yer emperor's backside some five, six years. He'd likely be real pleased with the orc who could boast he added the thieves' mangy hides to their own pile of skins. And when you hand over weapons the Wolfskinners stole from Crushbone orcs, the emperor's gonna swallow yer story without stopping to chew."

An appreciative grunt indicated the orc was envisioning this scenario and finding it very much to his liking. He pondered this extraordinary offer for a long moment before giving voice to his final question:

"You kill Mirdit, you die. Why you wanna do this?"

"I'm not one to leave a job unfinished," Trobe said softly. Again he traced his finger over the imaginary scar.

"This time," he said softly, "I'll make sure to cut a whole lot deeper, and I'll take whatever comes after as a bargain well made."

This information earned him a fierce grin. "And the elves? Why they come with you?"

"They've heard about the treasure hoard hidden under the mines, and they hope to plunder it," Trobe said in a curiously expressionless tone. As he spoke, he raised one hand to give his head a casual scratch—and to keep Xander from seeing him cast his eyes skyward in silent commentary on elven stupidity.

Dwarf and orc locked stares in a moment of perfect understanding. Then the centurion pushed himself to his feet and gave Trobe a curt nod. "See you in two days, slave," he growled as he hobbled away.

Xander, who had been observing this exchange with great interest and growing amazement, turned his incredulous gaze to Trobe.

The dwarf examined his fingernails in a parody of modesty, blew lightly on them, and then buffed them on his tunic. His playacting was not sufficient to the task of squelching a smug grin.

"That went well, don't y'think?"

"I think," Xander said slowly, "that you might have been mixing a great deal of truth into that tale you told the orc."

"Course I did," he readily admitted. "All the best lies hold at least nine parts truth for every one part deer scat."

"But what parts of the tale were true?" the elf persisted.

"Pretty much all of them," Trobe admitted, "excepting the bit about dying happy after the ogress gets hers. Don't you fret, elf; I got out of Crushbone once, and you can wager yer pointy ears I'll do it again."

"Haven't I already done that?" Xander said dryly, referring to the orc habit of tanning elven ears and keeping them as trophies.

The dwarf thought it over. "I reckon you got me there," he conceded.

11

Songs of Stone and Blood

CHANZOON NEXIS LINGERED IN THE DOORWAY to his forest tower long after the bandit leader had limped off into the night. The surrounding forest was uncannily quiet, for the wild creatures instinctively shied away from the restless dead. The undead, too, seemed to be quitting the tower to return to their interrupted slumber.

The unknown magic that had summoned them was fast fading away; the only undead still in motion were two human skeletons, latecomers pacing aimlessly through the small clearing as if trying to recall just why they'd come.

The necromancer turned them to crumbling dust with a casual wave of his hand. He stood there a while longer, projecting an image of arrogance and power to any who might be watching, be they dead or alive.

The sneering smile dropped from his face the moment his tower door shut out the night. He sank into a chair to ponder the mystery surrounding this strange occurrence and his erstwhile apprentice's part in it.

It *had* to have been Alisar who turned the tower into a beacon for the undead; after all, the gnome was the only other person who had known of this spot until this very day, when Chanzoon had sent out a magical summons to Davin the Dark. The bandit leader knew nothing of magic—the necromancer was quite certain of that—so the little gnome presented the only possible explanation.

But how Alisar had done it, Chanzoon could not begin to say. How she could have hidden her true nature and her considerable skills was a marvel to him.

Why had she cast this spell? Why summon undead creatures here, to this tower? Chanzoon had other lairs closer to farms and villages, the better to collect the materials he needed for his work. Why this place, and why now?

"Why now" was the easiest question to answer: some rare spells were triggered upon the spell-caster's death. Obviously Alisar had devised a magical lure to draw other walking dead to this place. Perhaps, the necromancer mused, to finish a task she had left undone?

Chanzoon had a general idea what that task might entail. Undead creatures were his study, so of course he knew of Mayong Mistmoore's search for a certain red harp. Chanzoon had been elated when he'd come across just such a harp during a bone-gathering trip to the Hills of Shade.

Magical research was costly, and the dark elf vampire was willing to pay handsomely for the harp. Yet Chanzoon was not yet certain he wanted to sell. After all, any object of interest to a powerful vampire might be of equal value to a necromancer.

It had been easy enough to claim this prize, as well as other objects that appeared to have been looted from some ancient tomb. The tomb robbers—a trio of dark elves—were already dead when Chanzoon found them. Among their possessions was a pair of small, bloody shackles, which suggested they'd recently had a captive with them. But though Chanzoon had searched the area diligently, he'd found no sign of either the dark elves' captive or their killer.

Now he suspected they were one and the same.

Come to think of it, Alisar had come to him shortly thereafter. Looking back, he recalled her fondness for the red harp. She had never tried to play it, but she always seemed to linger near whenever one of the captured bards tried to trigger its magic. After each failure, she'd carefully cleaned the blood from its silver strings, her small hands moving lovingly over its curving frame.

Chanzoon did not believe in coincidence. If a dark elf vampire wanted the red harp, he was motivated by something other than a desire to expand his collection of musical instruments. Three dark elves—servants of the vampire lord, perhaps?—had died with just such a harp in their possession. These darklings had taken a small captive, who apparently had made an escape. Shortly thereafter, Alisar had found her way to Chanzoon and begged and bought herself an apprenticeship. Chanzoon could not help but think all these events were connected.

The answer to this riddle had to be Alisar's marvelous dual state: vampire by night, she possessed the strengths of that greatest race of undead; mortal by day, sunlight held no terrors for her. No wonder Mayong Mistmoore yearned to possess the blood red harp! After all, the desire for more and still more power was not confined to the living.

Yes, the vampire lord's motives seemed clear enough

to Chanzoon, but Alisar's story was still largely untold, and that troubled him. Why didn't she take the harp when she escaped from the dark elves? For that matter, why didn't she take it from Chanzoon? She'd had ample opportunity to do so.

The necromancer pushed himself off the bench and strode to the room where the gnome had kept her belongings—a few changes of clothing, some trinkets. There was a small cot in this chamber, for this was the only one of Chanzoon's lairs in which Alisar deigned to stay after nightfall. Given the remote forest location, she had few other options. Whenever they were here, she spent the night in the tower.

Or did she?

Chanzoon threw aside the gnome-sized bed frame and peeled back the cheery red-and-yellow carpet that covered most of the chamber floor. He cast a light spell and dropped to his knees for a closer look.

Yes, there it was: a thin crack outlining a trap door. And there, cleverly disguised in the grain of the wood and hidden in a knothole, was a small wooden ring, just the right size for a gnome's fingers to grasp.

Chanzoon lifted the trap door and directed the magical light to precede him down a small tunnel. It was a tight fit, but he managed to climb down the ladder.

He found himself in a room that most definitely had *not* been carved by his original tree-death spell; in fact, this room was deep underground, with walls and floor of hard-packed soil.

It was a dungeon, and a most unusual dungeon at that. The cages and prison cells had been cleverly fashioned from tree roots.

The necromancer turned slowly, studying the room

first with fascination, then with growing consternation. Alisar had not only learned his tree-death spell, but she had improved upon it! The gnome had not simply re-arranged the roots to her liking; it appeared that the roots had actually done the digging of this dungeon.

Never had Chanzoon thought to seek control over a dead tree. It had never occurred to him that it might be possible. Surely the spells that animated a once-sentient being, a monster, or an animal would have nothing to do with a tree stump!

Yet here, all around him, was evidence to the contrary. For no reason that Chanzoon could explain, he found it deeply disturbing. Trees were alive, of course, and eventually they died, but who would think them capable of any sort of afterlife?

On the other hand, it explained how Alisar had torn a spike from the lift platform in Kelethin. Now that Chanzoon thought about it, the applications of such a spell were many and varied. If Alisar were alive, he'd demand that she teach it to him.

His gaze shifted to the large roots that formed the rafters of the dungeon ceiling, and he noted the circular opening where each of them met the soil. He climbed the bars of one cell to peer into an opening. There was a rippling motion within, not unlike the undulations of a many-legged caterpillar. Several moments passed before he understood what he was seeing: thousands of tiny tree roots moving soil along the tunnel and keeping the air vents open.

He dropped to the floor, mightily impressed. So *that* was how the dungeon had been dug without detection! The living tree had been massive, and its roots probably spread for hundreds of paces in all directions. No doubt there were many small openings in the forest floor, and beside them small piles of discarded soil. In the heavy underbrush, they would be almost impossible to discern. Anyone who happened upon one would probably dismiss it as the work of burrowing insects.

A thorough search of the dungeon revealed no hidden tunnels—at least, none large enough to admit an intruder. That was one consolation; his lair was still secure. If any of Alisar's kind came calling, there was no portal through which they might pass.

The twang of a harp string startled Chanzoon. He spun toward the sound and noticed for the first time a headless skeletal human leaning against the dirt wall of one of the tree-root cages.

Chanzoon came closer, noting the unusual height of the undead harper, the breadth of the shoulders, and, finally, the tarnished bronze medallion hanging over the ribcage. Though the necromancer had never seen this man without his cloak of flesh and skin, he recognized him as the first of the bards he'd captured and killed. Alisar had been charged with the body's disposal, but obviously she'd had plans of her own.

The skeletal bard pushed himself away from the wall and began to stroll aimlessly about the cage, plucking at the strings of a small wooden harp. The instrument was badly out of tune, but after a moment, Chanzoon was able to pick out a simple melody, one chanted by generations of children at play.

His brow furrowed in puzzlement. This man hadn't been able to play a harp; in fact, that had been the reason for his death. Chanzoon hadn't thought it was possible for the dead to demonstrate a skill they had not known in life.

But then, neither had he known that a necromancer could command an undead tree to dig a dungeon.

A glint of silver drew Chanzoon's eye to a second chain around the dead bard's neck. He reached between the tree-root bars and broke the chain with a quick snap.

Instantly both movement and music stopped. The bard fell to the floor with a clatter of bone and a jangle of harp strings.

The necromancer studied the small pendant hanging from the broken chain. It was old and badly tarnished. Shaped like a shield, it bore an elaborately carved design and some runes of gnomish origin. A heraldic crest, by the looks of it.

Chanzoon nodded in appreciation. It made sense; a personal object might indeed transfer certain skills from a necromancer to an undead creature under her control. Obviously Alisar was no stranger to the bardic arts, for how else could the blood red harp have worked its transformation over her?

He quickly climbed the ladder and hurried to his spell-casting chamber, the gnome's family device clutched tightly in one hand. Chanzoon had some small ability with the magical gates that connected the far-flung sites of Faydwer, but he'd never had reason to attempt transport to the gnome city of Ak'Anon.

After what he'd seen of Alisar's handiwork, however, Chanzoon didn't anticipate any problems. No doubt the surprisingly resourceful gnome had already established a gate. All that remained to him was finding it.

TWO DIRT-SMUDGED FIGURES LAY SIDE BY SIDE IN the narrow tunnel, gazing down at the floor of the cave below. Like Trobe's abode, it appeared to have been formed long ago when a giant tree fell and tore an inverted mountain of soil and rock up with it. Just enough early morning light filtered in through various small openings to enable Elizerain to make out the pile of melon-sized eggs that appeared to have been carved from some sort of smooth gray rock. They looked harmless enough, but the tiny stone figure cradled in Elizerain's hand gave silent testament to the dangers within.

She studied the stone pixie, marveling at the detail. Each tiny curl, every fold of her delicate skirts, even the tiny feathers on her butterfly wings were revealed with startling clarity. Despite the uniform grey hue of the stone and the profound stillness of the pixie's pert features, the little fey might have been alive.

Beside her, Trobe shifted uncomfortably. "I don't like this," he grumbled.

Elizerain shot him a quick grin. "I thought dwarves were fond of tunnels."

"Decent tunnels. *Clean* tunnels."

"Not exactly a reasonable expectation, considering this one's *made* of dirt."

"There you go," Trobe agreed glumly. He gathered a bit of soil and let it sift through his stubby fingers. "Stuff that moves around so easy is not the sort of building material yer wanting to find in a tunnel. Give me nice sturdy stone above and below, that's all I'm asking."

"Haven't you been living in a dirt cave?"

"I wouldn't call it *living,* exactly. *Staying,* is more like. There wasn't a lot of loose dirt about—mostly tree roots above and around, and the floor I paved with good solid river rock. Not exactly what I'd call a palace, but it was a damn sight better than this rabbit hole."

A sudden movement below caught Elizerain's eye.

She grasped the dwarf's wrist with her free hand, silently warning him to hold his complaints.

The floor of the small cave shifted and stirred, prompting a soft moan of distress from Trobe. Elizerain watched in fascination as dozens of large, iridescent black beetles fought their way free of the soil and crawled slowly over to the nearest round stone. They swarmed over it, sluggishly at first, then in escalating frenzy.

Slowly, ever so slowly, the stony shell took on a lighter hue, and the texture began to resemble a leathery eggshell.

"They're eating the outer shell," marveled Trobe softly, watching as the beetles moved on to the next egg. "And here I thought that pixie was still prank-playing with you. Damned if the talking bug wasn't telling you the truth!"

Those pranks still rankled with Elizerain, too, but she could understand why the pixie acted as she did. "She needed help, and she did what she thought she had to do to get our attention."

The dwarf's shrug expressed a profound lack of interest in pixie motivations. "So, when does the singing commence?"

"Any time now," Elizerain assured him.

In truth, she had no idea how long it took a basilisk to hatch. The beetles thinned several more shells down to the leathery inner lining before the first egg burst open.

A small, armored creature approximately the size of a housecat rolled free of the shell. Instantly a small swarm of beetles converged on the hatchling, licking it clean and lapping at the broken bits of shell.

This unusual meal seemed to be precisely what the beetles required. Once sated, the creatures began to chirp and fan their wings. One by one, they rose into the air and sought the openings into the forest—one of which was currently occupied.

"Bet the pixie didn't mention *this* part," Trobe observed snidely as he swatted at a passing beetle.

Elizerain shushed him, listening intently to the whirr and chirping in the cavern below. Slowly, a musical pattern emerged from the cacophony, a six-note melody embellished with an odd little trill.

Despite her fascination, Elizerain felt a stab of resentment toward the wizard who had "taught" this tune to the beetles. According to the pixie, this wizard's experiments with basilisks had nearly depleted the forest population. Clutches of eggs remained, but they couldn't hatch without adult basilisks to lick away the rocky outer shell. Belatedly realizing his mistake, the wizard meddled with another of Tunare's creatures—this time with a type of beetle that laid its larvae in caves and hollow logs. After the first couple of hatching attempts resulted in a quantity of beetle-shaped stone paperweights, the wizard created a restoration spell that would be released by the beetles' hatching song. Twisted, yes, but it seemed to be working.

Elizerain hummed the tune fragment several times to affix it in memory.

"Got it?" the dwarf prodded. "Because here comes something else the pixie didn't bother to tell you about."

Elizerain's eyes widened. Three basilisk hatchlings were scrambling up the wall of the cave, headed straight toward the tunnel.

"Go," she said tersely.

Trobe didn't require further prompting. There was no room to turn around, but he raised himself on his hands and knees, insofar as the low dirt ceiling allowed, and scuttled backward like a panicked crab. He kept his eyes squeezed shut, just in case one of the basilisks caught up with him.

The elf followed. Fortunately, the tunnel was short, and the moment she and Trobe rolled free of it, they were on their feet and running. According to the pixie, basilisk hatchlings, like the shell-eating beetles, required immediate nourishment, and the usually solitary creatures would form a one-time pack to hunt. Not knowing exactly what the hatchlings considered "food," Elizerain thought it best to remove herself and Trobe from consideration.

They found cover and watched as a dozen or more of the creatures scurried off into the underbrush.

"They instinctively form a pack, so that should be all of them," Elizerain said. She rose to her feet and brushed some of the dirt off her tunic. "The beetles return to the cave when it's time to lay their larvae."

"And the whole thing starts over again when the new beetles dig their way out," Trobe concluded as he fell into step beside the elf. "Strange, the way basilisks can live inside those eggs fer years and years."

"Stranger than their ability to turn people to stone with a glance?"

"There's that," he admitted. He glanced at the tiny stone figure in Elizerain's hand. "You sure you wanna sing that thing back to life?"

That stopped Elizerain in mid-stride. "Sweet Tunare," she whispered. "I never thought of it quite like that, but that's what the spell does, isn't it?"

Trobe reached up and gave her a reassuring pat on the shoulder. "Don't be looking like that. You can do it, though I don't mind admitting I can't see why you'd *want* to. The statue in yer hand is a lot less annoying than her prank-playing friend."

Elizerain waved his complaints aside. "But I haven't been a bard for very long. What was I thinking?"

"That whatever a beetle could do, you could probably do better?" he suggested.

That coaxed a chuckle from her. She squared her shoulders and took a deep, calming breath. "Well, here goes, then."

When the first note passed her lips, Elizerain's doubts disappeared. Magic flowed through her from dark, deep places in the forest, pouring life into the song-spell she sang. For one odd, exhilarating moment, the elf knew what it was to be an ancient tree, to watch and ponder the secrets of the forest and all who lived and died beneath her branches.

The moment passed all too soon, leaving her feeling slightly dazed, as if she'd just awakened from a dream she was already forgetting.

A soft rustling, like wind sighing through distant leaves, rose from the tiny figure in Elizerain's hand, and a network of delicate cracks skittered across the statue's features. Stone dust fell away, and the pixie—a fey lass with autumn-colored tresses and wings to match—burst into flight. She flitted away without so much as a backward glance.

Elizerain watched her go, a smile of deep satisfaction on her face and a sense of wonder in her heart. She wasn't surprised by the pixie's ingratitude—she had expected nothing more. What astonished her was the power a simple melody could hold.

So *this* was why so many people chose a bard's path!

Everyone knew there was magic in bard-song, and Elizerain had cast a few simple spells herself. But *this* was beyond anything she'd ever considered possible!

Magic was not what lured her to bard-craft; music and stories had always been her life and her joy. They had always been enough for her.

Or had they?

If music and stories were enough, why had she "gone bard," when she could just as easily have followed her parents as a rural harper?

"Now, *there's* gratitude for you!" complained Trobe. He took Elizerain's hand and deftly plucked out a splinter. A disgusted expression crossed his face, and he held out a tiny dagger for her to see. "The bug couldn't be bothered to say a word before flitting off, but it *did* take the time to cut you."

Elizerain regarded her bleeding palm and for the first time registered the sting. "It doesn't look too bad."

"It's not what it looks like that worries me, it's what it *smells* like. Don't want a scent of blood in the air," he pointed out, "because for all we know, those beetles still might be feeling a mite peckish."

Since several of the airborne insects seemed to be showing an interest, the elf conceded this point with a nod and gritted her teeth when the dwarf reached for his silver flask.

He poured a bit of liquid fire over her hand, which cauterized the wound as effectively—and as painfully—as forge-heated iron. Then he deftly bandaged her hand, tending the task so quickly that it was over before Elizerain had finished cursing him.

"You got in a few good hits there," Trobe noted admiringly, "and some real interesting misses, too."

The elf managed a wan smile and waved away his offer of a drink from the same flask. "Sorry about that."

"Don't be. The sharp side of yer tongue is mighty entertaining, even if I was the one getting flayed by it."

Trobe tucked away the dwarven spirits and sent her a grim smile. "Makes me look forward to hearing the songs you'll be singing after a few days in Crushbone."

THE ROAD TO AK'ANON WAS ALREADY CROWDED with morning traffic when Chanzoon Nexis emerged from the magical gate that connected his forest tower and the gnome city, several days' foot-travel to the south.

His sudden appearance was noted by a small flock of gnome children, who yelped in astonishment and scattered like startled birds. Fortunately no one else seemed to notice, and Chanzoon set off purposefully toward the nearest adult gnome—a farmer of some sort, trundling a handcart heaped high with early cabbages.

"You, there," he called. "I'd like a word."

The gnome glanced over his shoulder but didn't bother to stop. "You got a particular word in mind?"

Chanzoon gritted his teeth and reminded himself that information, not the slow evisceration such impudence deserved, was the more important goal.

"As it happens, I do. A name."

He lengthened his stride and overtook the little farmer in a few steps, then thrust Alisar's silver crest into his face.

"Do you recognize this device?"

The gnome glanced at the pendant. "I might. Depends on what your business might be."

"I'd like to return this to the family. The gnome who owned it died in my service. She never told me her family name."

At last the farmer stopped. He set down his cabbage cart and scratched his bulbous nose as he thought it over.

"I suppose that's a likely enough tale," he conceded. "The Kneebreakers been known to hire themselves out to all sorts."

"Kneebreakers," Chanzoon repeated, trying without success to equate this name with dainty little Alisar.

"You'll be wanting Fedric Kneebreaker. Not that *he's* a hired dagger—far from it! Likes his creature comforts too well, Fedric does, but when it comes to kin, he's the one to ask. Collects 'em, he does. Likes the display, he does."

An odd image flashed into Chanzoon's mind: Alisar's gnome relatives standing in a neat row, stuffed and mounted like hunting trophies. This unlikely scenario appealed to him, as it suggested a way of disposing of this annoying little fellow.

The necromancer quickly banished this pleasant thought and returned to the task at hand. "And where might I find this Fedric Kneebreaker?"

A small, soil-begrimed finger pointed down the road. "Keep on 'til you come upon the path to Redbird Hollow. You won't see the path, most likely, but keep an eye open for thirsty-looking gnomes. There's a fine inn down the path a bit. You won't see that, either, as it's hidden in a hillock. But Goodwife Kneebreaker brews a hopping good breakfast ale and bakes spice rolls afresh each morn, so you should be right enough if you follow your nose."

The gnome patted the large, rosy feature that dominated his face and cast a scornful look at Chanzoon's elegant profile, as if doubting that so small a nose could be equal to the task. "Or you could just follow a thirsty-looking gnome."

Chanzoon was beginning to see whence the wind blew. "I imagine pushing that cart is thirsty work. Be my guide, and I'll pay for your morning ale."

"Seems fair," the gnome allowed.

As it happened, the turnoff was just around the bend, and the hillock in question was in clear sight *and* distinguished from the surrounding countryside by quite visible windows and doors, not to mention a pair of merrily smoking chimneys.

A gnome woman, a tidy little soul with nut-brown hair tucked into a snowy white cap and a blue dress covered by a ruffled white apron, bustled out of the side door and greeted the farmer with a half-feigned scowl.

"*There* you are, Gorminar! The midday soup is already a-simmer, and no cabbages to be had. I was about ready to send Fedric foraging for greens—"

She stopped short when she noted Chanzoon's necromancer robes. Fear flashed over her round, rosy face, but it was quickly displaced by curiosity.

"Well now, who's this?"

"A fellow who hired himself a Kneebreaker some while back. Looking to talk to Fedric, he is, and thought the introduction was worth the price of my morning ale."

Well worth it, Chanzoon agreed silently, for he had no doubt whatsoever that he'd come to the right place. The gnome woman had Alisar's bright blue eyes and abundant brown hair, though hers was liberally streaked with gray. Her features were rounder and courser, and she was as plump as a pigeon, but there was no mistaking the resemblance.

"I'll fetch him," she promised and spun away into the hillock. She returned in moments with her husband, an amiable-looking little fellow who, judging by the rounded belly under his fine yellow waistcoat, was exceedingly fond of his wife's ale.

"I've come about your daughter Alisar," Chanzoon said without preamble.

The gnome couple exchanged puzzled glances. Fedric's eyes slid meaningfully toward the eavesdropping farmer, then toward the side door of the hillock tavern. A mutinous expression crossed his wife's plump face, but she bobbed a curtsey to Chanzoon and ushered the farmer toward the kitchen. It did not escape the necromancer's notice that she left the door conveniently ajar.

"There's been some sort of mistake," the gnome ventured. "We have no daughter, not by that name or any other."

"Don't waste my time with foolish evasions," Chanzoon said impatiently. "Alisar was the very image of your wife."

He chose his words deliberately, giving just enough emphasis to "was" to hint at Alisar's demise.

Understanding flashed onto the gnome's face, but it was not accompanied by either grief or shock.

"Come to think of it," he said slowly, "Nebbie's granddame had a sister by name of Allisandra. Famous beauty in her day, she was. Everyone says my Nebbie is Allisandra all over again. I'll show you."

He bustled into the hillock without waiting for a response. Chanzoon followed him through the front door and down a flight of stairs, stooping to keep from scraping his head along the low ceiling.

The tavern was surprisingly grand, given its humble exterior. The entrance hall was long and narrow, floored with bluestone tiles and lined along both walls with portraits in elaborately carved frames. The candles in the small wall sconces on either side of every picture filled the hall with light. There were three doors on each side of the hall and two flights of stairs at the end, one leading up to the top floor, the other descending to some pleasantly fragrant cellar. A cozy taproom was visible through an open door to Chanzoon's right, filled with small tables of highly polished wood and deep, soft chairs that looked exceedingly comfortable, provided one was gnome-sized.

Fedric stopped beside the sitting room door and pointed to the first picture, a younger, slimmer version of himself and his wife.

"Here's me and Nebbie," he said proudly. "And next one over is my brother Shadwick and his wife on their wedding day. Yonder's my father—"

"I have no interest in climbing your family tree," the necromancer broke in coldly. "Show me Alis—" He broke off and corrected himself, "*Allisandra's* portrait."

Fedric hurried about halfway down the hall and pointed a stubby finger at the opposite wall. Chanzoon followed, then crouched down for a better look.

Depicted with considerable skill was a blue-eyed gnome maiden, dressed in a pink satin gown that was probably the height of gnome fashion a few decades past.

For a long moment, Chanzoon gazed into the smiling face of his erstwhile apprentice.

"Nebbie's grand-auntie Allisandra," the gnome announced. "That's her betrothal painting. The marriage never took place, of course. She was gone soon after that was painted, but Nebbie's granddame always said it was a good likeness."

"What happened to Allisandra?"

A proud smile wreathed the gnome's face. "Went off adventuring, she did, and no surprise in that. My Nebbie is a Kneebreaker, too. It's a big clan, mind you, with as many branches as any tree in Faydark. Nebbie's side has a famous line of hired daggers going way back to—"

He broke off suddenly, having caught sight of the expression on Chanzoon's face. The hand he'd lifted to point down the hall to some ancestral portrait faltered, then dropped to his side.

"Anyhow, Allisandra bred true to the Kneebreaker name," he finished lamely.

Chanzoon gritted his teeth in frustration. He'd never met a creature who could natter on for so long without actually answering a question.

"How did she die?" he enunciated slowly and precisely, in a tone that hinted he might be seeking suggestions for his own use.

The gnome gulped audibly, then cupped his left elbow with his right hand, lifting a shaking forefinger to tap at his nose. After a moment he said, "Well, now, I'm sure I've heard that story, but it's just not coming to me. Nerves, you know," he continued apologetically. "It's not every day a necromancer comes to call. Nebbie?"

The door nearest the cellar stairs swung open, and Goodwife Kneebreaker bustled into the hall, making no effort to hide the fact that she'd had an ear to the door.

"Allisandra ran with the Seven Seadogs," she said briskly. "Humans, all of them, but they had her along because she was handy with a spell and knew what to do with the business end of a dagger. Pass as a human child, she could, with a bit of magic to help things along. I'd wager *that* came in handy more often than not, seeing as how the rest of them were fairly named. Seadogs, indeed, and a mangier pack of curs I've never seen."

Apparently Nebbie Kneebreaker was every bit as talkative as her husband, but Chanzoon found her conversation far more profitable.

"You've seen these people?"

"When I was a very young girl," she confirmed. "Not all of them, of course. Some of them had come to no good end by then, and the rest were old men. But they'd come around every now and again looking for Auntie Allisandra."

Chanzoon shot a quick glare toward Fedric. "You said she died young."

"Begging your pardon, but I said she went off adventuring," the gnome replied. "It was you who asked how she died, and the truth of *that* I don't rightly know."

Chanzoon cut him off with an impatient gesture and turned to the gnome woman. "What do you know of this?"

"Aunt Allisandra was swallowed up during one of those ground shifts that happen in the western lands. The Seadogs *said* they wouldn't lose hope of her until her body was found," Nebbie said, her sour expression making clear what she thought of *that* sentiment. "More likely, she had something they wanted when she disappeared, and they were hoping to get it back."

"Do you know what this 'something' might be?"

Nebbie shook her head regretfully. "Never heard it said, and believe you me, I kept an ear open."

"She does that," Fedric confirmed.

Chanzoon tried a different approach. "Your Aunt

Allisandra was renowned for her beauty; I suppose she was equally famous for her bard-craft?"

"Bard-craft?" Nebbie repeated, clearly astonished. "There's never been a Kneebreaker bard, best I know. Allisandra was a necromancer, and a good one."

The gnome grimaced, as if she'd just heard her own words and found herself out of agreement with them. "Well, she was not exactly a *good* one. No offense intended to yourself, but she was good at being bad, if you catch my meaning."

He did indeed. Clearly, Alisar had known more of the necromantic art than she'd admitted to.

With a curt nod, Chanzoon rose to his feet, insofar as the low ceiling allowed, and headed for the door.

"Gorminar said something about Allisandra's crest," Nebbie Kneebreaker said, despite her husband's best efforts to shush her. "Will you be returning it, then?"

Chanzoon shot a look over his shoulder that sent both gnomes reeling back a pace, clutching at each other for support. But the redoubtable Nebbie was not quite finished.

"Well, that's all right, then," she said faintly, "but my morning ale goes for two silver bits a tankard, and well worth the price it is. It's Gorminar's custom to have two tankards with his breakfast, but his thirst grows when someone else is paying."

Her persistence amused the necromancer. Or perhaps he found her misplaced courage admirable. It was also possible that she reminded him of Alisar, whose absence he felt rather more keenly than he would have thought possible. Whatever the reason, Chanzoon tossed the gnome a gold piece before he ducked out into the bright mid-morning sunshine.

12

Dead Wolves Don't Play Fair

XANDER WOKE AT FIRST LIGHT, AS WAS HIS custom. He preferred to stand the first watch each night and then catch a few hours of sleep before arising to tend the breakfast fire. But this morning he awoke to the sounds of a crackling fire and the rich scent of roasting meat.

To his surprise, Elizerain was already up, sitting cross-legged beside the fire she'd built in a circle of stones near the creek that bordered their campsite. She was deep in study of a small parchment scroll, which she tipped toward the fire to catch the small amount of light it shed.

The bard looked up as Xander approached, her amber eyes shining.

"This is the prize I got at the Songweavers' Feast," she said excitedly, waving the scroll at him. "It's a healing spell, and a good one!"

The ranger settled down beside her and carefully removed a skewer of roasted rabbit from the green-twig rack Elizerain had constructed. "You should eat something. We have a long day's walk ahead."

She obediently took a portion and set it aside to cool, then picked up the parchment again. "This spell really could come in handy. I doubt all of us will be able to get out of Crushbone without an injury of some sort."

This new, practical side of Elizerain appealed to Xander. He suspected it had something to do with the side trip she'd insisted on taking yesterday, and he rather regretted that Trobe had been the one to share it with her. But Xander had his duty, and leaving Nyson untended was not something he could do in good conscience.

He sent her a wistful smile. "I've never seen you so excited about a spell. Songs, certainly, and sometimes a tale or legend, but never magic."

"I've good reason! Did Trobe tell you about yesterday's adventure?"

"He said you fulfilled your pledge to the pixie, and he seemed relieved that the pranks would end, but nothing more."

In a few words Elizerain told him how the beetles' hatching triggered a spell that could reverse the results of a basilisk's gaze.

"A resurrection spell?" Nyson's voice came from behind them, his tone rounded with incredulity. "You learned a *resurrection spell* from *bugs*?"

Both wood elves turned toward the young Koada'Dal, who had just arisen and was shaking the leaves from his cloak.

"It worked," Elizerain said flatly.

Nyson inclined his head in a slight bow. "I meant no disrespect, Songmistress. I was surprised, nothing more. The sword you carry proclaims you a bard of considerable power, but I have never heard of a music-based spell that could restore a basilisk's victim to life."

That was a topic Xander had long wanted to raise. "About that sword . . ."

The bard shot him a quelling glance and shook her head to indicate "not now." To Nyson she said, "Perhaps we elves should spend more time conversing with pixies. Imagine what else we might learn."

Trobe strode into camp just in time to hear this last remark. "Suit yerself. Me, I'd rather talk to a swarm of gnats. They're less annoying."

The dwarf settled down beside the fire and claimed the bigger of the two remaining portions. He popped a morsel of sizzling meat into his mouth and chewed lustily, gave a grunt of approval, and followed it with another hearty bite.

A faint rustle came from the bushes on the far side of the stream, still some distance away but closing in fast.

Xander was on his feet first. In a few quick, fluid movements, he had an arrow nocked and ready. The two other elves were swift behind him, swords in hand.

Trobe carefully thrust one end of his skewer into the ground and hauled himself to his feet, grumbling about impatient elves and interrupted breakfasts.

The four companions fell back several paces to put some cover between themselves and whatever was swiftly approaching their camp. Ever mindful of archers, Xander waved Elizerain toward the thick truck of a large oak. After Nyson and the dwarf had each claimed a smaller tree as a shield, the ranger joined Elizerain in her refuge.

A pair of large gray wolves burst from the underbrush, tongues lolling. They paced back and forth alongside the stream as if seeking a dry path across. Even from this distance, Xander could smell the foul drool dripping from their muzzles.

"They won't cross the water," Nyson said confidently, stepping out from behind the tree. "Look at their patchy coats, and see that foam at their mouths? They're very sick, and their illness makes them fear water."

"Those wolves are long past sick," the dwarf retorted as he drew his axe from his belt. "They've been dead some good long while."

"He's right," Xander said. He sent a troubled glance in Elizerain's direction and said in a voice meant for her ears alone, "The necromancer's pets, mayhap?"

Her brow furrowed. "You think he's tracking me?" she replied, speaking just above a whisper.

"It's very possible."

She gave a single curt nod. "Good. I hope he finds us before we get to Crushbone. I'd rather face one human necromancer than a fortress full of orcs."

"Assuming the necromancer could be persuaded to remove the curse, I would agree. But we don't know what he wants. Stay out of sight and let the rest of us handle this."

Before she could reply, a loud splash drew their attention back to the stream.

"Enough with the whispering!" bellowed Trobe. "Dead critters, closing in fast!"

Xander stepped clear of the oak tree, drawing the bowstring taut as he moved.

Apparently the wolves had not been rabid, or perhaps death had wiped away the fear of water that sometimes came with the late stages of the illness. Or perhaps some dark compulsion forced them to attack despite their natural inclinations. One wolf was dipping a tentative paw into the stream, but the other was already wading ashore. It caught sight of Xander and kicked into a loping charge.

The undead creature closed the distance with a few strides. The ranger waited until the wolf was almost upon him, hoping that instinct had survived death, so that the creature would attack as it would have in life.

Sure enough, on its final stride the wolf reared up and pushed into a high leap, bared teeth reaching for Xander's throat.

The ranger released the arrow when the wolf was in the air. It took the creature through its dead heart with enough force to fling it over backward. The wolf landed on its back and thrashed about, rolling this way and that as it tried to regain its footing. But the long arrow shaft sticking from its chest effectively kept it from rolling over.

Trobe strode forward and finished the wolf with a single well-placed blow of his axe. He kicked the head aside and dropped into a battle crouch, pulling the axe up high over one shoulder in preparation to meet the second wolf's loping charge.

Xander's arrow got there first, whizzing past Trobe's ear—close enough to prompt a yelp of surprise from the dwarf—and then driving deep into the wolf's shoulder.

But the creature didn't so much as break stride. Trobe, who'd belatedly ducked away from the arrow, was left off balance. Still, he managed to swat the wolf with the side of his axe hard enough to send it rolling aside.

Nyson stepped into the creature's path, sword in hand, and waited for it to regain its feet.

"You're not fighting a duel, boy!" the dwarf howled. "Dead wolves don't play fair. Just *hit* the damn thing!"

An expression of distaste crossed the young elf's face, but he did as he was told. Muttering something that sounded suspiciously like "unsporting oaf," he swept his sword down toward the staggering, off-balance wolf.

It was a strong blow and skillfully delivered. Despite the moving target, Nyson cleanly sliced the wolf across the throat. Black blood, thick as tar, oozed from the gaping wound.

The wolf, however, was too accustomed to being dead to be inconvenienced. It got its feet under it and tamped down for a spring.

Xander's next arrow plunged into the open wound. There was a crack of bone as the arrow severed the spine, and the creature fell to the ground. A final twitch, and it lay limp and still.

The dwarf stalked over, axe held ready. But there was no need. The wolf suddenly seemed much smaller, and it looked as if it had lain there dead for a very long time.

Trobe nudged at the thing with his boot, wrinkling his nose at the stench that rose from the corpse.

He turned to the young elf, a sly look on his bearded face. "Smells bad enough to put you off yer feed, don't it?"

Nyson stopped cleaning his sword and returned the dwarf's stare coolly. "If you're thinking to claim my share of the morning meal, think again."

The dwarf blinked in surprise. Then he shrugged and stalked back toward the fire. "No matter. Yers is probably overcooked by now, anyway."

AFTER A LONG DAY'S MARCH, ELIZERAIN AND HER three companions settled down into the underbrush not far from the frog pond where Trobe had arranged to meet the orc centurion. Situated as they were on a small hill, they could watch for the approach of the centurion and shaman, yet remain out of view in case the orc proved treacherous.

Not all of them were agreed upon this course of action, and none was without doubts. Nyson, of course, expressed his most strenuously.

"Whatever possessed you, that you would assume an orc—an *orc*!—would keep his word?" he demanded.

Trobe folded his arms over his chest and glared at the young Koada'Dal. "He wants Mirdit Smallplague dead, that's why. Once you meet her, you'll understand."

"But the ogress is a slave master, an important personage in Crushbone, and apparently she has the favor of the orcs' so-called emperor. Won't your centurion reap the whirlwind once it's known Mirdit was killed by a slave *he* brought to Crushbone?"

The dwarf shrugged. "Why do you care? We'll be long gone by then."

"My opinion in this matter is of little importance," Nyson said grimly. He raised one hand in an abrupt gesture to cut off Trobe's ready agreement, then added, "The question is whether or not the centurion has thought ahead to this eventuality. If so, he might not be inclined to honor the deal you made with him."

"Nyson has a point," Elizerain said.

Xander nodded. "After all, the orc's had two days to think things through."

"Don't you worry about that," Trobe said robustly. "Didn't you mark the size of that bugger? I'd wager my last coin he owes his rank to his muscles, not his brains. Besides, if he grew some doubts over the past two days, I can scythe them down easy enough."

"If we must entrust our lives to this orc, we should at least keep our best weapons at hand," the high elf persisted.

"If we give over our weapons, what's to stop the orc from keeping them for himself? At the very least, the bard should keep her singing sword. If it comes to battle, the extra speed it could lend all of us might make the difference."

"There's that," Trobe agreed, eyeing Elizerain's sword approvingly. "Bound to be loose stones in the quarry. If we can heave 'em fast enough, we could probably hold off the orcs long enough to dive down the tunnel, even if we didn't have another weapon."

A quick flush stained Elizerain's cheeks. "But you and Xander are better fighters. If any of us is to have a weapon, it should be one of you two."

"I would agree," Xander said, his gaze on the bard's singing sword.

Elizerain shrugged off his disapproval and turned to Nyson. "How do you propose that *any* of us walk into Crushbone carrying hidden weapons? Wait a minute," she added slowly, as the answer presented itself. "You have *another* spell you didn't bother to tell me about, don't you?"

"It's called a ghost scabbard," he said, not looking at all abashed at being caught in yet another omission. "Once the weapon is sheathed, it is not only invisible but undetectable."

"Handy," Trobe admitted.

A bleak expression touched the young elf's eyes. "It's a newly created spell, not widely used. I consider myself fortunate to have known the enchanter who created it."

"Good luck for the rest of us, too," the dwarf said. He unbuckled the belt-loop that held his axe and handed the weapon over. "Let's see what you can do with this. Don't exactly keep it in a scabbard, but close enough."

Nyson looked dubious, but he accepted the weapon and began a deep, crooning chant. After a few minutes, he fell silent and handed the axe back to Trobe.

The dwarf buckled the weapon into place. Instantly the axe disappeared, as did the contraption of leather and brass that held it to his belt.

A bemused expression crossed the dwarf's face as he patted at his hip. "Can't feel it at all. You sure it's still there?"

"Reach for your axe with the intent of wielding it," Nyson instructed.

The dwarf's hand flashed to his hip, and came up with the axe clenched in his fist and ready to swing. A broad smile stretched his black mustache into a straight line.

"That's magic worth knowing," he said happily as he returned the axe to its hiding place.

"Do the harp next," Elizerain demanded.

The others turned to her, surprised by her vehemence.

"Well, Trobe made no arrangement for it with the orc centurion," she explained, "and who knows what they might do with it once we get to Crushbone—keep it as treasure, trade it for weapons, even burn it for firewood!"

"It's a harp," the dwarf said dismissively. "You'll get another."

He noticed the glances that passed among the elves, and his face took on a resigned expression. "Oh, good—there's more."

Elizerain quickly told him the story behind her quest: the curse placed on her by a vengeful necromancer and her need to find the true story of the harp's history.

Trobe stroked his beard as he listened but offered no comment until she fell silent. "And yer thinking the harp's story can be found in the treasure trove under Crushbone?"

The bard lifted her chin and returned his gaze squarely. "Evidence does seem to point in that direction."

But the sharp-eyed dwarf noted how her eyes had darted toward Nyson. "Is that a fact?" he mused, eyeing the young high elf.

He was about to say more, but Xander quickly cut him off. "If we're to keep our weapons, we should let Nyson get on with his business."

The young high elf quickly worked the spell on the harp, Elizerain's short sword, and Xander's bow and daggers. He was tucking his own jeweled sword out of sight when the crunch of heavy footsteps announced the approach of the orcs.

There were just two of them, as agreed: the centurion whom Xander had vanquished and questioned and a smaller, even uglier orc with one broken fang and a network of black tattoos that took in the entire expanse of his bared, green-skinned chest.

Trobe rose and stepped into the open, his arms full of weapons they'd taken from the band of orc thieves. He strode forward and spilled them to the ground, then motioned for the elves to keep back. They'd decided ahead of time that Trobe would speak for all, since he'd already cast himself as a sort of co-conspirator with the orc centurion.

"Good steel, all of it," the dwarf said stoutly. "Some of it has the Crushbone mark on it."

He toed one of the daggers closer to the orcs. The centurion picked it up and grunted in satisfaction when he noted the skull device that was the citadel's emblem. He showed it to the shaman, who held it up for closer examination.

"Belong to Umbrug Toothsmasher," the shaman decreed. "Never come back from patrol. Wondered what happened to him."

"Let's get on with it," Trobe prodded. "We got words to say, oaths to make."

The shaman tucked the dagger in his own belt, ignoring the scowl this prompted from the centurion.

"Hold arms like this," the shaman instructed, fisting both hands and holding them at eye level and shoulder width. "Not so close to nose," he scolded, when Trobe mirrored the posture imperfectly.

"Maybe he *want* to have ring through nose, like bearded pig," the centurion observed. The orcs shared a dark, grating chuckle over this incomprehensible jest.

After their mirth subsided, the shaman instructed, "You say words, I dance magic."

As the orc stamped and whirled, Trobe promised that he would not kill the centurion and that after he got to Crushbone, he *would* kill Mirdit Smallplague but harm no Crushbone orc, except in defense of himself or his three elven companions. And with each word he spoke, a ghostly link formed in a chain that stretched from one wrist to the other, and from both of them to the ground. Once the oath was made and the chant finished, the shackles faded away.

"Try to kill Farmid," the shaman suggested, tossing his head casually in the centurion's direction. "Just for fun."

The dwarf's fierce grin showed full agreement with this sentiment. He started to reach for his axe before he remembered the concealing magic. To cover his near-blunder, he gave his belly a leisurely scratch before stooping to take a halberd from the pile. He pulled it back with both hands and swung it hard in the orc's direction.

The swing was arrested in midair, and there was a distinct *chink* as invisible shackles stayed his hand. For a moment the dwarf stood with weapon in hand, visibly vibrating from the force of the invisible jolt.

He shook himself briskly and tossed the weapon aside. "That should do it."

"Now try to kill elf," Farmid suggested slyly, sending a hate-filled gaze in Xander's direction.

Trobe snorted. "I suppose you had to try, didn't you? Now *you* say the words: No harm comes to these elves by yer hand or deed or word until Mirdit Smallplague dies by my hand. And I want a pair of those links going through yer tusks, so you have to decide whether taking a swing, so to speak, is worth losing yer favorite teeth."

The shaman sent him an admiring glance. "Farmid keep blood oath or lose fangs—not bad thinking for dwarf. This orc shoulda thought of that."

"Well, that's the reason for places like Crushbone, innit? A fellow can only think up so much mischief on his own."

The orc grunted his agreement with this philosophy and began the magic that bound the centurion to his end of the bargain.

After the orc's invisible chains were cast and gingerly tested, Trobe picked up the halberd again. He studied it for a moment, then with a single quick sweep he brought it down and back, circling all the way around. The halberd's blade swept downward and came to rest deep in the shaman's tattooed chest.

The hideous creature died before he could finish a startled curse. His last breath was a gurgling wheeze, and he slumped to the ground in a spreading pool of blood.

Farmid stared at the dwarf over the shaman's corpse. "You took oath—"

"That I wouldn't harm any orc *after I got to Crushbone*," Trobe broke in. "Besides, it was a needed thing. What was to keep this shaman from bragging about his part in this? If he talked before I got a chance to kill the ogress, I'd be one dead dwarf. Not that I'm against dying for a good reason, but when I go, I mean to have ogre blood on my hands.

"And," he went on, turning an intense gaze on the centurion, "if I were to claim you brought us to Crushbone to kill the ogress, it would be yer word against me and those elves yonder, and who'd listen to the likes of us? It'd be another song entirely once the shaman started singing."

The orc looked decidedly unhappy with this logic, and with his own lack of foresight. "Shoulda thought of that," he mumbled.

Then, suddenly, he brightened as another possibility occurred to him. His gaze shifted to Xander, and his hand dropped to his sword.

"We not in Crushbone yet," he sneered.

"True enough, but you didn't say the words the same way I did," Trobe pointed out. "Even if you had, think on this: until we get to Crushbone, there's one of you and four of us. And you might notice that these three didn't do any oath-taking."

Farmid muttered something that sounded like an orc profanity and wheeled around. As he stomped off toward the orc citadel, his muttered words floated back to them:

"Shoulda thought of *that*, too."

FULL NIGHT HAD FALLEN BY THE TIME THE COMpanions shuffled into Crushbone, shackled together at wrist and ankle by stout ropes. Farmid had insisted upon this bit of theater, and Trobe readily agreed it would look odd if four able-bodied slaves walked into the citadel willingly.

Still, it was all Elizerain could do to stand still under the leering eyes and prodding hands of the orcs. Not that the creatures had any personal interest in her; they patted down all the slaves for treasure and weapons. They immediately stripped Nyson's rings from his hands and squabbled over the emerald and gold ring Davin had passed along to Elizerain. The contents of travel bags were poured onto the ground, where they were gleefully looted. One of them drained Trobe's flask without coming up for air. He belched mightily and bared his fangs in a broad smile. The smile held even as the orc toppled over backward like a felled tree.

Taking advantage of the burst of orcish jeers and laughter that greeted their comrade's fall, Elizerain leaned in closer to Xander and murmured, "We should have left the pixie's silver mosswort tea in my water flask. The poor fellows look thirsty."

The ranger's lips twitched, and the gaze he turned on her was frank in its admiration. "You've never lacked spirit, whatever might be said about your good judgment."

It was a left-handed compliment at best, but Elizerain was not inclined to disagree with it. After all, it had been her idea to come here.

She studied the orcs' fortress with growing dismay. Crushbone was a grim, artificial place, as dead and dry as an old scab. The hard-trodden ground was bare dirt, and the slaughtered trees had gone to build stockade fences and squat, ugly buildings. There might have been open sky above, but Elizerain couldn't tell. Oily smoke rose from torches thrust into skull-decked plinths, obscuring the stars.

And the orcs!

They were even uglier up close than they appeared at a distance, and the stench that rolled off them was reminiscent of rotting carrion.

Even so, Elizerain found her perception of them shifting in disturbing directions. She'd fought orcs before, of course, but never had she seen so many at one time, or at such close range. During forest skirmishes, she regarded them as she would any other monster or rogue beast, but the sly intelligence in their small, red eyes belied that comfortable delusion.

Nor was Crushbone the rough camp she expected. It lacked the beauty of form and the harmony with nature that characterized an elven settlement, but it appeared to be intelligently designed and certainly well defended.

The worst part was how small and insignificant she felt, surrounded as she was by tall, thick-bodied orcs, and how thoroughly, irrevocably trapped. Not even in Freeport's dungeons had she experienced so powerful a sense of walls closing in on her.

She fought back a rising wave of panic and turned a rueful smile to Xander. "This seemed like a good idea at the time." She tipped her head to one side and considered her words. "I say that a lot, don't I?"

"The dwarf knows what he's about," the ranger said softly, reminding her that they would soon be free of this place.

Elizerain nodded and glanced toward the orc centurion. "Trobe certainly took *that* one's measure."

Farmid, who had seemed to gain swaggering stature

the moment they entered the citadel, now held court amid a small throng of orcs and regaled them with his exploits. By his telling, he had brought down the band of orc thieves known as the Wolfskinners almost single-handedly, after the bandits had attacked and slaughtered his patrol.

As Trobe had predicted, the cache of weapons was readily accepted as evidence. Farmid attributed the death of the shaman, who apparently lived apart from the compound, to the dwarf and his elven "slaves," and loftily proclaimed the justice in enslaving the proud dwarf rather than killing him outright. What more humiliating punishment could be meted out, he noted, than forcing the dwarf to labor beside his own elf servants?

The loud jeers and huzzahs of agreement still echoed through the compound when the summons came from the emperor. Farmid sauntered off toward the wooden "palace" to tell his tale anew, not sparing so much as a glance toward his captives.

A hand fell heavily on Elizerain's shoulder. She glanced down at a huge, leathery brown paw with an odd tattoo on the back: the outline of a footprint, with the toes darkened in. Odder still were the thick nails, which were filed to a sharp point and painted a garish shade of orange.

Her captor whirled her around effortlessly. Elizerain staggered a bit, regained her balance, and gazed up—*way* up—into the face of an ogre female.

It could be none other than Mirdit Smallplague. Nearly seven feet tall, the ogress was impressive in her own way. A line of tattooed footprints marched up her muscled arms. Lavish curves were stuffed into a vast leather corset, which was also dyed orange, and her thin black hair had been skimmed back into a short tail and greased until it gleamed. Her ugly face was made horrific by a deep, badly healed scar that started above her hairline, gouged a deep furrow across one cheek, and traced her jaw to the other side of her chin.

"Few people could have survived a wound like that," Elizerain said bluntly.

Her companions caught their breath in a faint, collective gasp, but Mirdit Smallplague seemed to take the comment as it was intended: a compliment on her strength and toughness. The scant brows tracing her prominent brow-ridge rose as she considered the slender elf girl.

"And you," she said in a voice like a sword rasping against stone: "What damage could *you* survive?"

Elizerain dipped her head slightly in a gesture that ceded this particular contest to the ogress, but she kept her gaze steady and level. "Nearly two years in a dungeon, more tavern brawls than I can count, and a lifetime on the road. Hard work won't kill me, if that's what you're asking."

The ogress gave a curt nod and moved on to Nyson. A glance sufficed: she scoffed and turned to the young orc who followed close on her heels. "This one's good for nothing but the stewpots."

Trobe stepped between the young Koada'Dal and the slave mistress, his arms akimbo and his bearded chin tilted pugnaciously. "That could be the first sensible thing ever I heard you say."

Mirdit's eyes widened, then narrowed into evil slits. A delighted leer stretched her lipless mouth.

"*You!*"

The dwarf shifted one shoulder, a casual gesture that,

in combination with his bored expression, suggested he considered one person stating the obvious to be more than sufficient.

The slave mistress whirled toward her assistant. "Plenty of fun tonight," she exulted. "Take all four to the slave pits."

"Four?" balked Trobe. He jerked his head toward Nyson. "I thought you were gonna throw this scrawny excuse for a soup chicken into the pot."

Mirdit's little black eyes flashed to Nyson, noting his haughty bearing and the incredulous disdain with which he was regarding the dwarf. A sly expression crossed her scarred visage.

"You don't like this elf?" she demanded of Trobe.

"Not so you'd notice."

"Annoys you, does he?"

"Well, no more than any *other* festering boil I've had on my backside."

"Can he work? Will he be of any value to me in the slave pits?"

Trobe snorted. "With those white lady-hands? Not bloody likely."

Elizerain wouldn't have thought it possible, but the ogress's smile grew even broader.

"*Gooood*," Mirdit crooned. She turned to her orc assistant. "Shackle these two slaves together and make sure the dwarf works enough for them both.

"And tonight, if some of the elf boy's share of stripes fall on the dwarf," she added slyly, "so much the better."

A DEEP SENSE OF DESPAIR FILLED DAVIN THE DARK as he watched what was taking place just inside the gates of Crushbone. Even from this vantage, high in a tree and a safe distance from the citadel, he could feel the evil that lingered about the place like a foul mist.

Evil had never particularly bothered him, except when someone of low character and acquisitive intent stood between him and something he wanted, but the thought of pretty, life-loving Elizerain in that horrible place hit him like a fist to the throat.

There was no getting around it: Elizerain was lost to him. To the best of Davin's knowledge, no elf who'd set foot in the orc slave pits was ever heard from again.

Why, then, had she and her band of companions walked willingly into Crushbone? What did she expect to find in there that was worth dying over?

And, blast it all, *what had she done with that bloody harp?*

Davin had picked up Elizerain's trail from the dwarf's camp and followed her every step of the way, and he felt as certain as it was possible to be that she hadn't left the harp behind. He'd even crawled into the dirt tunnel that she and the dwarf had spent half a morning in without seeing any sign of the little red nuisance.

Yet he was equally certain she hadn't brought it into Crushbone. From his perch, he could see quite clearly the tiny figures in the outer courtyard. He watched, gritting his teeth until his jaws ached, as Elizerain was stripped of her cloak and tunic and boots, rudely searched from head to toe for items of interest to the orcs. And Xander Fletcher, may all gods damn him, just stood there and did nothing to stop it. Why, if Davin had been in his place, he'd have—

He'd have done *what*, precisely?

By now the new slaves had been moved deeper into the citadel, into the stone quarry where they would live and work out their last days. Davin could no longer see them, but the faint crack of whips against naked flesh rose into the night air, punctuated by jeering bursts of laughter and brief periods of sickening, silent anticipation.

Davin squeezed his eyes closed, as if doing so could shut out the image these sounds conjured. Self-loathing swept through him like waves of nausea, but he could not deny what he knew to be true:

If he'd been the one standing beside Elizerain in Crushbone, he'd have done exactly what he was doing now, and what he had always done:

Whatever best served his own interests.

Even so, his heart was heavy as he climbed down from his perch and slipped off into the night to seek out the necromancer and report his latest failure.

13

The Truth of the Tale

CHANZOON SPENT THE DAY IN HIS FOREST LAIR, warding his tower and arming himself with spells for the visitation to come. That darkness would seek his door with the coming of night, he had no doubt.

Yet twilight came and went, and night passed quietly enough. Midnight was long gone when the necromancer heard the first strains of music.

A woman's voice, low and sultry, beckoned from the forest beyond. She sang of love hopeful, and something in her voice promised that whatever the listener desired, be it love or fame, passion or power, could be found in the waiting darkness.

Chanzoon carefully renewed his warding spells and slowly opened the door.

The bramble hedge outside his tree-trunk tower had been trampled flat by dozens of undead feet. What remained had burned to ash along with the corpse of a particularly stubborn zombie. A bit of moonlight took advantage of the rare opportunity to touch the forest floor. Standing in the center of the newly expanded clearing, illuminated by that faint spill of moonlight, Chanzoon's visitor flamed like a candle in a cavern.

She was a small, slim woman, dressed in a white gown that clung to her slender frame and swirled about her legs like wind-stirred mist. Red hair spilled around her bared shoulders, and her lips were a startling crimson in her too-pale face. Even surrounded as he was by wards and fortified with charms, Chanzoon could feel the power of her otherworldly charm.

"I suppose you've come for the harp?" he said indifferently, raising his voice to be heard over softly crooned temptation.

The song broke off abruptly, and an expression of very human pique crossed the singer's face. She quickly mastered her countenance and sent him a slow, teasing smile.

"I had heard Chanzoon Nexis was wed to his art and thus immune to the charms of women. Tell me, did my song suggest *nothing* that you might desire?"

Never had the necromancer heard a more thoroughly seductive voice: dark and velvety, rich with melody and magic, warm with promise. It cost him some little effort to keep his feet firmly planted on the safe side of his threshold.

"What could I desire from your song?" He considered the question for a moment, then tipped his head slightly to one side and shifted one shoulder in a gesture of profound indifference. "A keener sense of rhythm, perhaps? And now that you mention it, your intonation was a bit off, as well."

He wouldn't have thought it possible, but fury leached still more color from her pallid face. Her red lips peeled back from her teeth in a feral snarl, revealing slender white fangs. She blazed forward, quick as thought, coming to a stop just short of the great tree. Had Chanzoon wished to do so, he could have reached out and touched her.

"Come to me," she commanded, her voice low and vibrating with power.

The necromancer examined the back of his fingernails. "Oh, I think not," he said casually.

"Do you fear me so much, *great necromancer*, that you refuse me on the doorstep of your place of power?"

Chanzoon wasn't even tempted by this type of bait. "Easier to refuse you on the doorstep, I dare say, than in my hall."

Her lips twisted in a sneer. "What sort of man are you, to admit weakness so readily?"

"What is false pride," he asked calmly, "but another form of weakness?"

The vampire blinked, an oddly human gesture. In that instant, her otherworldly power and glamour winked out like a snuffed candle, leaving her looking much as she must have in life.

"True," she said in a voice that was almost as thin as any mortal's, and oddly accented. "Too bloody true, and a lesson I was late in learning."

Chanzoon folded his arms. "There's a bit of dwarven inflexion to your speech. Did you live in the Butcherblock Mountains? And perhaps make an occasional venture into the Hills of Shade?"

The eyes that focused on his face held none of a vampire's compelling power. "Ask me what you truly wish to know," she said wearily. "Ask me about Allisandra."

"I knew her as Alisar."

The vampire nodded. "She preferred that to her given name. She thought it an odd custom that the shorter the person, the longer the name seemed to be, while giants all seemed to be named Og or suchlike. But that's neither here nor there. Alisar's dead, I suppose."

"So you know of the spell she laid on this place," he said. "Coming here was not a mindless compulsion for you, as it was the others."

"What others?" she demanded.

Chanzoon grimaced. "Every walking, flying, or crawling undead creature within a day's travel, whether it be rotten or dust-dry bone. You're the first vampire, if that's your concern."

"I won't be the last," she promised, "as I wasn't the only treasure hunter in Lord Mistmoore's hire."

The necromancer folded his arms and regarded her coldly. "So you were the last bard to play the blood red harp. It was you who transformed Alisar into what she was."

The vampire's auburn brows lifted. "I'm impressed. Most people think it's the bard who becomes Dawnwalker: mortal by day, vampire by night."

Chanzoon didn't see any reason to admit he'd just changed his opinion on that matter. "You traveled with the Seven Seadogs."

"I hired them," she said grimly, "for they told a tale of a red harp they'd seen in an opened tomb, deep in the Hills of Shade. Or, to be more precise, Alisar was the only one who had seen it, as only she could fit into the narrow passage."

"Only Alisar and *you*," he added, seeing how this story might end. "And apparently the Seadogs needed a bard's magic to get at the harp, or they would have raided the tomb and gone on their way."

The vampire nodded. "And as you have already concluded, the hills shifted yet again, sealing the two of us into the hill tomb and carrying it away. The magic took us somewhere marshy and wet, so we had water enough to live on for some time."

That fit what Chanzoon knew of the harp's history and also described the place where he'd found the slain dark elves.

"And to pass the time in this captivity, you taught yourself to play the harp, which slowly revealed its true powers. In doing this, you created Alisar."

"I created Alisar, who in turn created me." She paused for a bitter smile. "Or should I say, she fed on me, which in time made me what I am."

A normal vampire, Chanzoon surmised—if indeed the word *normal* could be applied to any sort of undead creature. The former bard was a nightwalker, with all the powers of her kind but none of the special gifts Alisar had gained from the blood red harp.

In short, he had little to fear from her.

But he was a prudent man, and a few questions remained unanswered. "I have always understood that there is but one way to become a vampire: one must be bitten by a vampire of Mayong Mistmoore's lineage."

"Why do you think my lord seeks the harp?" the vampire said teasingly. "Since my transformation, I have learned many things. Shall I come in and tell you about them?"

"I am quite content with our current arrangement. Tell me of the dark elves who opened your tomb. Were they agents of the vampire lord?"

A bleak expression crossed her face. "I wouldn't know

who opened it. I was a new vampire, so even locked away from the sun, I slept during daylight hours. Tell me, have you ever seen a vampire asleep?"

"Yes." He'd dispatched a few, but saw no reason to mention that. Her point was well taken: during the daylight hours, a vampire simply looked dead. Some vampire "corpses" aged in a manner consistent with the passage of time—rotting and moldering with the coming of each new day, arising anew with each night.

Chanzoon could imagine what the dark elf tomb robbers found: a human corpse, and a terrified but beautiful gnome maiden clutching the harp they sought. They probably considered Alisar an added bonus, a potential sale to pirates or slavers.

"Dawn isn't far away," he told the vampire. "Don't you need to feed and find shelter before daybreak?"

"I've fed, and I have shelter prepared," she said quickly, but Chanzoon didn't miss the worried glance she sent toward the open patch of sky.

"You might as well come in," he said, moving away from the doorway. "I offer shelter, in exchange for all you know of the harp. Let there be a truce between us."

"Truce," the vampire agreed. She quickly stepped into the tower and shut the door behind her. Her dark-eyed gaze swept the hall and came to rest on a small table holding a wine decanter and several goblets.

Chanzoon filled two goblets and handed one to her. "You'll forgive me if I don't offer you the traditional libation."

She smiled faintly. "I've had blood enough for one night. I can only drink a sip or two of wine at a time, but I still enjoy the taste."

Apparently so, for over the next few hours Chanzoon filled her goblet more than once. The story that emerged between sips was well worth the expensive vintage.

By the time the necromancer had learned all his visitor knew of the harp, the sun was cresting the trees and shining directly into his little clearing. He knew that because a thin stream of light poured from a knothole placed strategically high on the eastern wall. The vampire saw it, too, judging from her soft hiss of surprise, followed by the scrape of her chair against the floor as she moved away from the light.

Her reaction increased Chanzoon's sense of pleasurable anticipation. He set aside his goblet and began the gestures of a spell.

His first chanted words brought the vampire leaping to her feet with a cry of protest. But by then, it was too late—she was thoroughly caught in a charm that held and commanded the undead.

Chanzoon rose and came to face her, taking enjoyment in the fury and frustration burning in her eyes. Then, with a casual flick of his hand, he indicated the door. It swung open, and morning sunlight spilled into the room.

For a moment the vampire's power flared out at him—a scorching blast of invisible flame. But the necromancer's magic held. The vampire spun away from him and started a slow walk toward the door.

Her gown began to smolder, and her red hair writhed about her shoulders in a manner that anticipated the flames to come. But she walked steadily from the room. The moment she stepped into the clearing, she was engulfed in a burst of crimson fire.

The vampire's death was over before Chanzoon could

begin to enjoy it. Eager to savor the moment, he rushed into the clearing and knelt beside the vampire's ashes.

They were already cool to the touch. Gathering up a handful, he let them sift through his fingers.

And in that moment, a new and terrible ambition was born.

Someday very soon, he would hold Mayong Mistmoore in his hands, just like this, and scatter the dark elf's ashes from the ramparts of Castle Mistmoore.

And then he, the last and greatest of the harp-spawned Dawnwalkers, would take the vampire lord's place.

14

CRUSHBONE

ELIZERAIN WAS DIMLY AWARE THAT SHE WAS caught in the grip of a particularly strange and unpleasant nightmare. How else to explain the sensation of swimming up through deep, dark water, coupled with the pain that attended each breath? She was breathing; therefore, if she were awake, she'd surely be drowning.

And only in nightmares could the surface of the water burn like a bonfire; only in nightmares would she be foolish enough to swim toward the flame despite the kindling pain searing across her back. And no fish she'd encountered in any waking swim had been as aggressive as these. Large, blunt-nosed sea creatures thudded painfully into her ribs, again and again.

Then, suddenly, Elizerain broke the surface. Pain seared across her back, but the fire was nowhere to be seen. In fact, inexplicable darkness surrounded her.

"Wake *up*, you lazy wench!" commanded a deep and somehow familiar voice.

Elizerain realized she was lying face down on a hard,

cold surface. With great effort, she turned her head toward the sound. The pain throbbing behind her eyes blurred and distorted the speaker, but Elizerain's keen night vision enabled her to make out the outline of a very large, very irritated ogress.

The events of the night before came back to the elf girl in a sudden surge. She and her companions had been taken to Crushbone, where they'd each been welcomed with 13 stripes from a dragonhide lash. Elizerain had been the first to endure the lash.

The memory of that first burning stroke was as keen as the pain it had left behind. Equally vivid was the echo of 100 jeering orcs. But Elizerain had lost count after 9 stripes, and she only dimly remembered being dragged to the slave quarters and dropped to the hard-packed dirt floor.

At least she'd been spared the torment of watching her companions suffer.

Panic welled up into her throat, riding a wave of bitter bile. How had the others fared? Had they all survived, or had the orc centurion found a way to evade his oath and take vengeance on Xander?

The ogress tossed a crumpled wad of cloth at Elizerain. "Here's your tunic. Dress yourself, and be ready to work by the time the others awaken."

It suddenly occurred to Elizerain that she was naked from the waist up. Normally that would not be a matter for great concern, as modesty was not one of her defining traits. But for some reason, it was deeply troubling . . .

"The harp!" she gasped as she leaped to her feet.

Sudden movement proved to be a mistake. The floor tilted to an alarming angle, and the small cave spun around her. For a long moment she leaned against the stone wall, holding herself upright with both hands. Her thoughts whirled as giddily as her surroundings.

What had become of her harp? She didn't remember the orcs taking it from her. Was it possible that Nyson's magic kept it bound to her back, even after they'd taken her cloak and stripped off her tunic? Had the magic protected the harp from those 13 lashes, or had it taken the brunt of the beating?

The elf who'd slept next to her, an aging wood elf male wearing tattered, forest-colored garb, was still sitting on the floor of the cave. He sent a glance her way, then quickly averted his eyes.

"How bad is it?" she asked softly.

"Not very," he said in a voice that had been worn down to a dry, dusty rasp. "Welts only. No blood."

Elizerain cautiously pushed away from the wall and found that she could stand on her own. Her fingers itched for the reassuring feel of harp strings, but Mirdit Smallplague stood at the mouth of the small cave, hands on her ample, corset-clad hips as she harangued the young orc charged with waking the other slaves. With the ogress still within sight, Elizerain didn't dare to test the harp's concealing magic.

She stooped and picked up her tunic, which she shrugged on, gritting her teeth against the pain. As soon as she was dressed, she extended a hand to the old elf.

Pride flared in his eyes, but after a brief hesitation his thin, calloused fingers closed on hers. She helped the elf to his feet, then stepped in close.

"Did you see the whipping?" she asked softly.

He dropped his gaze as if to indicate that he would have respected her privacy had he been given the choice. "Aye. They make us watch."

"Did they take a harp from me? A small red harp?"

The old elf glanced up at her. "You play a harp? But the red-haired elf said you were a bard."

The mention of Xander sent a wave of shame through Elizerain. Her first words should have sought news of her friends' welfare, not the well-being of a musical instrument!

She clutched the old elf's arm. "Is he alive?" she whispered urgently.

"Aye."

Something in his face made Elizerain's throat tighten with dread. "And the others? The Koada'Dal, the dwarf?"

"No talking!" Mirdit snarled, shooting a glare over her shoulder. "To the pits, or taste the lash."

Apparently Elizerain would find out the answer to her question soon enough. She fell into step behind the three elves who shared the sleeping cave with her. In addition to the old male, there were two females whose ages were impossible to guess, for both had been worn down by hard work and despair. Very little flesh remained on their bones, and their hair had gone lank and thin. When the bard whispered her name to them by way of greeting and introduction, the eyes they turned in her general direction were dull and uncomprehending.

The slaves filed past Mirdit's assistant, a young orc whose hide was a strange yellowish hue, accepting the small hand picks he handed out.

They followed the ogress along a narrow canal. Elizerain studied the water and the stone walls that contained it. This appeared to be a reservoir of some sort, and the water was as clear and fresh as the pristine lake that shared Elizerain's name. No doubt this reservoir was supplied by some deep spring. Perhaps, she mused, that opening would be the path to the treasure trove? She hoped not; Xander was not much of a swimmer. She didn't know about Nyson or Trobe, but most dwarves swam about as well as any river stone.

Still, she was impressed by the workmanship of the reservoir and the amount of water it held. It was said that Crushbone could withstand a siege for many months. If their food and weapons supplies were as well designed as this, Elizerain suspected that for once, rumors spoke the truth.

The dull thud of metal against rock drew her eye farther down the path. There stood Xander and Trobe and behind them three tall elves. Relief washed through Elizerain, and she sent Xander a brilliant smile.

Just then one of the elven strangers bent to gather up rocks into a basket. Elizerain's smile faltered as she noticed that the elves working behind him had dark brown hair. Nyson was not among the workers.

She edged closer to the yellow-skinned orc. "Where is the other elf—the lad with the fair hair?"

"No talking," growled the young guard.

Elizerain noted with dismay the growing smirk on the orc's sallow face. Whatever Nyson's fate had been, this grinning bastard found pleasure in it. In Elizerain's experience, a happy orc was never a good sign.

She watched for an opportunity to learn more as the sun slowly crawled across the sky, beating down on the hard-packed ground with a ferocity that Elizerain, accustomed as she was to the warm, mist-laden forest, found strangely uncomfortable. Nor was she the only one. By the time the sun reached its zenith, Trobe's bald head had turned a painfully bright shade of pink.

Finally, as sunset colors began to paint the sky in similar hues, Elizerain saw a chance to talk to Xander. Noting that his basket of stone chips was nearly full, she quickly traded her nearly empty basket with that of the old elf. He sent her a startled look and then shot a quick glance toward the ogress. Fortunately, Mirdit's attention was fixed on her yellow-skinned assistant, who was glumly surrendering to her what appeared to be his dinner.

The old slave met Elizerain's eyes. "Konnik," he said softly, touching one hand to his chest.

"The mushroom hunter?" she asked in surprise. When she'd departed Kelethin for adventure in Antonica, Konnik Oakroot had been well known for his uncanny ability to find the underground hiding places of certain elusive fungi. His dried mushrooms were much sought after as trail food, for a small handful and some wild onions made a fine pot of stew, with or without meat. Elizerain had even gone to his shop a time or two and remembered him as an elf in vigorous middle years. Never would she have recognized that robust elf in this aging, skeletal slave.

Konnik acknowledged his past life with a faint nod as he turned back to tapping at the wall. Elizerain hoisted his full basket and hurried after Xander, who was following one of the orc guards.

Chipped stone had many uses in the citadel, and they'd been toting it from one place to another throughout the day. This time the guard led them to a remote corner behind the barracks and pointed to a pit encircled by a low, stone wall. Nearby was a shallow mound of dirt about the same size across; no doubt a pit that had been filled in completely. The new one was some ten feet deep, not counting however much was already covered in gravel.

A new midden, Elizerain guessed, surprised once again

by the orcs' ingenuity. The stones would act as a filter, and adding a daily layer could cut down on the stench and the flies that usually attended an open privy.

Xander was emptying his basket into the pit, a handful at a time. She hurried to his side, keeping her back to the bored-looking orc who'd accompanied them.

"Nyson?" she asked softly.

The ranger glanced at her, his face grim. "He and Trobe were shackled at the ankle before the beating. Nyson took the worst of it, even though the ogress told her yellow minion to land most of the stripes on the dwarf. The fool boy deliberately shielded Trobe."

Elizerain understood at once. "He's high elf to the bone, too proud to let another person take his share."

"Aye."

"How is he?"

The ranger glanced at her, a world of frustration in his dark eyes. "He did not awaken this morn, and they left him lying in the dirt, untended. If no fever sets in, he may live."

"You, there!" bellowed the orc. "Move it along, or there'll be no soup left for you."

Xander upended his basket into the pit and reached for Elizerain's. They headed back to the quarry, the orc grumbling behind them and hurrying them along with an occasional rough shove.

The quarry was deserted by the time they arrived. They handed over their baskets and picks and were marched back to their sleeping quarters. The evening meal was a thin soup simmering over a fire between the two slave caves. The other elves had already dipped up their portions and were sipping directly from the bowls. Nyson was not among them.

The ogress rushed the slaves through their meal and herded them into the tiny caves. To Elizerain's relief, there would be no "entertainment" tonight—at least none that need concern the captured elves.

A single guard slumped down beside the dying fire, watching glumly as his comrades hastened to the large wooden building that served as Emperor Crush's palace.

Konnik Oakroot and the two females whose names Elizerain had yet to learn fell asleep almost immediately. Elizerain, though she felt bone-tired, lay awake, straining her ears for any sound that might carry news of the young Koada'Dal's condition.

But the only noises carried by the night breezes were the distant rumble of voices coming from the palace. The cadence rose and fell, ranging from near silence to a bestial roar.

A debate? wondered Elizerain. Or mayhap an audience responding to some sort of oration?

Whatever the orc meeting entailed, it ended some time after the moon had risen into the open sky above Crushbone. Silence quickly descended over the camp, but sleep continued to elude Elizerain. For what seemed like hours, she listened to the unhealthy wheeze coming from the old elf and what sounded like a louder, grating snore from the orc guard outside.

She cautiously crept to the mouth of the cave and peered out into the night. Yes, the guard was soundly asleep; his mouth hung open, and drool dripped from his pock-marked yellow chin.

The bard slipped out of the cave and carefully circled the snoring guard. She ducked into the other cave.

Xander and Trobe were awake, crouching over the

prone high elf. They glanced up as she edged past the three other wood elf slaves and moved quietly to their side.

A glance told the whole tale. Even in the darkness, Elizerain could make out the marks of the lash on Nyson's back, and the ridges on either side of each cut. Already the wounds had turned angry—dangerously so. The young elf shook with fever. Elizerain touched her fingertips to his skin and recoiled in surprise from the heat of it.

Water? she mouthed silently.

Xander upended a water flask—saved from his ration for the hot day they'd just spent—and shook his head to indicate that he'd already emptied it on Nyson's behalf.

After a moment of silent debate, the bard reached for the place on her hip where her singing sword usually hung. To her relief, her hand closed around the silver hilt, and she drew the sword smoothly from the old leather scabbard.

She shook her head at Xander's silent question and unbuckled her belt, then turned the scabbard upside down and gave it several shakes. A roll of parchment slid out.

Elizerain quickly tucked the sword away. To her infinite relief, the magic held, and the weapon once again disappeared from view. The dwarf's soft sniff expressed better than any words his opinion of the risk she'd just taken.

She unrolled the parchment and held it up for Xander to see. His eyes widened when he recognized the healing spell.

"Bard spell," he told Trobe softly, by way of explanation.

The dwarf thought this over. "Noisy business," he concluded. "She'll be needing a diversion."

Without waiting for Xander's reaction, Trobe rose and swaggered from the cave, casually treading on the sleeping elves as he went. When he reached the cave's mouth, he whirled back and glared at the ranger.

"Come outa there and say that again, if you got the stones fer it!"

Xander seized Elizerain's hand and gave it a quick squeeze, then pushed his way through the trio of suddenly wakeful elves and out under the open sky. He went toe-to-toe with the dwarf and gazed down at the pugnaciously upturned face.

"I *said* sunburn suits you; that shade of pink makes you look like a pixie-kissing gnome," Xander said distinctly.

Trobe blinked with surprise and passed a hand over his bald pate. "Good one," he murmured admiringly.

Then, for the benefit of his audience—the suddenly wide-awake guard, a couple of orcs on their way back from the midden, and the trio of elven slaves clustered around the mouth of the cave—Trobe poked Xander's chest with a stubby forefinger and loudly announced, "That's it: I'm fixing to kick yer flat arse up between yer sorry excuse fer shoulders. *Shoulders*, did I say? Bah! Elves are all neck, from chin to flanks."

He went on in this vein for some time, but Elizerain had ceased to pay attention. She glanced at the three dark-haired elves, noting with gratitude that they were purposefully blocking the cave's entrance.

The orcs had taken her hand drum, and the spell required instrumental accompaniment to reach its full power. Elizerain's heart pounded in anticipation as she reached for the place on her shoulder where the harp's strap would be. A sigh of relief escaped her as her fingers closed around a strip of worn leather.

The bard swiftly shrugged off the harp and drew it into her lap. She smoothed the scroll out flat on the dirt floor. As softly as she could, she sang the words of the spell while her fingertips nudged the faintest whisper of song from the harp strings.

The result was swift and dramatic. The deep furrows on Nyson's back smoothed out, and the stripes faded into the smooth, golden hue of his high-elven skin. The young elf groaned and rolled over onto his side, his blue eyes blinking as they adjusted to the sudden flare of torchlight just beyond the cave opening. By now the feigned altercation had progressed to a brawl, and by the sound of it, several more orcs had wandered over to enjoy the show.

"What—"

Elizerain slapped a hand over Nyson's mouth, cutting his question short. She raised a warning finger to her lips, then released him so she could return the harp to the hiding place the young Koada'Dal's magic had created.

"Put on your tunic, so they won't know you've been healed," she whispered.

She saw memory and understanding flash through the young elf's eyes. He did as he was bid, then began a magical chant of his own.

To Elizerain's surprise, her hands began to fade away. The rest of her swiftly followed. She held her hands up before her eyes, turning them this way and that, and could perceive only the slightest outline, as if she had been turned to glass.

"Stay out of the light," Nyson advised. "The spell will last until you say 'bubbleburst' aloud."

The roar of an irritated ogress rose about the tumult,

which swiftly faded as the impromptu entertainment came to an end. The three elves who had blocked the view of the spell-casting bard stumbled back as Xander and Trobe were shoved into the cave, both of them looking rather the worse for wear.

Mirdit Smallplague thrust her face into the cave. "Since you're determined to entertain the troops, you can fight again after tomorrow's nightfall," she said. "See that you both get some sleep. I'm expecting a full day's work from the both of you and a brisk battle after."

She withdrew just as abruptly. The sound of heavy footsteps and the glare of torchlight swiftly retreated. A thump and a grunt of pain suggested she'd dealt a final kick to the orc guard who'd allowed the fight to occur under his watch.

Trobe gave a grunt of satisfaction at the sight of a revived Nyson and nodded knowingly as an unseen Elizerain brushed past him. He passed the back of his hand over his mouth and leaned aside to spit blood. Despite his split lip, his grin was wide and genuine as he turned to his elven "opponent."

"Next time," he advised Xander, "try a little harder to make it look *real*."

EARLY THE NEXT MORNING, DAVIN THE DARK paused at the edge of the fire-ravaged clearing that surrounded the giant tree stump. The necromancer's tower had been blackened by the blaze. No sign of life—or, for that matter, *former* life—was anywhere to be seen.

The bandit leader allowed himself to hope. Perhaps Chanzoon Nexis had died in the fire. Perhaps—

This cheerful line of thought stopped dead at the sight

of a doorway swinging inward, revealing the faint light within the tree-stump tower.

Davin gritted his teeth and strode toward the necromancer's lair. Best get it over with and take whatever steps necessary toward getting back the life he'd known before meeting Chanzoon Nexis.

The necromancer awaited him, seated hearthside at a small table supplied with a bottle and two goblets. He glanced up and began to pour out two portions of crimson wine.

At least, Davin *hoped* it was wine! Who knew what a thrice-damned ghoul like Chanzoon drank?

"Well?" the necromancer inquired.

Davin took a seat and quickly gave his report. "And that's the end of it, I'm afraid," he summarized. "The harp is gone, and so is the bard."

The necromancer received this grim recitation with amazing composure, sipping his wine the while. He poured himself a second glass of wine and leaned back in his chair. "Oh, I think not."

"Elizerain is an elf," Davin said flatly. "No elf has ever come out of Crushbone's slave pits alive."

"Perhaps not, but a *dwarf* has," the necromancer told him. "You mentioned a dwarf by the name of Trobe. I happen to know he has been in and out of the orc citadel. Apparently your former wife knows that as well and hired him to lead the way out."

A glimmer of hope returned to Davin's heart. "But why would she enter Crushbone in the first place?"

"No doubt she's seeking the story behind the harp she carries."

"In *Crushbone*?"

Chanzoon shrugged negligently. "One place is as good as another. It matters not, as long as she carries and plays the harp. In time, it will reveal its story to her."

"But she didn't have it with her. I told you that."

"So you did, but I beg to differ."

The necromancer rose and walked across the chamber to an ornate iron tripod, upon which rested a large, shallow bowl filled with dark liquid. He moved one hand over the bowl and murmured a few words that Davin did not understand and, as was common with overheard spells, immediately forgot.

"I didn't think it prudent to rely entirely upon your services," Chanzoon said. "As a precaution, I placed a spell focus on the harp that enables me to learn its location. And I assure you, the harp is in Crushbone."

Davin came over to the scrying bowl and glanced at the dark liquid. He was rewarded with a stabbing pain between his eyes. Quickly averting his gaze, he asked, "What if the bard finds and removes this device?"

"Not likely, as the spell focus was placed upon one of the harp strings. When the harp moves, I'll know."

"And you'll pass that knowledge along to me, I suppose," Davin said resignedly.

"On the contrary; your services are no longer required."

The bandit's gaze snapped to Chanzoon's face. "What?"

Chanzoon's smile was profoundly unpleasant. "I believe I know where the bard will go next. You know these forests, and thus you have been of some use to me. That usefulness has come to an end."

"And the compulsion?" Davin persisted.

"Gone." The necromancer grimaced. "Obviously

gone, for if you were still compelled to follow my every inclination, you would have already quit this tower."

The front door swung open again. Chanzoon glanced from it to the bandit and pointedly lifted one brow.

Davin needed no further prompting. He turned and strode from the tower, and once he was past the clearing, he broke into a run.

He kept that pace throughout the day, setting a direct course toward Crushbone.

Chanzoon Nexis might be through with Davin the Dark, but that didn't mean *Davin* was through with Elizerain!

15

Strange Alliances

THE NEXT FEW DAYS PASSED IN A HAZE OF PAIN and exhaustion. Every morning, Elizerain was kicked awake before dawn and put to work alongside a handful of other stolen elves until long past nightfall, tapping with a small hand pick at the solid gray wall, carefully freeing stones that then had to be carried from one incomprehensible pile to another. Elizerain assumed they were mining for something of value, but she was never able to detect what that might be.

At day's end, more often than not, the slaves would be tormented for the enjoyment of their captors or forced to fight each other. Those who resisted participation in this new entertainment were beaten into unconsciousness and tossed aside, to survive or die according to the whim of indifferent gods. Two of the wood elves in Xander's cave—brothers, apparently—had died rather than fight each other, and the rest of the slaves carried an ever-growing assortment of bruises.

Yet each evening, when the quarry slaves gathered around the single, too-small soup cauldron for their one meal of the day, Trobe, who was once again shackled to the young high elf, shook his head to indicate *not yet.*

Elizerain figured the dwarf hadn't had a chance to take on Mirdit Smallplague, or perhaps he was having difficulty with the opening to the treasure trove. Either way, she wished he would get on with it.

In the meantime, she tried making friends with her fellow captives, but both of her female cave-mates were reaching the end of their endurance and had little spirit for anything but survival. Konnik Oakroot, the aging mushroom hunter, spent his days struggling with never-ending rock and his nights wracked by an increasingly wet, rattling cough.

Though his suffering smote Elizerain's heart, there was little she could do for him. The orcs had taken her travel supplies, including her small hoard of herbs and remedies. There was, of course, the bard-song healing spell, but whenever Xander caught her sympathetic gaze resting upon the old elf, he shook his head in silent warning.

Elizerain knew he was right—the chances of another "diversion" succeeding were exceedingly slim—but it grated on her to stand by and do nothing when she had the means to help a suffering elf.

On the third night, she could stand it no more. Like most bard-spells, hers required the accompaniment of an instrument for full effectiveness, but she dared not reveal the harp again for fear of losing it and unleashing the necromancer's curse. Perhaps the song itself would ease Konnik's suffering.

But as the first few notes passed her lips, the orc guard stormed into the cave and dragged her out. He proceeded to kick and beat her into silence. Even above the thud of the orc's fists and his angrily hissed threats, Elizerain could hear the fierce scuffle in the cave beyond as Trobe kept Xander from rushing to her defense. Apparently the ranger was not quite as good at following practical advice as he was at giving it!

At last the orc threw her back into the cave. Konnik Oakroot silently handed her his water flask and a bit of rag.

"Tend your hurts. A bit of water won't make much difference to me," he said simply.

Elizerain held Konnik's eyes for a long moment and saw that he was speaking simple truth. With a nod of thanks, she poured a little water on the rag and dabbed at a cut below her eye. Accepting the dying elf's gift was the only kindness she could offer, but judging from the smile on Konnik's wasted face, he accounted it no small service.

HIGH ELVES WERE GENERALLY REPUTED TO BE proud people, justly prizing their many talents and relishing opportunities to give them full play. Xander had often noted this trait in the Koada'Dal, and he was not above taking advantage of it when it suited his purposes.

It had been a small matter for the wood elf ranger to convince Nyson to cast a spell of invisibility upon him. The young high elf had also created a shadowy image of Xander asleep in the cave. Thus the ranger could leave the slave quarters to venture out into the orc citadel, and as long as neither orc nor ogress looked too closely, all would be well.

Wearing a form as insubstantial as a soap bubble, Xander slipped out into the night and followed Mirdit Smallplague to the palace, taking care to keep beyond the revealing glare of torchlight. Once inside the building, he ducked into the shadows and regarded the capacious interior with dismay.

He'd expected a dank, barnlike interior, but the palace possessed a certain austere elegance—and it was remarkably well lit. If Xander followed Mirdit into the emperor's presence, his glassy outline would reflect light like a well-polished crystal goblet.

He gave the hall a quick, sweeping study, noting the rafters overhead. The lamplight didn't reach so high, and in the darkness he would be able to move about unseen.

Xander skirted the wall to the nearest corner and quickly climbed, finding small handholds between the boards when he could, bracing himself against the two conjoined walls when he could not.

Once he reached the ceiling rafters, his progress was much easier. He hurried after the ogress and her escort, following her into the presence of the largest, ugliest orc he'd ever set eyes upon.

Emperor Crush presided on a vast throne, and he was not alone. A second person had been given a place of honor beside him. Xander's blood chilled as he studied the orc chieftain's guest.

The ranger seldom had any need to step beyond the forests of Faydark, and the Teir'Dal seldom had reason to enter Faydark; accordingly, Xander's experience with dark elves was limited. This tall, elegantly dressed darkling struck him as particularly vile, and not just for the expression of cold calculation on his ebony-skinned face. Where Ambassador D'Vinn went, other Teir'Dal were likely to follow.

Xander crept as close as he dared and flattened himself on a broad beam to listen and learn.

"Message come from Teir'Dal queen," the emperor was telling Mirdit. "D'Vinn tell you all."

"Thank you, Your Eminence," the ambassador said in a cultured, oddly accented voice.

Turning to the ogress, he announced, "Your offer of alliance has been approved, upon certain conditions. You may return to the Butcherblock Mountains at your earliest convenience, where you will regroup with the Mudtoe clan and resume your attacks on the dwarves of Kaladim. Weaken the dwarf resistance, and you will prove yourself a worthy ally."

"We can do that," Mirdit said stoutly. "What can we expect from Crushbone and Neriak in the way of weapons and troops?"

The orc chieftain grew a sly smile. "Kill dwarves, take their weapons," he advised her.

The ambassador of Neriak's dark queen didn't bother to answer at all.

It seemed to Xander that Mirdit was not at all surprised by the lack of forthcoming support, nor particularly aggrieved.

"We can do that," she repeated.

Xander had heard enough. He quickly retraced his steps and hurried back to the slave quarters. The ranger had expected Trobe to wait for news of Mirdit Smallplague's encounter with the orc leader, but the dwarf was sound asleep and snoring lustily.

Annoyance shimmered through the ranger for the second time that night. As much as it pained him to admit it, Trobe had been right to keep him from coming to Elizerain's aid when the guard beat her. But he could not understand the dwarf's apparent lack of interest in carrying out his oath-bound duty.

Time was growing dangerously short. They had to do what they came for and do it soon, or Mirdit Smallplague could well be the only non-orc to leave Crushbone alive.

THE NEXT DAY DRAGGED ON LONGER THAN USUAL, for Elizerain's every movement was stiff and slow. Xander tried to keep her spirits up with an occasional nod of encouragement, and once he managed to catch her hand for a quick squeeze. Even those small gestures helped immeasurably, and by noon she felt more like her usual self.

On her way back from dumping the latest basket of stone chips, she noted Nyson and Trobe standing off to the side, half-hidden behind one of the skull-bedecked plinths that "decorated" the orc compound. After a quick glance around, Elizerain hurried over.

"What about the other elves?" Nyson was saying in his imperious fashion. "Surely there must be some who labor in places other than the quarry. Kitchen staff, perhaps, or chambermaids? Or even . . . courtesans?"

Elizerain couldn't make out the response, but the gruff tone stopped her in her tracks.

An *orc*. Nyson was demanding information of an orc!

She'd expect this sort of arrogant stunt from a young Koada'Dal, but surely *Trobe* knew better!

She hurried around the plinth, ready to treat them both to the sharp side of her tongue.

The dwarf stood calmly by Nyson's side, neither moving nor protesting. He was standing *too* still, come to think of it, and though silent, his red face and bulging eyes spoke of words clamoring to burst free.

And for that matter, the orc seemed oddly content to pass the time chatting with a lowly elf slave. Elizerain noted the dazed expression on the ugly green face and seized Nyson's arm.

"I don't know what spells you're using on these two, but I want you to release them both," she said softly but firmly. "You're going to get us all killed."

Nyson yanked his arm from her grasp and spun toward her, blue eyes blazing. "Is that all you care about?"

"No, but I figure being alive makes it possible for me to care about *other* things. What's *your* immediate concern?"

"I want to make sure that when we leave, every elf in this citadel goes with us."

Her eyebrows rose. "That's a dangerous streak of idealism you're developing. Keep talking that way, and none of us will get out."

"Perhaps that is true, but there would be more honor in fighting to the death than in turning our backs on our own people," he insisted.

It was on the tip of Elizerain's tongue to agree with him. She'd gone over that same path time and again and had come to realize the futility of it. The elves who shared her quarters were too near death to make escape a possibility.

But it would take too long to convince the young high elf of that. Instead, she mustered the most commanding tone she could and icily informed him, "Speaking of honor, might I remind you that you pledged to follow my command? *I* am head of this expedition, and *you* will do what you're told."

For a long moment Nyson held her gaze. He spun away abruptly and made a quick, complex gesture with one hand.

The orc suddenly blinked, yawned, scratched at his chest, and ambled off without a backward glance. But judging from Trobe's quietly sputtering fury, the dwarf had come through the spell with his memory intact. Muttering imprecations, he seized Nyson's arm and quick-marched him back to the quarry.

Elizerain was about to follow when a gruff female voice hailed her with a brusque, "You! Elf girl!"

Her heart took a panicked leap skyward at the sight of Mirdit Smallplague stomping over. How much had the ogress seen? What had she heard?

Mirdit closed in, looming ominously over the smaller elf. "Did I hear you say that you were in command of the three who came in with you?"

The ogress seemed more interested in than incensed by this information. Elizerain gave a cautious nod.

"But Farmid, the centurion who brought you in, said that you and the two male elves were the dwarf's servants."

The bard spread her hands, palms up, in a "What can I do?" gesture.

"Show any orc a party made up of three elves and a dwarf, and what conclusion will he come to?" she asked.

Mirdit grunted agreement. "That thinking doesn't stop with elves. Orcs don't put much stock in females of any kind."

There was an oddly confiding note in the ogress's voice and visage. This, Elizerain had not anticipated. She swiftly made the mental adjustments necessary to exchanging girl talk with her jailor.

"That might be true, but being an ogress has its advantages."

"Of course it does," Mirdit agreed. After a moment, she added, "What particular advantages were you thinking about?"

"You hold a position of power, and you have the ear of Emperor Crush."

"But they still think of me as a servant," she grumbled.

"You're a slave mistress," Elizerain said bracingly. "Do any *orc* females hold similar rank in Crushbone? For that matter, how many orc females are there in the citadel?"

Mirdit's scarred face twisted in a sneer. "You answered your own question, elf. There are no orc females to do this lowly work, so they give it to me."

"But aren't you higher in rank than some of the orc males? Don't you have assistants to carry out your orders? Does anyone object when you chastise your yellow-skinned underling, and isn't he an orc male? Even some of the soldiers who don't report to you show you the same respect they do their officers. They fear you; I've seen it in their eyes."

The ogress nodded slowly. "All that is true. But there are things you don't know."

It was on the tip of Elizerain's tongue to invite confidence, but that would surely cause the ogress to retreat. She settled for, "It's not always a bad thing for people to think you are less than you truly are."

"That's probably the canniest thing I've heard since coming to Crushbone," Mirdit grumbled, "but no easier to take for all that."

She glanced down at Elizerain, and a strange expression crossed her face. Whatever she had intended to say was swiftly tucked away behind a cruel grin. "Just make sure you don't pretend to *work* less than you can."

Mirdit sauntered toward the slave pit, giving a casual

flick of her whip across the shoulders of the old elf. The blow was light, but it sent Konnik staggering to his knees. The ogress's mocking laughter drifted back to them.

The tall, dark-haired elf slave helped Konnik to his feet and sent an accusing glare in Elizerain's direction, as if to imply the old elf's troubles were the direct result of this consorting with ogres.

Elizerain wasn't sure he was wrong. She sent the pair an apologetic look and inclined her head in a slight bow. The younger elf turned away without response; the older one was beyond noticing.

She hurried back to the quarry and attacked the wall with renewed vigor. It actually felt good to be able to hit something.

16

The Treasure Trove

MIRDIT SMALLPLAGUE SEEMED UNUSUALLY jovial for the remainder of the day, leaving Elizerain with a sinking feeling that when evening came, the brutish slave mistress would be in the mood for entertainment.

Sure enough, shortly after the "tools-down" command, the ogress strolled into the slave quarters, where Crushbone's laborers gathered around the soup pot. Konnik Oakroot was the only one not eating. He stood off to the side, leaning against the stone wall near the cave and looking as if he had fallen asleep on his feet.

An evil smile creased the ogress's scarred face. She strode over and dropped a heavy brown paw on the old slave's shoulder. His eyes fluttered open and fixed on his tormenter with resignation.

Mirdit pointed to the largest elf among the slaves, the tall male who wore his dark hair in two long braids.

"Your turn to fight, Two-Tails," she said, employing one of the casually insulting nicknames she used instead of names. "You and the old one."

Nyson's wooden bowl clattered angrily to the hard ground, and he took two steps forward before the chain binding his ankle to Trobe's stopped him. "Leave him be. Can't you see he's too sick to fight?"

The ogress's smile broadened into a leer. "If he's too sick to fight, he's too sick to work," she said meaningfully.

"I'll take his place," the high elf said quickly. "You want a good show, don't you? Give me and my opponent swords, and I'll see that you get one."

Mirdit sneered, and her gaze swept the watchful elves. "Are all your younglings taught stupid arrogance at their nursemaid's knees, or did this one purchase *his* by the pound?"

"My last sword master sought adventure in his youth as Zimapol Stormsong," Nyson said softly. He lifted one golden brow. "I believe the ogres of Faydwer have reason to know that name."

For a long moment the ogress stared at the young elf. Finally she nodded, slowly.

"Swords," she agreed.

"Now, hold on a mite," burst out Trobe. He lifted the leg that was shackled to Nyson and gave the chain a little shake. "If the boy wants to bleed, that's his choice, but I'd just as soon keep my skin in one piece."

Nyson responded with a disdainful sniff and turned to the ogress. "Cut me free of this craven dwarf, and I'll happily fight alone."

Mirdit grinned. "You tired of living, elf boy? Four orc soldiers ambushed Two-Tails, and he brought three of them down before the last one dragged him into this fortress. You sure you want to fight him?"

The Koada'Dal inclined his head to the watchful wood elf in a gesture of respect. "I don't wish to fight him, no."

The ogress's smile faltered. Before she could speak, Nyson added, "I wish to fight the orc soldier who captured him."

Murmurs of approval and excitement drifted through the gathering crowd, and more than one orc stepped forward to lay loud claim to this feat. The orcs were forbidden to kill slaves, so the promised battle offered an unusually satisfying entertainment.

"That would be Farmid," Mirdit said. Her small eyes shifted over the crowd, seeking the big centurion.

Hoots of encouragement rose from the orcs. Farmid was seized, hoisted aloft, and passed hand to hand over the heads of the crowd. In moments he was standing before the calmly waiting Nyson.

A soft growl of protest came from the dwarf. Mirdit silenced him with a backhanded swat to the head.

"You had your chance to fight your captor, and you gave it up," she taunted him. To her assistant she said, "Cut the short one loose and get him out of the way. Let him watch the fight; I want him to drool like an ogre youngling at a hog slaughtering."

Farmid swept a contemptuous glare over Nyson, and his thin lips twisted in a sneer. He balled his fist and thumped it against the insignia on his chest.

"Why orc centurion want to fight girly-boy elf?" he rumbled scornfully.

Mirdit's ugly face took on an expression of exaggerated surprise. "Since when did any orc need a reason to kill an elf?"

The cheers and hoots of agreement that rose from the

orc crowd surrounded the would-be opponents like a rising tide, sweeping them inevitably toward the battle. Eventually Farmid flung one arm up high to command an end to it. Silence fell, broken only by the sound of a sword scraping free of the baldric slung over the big orc's back.

Farmid took his time drawing the weapon, sliding it slowly out of the scabbard, gradually extending his long arm up and up. Finally he tossed the blade to Nyson, who deftly caught the hilt and then stumbled a little under the weight of the weapon.

Elizerain caught her breath on a small, quiet sob. The sword was longer and heavier than anything the young elf could reasonably be expected to wield. It was a bludgeoning weapon, with a bluntly rounded tip and hardly an edge. In the hands of a large, powerful orc, it could do considerable damage in a melee, but it was such a far cry from Nyson's jeweled dueling sword that it might as well have been a battle axe.

"Sword's name is 'Foresworn,'" the orc said, casting a baleful glance at the dwarf. Still holding Trobe's eye, he drew a second, smaller weapon as a sly grin spread across his face. "This one called 'Spellscythe.' It cut through magic."

"Call it 'Dungspade' and cut through your stalling words," Nyson said distinctly as he raised the heavy sword to high guard position.

This insult drew a few sputters of surprised laughter from the watching orcs. Farmid scowled and mirrored the young elf's salute. The combatants began to circle each other as the watching orcs fell back to give them room.

Elizerain edged closer to Trobe and leaned down to whisper, "Do you think Farmid is bluffing?"

"Wouldn't know," the dwarf grunted. "Never played cards with orcs."

Three sharp, metallic cracks drew her eyes back to the makeshift arena. Farmid was displaying his fangs in a wide grin. *Pointedly* displaying them.

It seemed to Elizerain that there was as much relief as triumph in the orc's face. Apparently he hadn't been entirely certain the sword could cut through the invisible chains the shaman's oath-spell had forged between the orc's sword arm and his fangs.

"That answer yer question?" Trobe muttered.

Elizerain's answer was lost in a sudden clattering flurry as the orc pounded the slender elf with blow after blow. She held her breath, certain that the next heavy strike would drive Nyson to his knees.

But the Koada'Dal moved like a leaf in the wind, light and quick, anticipating each attack and meeting it early, before the orc could bring his full power behind it. He was doing something with his parries that Elizerain had never seen before—never meeting a blow squarely, but always turning his sword slightly so the orc's blade slid down the heavy sword—and always at a different angle.

Elizerain glanced at Xander, who was nodding approvingly as he watched. "See how he changes the orc's timing," he murmured. "Ending each attack early, slowing the disengage. He is forcing the orc to fight in an unfamiliar rhythm, and the short glancing parry keeps the orc constantly off-balance."

The centurion's frustration with this tactic was growing by the moment. Finally he broke off the futile engagement and backed off, swiping the back of one hand across his low forehead to dash away the sweat.

Nyson continued to circle, keeping a watchful eye on the orc and a small arrogant smile on his lips.

And then he laughed.

Not a burst of mocking laughter, but a single small, contemptuous *hmph* through closed and sneering lips.

"Here it comes," Xander said softly.

Farmid erupted into a sudden roaring charge, sword clenched in both fists and held high overhead. He brought the blade down in a mighty sweeping attack that seemed destined to cleave the elf in two.

But Nyson was no longer there. He spun aside lightly, letting the weight of his borrowed sword carry it down in a sweep that hamstrung the orc and sent him stumbling. Before the centurion could hit the ground, Nyson had circled around to face him. He dropped to one knee and flipped the heavy sword, slamming the hilt into the ground and angling the point to meet the falling orc.

Farmid landed squarely on the blade with a sound like a fist slamming into leather armor. A moment later, he hit the ground face down. The bloody sword rose from his back like the mast of a small, malodorous ship.

Stunned silence ruled the compound for a single moment before a lone voice broke into a crow of laughter.

All eyes turned toward Mirdit, who was pointing to the old elf and guffawing so hard she had to bend over and clutch at her corset-clad belly.

Konnik Oakroot was still standing in the same place he'd been when Mirdit sentenced him to what would certainly be his final battle. He still leaned against the wall, and his eyes were open . . . and sightless.

"Too bad he missed the fight," Mirdit gasped, wiping tears from her eyes. "Oh, this is good. The oh-so-noble elf boy risks his life to save a *corpse*."

"Centurion Farmid is dead," an orc wearing a centurion's insignia reminded her coldly.

"And I'm sure we'll all shed tears later," she lashed back, all traces of mirth gone in an instant. "Any of you want to avenge him, step forward."

"No more fighting," the centurion said, speaking quickly to forestall a challenge—or perhaps, to cover a possible hesitation. "*Ogress* punish slave. Soldiers got better things to do."

He spun on his heels and stalked off. The others followed, some with obvious regret, others with scowls that didn't quite mask their relief. Dying in battle was one thing, but humiliation at the hands of a young high elf was not the sort of end any self-respecting orc sought.

"You there," Mirdith said, pointing toward her sallow-skinned assistant. "Show elf boy where the death pit is. He and the dwarf can carry the old one."

"I'll help elf boy," Elizerain said quickly, noting the scowl on Trobe's face and not quite trusting that the dwarf wouldn't toss Nyson in, too.

The ogress turned a scowl in her direction, then shrugged.

Elizerain and Nyson gently lifted the old elf and fell into step behind their orc guide. The pit to which he led them was smaller than the bard had expected, given the number of slaves and curious adventurers who ended their days in Crushbone.

Odder still, no scent of death rose from it. The only aroma in the air was the savor of roasting meat wafting from the nearby barracks. The young orc snuffled the air longingly, then cast an impatient glare at the elves. He shifted his weight from one foot to another as hunger warred with duty.

Hunger won. He set off at a trot, calling back over his shoulder, "Throw old one in, go back to slave cave."

When they were alone, Elizerain caught Nyson's eye and nodded. They dropped Konnik's body into the pit and braced themselves for the thud of impact.

No sound came from the pit. The bard peered in, and saw only a layer of the ubiquitous crushed stone. She glanced up at Nyson, who stared into the empty pit in stunned silence. The naked grief on his face told an unexpected tale.

"Whom were you hoping to find?" she asked softly. "Or should I say, *dreading* to find?"

He looked away. "She was a high elf of Felwithe," he said simply. "She deserved a better end."

Elizerain placed a gentle hand on his shoulder. "I'm sorry."

"*Are* you?" Burning blue eyes flashed to her face. "Why pretend to care about a dead elf when you have no regard for the living? If you did, every elf in this place would leave with us!"

Elizerain sighed. "I'd like nothing better, Nyson, but we need to face reality. None of the slaves are in good enough condition to make an escape. If we tried, they'd die during the attempt and take us with them."

She nodded toward the pit. "What you did for this unfortunate elf was brave and noble, but his death was already a certainty."

"But the others—"

"Neither of the elf women in my cave would survive the trip out," she said bluntly. "That leaves Two-Tails, and I'm guessing you refused to fight him for the same reason you offered to take Konnik's place. You knew he was in no condition to fight."

Nyson made no reply, but Elizerain saw the answer in his eyes.

She slipped an arm around his waist. "We'd better get back to quarters before Merry Sunshine finishes his dinner and comes looking for us."

The incongruous nickname for the glum, yellow-skinned orc brought a flicker of a smile to Nyson's lips. They walked back in silence to find Xander and Trobe waiting for them at the mouth of the cave, their faces grim. Behind them, the cave was empty.

"Where's Two-Tails? Where's the guard?" Elizerain asked.

"Surprised you didn't pass them on your way back," the dwarf muttered. "Elf couldn't take no more, I'm guessing. He pretty much just turned up his toes and died. The ogress made the guard haul him off."

Trobe eyed the young Koada'Dal, his small eyes surprisingly shrewd. "You got what you came for?"

Nyson blinked away his surprise. "In a manner of speaking."

The dwarf stood and rolled his shoulders. "Well, then, let's be off."

"Just like that? What about Mirdit?" demanded Xander.

That prompted a nasty smile. "Don't you be worried about the ogress. She'll get hers."

Trobe went to the back of the cave and moved a stone, revealing a small opening.

"Don't tell me the tunnel was here all along!"

The dwarf shot Elizerain a dirty look. "Supplies, girlie. Take these."

He drew several sacks and a length of rope from the small opening and tossed them at her. That accomplished, he led the way from the slave pits to the hut Mirdit occupied. Standing on tiptoe, he peered into a small knothole, then gave a curt nod.

Elizerain eased open the door, wincing at the creak, and slipped into the hut with the others close on her heels.

"Used to be a well house," Trobe said briskly as he pried open a section of wooden floor. "Don't many orcs remember that, seems like."

The bard peered down the narrow shaft. The elves would have no problem, but she wasn't sure the shaft would accommodate the dwarf's girth. If Trobe were as stocky as most of his kind, there would be no question.

"You sure you can fit down there, Trobe?"

"Done it before, just barely. Who's first?"

Elizerain firmly laid claim to the role of scout. She eased into the hole and slid down the rope to what Trobe said would be the first landing.

The ledge felt sticky underfoot. Curious, Elizerain touched the wall. The telltale feel of spider silk—thick and freshly spun—sent her heart leaping skyward in a single painful bound.

An angry chittering erupted from the nearby darkness, followed by the skittering rush of many legs. Elizerain's hand reached for her hidden sword and closed around the hilt.

She swept it out in front of her. Tiny blue notes wafted from the sword, and the sudden spill of azure light revealed the biggest and ugliest spider Elizerain had ever seen. Its head was nearly the size of her own, and its long, hairy legs were probably longer than she was tall.

Unlike the furred black giants of Faydark, this one was a sickly white. Its skin appeared to be covered in tiny scales, like the underbelly of a fish, and its multifaceted eyes were a dull pink. It was probably blind, for the sudden burst of light didn't seem to startle or slow it in the slightest.

Those eyes might not work, Elizerain reasoned, but surely they could still feel.

She slashed out wildly, aiming for those sightless pink eyes.

The spider shrieked and reared back on its hind four legs, while the front limbs pawed frantically at its ruined eyes. One of those flailing arms struck the elf and knocked her onto her backside. She hit the stone hard, and her sword clattered to the stone. The tiny blue lights winked out.

A heavy, sickening weight swarmed over her, forcing her onto her back. Mandibles clacked in anticipation as the smell of carrion swept over her like an evil wind.

Elizerain flung her head to one side and felt the mandible graze her cheek and close on a thick lock of hair. The creature spat out its bloodless mouthful with a sound eerily similar to a human expression of disgust—a sound that rose into a keening and decidedly inhuman shriek.

Warm, sticky fluid rushed over Elizerain, and suddenly the spider's weight was gone. A faint light illuminated the tunnel, casting a blue glow over her three companions. Nyson's work, no doubt—and yet another spell he hadn't bothered to share with her.

Xander, his sword still in hand, extended his free hand to Elizerain.

She let him pull her up, then brushed at her clothes, grimacing at the stickiness of her tunic. "I'm covered in spider goo."

"There's worse ways to get acquainted with the inside of a giant spider," Trobe observed.

He dropped to one knee and heaved at the scaly white body with both hands. It rolled over once, then again, then dropped out of sight. In the faint light, Elizerain could make out the jagged edge of the stone ledge just beyond Trobe's boots.

The dwarf cocked his head and listened for several moments, then nodded in satisfaction at the soft thud far below.

"Distance is about the same as I remember."

"That's a long way down," Nyson said in dismay.

"It'd be a lot farther if we had to *dig* our way through," the dwarf said tartly. "What with all that tapping and pounding up in the quarries, there's always a risk of tunnel collapse down below. Damn fool orcs wouldn't know where to look for a tunnel if they were born with maps on the backs of their hands."

"They're looking for the treasure trove?"

Trobe shrugged. "What else? You see anything in all that rock that's worth mining? Let's get on with it."

He wriggled through a small opening that led into a side tunnel, a rough passage that was frequently low enough to force them to crawl on their bellies.

Finally they came out in a tiny cavern and rose gratefully to their feet. The soft blue haze of Nyson's spell revealed four tunnel openings.

"That one," Trobe said decisively, pointing.

"How do you know where to go?" Nyson asked.

The dwarf dug a bit of rock from the mouth of the tunnel and showed it to the young elf. "What do you see?"

Nyson studied the rock for a moment, then shrugged.

"That's right!" the dwarf said and swatted the Koada'-Dal on the shoulder. "Nothing *to* see."

"I'm not sure I understand," Xander prompted.

"Nothing to see," Trobe repeated, running one finger across the smooth stone. "No sign of anything that might have come from the forest. Moving water made all four of them tunnels. Some of that water started in the forest and made its way down, some comes up from deep in the stone. You can tell which is which by the signs it leaves on the stone."

"So that tunnel leads to an underground water source," the ranger said.

"It's a bit of a walk, but yes. That first shaft we came down used to be a well. Wells have been known to go dry," Trobe explained patiently. "I'm guessing when it happened, the orcs didn't waste much worry on it."

"The reservoir," Elizerain said.

"That's right. There's water aplenty under the orcs. *Fresh* water, and that means it's moving. And when water moves, it shapes the stone. The well we came down was spring-fed. Yonder tunnel was the source. But the stone shifted, as stone will do, which is why that ledge with the spider was our first stop, instead of a dead-end bottom of a well. As fer those other tunnels, well, they're all come-lately, made by water working its way down through the rock. Useless fer our needs, as they'll narrow up to next to nothing in no time. The story's in the stone, if'n you know how to read it."

"So we're heading for an underground river," the Koada'Dal summarized.

"Won't be needing to go that far down. We're looking fer a side tunnel—or better said, a lot of side tunnels," the dwarf amended. "Could take a while. Water don't seem to like a short, straight path."

These words proved prophetic. For what seemed like days they crawled through a maze of stone passages or hugged rock walks as they edged their way along narrow ledges. Time became an oddly shifting thing. They rested when they needed to, ate the occasional fungi that Trobe deemed fit for consumption, and drank from plentiful sources of water.

The last tunnel did indeed lead up, and at an angle that at times was little different from climbing a sheer rock wall. Finally they crawled out into a level, open cavern. Nyson renewed his flickering light spell, and suddenly the world around them was aglow.

They stood in silence and gazed at the ancient hoard. Dust and cobwebs obscured some of the glitter, but the gems and gold shone through clearly enough.

A wide grin stretched across Elizerain's face. "This is the first time I've known treasure hunters to err on the side of pessimism."

"Who could have thought the legends might be true?" Nyson marveled.

The bard shot him a quick, assessing glance. "You're the one who said the harp's story could be found here."

"The spell yielded a riddle," he reminded her. "This seemed a likely solution, but spell-sought answers are notoriously cryptic."

Since Elizerain had no answer to that, she set to work searching for the story of the blood red harp. She paged through a small, crumbling lore book, upended golden urns to check for hidden scrolls, lifted lids of silver boxes. With the two elves helping her, they soon went through the treasure. Wealth there was in great plenty, but there was nothing about the harp to be found, not anywhere. Not a word.

Several questions that had been nothing more than an itch in the back of Elizerain's mind took on a sudden, unpleasant clarity. She tossed aside a gem-encrusted vase and raised her eyes to a suddenly watchful Nyson.

"There's nothing here to find, is there? You made the whole thing up so we'd help you rescue your high elf girlfriend."

"Yes."

Anger began to rise in her like a fever. "And if your path is littered with bodies, what is that to you?"

His chin lifted. "It was never my intent to put you in danger. My friends and I planned to rescue Cyntharia Starflower, an enchantress of Felwithe. When I learned of your . . . unfortunate attachment to the harp, I knew you would seize at any chance to rid yourself of the curse. I'd hoped you would employ your bardic talents to recruit others to our cause, but I fully planned to leave you behind once you had raised an army. The ranger, however, devised a better plan, and it seemed prudent to follow his lead. Indeed, by that time I had little other choice."

Elizerain's fist flashed toward the Koada'Dal's face. She caught him squarely on the jaw, a solid punch that sent him staggering back several paces.

Later, her hand would no doubt hurt, but at the moment she was too angry to care about anything but the burning desire to wipe that expression of cool, arrogant certainty off Nyson's face before the necromancer's curse overtook her. Judging by the itch and tingling in her scalp, she'd have to hurry.

Xander stepped between her and Nyson just as she

was hauling back for a second punch. The wood elf took her by the shoulders and gave her a shake.

"Elizerain, we will find the answers you seek," he told her. "Never doubt that for a moment."

Her ire began to slip away, and the curse with it. She lowered her fist and stared searchingly into Xander's face. "You would stay with me?"

"Was there ever any question of it?"

She dropped her head onto his shoulder. "You're the truest friend I've ever had," she mumbled into his tunic.

"Nor will I be the only one," he said firmly. "Nyson will continue with us until your quest is complete."

Elizerain pulled away. "I don't want him."

The young elf bowed stiffly. "I understand your reticence, Songmistress, but the good ranger has the right of it. Honor demands that I continue with you."

She met his gaze squarely. "You'll forgive me if I'm not terribly impressed by that sentiment. Your behavior so far isn't exactly what I'd call honorable."

"Then take *my* word on it," Xander said. "Where I go, Nyson goes. It's my sworn duty to protect the son of Lady Niola Impholder."

The color drained from Nyson's face, leaving angry splotches on his high cheekbones. "On whose orders?"

"Regren Steelforger, captain of the Emerald Guard," the ranger informed him. "As a protector of Kelethin, I do as my commander instructs. Your mother did not hire me, if that is your concern."

The young elf looked somewhat mollified, but his skeptical expression remained. "You were ordered to accompany me beyond the boundaries of Kelethin?"

"I promised to do all that was in my ability to bring you safely back."

"But—"

"Enough," Elizerain broke in, thoroughly tired of the self-absorbed Koada'Dal and the entire pointless adventure.

Pointless indeed! The young elf should have known his ladylove was dead when he found her pendant in the hands of orc thieves. In fact, he'd held in his hands proof that his Cyntharia never made it to Crushbone. That didn't stop him from dragging them all into the orc citadel.

Elizerain shook her head in disgust. "Take us out of here, Trobe."

But the dwarf was busy with an agenda of his own, kicking aside priceless treasures to palm the stone wall.

It occurred to Elizerain that Nyson was not the only one to harbor secrets.

"Why did *you* come to Crushbone, Trobe?" she asked wearily.

"Lost me an axe, last time I was in these parts," he said. "It's an old one, even as dwarves reckon such things, and worth the trouble to retrieve. Ah, here we go," he announced happily. "Help me move this box."

The "box" was an enormous sea chest bound in brass and covered with some sort of reptilian hide. Nyson came to help the dwarf, while Elizerain and Xander positioned themselves on the other side. They took hold of rusted bronze handles, and on Trobe's count, they all heaved.

The lid flew open, and a small dragon darted out. High, piping shrieks burst from it like waves of audible light. Its shrill keening tested the upper edges of the elves' hearing—as well as the integrity of the ancient cavern. Stone dust started to fall from the ceiling like gray mist.

"Kill the damn thing before it brings down the stone!" Trobe howled, clamping his hands to his ears.

Xander reached over his shoulder for the bow Nyson's magic had obscured. He pulled it from the quiver, which also reappeared, and quickly snapped the string into place. With a single smooth, fluid motion, he fitted the first arrow and let fly.

The arrow struck its target cleanly, right under the wing—the reptilian equivalent of a man's armpit. The creature shrieked again, and the cavern floor trembled. It was a lethal shot, for it pierced the lung. In time, the creature would drown in its own blood.

Another cry shrilled through the treasure cave, and rocks started to roll and skitter down one wall.

"Finish it!" Trobe howled.

Xander's next arrow tore through a wing. The creature seemed to stagger in midair, then righted itself and came straight at the elf in a dive, jaws flung open and talons arched forward like those of a hawk swooping down to snatch up a hare.

The elf stood his ground, a third arrow ready. When the dragon was almost upon him, he let fly and then dived aside.

His arrow plunged deep into one glowing eye. The dragon crashed into the pile of treasure.

Trobe's axe appeared in his hands as he charged forward. He lifted the weapon high and brought it down with all his might on the back of the dragon's neck. The head rolled down a pile of coin and came to rest against the bronze statue of a winged cat.

The ranger rose to his feet and regarded the decapitated corpse. "If ever I need to track you," he said dryly, "I'll simply follow the unattached heads."

"Best way to make sure," the dwarf said briskly, kicking the creature's head away as if it might reattach itself if left too close to its body. "Now, let's have another go at this box."

Even empty, the trunk was heavy enough to require all four to lift it. When they'd moved it aside, a small opening was revealed in the cavern's wall.

Too small, Elizerain judged, for the dwarf to pass through.

Obviously Trobe had come to the same conclusion, for he was eyeing Elizerain appraisingly. "You're about the right size for this tunnel. Go on in. The axe will be in there."

She dropped to her knees and peered in. The tunnel was extremely low, barely large enough for her to wriggle through. "You're sure of that?"

The dwarf sent her a disgusted look. "I saw it drop down the shaft. Heard it fall with my own ears. That's where the shaft ends. Where else would the durned axe be?"

Elizerain didn't see how it was possible for Trobe to know that, but she held her questions and wriggled into the small tunnel.

Sure enough, there lay an ancient axe. A tiny glimmer of light spilled from the opening far above, enough to give her a clear view of the weapon. Dwarven runes were carved on the blade. The handle was fashioned from the bone of some large creature, yellowed with age, and marked with many trophy notches.

Dragging the ancient thing behind her, she carefully backed out and handed the axe to Trobe. He immediately tossed aside the axe they'd retrieved from the Wolfskinner orcs and tucked the older weapon carefully into his belt.

"Time we were getting on," he said. "Xander, how about you pick up those pikes over there and tie them into a bundle. Bard, fill these sacks with every sheathed knife and dagger you can find. The boy knows his swords—let him pick the best of them, as many as he can carry. I'll take the axes and halberds and suchlike."

Elizerain's eyes narrowed. "That's a lot of weapons for a solitary dwarf. It's not as if you're equipping an army."

"Seems to me like the more solitary you are, the more weapons you need. Can't never have too many."

"We did say he would be paid from the trove," Xander pointed out.

The bard shrugged and began to sift through a pile of loose gems. She'd never been particularly drawn to wealth, but some spells required the sacrifice of a costly jewel. No spells that she could cast, just yet, but someday . . .

She drew her sword and dropped a handful of gems into the scabbard. The sword didn't seat as deeply into the sheath, but the magic was still sufficient to conceal the weapon. That accomplished, she quickly filled three sacks with small edged weapons and, at Trobe's bidding, tied two of them together and slung them over his shoulder. Just as well—the weapons were heavy, and one sack was about the extent of Elizerain's strength.

Nyson, however, was giving more attention to his task than the dwarf's patience allowed. Each sword had to be examined, checked for balance, and tested by sweeping it through a short, elegant, deadly dance. He would not be hurried in this work, no matter how Trobe huffed and complained.

"That's it," the dwarf finally announced. "Did I tell you the way out is hidden underwater during the full moon tide?"

Nyson stopped in mid-spin. "I believe you neglected to mention that."

"Gather up what you've got and grab a few blades yet untested," Trobe instructed. "If we set a brisk pace, we'll just about make it."

"How can you possibly tell what time it is, or for that matter what day it is, after all this time underground?" Nyson wondered. "We've been wandering these tunnels for . . . what? Three or four days?"

"Something like that, and there's more of the same ahead." The dwarf shifted the sacks higher onto his shoulder. "Less talking now means less swimming later. Let's go."

Fortunately, the passage to the surface was high enough to allow them to walk upright, and smooth enough underfoot to allow them considerable speed. Laden with warlike loot, they hurried along, listening in trepidation to the growing roar awaiting them.

Elizerain had never had much to do with the sea, other than the voyage to and from Antonica. She was a strong swimmer—most elves who grew up on the shores of Lake Elizerain could swim before they could walk—but the notion of a tunnel that opened into the sea was terrifying. She kept shaking off vivid images of water pouring into the tunnel, sweeping them away like rats in a flooded cistern.

Trobe's assurances that the tunnel entrance was not only sealed but located well above sea level, except at full moon tide, did little to settle the school of fish that seemed to be having an agitated swim in Elizerain's stomach.

And how *did* the dwarf know when the tides occurred?

The last part of their journey—or so Trobe promised—was a long, steep climb, followed by an equally steep descent. Elizerain began to understand how the tunnels kept dry, despite opening into the sea.

They made their way down the slope and came at last to the end of the path. Trobe set to work prying apart what appeared to be a solid wall of stone. Soon sea wind was whistling through the opening, crisp and clean and salty—and best of all, wonderfully dry.

The elves couldn't leave the tunnel fast enough. They emerged to find themselves on a sea cliff, standing on a small, rocky ledge. Trobe swiftly replaced the stones, artfully tucking clumps of sea grass here and there to obscure the recent opening. He worked quickly, glancing up at the sun from time to time.

When he was finished, they made their way up the cliff, the rising tide nipping at their heels like a vast hound. Trobe called a halt when they reached a fairly large ledge not far from the cliff's edge.

"There's a path yonder leads to the forest," Trobe told them. "Dump the loot here and be on yer way."

"But what about you?" Elizerain asked. "You can't carry all this on your own."

"I'll manage. Go, and be quick about it."

The sound of loose stones skittering down the cliff drew their gazes upward. Elizerain let out a low, fervent curse.

A band of orcs half-walked, half-slid down the path Trobe had indicated. By now Elizerain had grown adept at picking out the differences between what had once seemed indistinguishable members of a uniformly ugly race. These orcs were familiar, and they were not clad in Crushbone armor.

"The Wolfskinner bandits," Xander said bitterly. "I *knew* that battle went too easily!"

"It couldn't have been Davin who sold us out," Elizerain murmured. "If he knew about the treasure trove, he would have plundered it by now. That leaves—"

"Hail, Trobe!" called a familiar voice. A couple of the orcs stumbled as Mirdit Smallplague shoved her way past them to the front of the band.

"Ye're early," the dwarf said flatly.

"Apparently I'm just in time," she countered, her gaze dropping to the pile of weapons on the ledge. "These elves seem to think they're finished. In fact, it looks to me as if you planned to let them go free. When you promised to bring some slaves back to Crushbone to help haul out weapons, that wasn't part of the deal."

Three pairs of accusing elven eyes turned to the dwarf. Trobe met their gaze coolly and turned to Mirdit.

"The elves served their purpose. Might as well let them go. There's nothing more to be gained by keeping them around."

"Oh, I can think of a purpose or two they might yet serve," Mirdit said airily. "We've a battle ahead, so there will be auguries to be read and sacrifices to be made. A few elves would be a fitting sacrifice to ask the ogre gods for their blessings—"

She broke off and sent Trobe a horrible grin. "And a good meal, afterward."

17

BETRAYAL

THE STUNNED SILENCE THAT FELL OVER THE elves gave way to sudden, surging wrath. Nyson was first to respond; he reached for his magically hidden sword and would have drawn it, had not Xander been quick enough to grab his sleeve and pull his hand away from the invisible weapon.

"Not yet," the ranger said softly and urgently. "Save it for a better time."

"To what end? The dwarf knows all and will betray us whenever it pleases him to do so," Nyson bitterly retorted. "I would rather die with my weapon in my hand, at a time of my own choosing, and take an enemy with me!"

His voice rose to a shout as he spoke, and as the last words left his lips, he hurled himself at Trobe. They went down together in a rattling crunch of loose stone and a flurry of fists. The orcs fell back a pace or two to form a small, makeshift arena on the ledge.

"I wouldn't have taken elf boy for a brawler," Mirdit said, grinning broadly as she hopped beyond range of a swinging fist. The ogress's smile disappeared as the high elf's hand closed on one of the daggers that had spilled from the sack of weapons Elizerain had carried from the trove. She leaped away from Nyson's first sweeping cut, showing astonishing agility for one of her size.

Nyson's first swing was deliberately wild, so as to shake the weapon free of its sheath. But the old leather flew away easily, and the blade slashed a rising line across the shin of a Wolfskinner bandit.

The orc thief howled in pain and rage as he aimed a fierce kick at the pair of combatants. His timing was unintentionally superb; he caught Trobe in the ribs just as the dwarf heaved himself and the elf over, attempting to pin Nyson beneath him. The kick added momentum Trobe hadn't counted upon; he rolled right over the elf and kept going—to the very edge of the stone ledge.

For a moment Trobe teetered there, unable to catch himself because he needed both hands to hold Nyson's blade away from his throat. For his part, the elf seemed grimly content to go over the edge with Trobe if that was the required way of settling this dispute.

They both would have fallen into the sea, had not Mirdit grabbed Trobe with one massive brown paw and dragged him back to safety. Xander took hold of Nyson—who still clung doggedly to the dwarf with one hand and the dagger with the other—and pulled him away.

Elizerain seized the wrist of Nyson's weapon hand and twisted it into palm-up position. She gave his forearm a sharp, quick blow just below his elbow. That relaxed his grip for a moment—long enough for her to snatch the dagger and toss it aside.

At last the high elf subsided. But the fulminating rage

on his face as he regarded the treacherous dwarf convinced Xander and Elizerain to keep a firm hold on him, just in case.

The orc Nyson had cut stopped probing his wound long enough to sweep a bloody finger toward his attacker. "That one *mine*. Nobody else kill."

"*No one* will kill that one," Mirdit commanded. "He could be useful to me later."

"What about other two?" the orc persisted, his gaze shifting to the two wood elves who'd subdued the young Koada'Dal.

The ogress regarded Xander and Elizerain for a moment. "I'll take them along. Someone's got to play nursemaid to elf boy, and they'll do as well as any. Ah, here comes our boat, right on time."

Elizerain followed the ogress's seaward gaze. An old fishing vessel with a single mast was turning away from the wind and dropping its much-patched sails. Sailors lowered two small wooden rowboats over the side by rope and pulley. Apparently the larger ship would stay well away from the shore.

The reason was obvious, even to the bard's inexperienced eyes. Wave after wave broke against jagged rocks jutting out of the surf, and now, at high tide, surely many similar hazards lay just below the surface.

"You pay us now," the pot-bellied orc told Mirdit. The ogress Mirdit glanced pointedly at Trobe.

The dwarf removed a small sack from his tunic and handed it over. Elizerain's eyebrows rose as the dwarf poured a small fortune in old coins into the orc's large green palm. She hadn't noticed Trobe collecting treasure and wondered, briefly, what else he might have picked up in the trove.

But there was no more time for speculation. At Mirdit's instructions, the orcs looped a rope under Elizerain's arms and lowered her toward the waiting boat. The big, brown-skinned sailor who manned the oars greeted her with a cheerful leer, revealing a few dark stubs where once his teeth had been.

"Sweet Tooth," he said by way of introduction as he helped her out of her impromptu harness. "Welcome aboard, lass. Sit you down in the prow and keep as still as you can. It'll be tricky business getting old Mirdit aboard this tub."

But the ogress was being lowered into the second, stronger-looking boat, and the dwarf with her. While Mirdit supervised the loading of her new weapons into the larger craft, the three elves settled down on the floor of the leaky, low-sided boat. Sweet Tooth pointed out the bailing buckets and then set off for the ship, roaring out an off-tune ballad that kept time with the powerful sweeps of his oars.

A particularly strong wave dashed over the side, drenching Elizerain to the skin. The wind was picking up as they moved out of the cliff-protected cove, and her teeth started to chatter from the chill.

"Tell me again why it was a good idea to put our lives in that dwarf's hands," she asked Xander.

The ranger paused in the act of bailing and shot her a somber glance. "There are things about Trobe you don't know."

"So tell me."

When he didn't respond, she tipped her head to one side and considered him for a long moment. "You don't have enough trust in Elizerain *Greenleaf* to confide in me, do you? How long will you hold Davin the Dark against me? *Talk* to me, Xander!"

"I have made certain oaths and promises."

"That's not an answer!"

"It should be."

Elizerain thought this over and found she had no argument. Perhaps her time with Davin *had* changed her, if she'd forgotten what honor meant to an honorable person. "Very well, then, if you can't talk about Trobe, ask Nyson here about his high elf ladylove. Ask why he *still* led us into Crushbone after he found his lady's pendant in the hands of the orc bandits. Tell me why that discovery didn't prove to him she'd been killed long before she got to Crushbone."

The wood elves waited for Nyson to answer, but the young high elf stared adamantly out to sea. When it was clear that no response would be forthcoming, Xander suggested, "Our belongings were taken from us when we entered the citadel. Mayhap at some earlier time, the ogress paid the Wolfskinners from her share of other prisoners' stolen possessions. The blue pendant could have come into their hands in that manner."

That stopped Elizerain, but only for a moment. "But how did Nyson *know* this? How did he know the elf woman he sought had made it to Crushbone? Did Trobe tell him, or did he already have reason to know of a connection between the ogress and the orc bandits? And for that matter, why was Nyson's lady bound for Crushbone? High elves tend toward arrogance, but they are rarely suicidal. What reason had she to believe she could survive?"

Xander turned to the young Koada'Dal, his rugged

face set in grim lines. "These are good questions. I strongly suggest you answer them."

"You are hardly in a position of *strength*," Nyson pointed out, not bothering to shift his gaze from the sea, "and given our circumstances and your unfortunate choice of guide, you'll forgive me if I'm not inclined to take any more of your *suggestions*."

His haughty tone pushed Elizerain's temper to the end of its tether. She brought to mind just how the skystone pendant had swung free of Nyson's tunic when he leaned forward to accept a bowl of stew that night they had shared a campfire. She caught a handful of his pale hair and yanked his head down to duplicate that posture. Her free hand darted out and came back with a blue and silver pendant clenched in her fist.

A sharp yank broke the delicate chain. Elizerain flung her hand out over the low side and dangled the token over the sea.

"If you don't like Xander's *suggestions*, let's go straight to *threats*. Tell all, or I drop this."

Nyson's handsome face turned pale with anger, and his lips firmed into a thin, straight line. After a moment, he gave a curt nod of surrender.

"I knew Cyntharia was bound for Crushbone, but she refused to tell me what business she had there," he said softly.

"So you followed her, hoping to find out."

"I followed her, intending to aid her in her purpose," Nyson corrected. "The three friends who came with me knew this. They were as committed to this adventure as I, come what may."

"Pity you weren't quite as open about your plans with Xander and me," Elizerain observed.

"Indeed," he said softly. "You and the ranger were brought into this undertaking under a pretense. It seemed prudent at the time, but I regret . . ."

His voice trailed off. It was more apology than Elizerain had expected. Most of her ire melted away, and she reached out to give his shoulder a quick, light squeeze.

"After I found the pendant, I had to know if Cyntharia had made it to Crushbone or perished along the way," he said softly. "To that end, I confided in the dwarf. As you pointed out, it would have been selfishness and folly to lead others into the orc citadel, otherwise."

With difficulty, Elizerain refrained from commenting on the young elf's notions of altruism and good judgment. "Trobe saw your friend the last time he was in Crushbone?"

The young elf nodded. "He told me that she came in shortly before he escaped. This knowledge only increased my determination. I had to get her out if I could or find out what happened to her if I could not. I thought Trobe would understand and support this quest, as dwarves are clannish folk who prize loyalty highly." He paused for a brief, bitter smile. "Or so I have always been told."

"What did the dwarf have to say for himself? Do you have any idea how he got mixed up with Mirdit?"

"What does it matter?" Xander broke in. "Let the past lie as it fell. We need to bend our thoughts and efforts toward getting through this alive."

A shadow passed over the young Koada'Dal's face. He glanced toward the setting sun, as if the day's fading stood as a fitting symbol for the end of his hopes and dreams.

"For some of us," he said softly, "it's a bit late for that."

DAVIN THE DARK COULD TRAVEL THE FOREST AS quietly as any ranger, for hadn't his father raised him to follow that particular path? Perhaps the lure of women and wealth was strong enough to draw him out of the forest shadows from time to time, and perhaps his feet were fashioned to walk the twisted and self-serving path of a rogue, but still he knew Faydark as well as most elves. When something was out of place, he knew it, and nothing he'd seen in his long years among these trees was as inherently wrong as the sight of an ogress slipping away from Crushbone.

First off, orcs and ogres were unlikely to share a table and raise tankards together. Second, Crushbone was a male stronghold, and what business an ogre sow might have there was beyond Davin's ken. Stranger still, the guards let her walk out with nary a challenge.

Curious, Davin had taken Grib—the oldest member of his band, yet still the fleetest of foot—and followed the ogress to an encampment of orcs.

Familiar orcs, and not those of the Crushbone variety. These were the Wolfskinners, and if Davin's eyes served him right, that big pot-bellied brute was the orc that Elizerain's friend Trobe had stomped into insensibility during the attack meant to retrieve his axe. A rather common-looking axe, come to think of it, with nothing special about it.

Davin recalled the way the dwarf had stormed the orc encampment alone, before the signal was given. His charge had taken everyone by surprise, orcs and attackers alike. The orcs hadn't had much fight in them—they'd pretty much turned tail and run right after Trobe's initial charge. Davin hadn't thought that particularly odd at the time, and he wouldn't have reconsidered the matter now, except for the fact that the dwarf's "first kill" was walking around looking healthier and happier than any orc had a right to be.

So for nearly five days he and Grib had followed the ogress and her orc cohorts, traveling from Crushbone to the very edge of the northernmost forest. When their quarry left the forest shadows for the lichen-strewn rocks of the seacoast, the Greenleaf bandits climbed high into the last of the tall trees. They settled down in a perch that afforded them a clear view of the sea.

The bandit leader held out one hand. "Let's have it."

Grib reluctantly handed over an old sea glass—a treasured reminder of his pirating days. Davin held it to one eye and swept the horizon for a few moments before he found what he sought.

"There's a boat just beyond the shoal. Small, old. I can't make out much more than that."

The old thief reclaimed his property and held it to his single remaining eye. "A trawler, by the look of it," he said briskly. "Hang on a tick; there are markings on the hull."

He studied the boat for several moments before lowering the glass.

"*Prawnbane?*" he said incredulously. "What kind of captain would give his boat a damn fool name like that?"

"A captain who'd rather folks react to his boat with a smirk than with suspicion, would be my guess. If he's carrying cargo or passengers that wouldn't bear close scrutiny, it's not a half-bad ploy. Many a pirate would outlive their parrots if only they'd name their ships after something big-eyed and furry, like *Sea Otter* or *Seal Pup*, instead of *Wind Reiver* and *Deathdealer* and suchlike."

"Suppose so," the old man said grudgingly. "But still."

"There's something moving in the water there near the ship. See if you can make it out."

Grib obligingly lifted the glass again. "Two rowboats pulling up to the trawler. The big ogress is getting herself hoisted over the side. And there's your elf girl!"

"*Elizerain* is with them? You're sure?"

"Ought to be. Traveled with her for more than a year, didn't I? Looks to me like she's fixing to take another sea voyage."

"Whether she wants to or not," Davin murmured. "Can you get word to any of your old cronies, maybe find out where the *Prawnbane* is headed?"

The bandit looked doubtful. "That'd take time. And if you're right about the kind of cargo and passengers that boat's taking on—and since they're hauling an ogress, I'm guessing you are—the crew's likely to be a little closed-mouthed about the what and where of things."

"Then see if you can find out anything about a man by the name of Chanzoon Nexis. Tall fellow, probably about my age—"

Davin broke off, grimaced, and conceded reality by saying, "Well, not much more than ten years younger, anyway. He has long black hair and the palest blue eyes you're likely to find, and he might be considered good looking until you get to know him. He's likely to draw eyes, and he's easy to pick out of a crowd. He'll be following the *Prawnbane*. And he's a necromancer," he added in the casual tone usually assigned to inconsequential afterthought.

Grib snorted. "Saved the best for last, did you?"

"Well, I thought you should know, as it tends to come up in conversation sooner or later."

The old man shook his head in disbelief. "Elizerain's a

good lass," he said grudgingly, "but no female's worth this much trouble."

"Rain is only part of this tale. I've a good mind to kill this Chanzoon Nexis, and a good reason, too."

Women might be a mystery to the old bandit, but revenge was something he understood well enough. He slapped Davin's shoulder bracingly.

"I'm off, then. Meet at the usual place?"

"Aye. Mind those orcs, now. They're in our line of work, which would make them cannier than most."

Grib snorted, but whether at the notion of intelligent orcs or the wisdom of following a bandit's path, Davin could not say.

18

At Sea

XANDER STOOD AT THE STERN OF THE SHIP, carefully emptying the night pots and kitchen leavings over the rail. It was one of his shipboard duties, and he had carried it out for the past three mornings. It seemed wrong to him, for no ranger would befoul a stream or pond in this manner. Though he knew the vastness of the sea made a considerable difference, it just didn't sit well with him.

On the whole, however, Xander had little reason for complaint. He and his fellow elves had been treated well enough by the captain and crew of the *Prawnbane*. The sailors had shown no surprise when Mirdit referred to them as her captives and no inclination to intervene on their behalf, but shipboard life had an equalizing effect of its own.

Everyone aboard was expected to pitch in with the work. Mirdit immediately made herself at home in the galley, and she and Sweet Tooth split between them the task of feeding the crew. Elizerain had been put to work as a rope runner, scampering up the web of lines to tie a slackening knot or repair a fraying bit of rope. She seemed to take it in stride and assured Xander it was not so different from climbing trees. Still, it seemed strange to see a wood elf perched barefoot on a slender hemp line, silhouetted against sea and sky.

Indeed, that vast openness was the strangest thing of all. The ship seemed somehow naked to Xander, exposed as it was to the whims of sun and winds. A storm had blown through last night, and the rain that lashed the old trawler in stinging torrents and wind-driven sheets had been nothing at all like the soft, heavy mist that filtered down through the forest canopy. Equally fierce was the sun, with its unrelenting golden glare.

Still, Xander found this strangeness preferable to their tiny quarters below decks. He savored this moment of solitude—and the privacy needed to tend an important personal task.

A small flock of seabirds was following the ship, hoping for a breakfast of fish offal. Xander did not disappoint them: he emptied a large bucket of fish heads and slimy innards into the sea, leavings from last night's stew. Immediately the birds set up a contentious racket, loudly laying claim to the best bits as they swooped toward the water.

Xander took advantage of the racket to let out a high, ringing call of his own—indistinguishable from the seabirds' calls, except to the ears of a ranger, a druid, or another seabird.

A large white-and-gray bird peeled away from the flock and swept in to land on the rail a mere arm's length from the ranger. The bird dipped its head slightly as if in greeting and waited, black eyes bright with intelligence.

Xander quickly tied a small scroll to one of the bird's legs and gave it a few words of instruction. After gulping down the several small fish Xander had put aside as a reward, the bird unfurled its wings and leaped into the sky, winging steadily toward the east. There it would find an old elf who knew what to do with such messages.

With a sigh, Xander sank down to the morning-cool wood of the deck. He pulled his knees up to his chest and leaned back against the curve of the ship's wooden side, enjoying the shadows it cast over him. For a pleasant moment, he allowed himself to dream of tree-shaded paths.

The creak of old wood drew Xander's eyes toward the aft hatch. A small, square opening led down to the elves' quarters, and from it thrust a rickety old ladder. Nyson's golden head emerged from the hold, and the young elf leaped nimbly to the deck.

He walked quickly to the stern on some errand of his own. Xander noted the small sack in one hand, which appeared to be full of soft, lumpy objects. Nyson dropped this sack over the rail. For a long moment he clung to the side of the boat with both hands, and the expression on his face suggested that he was about to toss his last meal overboard, as well.

"Are you ill?" Xander asked.

Nyson spun around quickly, apparently startled by the unexpected voice. He quickly gained his composure.

"I am quite well and glad to find you here," he said. "Elizerain has taken ill. The necromancer's curse is settling upon her again."

Xander met this announcement with a stoic face and sinking heart. In truth, he'd been expecting it, but several days had come and gone since their "escape" from Crushbone, and three more aboard ship. When the curse did not come, he'd allowed himself to hope its time was past.

"Do you have any magic that might ease her?"

The high elf shook his head.

"Are you sure?" Xander persisted. "I am not learned in the art of magic, but it seems to me you have a strangely wide variety of spells."

"I am quite sure, else why would I have sought you?" Nyson retorted. His ire swiftly faded, to be replaced by frustration. "We are none of us healers, and the best the shipboard doctor can do is to douse her with some of the spirits he's forever drinking and then offer to cut off a limb."

Xander had nothing to add to this bleak but accurate assessment. After a moment the high elf tentatively offered, "She improved when we headed to Crushbone, even though there were no answers to be found there."

The ranger nodded thoughtfully. "Could it be that the curse is satisfied as long as the seeker believes she is moving toward an answer?"

"That would make sense," Nyson agreed. "Some curses are fueled primarily by the mind of the one cursed. In fact, from what I have read of necromancy and what I have observed of Elizerain, it seems more than likely to be true of this situation."

Xander wondered briefly what business a Koada'Dal youth had with curses and necromancy, but he tucked these questions away for another time.

"In that case, you'll tell Elizerain what you 'really saw' when you cast that spell. If she thinks she's moving toward an answer, she might yet survive this sea voyage."

An expression of distaste crossed the young elf's patrician face. "You want me to tell a lie."

"It wouldn't be the first time, would it?" Xander pointed out.

Up came the Koada'Dal's chin. "I had good cause," he said coldly.

"Better cause than this? Once again, an elf woman's life is at risk, and do I need to point out that Elizerain came to Crushbone on your say-so? If you hadn't intervened, she might be well along the path to a real solution."

Nyson stood in silence for several long moments. "I don't know what to tell her."

"Tell her we're heading toward the Butcherblock Mountains."

"Why should she believe what I tell her?"

"Her own eyes will tell her you speak the truth. We set sail from the northernmost part of Faydwer, to the northeast of Crushbone, and we're heading west. And since I have never given her cause to doubt my word, she will believe me when I tell her Mirdit Smallplague intends to unite the ogres of the Butcherblock Mountains and march toward Kaladim."

The high elf's gaze sharpened; Xander's words held the ring of truth, and Nyson was canny enough to hear it. "How do you know that?"

"It was my business to find out," Xander said simply. "We all had our own reasons for walking into Crushbone."

The young elf studied him for a long moment, his blue eyes thoughtful and assessing. "You're far more than just another bodyguard, aren't you?"

"Where you are concerned, I should think that would be challenge enough," Xander said, "but no, I am not just your bodyguard. The elves of Kelethin are concerned about the alliance being brokered between the orcs of

Crushbone and the dark elves. Apparently the Teir'Dal's ambitions are wider than we feared. The ogres are being considered for inclusion in this treaty. For good or ill, they apparently require Mirdit to first prove herself an ally of value."

"And Trobe is leading the ogress to his own people," Nyson said bitterly. "He betrayed us and will turn traitor yet again."

"Before you cast such accusations, consider this: had we left the treasure trove when Trobe urged us to do so, we would have been well away from the cliff before the ogress and her band of orcs arrived."

The young elf's face flushed as he recalled the delay he'd caused when choosing swords.

"So this—" Nyson waved his hand in a gesture that encompassed their dilapidated seagoing prison. "—is my fault, as well?"

"I had no thought to assign blame; I merely suggested that *you* should not be so quick to do so. But we must speak of this another time," he said briskly. "Elizerain is in pain and in need. You will do what is needed, or you will answer to me."

The young elf inclined his head in a small, curt bow and spun away. Xander followed closely as Nyson made his way down the ladder into the hold of the ship.

Elizerain lay still in her hammock, her thin blanket twisted around her, evidence of a tormented sleep. Her face was flushed and damp with fever. Trobe stood beside her, wringing out a cloth he'd just dipped in a bucket of cold seawater. He placed it on her forehead and smoothed a strand of hair off her cheek.

Nyson's face clouded with anger. "I should think you've done quite enough."

"If you can do better, yer welcome to try," the dwarf snapped. "In fact, it's about time you did something useful."

Trobe reached for Elizerain's hidden sword with a sure hand. His short fingers closed around the winged hilt. "Don't be getting ideas, boy," he said without turning around. "There's something in Rain's scabbard yer needing. I'm not drawing a sword on you, so you can put that pointy jewel box away."

Nyson slid his half-drawn sword back into its sheath, but he kept one hand on the hilt as he watched the dwarf unbuckle Elizerain's belt and gently tug it out from under her. He removed the winged sword from the sheath, which he turned upside down. A handful of jewels clattered to the wooden floor, followed by a tightly rolled scroll. Trobe caught this as it fell and handed it to Nyson.

"It's a healing spell," the dwarf explained.

The high elf unrolled the scroll and glanced at the runes. "I'm no bard," he said hesitantly. "This spell is meant to be sung."

"Do you know enough of bard magic to make out the tune?" asked Xander.

Nyson studied the symbols for a long moment. "It seems . . . familiar," he said hesitantly. "I could sing it, after a fashion, but I'm not trained, and there are no guarantees—"

"Sure there are," Trobe broke in, his small eyes glinting. "I can guarantee this girl will die unless one of us does something other than flap his jaws. Now, get to it!"

PAIN BUFFETED ELIZERAIN THE WAY LAST NIGHT'S dimly remembered storm had tormented the ship. It beat at her, howling and fierce and unrelenting.

Yet dimly, slowly, she became aware of a thread of melody amid the cacophony. A song pushed at the pain, no more effective than a child's attempts to extinguish a campfire by blowing upon it, but it caught Elizerain's ear, and her mind quieted somewhat as she listened. The voice was strange, yet somehow familiar—a deep baritone, young enough to retain a bit of puppy-dog growl in the lower notes.

Nyson, thought Elizerain. Nyson was singing her healing spell—and singing it badly. Clearly the young high elf had little aptitude for the bardic arts and not even much of an ear for music, but she thought it was extraordinarily nice of him to try.

Then he reached for a high note, and his voice cracked in a strange, yodeling leap down and back.

With great effort, Elizerain managed to lift one hand and gather up a handful of his tunic.

"Stop," she croaked. "I've heard better music coming from a cat orgy in a Freeport alley."

She heard Trobe's distinctive snort, and a sound that suggested he'd just swatted Nyson on the back.

"And here you said you couldn't put her to rights!" the dwarf exclaimed happily.

By now Elizerain had managed to open her eyes, and she noted the scathing look the young Koada'Dal sent the dwarf. Nyson elbowed Trobe aside and leaned over her hammock.

"Listen to me, Songmistress," he said urgently. "I must tell you what I really saw the day I cast the seeking spell in Kelethin."

Elizerain did her best to focus as the high elf promised that the true answer to her quest lay in the Butcherblock Mountains, in the depths of fabled Kaladim.

"The dwarf city?"

"That's right," he confirmed.

She thought that over. There was something wrong with this notion, but her pain-wracked mind couldn't quite grasp it. "Trobe?"

"He's here," Nyson said flatly. He turned a cold stare toward the dwarf. "And I'm sure he's anticipating quite the reunion with his kinfolk."

Her still-hazy gaze sought out the dwarf. "Why would your folk know about my harp? The instrument isn't part of your culture."

"The playing of them, no," Trobe admitted, holding up his hands to display his short, thick digits. "We don't have the right tools for that. But the *making* of them, well, that's another thing altogether. Dwarves have long memories, and I'm thinking there's a crafter or two in Kaladim could tell you who had the making of that harp. Could be she's still alive and can tell you the story of it herself."

"She?"

"Well, sure. When you think of dwarf-craft, it's stone and metal that comes to mind, but some few dwarves work with wood. Generally they are womenfolk, as trees and suchlike are women's doings. No offense intended," he said, tossing a glance at Xander—and a longer, more pointed one at Nyson.

"None taken," the ranger murmured.

"It's just that elves are sort of, well, *girly*," the dwarf went on aggressively, glaring at the young high elf in a manner that suggested he had grievances of his own and was anxious for an excuse to air them.

Nyson lifted one brow. "Offense intended?"

"Just telling you what I'm seeing, is all," Trobe said.

He turned pointedly to Xander. "Yon high elf lad, now, is a walking posy—a long-stemmed bunch of skyflowers and yellow meadowsweet, tied in the middle with a fancy blue ribbon. Sure, that ribbon might be a weapons belt, but that makes no real nevermind to me."

"This 'walking posy' killed an orc centurion in single combat," Nyson reminded him.

That brought Trobe spinning back to face him. "*Fair* combat?" the dwarf taunted. "You knew the orc was spell-bound against killing you when you challenged him. That was about as sporting as running a pike through a boar that's been caught, penned, and hog-tied."

"I didn't know Centurion Farmid was the orc who'd captured Two Tails until the ogress told me," the elf said quietly. "If I had known, your rebuke would be well deserved. But once the challenge was given, I could hardly withdraw it without revealing our arrangement—a deal, I might add, that *you* made. And if truth be told, I'm not sorry the orc is dead."

"Nor am I, but what about my pledge?" Trobe persisted. "I promised not to kill any orcs in Crushbone."

"As you did not, you may consider your pledge fulfilled. You don't speak for me."

"We agreed that I would speak for all, as the orcs would sooner kill an elf than listen to him."

"I am surprised to learn your word means so much to you," the young elf said coldly.

Trobe thrust his bearded face pugnaciously close to the young elf's. "Let's just say I do what I set out to do. The ranger hired me to get you three into Crushbone and out again. *I* kept my promises, *and* I left with what I came for. Too bad you can't say the same."

A red flush of anger crept over the Koada'Dal's face, and his hand tightened on the grip of his sword.

Before he could draw it, Xander's hand flashed forward, seized the high elf's wrist, and slammed the now-visible weapon back into place.

"Don't be so eager to die," he said firmly. "That will come soon enough."

A strange expression crossed Nyson's face. He spun around and strode over to the ladder, which he climbed without a backward glance.

Trobe gave the two remaining elves a weak smile. "Thought he'd never leave," he quipped as he turned back to his patient. "How fare you now?"

The elf girl was regarding him with puzzlement. "Well enough to start remembering," she said slowly. "You had a deal with the ogress."

Trobe shrugged. "Never said otherwise, did I?"

"It just never came up in conversation, is that it? What else have you neglected to mention? Is my harp truly dwarf-crafted?"

"Don't know for sure," he admitted, "but it seems likely. Strings hold a tune, don't they?"

"Yes, but I figured that was the result of a spell."

"Could be, but there's more magic in good dwarf metalwork than in many a mage's spell books," Trobe asserted. "Elves don't like to brag about this, but when they want fine metal strings for their lutes and suchlike, they usually get them from Kaladim. I'll wager that at least half the strings sold in your elf cities are dwarf-crafted."

"Well, that's probably true," Elizerain admitted.

"Sometimes the fine-metal workers build instruments on the side, as some buyers like to test wares before they put down coin. Could be yer harp was dwarf-crafted. If we can't find out who made it, there's still a good chance someone will know whose work went into those strings. From there, it's just a few questions and maybe a little bookwork to find out who did the buying of those strings."

Elizerain nodded slowly. "That makes sense. Now, explain to me what you're doing with that ogress."

"That's a tale for another day," the dwarf told her briskly. "You feeling up to walking a bit? The elf lad's been talking up your harp playing, and I mentioned you knew a tale or two. There's some sailors looking forward to hearing you play, all the more so when I told them you were a dab hand at making up new ballads." Trobe lifted one side of his single black brow. "Seems a few of them think they done things would make stories worth singing."

DAVIN THE DARK KNEW THE PATHWAYS THROUGH the forest and those who ran them. So he and his men set up a watch for the messenger who carried messages from the seaside hut of a certain hermit.

He read the message now, one booted foot propped on the body of the elven runner who'd carried it. The eyes he raised to old Grib's expectant face were grim.

"There's news here that should be sent along to Kelethin. Pick a man to carry it."

"And you?"

"You said the *Rusty Cutlass* was looking for a few good swords. I'm thinking the sea air will do me good."

"Might could use some of that myself," suggested Grib.

The bandit leader clasped his old friend's shoulder. "I

appreciate the offer, but I need you boys to return to the Gallows Tree and tend to business. This trip will empty my coffers."

"Then why go?"

Davin's smile was wry. "Debts have a way of piling up. Much as I hate to say it, sooner or later, somehow or other, they've got to be paid."

19

Shipwrecked

The day at sea passed pleasantly enough, with a comfortable haze over the sun and a slow and steady wind. The *Prawnbane,* despite its silly name and ancient, creaking timbers, was a solid boat manned by a skilled crew.

But in these placid seas there was little enough to do, and several of the sailors gathered around the elven bard to hear the singing of tales. Those most fascinating to them were the ballads Elizerain made up on the spot, setting to music tall tales of their own exploits, often with newly improvised endings that had them shouting with laughter. With each song, the small crowd grew.

Even the big ogress wandered over, curiosity writ large on her scarred face. She'd kept to herself for much of the trip, though occasionally her loud disputes with Sweet Tooth—frequently punctuated by a clang of ladle and tong that suggested a cutlery duel raging below decks—could be heard during the meal preparations.

The impromptu session was exactly what Elizerain

needed. Her head still throbbed a bit, but the necromancer's curse had subsided, and her spirits rose with each song she played. It was good to have people around to sing and laugh with, even if they were a decidedly unwashed and unshaven lot.

Xander, of course, took no part in the afternoon's revels, but the bard was pleased and a little surprised that Nyson stayed at her side throughout, listening attentively and with apparent pleasure to her songs.

But Mirdit's arrival cast a cloud over the pleasant gathering. Even the sailors exchanged uneasy glances as the big ogress settled down on a barrel to listen to a tale of piracy gone comically wrong.

When Elizerain paused for breath, Mirdit said, "Few songs are sung of ogres, except as foes to be vanquished. We have our stories, mind you, but we don't set them to music. I think I would like to hear such a song."

She sent an inquiring look in Elizerain's direction. The bard nodded cautiously.

"It's a tale of slaughter and vengeance, as all good stories should be," the ogress went on. "The villain is a dwarf war chief by name of Trondle Ogrebane. He made it his business to rid the Butcherblock Mountains of ogres. It was his particular goal to slaughter the Mudtoe Clan, down to the very last ogre." Mirdit bared her fangs in a sneer and ran the painted talons of one hand over the brown footprints tattooed along her brawny arm. "As you can see, he did not quite succeed.

"But not for lack of trying! The wretch harried us as we went about our warfare and peaceable business alike, hunting us even in our dens and caves. Finally we gathered every Mudtoe ogre that remained for a valiant stand. But the treacherous dwarf ambushed us on the way to our chosen battlefield, throwing us into disadvantage.

"The slaughter was terrible," she said grimly. "I saw my father fall, my sister, my sons. But I fought on. I knew Trondle Ogrebane by his brazen helmet and long, braided beard, and I fought my way to him, cutting through his dwarf guards as if they were nothing more than squat, ugly mushrooms growing between me and their leader."

She raised a hand to trace her long, livid scar. "We fought. He was lucky," she sneered, summing up their confrontation in five terse words. "But before I fell, I tore his axe from his hands and dealt him a deathblow with it—or so I thought at the time. Later, when I came to myself, no dwarf bodies lay upon the field. Dead ogres in plenty, of course, but my two brothers were not among the slain. I tracked them deep into the mountains, where they'd fled after they saw me fall. They saw the dwarves bear Trondle away and thought that he yet lived. The axe the dwarves did not take, as it was hidden beneath my body. That day I vowed to see Trondle Ogrebane slain by his own axe."

As Elizerain listened, several pieces fell into place.

"So you went to Crushbone to seek allies?"

Mirdit shot her a quick glare. "Who's telling this tale?"

"Sorry."

"Do you see orcs aboard ship?" the ogress persisted. "No, it was weapons and treasure I wanted. Weapons and treasure will lure solitary ogres to join with the Mudtoe clan."

Questions danced on the tip of Elizerain's tongue, but she dared not ask them. How did the ogress know of the treasure trove? The only axe in Mirdit's hoard was the one Trobe carried—and that one was hidden by Nyson's magic!

"And yet you left Crushbone without that axe," Elizerain ventured.

Mirdit's smirk was faint and fleeting, but the elf noted it well. So, the ogress *did* know of Trobe's hidden axe. Moreover, she seemed content to let him carry it. Perhaps she thought he had a better chance of getting close to the dwarf hero than she did?

"Well, elf, get on with it," the ogress said brusquely. "Sing that story."

Elizerain's fingers poised over the harp strings, waiting for the music to come to her. But she knew of no tune that would fit such a tale.

Following her instincts, she began to pluck out a harsh melody, punctuated by an occasional biting chord. She did not sing the song, for no melody seemed to fit an ogre-told tale. Instead, she retold the tale in a dark chant, tuneless, yes, but as insistently rhythmic as war drums. Some of the sailors shifted uncomfortably during the telling, but the ogress seemed well pleased with it.

Nyson leaned closer when the strange ballad ended and murmured, "That was not the sort of music any elf should enjoy."

She burst out laughing at his puzzled expression. "But you did, and that surprises you?"

"Not so surprising, I suppose," he mused. "I like to hear you play. I *need*—"

He broke off suddenly, and his gaze shifted to the western sky. The sun had sunk low, and the silver ripples of the sea were tipped with sunset pink.

"I had no idea I'd tarried so long," he said as he pushed himself off the deck.

"Stay a while longer," she urged him, smiling. "The water turns such beautiful colors at dusk."

The high elf merely shook his head and hurried toward their shared sleeping quarters. Elizerain rose and stretched, catlike, and the others, seeing that the entertainment was at an end, began to wander off to tend to evening chores.

She stopped in mid-stretch as her gaze fell on something out in the waves.

"What's that?" she demanded, pointing toward the north.

Sweet Tooth squinted in the general direction. "Don't see anything but water. Cymron, bring those hawk's eyes of yours over here!"

The young boatswain hurried over and shaded his eyes with one hand. "I can't make it out," he admitted. "Most likely a bit of flotsam from last night's storm."

But Elizerain's eyes, always keener than a human's, were starting to adjust to the longer distances at sea. "It's a raft," she realized, "or more likely, a piece of wreckage. It looks as if there's a man lying on it. Yes, I'm sure there is!"

She turned expectantly to the sailors and was met with a bland stare.

"Shouldn't we pick him up?" she said, incredulous at this apparent lack of concern. "Isn't there a code of the sea, or some such thing?"

"You heard tell of a code, Cymron?" asked Sweet Tooth, grinning broadly at the notion.

The boatswain, an exceptionally humorless lad, gave the question serious consideration. "When you say 'code,' do you mean a cipher? There's some captains what use ciphers in their ships' logs, so's other people can't read what's writ."

Elizerain tried again. "What if it was one of you out there?"

"Offhand, I'd say we'd be buggered but good," concluded Sweet Tooth. Two passing sailors guffawed and slapped their knees.

"Fact is, there's no gain in it," the boatswain offered bluntly.

"Mayhap there's some gold in his teeth worth picking out," she said, sarcasm dripping from every word.

The sailors exchanged glances, shrugged, and started to untie the lines to the old rowboat.

"It is impossible to underestimate the paucity of human character," murmured Xander.

Elizabeth jumped, startled by her old friend's voice so close to her ear. In her concern for the shipwrecked man, she had not heard the ranger approach.

"Well, in you go, lass," Sweet Tooth said cheerfully, gesturing to the rickety little craft.

The bard stared at him.

He sent her a gap-toothed grin. "You want him so bad, you go get him."

"I'll do it," Xander said quickly.

Elizerain shot the ranger a quelling glance. "No offense, but you swim like a stone."

Before he could argue, she climbed into the little boat and gripped the sides with white-knuckled hands as the sailors lowered her in short, jerky bursts.

Elizerain quickly untied the ropes and rowed purposefully toward the makeshift raft. It took several moments to get the feel of the oars—how deep to dip, how hard to pull—and the going was harder than she'd anticipated.

The water was still rough from yesterday's storms. Waves splashed over the low sides of the boat, stinging her with cold, salty spray. But she threw all her strength into the task, mindful that these same waves could easily capsize the raft. Once she had the man safely aboard, she'd worry about bailing out the water that already lapped at her ankles.

The man sprawled face down, one hand trailing limply in the water; but Elizerain noted with relief the slight movements of shoulders and ribcage. He was still breathing, whatever his hurts might be. He was bigger than she'd expected—humans often tended to be—and further weighted down by layers of dark, heavy clothes. She pulled alongside and got a good grip on his cloak.

By Tunare, humans were heavy! Elizerain tugged and pulled, trying to roll him over the low side of the rowboat. She might have managed, had not a particularly large wave caught her boat and sent her pitching forward. The rowboat capsized, spilling them both into the sea.

The cold water closed over her in a rush. Ignoring the salty sting, she opened her eyes and looked about for the shipwrecked man. There was no sign of him.

Small wonder—she was small and slim, lightly clad, and had been raised to swim like a river otter, whereas the man was much larger, a dead weight further weighted down by his clothes. Before she could worry overmuch about whether or not she had the strength to drag him to the surface, Elizerain flipped in the water and began to swim straight down.

She didn't need to go far, for her seeking hands tangled in the long, floating strands of his hair. As she drew him up, his eyes snapped open and stared into hers.

Even in the dark water, she could see that his eyes were pale blue, cold as the sea itself.

And very, very familiar.

For a long moment, Elizerain stared into the face of the necromancer who had cursed her.

NEWS TRAVELED FROM KELETHIN TO FELWITHE ON swift feet—usually, quite literally. Messages of great urgency, however, were sent through magical means, often to a room deep within the Arcane School. Niola Impholder spent long hours in that room, neither eating nor sleeping, as she awaited word of her son.

Finally she was sent home by a small delegation of concerned wizards and magicians. By then Niola had become too weary to argue, and in truth there was really no point in doing so. Runners from the Arcane School came and went at all hours, and any delay in receiving a message would be slight. So she returned to her home and did her best to resume something resembling a normal routine.

Still, the days crept by. Just as Niola was certain she would go mad if another silent day slipped into sleepless night, the chime that announced an Arcane School runner sounded through her entry hall. She ran to the door and all but snatched the scroll from the messenger's hands.

His sympathetic smile forgave her, and he accepted without comment the circlet of blue pearls she drew off her wrist and pressed into his hand. Later, he would see the bracelet properly returned—no runner would accept such a valuable token—but this was hardly the time to trouble Lady Impholder with trifling concerns.

Niola hurried up to Nyson's rooms. She had been spending some of her hours there, first in an attempt to learn more about her son's recent activities and then in an effort to feel his presence. She sank down into a chair beside a small, ornately carved writing table and unrolled the scroll with trembling fingers.

Xander's first words filled her with joy and relief. Her son was safely out of Crushbone!

Nyson's quest, however, had not met with success, for the elf woman he sought was dead.

Niola lowered the parchment and lifted her eyes to the window. Nyson's rooms afforded a view of the towers of the Arcane School, where Cyntharia Starflower had taught. The lovely young enchanter had been very gifted, and her loss would be felt.

No doubt Nyson felt it far more keenly. First love was never easy, however it ended.

Niola read on: *It is with deep regret that I inform you of Nyson's deception. No information about Elizerain Greenleaf's red harp was to be found in the treasure trove beneath Crushbone. Nyson deliberately misled her, hoping to add the services of a bard to his little band of adventurers.*

A pang of guilt smote Niola. She had suspected it at the time; indeed, she had welcomed the opportunity to ensure that more seasoned elves accompanied her son.

I beg your discretion concerning the treasure trove, which not only exists but surpasses legend. It seems likely the orcs are aware of it, but they are making little headway toward finding a passage. I agree that future secret forays into the orc citadel to ascertain progress would be prudent, but the fewer ears that hear this tale, the fewer greedy adventurers will die on orc weapons.

Niola frowned. That was a concern she had not considered. Nyson's three friends knew he was bound for Crushbone, as did the elves in Kelethin who heard the riddle his "spell" had yielded. His return to Felwithe would raise much speculation.

I will not abandon Elizerain with her quest unfinished. Since my duty demands that I continue to guard your son, he will accompany us. I am sure you will agree this is the most honorable course for all concerned.

Niola couldn't deny that, but the dull burning just below her ribs—her constant companion since the events of the Songweavers' Feast—flared into bright heat.

She reached for the decanter that held the soothing potion she'd been sipping throughout her days and nights and poured a small portion into a goblet. Her hands were still unsteady, however, and a bit of the precious liquid spilled onto the table.

As she wiped it away, she felt a small, subtle movement under her fingers and heard a faint *click*. A hidden drawer slid soundlessly open, revealing a slim book bound in night-blue leather.

Curious, Niola opened the little tome and began to page through it. It was Nyson's personal grimoire, filled with pages of precise runes. With growing amazement and pride, she read spell after spell that her son had mastered—spells far beyond the level of mastery he would have been expected to achieve during a comparable time in the Arcane School. Not only was he precocious, he was creative. There were several new spells that he and Cyntharia had devised together.

The final entry, however, stole the proud smile from Niola's face. She read the spell again, slowly, and then a third time, hoping against hope that she had been mistaken.

At last she returned the book to the drawer, which she slammed shut hard enough to set the potion bottle rocking crazily. It fell to the floor, where it shattered with a tinkling crash. Niola spared it neither thought nor glance.

"It is well that you are dead, Cyntharia Starflower," she murmured in a voice she barely recognized as her own, "for otherwise I would kill you myself."

20

Dead Until Dawn

ELIZERAIN STARED INTO THE FACE OF THE MAN who'd cursed her, too stunned to move. Before she could recover from the shock of recognition, the necromancer seized her belt and began to drag her toward the surface.

They rose through the cold sea with effortless, impossible speed. As soon as they broke the surface, he slung her face down over the capsized rowboat. He seized her chin with long, strong fingers and turned her face toward his.

"It *is* you. Well, I suppose I should thank you for the 'rescue,' as I was beginning to wonder if those two-copper pirates were planning to just sail on by."

Elizerain twisted free of the necromancer's grasp and spat a mouthful of sea water in his general direction. "I should have let them."

"Oh, I think not. I know other ways to draw attention, none of them as subtle as this."

He glanced toward the *Prawnbane* and smiled. "Ah,

splendid. They're coming around and sailing this way. A pity the captain will never know the fate he just averted."

Elizerain glanced toward the trawler, which was indeed coming their way. "Why are you following me?"

"At least you're bright enough to realize our meeting is no coincidence. That is heartening."

The calculation in his ice-blue eyes was starting to unnerve her. "If you've come for me, you should know there are people aboard that ship who might have other ideas."

"Those people needn't know what passes between you and me. If you don't speak up, they'll be none the wiser."

"I won't lie to them."

"Not even to save their lives?" He reached into his sodden tunic and pulled out a slender black tube, a miniature version of a seaman's glass. "This will enable you to see through the cloaking illusion on my ship. Look to the east."

Elizerain took the glass and raised it to one eye, sweeping the horizon. A shimmer on the water suddenly began to take on substance, like a ghost materializing from shadow and moonlight.

It was a ship, all right, and an impressive one. Red runes on the black-painted hull proclaimed the ship to be the *Sea Witch*. The sails on three masts swung loosely in the wind, needing only a slight leeward turn and a quick tightening of ropes to send the ship into sea-skimming flight. The *Sea Witch* looked to be heavily armed; Elizerain could even see what appeared to be a giant ballista mounted in the stern.

She flung the glass into the sea, where it landed with a satisfying *plop*. "What do you want from me?"

"As it happens, I require the services of a bard."

"To what end?"

"That is hardly your concern. Swear that you will do as I say, and I will lift the curse."

"An unknown price usually ends up being far too high," Elizerain observed.

"Nevertheless, that is my offer."

"In that case, never mind. I can handle myself."

His gaze sharpened. "Can you? Are you willing to risk that any song you sing, any tale you tell, might be false, or even less than the whole truth? I see three choices before you: enter my employ, give up barding, or be dead before the new moon."

That last thought seemed to please him, for a cruel smile curved his lips.

Elizerain suppressed a shudder and spoke with a bravado she did not feel. "Looking for your next dead bard, are you?"

The necromancer's smile disappeared. "If I wanted a singing meat puppet, I would have kept Manarla Willowmere around. Her voice was far superior to yours, you know. In all fairness, she should have won the competition."

"And she might have, if you hadn't killed her."

The necromancer shrugged aside this accusation with extreme indifference. "You heard the ballad Manarla sang. I would like to hear it sung with harp accompaniment. A simple matter, one might think, but have you any idea how difficult it is to find a harp-playing bard?"

Under most circumstances, this topic lay near to Elizerain's heart. At the moment, however, her thoughts were busy with more pressing questions.

"How did you follow me?" she wondered. "Was it the curse spell? Does that leave a . . . a *scent* of some sort? Or was it the harp? It's the harp, isn't it? Manarla sang of a blood red harp, and you were angry about the song I made up about mine. The instruments are one and the same, aren't they?"

Then a new, terrible thought occurred to her. "*You're* the spell-caster in that dreadful ballad she sang!"

He had the nerve to look affronted. "What was wrong with the ballad?"

"Apart from being long enough to try the patience of a dwarf?"

By now the ship had pulled up alongside. Ropes dropped into the sea beside them. Elizerain tied them to one side of the rowboat.

"What are you doing?" the necromancer demanded.

"You don't think they'd pull us up and leave the boat, do you? Just hope they toss out a second line, after."

But the necromancer was not willing to take this chance. He took a firm grip on the rowboat with one hand and Elizerain with the other. They rose from the sea in sharp, jerky bursts. Leathery, sun-browned hands dragged them over the rail—after the small boat had been secured.

"Where is the captain?" the necromancer demanded as soon as his feet touched deck. He pulled a fine onyx and silver ring from his hand and held it up. "I wish to thank him for my rescue and pay for my passage."

The captain, a laconic man who kept mostly to the wheel, ceded his place to the mate and ambled over in the peculiar rolling gait of one who was seldom ashore. He swept a measuring eye over the newcomer.

"Your name and business?"

"Chanzoon Nexis is my name, and my business is my own," the necromancer said firmly. "Fortunately for me, Captain Ambrosh Saltwind is known to respect the privacy of his passengers."

The captain lifted one shaggy eyebrow, and his gaze sharpened. "We've not met, I'm thinking."

"No, but I have heard your name spoken by certain reliable, confidential sources." Chanzoon held out the ring. "Provide me with safe passage and discretion, and you shall have another ring like this one when we reach port."

The captain took the ring and examined the large stone. "A fair price," he admitted.

"Then we have a deal. Where are we bound?"

"Westward. Butcherblock Mountains."

"That is satisfactory. As it turns out, I have business in western Faydwer. Two things more: I shall require private quarters, and I would like to engage the services of a bard for some confidential business of my own. If you have one aboard, I will make it worth your while as well as his."

All eyes turned to Elizerain.

"She'll do it," announced a gruff female voice. "And you'll settle up with me."

Chanzoon locked stares with the big ogress. A small, strange smile crept over his face. "Very well. Now if someone will show me and the bard to my cabin?"

"Take them to mine," the captain said gruffly. "I'm never there."

Xander pushed his way through the knot of sailors

gathered around the dripping newcomer, placing himself firmly between the necromancer and Elizerain.

"Captives we elves might be, but we will not stand quietly by while any one of us is mistreated."

He spoke quietly, but something in his face made the sailors fall back a pace or two. The necromancer, however, burst into scornful laughter.

"I've no designs on the wench, if that is your concern. I have trouble sleeping, that is all, and find it helpful to have soft music playing to ease my thoughts. It is difficult for me to sleep under the best of circumstances, and after so harrowing an ordeal as a shipwreck . . ."

"I'll do it," Elizerain said curtly. "Let me dry off and get my harp."

She spun away and stalked toward the back of the trawler. Xander fell into step with her.

"Elizerain, this is not wise," he said in low, urgent tones. "That is the man who accompanied Manarla Willowmere into the tavern that first night of the Songweavers' Feast."

"I know."

Something about her tone stopped him in mid-stride. He seized her arm and spun her to face him. "Is that—"

Elizerain cut him off by planting a kiss firmly on his lips. "Yes," she said softly as she slipped an arm around his waist and turned him toward the hold. "That's him, the necromancer who cursed me. Don't look back, don't give even a hint that you know who he is. He's got a warship following us, under a cloaking spell of some sort."

The ranger scowled, but he did not pull away. "A warship," he said scornfully. "I've had sharper swords at my throat. The necromancer can hardly order it to sink us when he's aboard."

"You'd think," she agreed, "but really, if he can cast a cloaking spell that can conceal an entire ship, who knows what *else* he can do?"

Xander acknowledged this point with a short, grim silence. "What does he want with you?"

"Mayhap he's repented his evil ways and has come to lift the curse," she said lightly.

"Unlikely, but it does raise another question: *how* has he found you?"

"The spell he cast upon me probably leaves a trail. Who knows for sure? But I don't see I have much choice but to play along."

They stopped at the ladder that led down into their tiny sleeping quarters. Elizerain gestured for Xander to precede her, then scampered down after him.

Nyson was not yet in his hammock; most likely he was brooding in the cargo hold again. Since they'd come on board, he'd spent much of each night amid the kegs and sacks or standing at the rail, staring out to sea. He claimed he couldn't sleep and said he wished to be alone. He'd acted much the same during their time in the tunnels, and they'd left him to deal with his grief in his own way.

Elizerain peeled off her wet clothes and dug through a small chest holding items left by previous occupants. There she found a white chemise that looked as if it might fit and a red leather stomacher that was sized for a human child. She pulled the flowing garment over her head and quickly cinched it around her waist with the wide belt. Xander, she noted with a grin, had carefully averted his eyes during this process. At any other time, she would have delighted in teasing him, but . . .

She sighed and untied the cords that fastened down the harp. "Might as well get this over with."

Xander turned to face her. "Is there nothing I can say to dissuade you?"

Her smile was wistful. "You know, I really wish there was."

With that, she hurried up the ladder, tripping once or twice on the unfamiliar skirts.

Chanzoon Nexis awaited her in the tiny cabin, dressed in the same clothes—albeit dry, clean, and pressed. His dark cloak hung neatly on a peg.

"That's a good trick," she commented, nodding toward the dry cloak. Without waiting for a response, she plunked herself down on the narrow bed and folded her legs under her. "So, tell me about the harp."

"You heard the ballad," he said stiffly.

Something about his reaction prompted a strange thought. "And if someone were to cast a truth spell during the singing of that ballad?"

The expression on the necromancer's face told her that her shot had found its target.

"I *thought* I heard the ring of wishful thinking in that tale!" she crowed. "You can usually tell when a poet is creating some grandiose version of himself."

She sobered abruptly. "Why did you curse me to seek out the story behind my harp, if you knew yours was not the true version? And why did you make up a story about it in the first place?"

"I have my reasons," Chanzoon replied coolly. "They need not concern you now. At the moment, I would like you to learn a rather rare bard-spell, one that requires a harp as accompanying instrument."

Elizerain had never heard of such a spell. She eagerly took the parchment he offered her and smoothed it out. The spell was ancient, inscribed in faded ink on vellum that passing years had turned a deep shade of gold. The writing style was also archaic, but after a few moments of study she found she could make out the words and melody.

She attended herself to the melody first, humming it softly until she had affixed it in memory. No easy task—it was a strange melody with odd leaps and a jagged, ever-changing rhythm. Mastering it took time, and only then did she read the words, silently mouthing them in the odd cadence demanded by the tune.

Finally she raised her gaze to the necromancer's face. "This is a terrible spell," she said in hushed tones. "I don't think I can cast it."

His lips twisted in a sneer. "What, freedom from this curse is not sufficient inducement to cast away your scruples?"

"Well, there's that, but what I meant is that I don't think I *can* cast it. It's a very difficult spell."

He waved her hesitation away impatiently. "Your skill on the harp is remarkable. Any bard who has reached that level of achievement on an instrument should be able to cast this spell handily."

"It doesn't work that way," she said miserably. "As you've observed, few bards bother with the harp. I played the harp for years and years before I thought about being a bard. This skill was of no use to me in the Songweavers' Guild, so I started the same way any between-age elf might begin: singing and playing simple rhythm accompaniments on a hand drum."

"But you *are* a bard, and you play the harp exceedingly well. Aren't you curious to see whether or not your skill with the harp will enable you to cast a high-level spell? For that matter, don't you wish to know whether or not a harp *can* be used to cast bardic magic?"

Elizerain had already answered the latter question when she cast the healing spell on Nyson, but she saw no reason why the necromancer needed to know that. His other question, however, intrigued her.

"So it's possible that I'm not just a beginning bard," she said slowly, "but one who possesses real power."

"What you hold in your hands could answer that question."

Elizerain considered the old scroll. "I suppose there's no harm in trying it. It's one of those spells that doesn't . . . *happen* until the caster says the key word."

She looked up sharply. "That's it, isn't it? You want me to learn this spell and have it ready to cast. You want me to kill someone for you."

"I'm quite capable of handling such matters on my own," he said dryly. "You, on the other hand, would do well to have a spell or two of last resort. If you are going to stay alive long enough to be of use to me, you will need better defenses."

"But melting the bones in a person's arms and legs?"

"What better way to stop an attacker, short of killing him? And if killing is your goal, the spell greatly simplifies that task." His expression hardened. "Enough talk. Do it."

The cold command in his last words had Elizerain reaching for her harp before she had time to think it over. When she hesitated, the telltale itch and tingle began to crawl over her scalp.

She bent over the harp and began to play and sing the strange melody. Sharp, dark energy flowed through her veins the moment her fingers touched the strings. It built into a potent tension, like a longbow drawn taut and ready to fire.

Finally she set aside the instrument. The power of the spell drifted to the back of her mind. It was undoubtedly ready to unleash, but the urge to do so was no longer quite so imperative.

Chanzoon lifted one elegant black brow. "Well?"

"It worked," she said curtly.

He nodded in satisfaction, and a peculiar expression crossed his face. "Your performance was unexpectedly . . . stirring. I think perhaps you will stay a little longer."

Without warning, he reached for the neckline of her chemise and dragged her off the bed, using both hands to draw her to him in a sudden, powerful jerk. Before she could react, he ripped the thin garment to the waist. The single word he spoke was lost in the sound of tearing cloth.

Elizerain's first impulse was to snatch the torn edges of the chemise together. That surprised her, for she was not particularly modest. But she *was* practical and as a result had learned a dozen ways of turning aside unwanted male attentions.

Try as she might, she could call upon none of these well-practiced attacks. She couldn't lift her hands to the neckline of her chemise. Her bare feet seemed to be nailed to the floor. Her body adamantly refused to obey her urgent, silent commands.

Chanzoon moved away from her, leaning against the wall and observing her fruitless struggles with a smile of cool amusement. When he lifted one hand and flicked off a casual gesture, her hands at last began to move.

A will not her own lifted her hands to her chemise and made them drift slowly apart, spreading the torn garment. Her clenched fingers opened, flexed, and reached for the ties on the red leather belt. Another gesture from the necromancer, and her treacherous hands began to undo the ties.

"Stop it," she said through clenched teeth.

His eyebrows rose. "Interesting. You're the first person I've encountered who could speak while under this particular compulsion spell. Let's see what else you can resist."

Despite Elizerain's best efforts to stop them, her hands kept moving, steadily and surely. The leather belt dropped to the floor, quickly followed by the ruined garment.

But the necromancer was not yet done with her. A shimmer of lust rippled through her, a dark and ugly shiver that was equal parts terror, hatred, and madness. Elizerain had never experienced its like—had not known such ugly feelings could exist.

A wave of pure fury followed—an emotion that was entirely her own and more powerful than anything the necromancer could impose on her. It carried away the dark sickness, leaving her trembling with wrath.

"I'll kill you," she said softly. "By Tunare's sacred blood, I swear it."

Chanzoon laughed, softly and mockingly, and raised his hand to command yet another humiliating surrender.

He never got that far. Acting more on instinct than intent, Elizerain spit out the harsh, foreign word that launched the dreadful spell.

Power burst from her, and the backlash was enough to tear her from the necromancer's magical grasp and send her reeling backward. She hit the wall hard and slumped to the floor, watching with mingled horror and triumph as Chanzoon Nexis melted into a screaming, writhing puddle of human agony.

ELIZERAIN WOKE SUDDENLY AND FOUND HERSELF looking up into three concerned faces.

She was back in her hammock, wrapped in a blanket. Xander, Nyson, and Trobe were gazing down at her with a fixed stare that made them look oddly akin to a trio of curious cats.

"What happened?" she mumbled.

"Might be you could tell us," Trobe suggested gruffly. "They heard the human hollering and ran in to find you mother-naked, beating him senseless with the captain's ale tankard."

"I really did that?" she said, not sure whether to be alarmed or gratified by this news.

"That and more," Trobe said approvingly. "Could fairly be said that you were a mite riled up. Took the three of us to drag you off the bugger."

Memory returned to her in a sickening rush. "Did he have bones in his arms and legs?"

Her three guardians exchanged quick, wary glances. "We saw no reason to suspect otherwise," Nyson said cautiously.

"None of 'em were out in the open, so to speak," the dwarf added. "But he was moving around well enough. More's the pity."

"What happened?" Xander asked, his eyes searching her face.

"I'm not exactly sure," Elizerain said slowly. "He taught me a bard-spell. An attack spell he said was for my own defense. Then he . . . made me angry, so I used it on him."

Nyson frowned. "That probably wasn't wise."

The dwarf's hand found hers and gave it a little squeeze. "Maybe not," he said bracingly, "but I'm guessing it was damn satisfying."

THAT NIGHT ELIZERAIN LAY AWAKE FOR A LONG time, and sleep, when at last it came, was an uneasy and restless visitor.

She was dimly aware that she was asleep and dreaming, but that knowledge only served to make her dreams more disturbing. At the moment she was on a raft in the middle of the sea, surrounded by undrinkable water. Her throat burned with thirst.

Suddenly, inexplicably, a rat scurried by. She could hear the soft, swift percussion of its heart, like raindrops falling on leaves. She snatched up the creature, moving faster than she would have thought possible, seizing it by the scruff of its neck.

For a long moment, bard and rodent stared at each other. A sound like rising surf pounded through Elizerain's head, matching the rhythm of the living blood pulsing beneath her fingers. The thirst rose in her like an overwhelming lust.

Then the rat twisted in her grasp and sank its long yellow teeth into the soft web of flesh between her thumb and forefinger. The disturbing spell broke, and Elizerain woke to find herself sitting on the floor of the hold, a ship rat squirming in her hand and blood running down her arm.

Elizerain yelped and dropped the creature, which promptly scuttled away.

The small disturbance brought Xander awake. He leaned from his hammock, staring down in puzzlement at the bard. She scrambled to her feet, keeping her wounded hand behind her.

"I fell from the hammock," she said with a shrug. "Bad dream."

He nodded gravely. "Considering the evening you spent and the company we're keeping, it's a wonder any of us can sleep."

"Aye," she agreed hastily, hoping he'd accept that explanation as the whole story. "There's no hope for me tonight, but you should rest if you can."

Not waiting for his reply, she snatched up her harp—apparently one of her friends had thought to retrieve it from the captain's cabin—and climbed the ladder to the deck.

Other than two or three sailors on night crew, the deck was deserted. A fat gibbous moon rose high above the water. The moon-cast shadows of mast and forecastle, keg and high-piled ropes were long, ghostly things that seemed to move about the silent ship on some secret business of their own.

Elizerain found a place between a stout coil of rope and a barrel of pitch and settled down to play. Her fingers moved without an act of will on her part. After a few moments, she began to sing in a voice that was barely above a whisper:

Sing it ever more softly, and slow the cadence
Until rhythm fades away, as imperceptibly
As day yields itself to darkness.

Do not fear the night.
There is more music in silence than you know,
And more to life than a single day's death.

Remember the melody; you'll soon sing along
with the Dawnwalker's story: merely dead until dawn.

In the captain's cabin, a perfectly whole and healthy Chanzoon Nexis listened, a slow smile spreading across his face. It seemed that the harp did indeed reveal its legend, provided it was played long and well enough. And apparently Elizerain Greenleaf played well enough, despite her unconventional approach to bard-craft.

The elf girl had surprised him more than once this night. Oh, not with her ability to speak through the compulsion spell. Whatever he might have said, that was expected and planned. He'd taken her for a shallow, ambitious wench, for wasn't she a bard? And what female of character would espouse a man like Davin the Dark?

Yet Elizerain had risked herself to rescue what she thought was a drowning man. She had faced him alone, rather than confide in her friends and risk their safety.

In fact, she showed a rather incomprehensible regard for the value of life. Chanzoon had expected her to unleash the "disabling spell" the moment he dragged her off the bed. It had taken far more goading than he'd expected to get her to strike out at him.

The memory of that careful manipulation, that web of spell within spell, that mingling of illusion and compulsion, brought a smile to his face. He'd planned it out, to the last detail—even to covering the fact that magic was used at all.

Sailors were notoriously wary of necromancers, so he'd presented a scenario they could understand: a man alone with a maid had given in to temptation, and his advances had been soundly rejected. He would no doubt bear the brunt of whispered jests and sly smiles for the rest of the journey, but the opinions of ignorant sailors were nothing to him.

What mattered, *all* that mattered, was claiming the power of the blood red harp.

A wry smile curved the necromancer's lips. Given the bard's unwonted respect for life, it was well that he'd manipulated her into casting a spell on him *before* she learned too much about the harp!

21

Sky Stones

An elf woman slipped through the shadows of Faydark, swift and silent as any forest creature. Yet if any elf could be said to look out of place amid these trees, it would be she.

She was clad not in the practical garb of the wood elves, but in diaphanous skirts of delicate pale blue silk and a short, belly-baring tunic of the same hue, richly embroidered with silver thread. She wore slippers of buttery soft leather dyed to match and decorated with blue seed pearls. Her flaxen hair fell over bared shoulders in thick, shining waves. With her pale gold complexion and blue, blue eyes, she looked like a bit of sky and sunshine, inexplicably fallen to the forest floor, undimmed by the deep green gloom.

The high elf made her way to the base of an ancient tree and sank down to rest on a deep cushion of moss. She leaned back against the tree and closed her eyes. Her face, which was lovely but taut with watchfulness, began to relax as she drifted toward slumber.

The crack of a broken twig jarred her from her

reverie. She looked up into the face of an exceptionally large and ugly orc. Broad as an ogre and heavily muscled, he was also amply fleshed. A prodigious belly rolled over his weapons belt, and a gray-green droop of jowls framed a trio of chins. Yet the creature was undoubtedly powerful, and he held a well-tended sword with the air of one well versed in its use. He loomed over her, so close that the elf could smell the carrion stench of his breath.

She rose calmly to her feet and faced the orc down.

"Tell me," she commanded.

"Ogress has weapons and treasure. Dwarf bring, just like he said." The creature shook his ugly head in wonderment at the concept of a trustworthy dwarf. "He go on ship with ogress."

"And the elves?"

"Them, too. All happen just as you say."

"You've done very well."

There was dismissal in the elf's tone, but the orc lingered, shifting his weight from one foot to the other as he weighed his next words.

"You take off make-do magic now?" he said tentatively.

"Not just yet," she said. "But I will release you from this compulsion spell soon, this I promise."

The big orc's shoulders rose and fell in resignation. "You pay now," he countered, thrusting out his hand. His small, porcine eyes dropped to the glittering bracelet on her wrist.

The elf undid the clasp. For a moment she held the bracelet up, turning it so that the sky blue gems and delicate silver filigree sparkled in the faint light. Something almost like regret crossed her face, but she dropped the delicate bracelet into the orc's outstretched hand without further hesitation. After a moment, she took a matching ring from one slender finger.

"Since I've already given you necklace and bracelet," she said as she handed over the ring, "you might as well have the whole set."

GRIB PICKED HIS WAY ALONG THE HALF-SUBMERGED rocks that formed a walkway to the pirate dock, a large, free-floating raft towed close to Faydwer's northern shore at certain times and places, according to a complicated pattern that law-loving types had yet to fathom.

To his relief, the *Rusty Cutlass* had yet to weigh anchor. The sleek vessel, notable for her red-and-white-striped sails—and the false floor in her cargo hold—was docked beside the seaward side of the platform. A few men milled about on the dock, making trades and loading goods on and off the ship.

There was no sign of Davin, but then, there wouldn't be. No doubt the bandit chieftain was already aboard, throwing dice with the sailors or tumbling a wench on a bed of stolen pelts.

The thought brought a gap-toothed smile to Grib's face. He lived well, did Davin, which was one of the reasons Grib had followed him for these many years.

And follow he would. Davin had told him not to come, but Grib figured a man stood by his friends whether they wanted him to or not.

Besides, wouldn't it be fine to feel the salt spray on his face again?

A familiar figure swung lightly over the side of the ship and walked with a bouncing stride down the plank that served as a walkway between the raft and the *Cutlass*.

Grib knew the sailor at once by the red-and-white-striped bandanna he wore on his head. Proud of his ship, and rightly so. He'd been a cabin boy when Grib first sailed with him, and he'd worked his way up to mate.

"Hail, Weasel," the old bandit called out.

The man looked up. Weasel was well named: a sharp-featured man of about 40, exceptionally lean, and as brown as the animal he resembled. A smile of recognition creased his face—vastly increasing his resemblance to that sly animal—and he raised a hand in greeting.

"Hail yourself, Grib!" he bellowed. He crossed the distance in a few long-legged strides and struck the old bandit a companionable blow across the back. "What brings a Greenleaf to the wharf? Run out of land-loving folk to rob?"

"What brings a Greenleaf here?" the bandit repeated, incredulous. "Davin's not aboard? Davin the Dark? Big man, curly hair?"

Weasel grimaced. "I know the man, better than I'd like, and no, he's not aboard."

"You're sure?" Grib pressed.

The pirate let out a burst of humorless laughter. "He owes me money. You think I wouldn't leap at the chance to collect?"

At last the old man nodded, convinced. But his puzzlement remained. "He told me he'd taken the notion to sign on. Said you folks were looking for hired swords."

"Well, that last part is true enough. Maybe he ran into trouble on the way."

"He usually does. That don't stop him from getting where he wants to go."

Even as the words passed his lips, Grib knew the answer. Davin had never intended to take the pirate ship westward. Oh, he'd find his way to Elizerain, but on a different path. Most likely he knew Grib would follow the trail he'd marked out and was counting on the ship having set sail before the older bandit could reach the dock. And while Grib was off chasing shadows, Davin was slipping away to tend to business, alone.

Not bloody likely.

The bandit squared his shoulders. "You want my sword, it's yours."

Weasel slid a measuring eye down the older man, noting his sinewy muscle and well-honed weapons. "You're a good man in a fight, but you haven't been to sea for long years. We'll take you on at half-share."

The offer bordered on insult, but Grib didn't care. "Keep your coins, and never mind my share of booty. I'll sail for return passage. For two." He remembered Elizerain, and added, "Better make that three. Fighters all."

Weasel didn't even try to keep the delighted grin from his face. "Done. Here's my hand on it, before you come to your senses."

The pirates spat in their palms and sealed the deal. Grib followed his old comrade up the plank, as surefooted as a squirrel on a tree limb.

He set to work alongside a pair of younger men, hauling boxes down to the cargo hold. The roll of the deck beneath his feet felt pleasantly familiar, and the sharp scent of salt air, wet rope, and stale bodies carried him effortlessly back across the gap of years.

Yet as the ship pulled away from the floating dock, he paused to gaze back at the green shore. The strangest feeling assailed him, and as he stood there, a cask of greenberry cordial in his arms, a silent voice spoke words for his ears alone.

Grib was not a superstitious man, and he gave the gods no more than their due, but at that moment he believed the truth of those words:

He was seeing the Faydark for the last time.

The old bandit shoved the cask into the arms of a passing sailor, ignoring his protests. He went to the rail and gripped it with gnarled fingers. There he stood, eyes fixed upon the diminishing shore, until the sea mist closed around the ship and there was nothing to see but the endless silvery gray of sea and sky.

NIOLA IMPHOLDER STARED AT THE RING HER SERvant had just dropped into her open palm, a thick gold band set with a single large emerald. This ring had been one of Nyson's favorites. It had been his father's, and Niola had never seen it off her son's hand since the day his father had died.

"A human brought it," the elf maid said tentatively. "He wishes to speak with you but would not give his name. I wasn't sure what to do, so I bid him wait in the entry hall."

"You did well, Finlea. Give me a moment and then send him in."

Niola took the time to compose her thoughts and gather up the papers she'd been studying. She was shutting them away in the writing table drawer when the human came to the open door of her study.

He was a large man, nearly tall and broad enough to fill the doorway. Dusty from what appeared to have been a hard journey and smelling faintly of horse, he was nonetheless of good appearance. Curly brown hair spilled over the collar of his forest green tunic, which was of good cut and cloth. His boots and weapons appeared to be of good elf-craft, and gold glinted on his fingers. His smile was practiced, confident, and no doubt many females found it charming. Niola, however, was utterly unmoved.

"May I know your name?"

He dropped into a low bow, complete with hand flourish. "Davin the Dark, at your command."

The high elf leaned back in her chair and folded her hands on the table. "Quite the opposite, I should think. What can I do for you?"

He straightened and treated her to another roguish smile. "First, allow me to apologize for sending you young Nyson's ring without a word of explanation. I wasn't sure you'd agree to see me unless I caught your interest."

His familiar use of Nyson's name set Niola's teeth on edge. "You've accomplished your purpose. What do you know of my son?"

Davin sank down into a chair without waiting to be asked. "He was alive and well last time I saw him. And in case you're wondering, he gave me the ring in exchange for some gems he liked better: an unusual necklace made of sky stones in a fancy silver setting."

Niola kept her face impassive, but the effort cost her. The human had just described a family heirloom, which passed to Nyson with the understanding that he would bestow it upon the elf woman he wished to wed.

A thousand questions danced on her tongue, but none that she dared ask a human rogue.

She held out the ring. "Then this is yours, fairly bought."

"I'll take it in trade," he said, taking the ring from her hand and replacing it with a tightly folded note.

The magician's heart leaped as she recognized the

Watcher's seal on paper made from beaten sea grass. Another message from Xander Fletcher?

She unfolded the note and saw at a glance that it was no second missive. Rather, it held the information that had been sent to her magically from Kelethin and much, much more. And it was written in the Watcher's own hand.

She lifted her eyes to the rogue's face. "How did you come by this?"

"I found it on the body of a young elf, lying just off the main path. It looked important, so I sent the news about your son on to Kelethin, along with some other bits and pieces. The rest I thought I'd deliver in person."

This visit was beginning to make sense. "What do you want?" she said bluntly.

One side of the human's lips lifted slightly, turning the well-rehearsed smile into something wry and bitter and completely genuine.

"Ever been in debt, my lady?"

"Never," she said firmly. "I pay as I go."

The rogue's eyebrows shot up. "Well now, that might work for some. If I followed that plan, I'd be long dead."

The high elf took a deep breath and a firm grip on her patience. "So you want money."

"I didn't say that. Not every debt can be paid with coins and gems."

Niola studied him, beginning to be interested despite her better judgment. "Go on."

"Sounds to me like the dwarves of Kaladim are going to need some help."

She had come to the same conclusion when she read Xander's message. If the ogres of the Butcherblock Mountains united, they could be a formidable force. At first opportunity, she would hasten to the high elf king and lay this out before him. But that was hardly information a stranger and human needed to know.

So she lifted her chin and said in her haughtiest voice, "The dwarves will manage."

"And what of young Nyson? Are you just going to wish him well and hope for the best?"

Niola kept her gaze steady. "He is no stranger to the sword. I am quite sure he will acquit himself well."

Davin nodded approvingly. "Good. Glad to hear it. I'd hate to see a fine city like Felwithe laid waste."

"What threat is this?" she demanded.

The human leaned to one side and draped one arm casually over the back of his chair. "Well now, that's the question, isn't it? Does it seem likely to you that the Crushbone orcs would let an ogress come and go, unless it serves some purpose of their own?"

"Since you've read this message, you should know the answer to that question," she pointed out. "According to Xander Fletcher, the ogress was charged with weakening the dwarves' defenses of Kaladim."

Davin leaned forward, his eyes intent on hers. "So you think the dark elves have their eyes on Kaladim? Why, then, are they making an alliance with Crushbone? I'm telling you, this business with the ogress is a diversion."

Niola heard the uncomfortable ring of truth in these words but was not quite ready to admit it. "So you're an expert on tactics?" she said coolly.

"I'm a scoundrel," Davin said bluntly. "I know how to separate people from their treasures, play them for fools. Long years of practice have sharpened my eye, and I can usually tell a game when I see it."

The high elf sat in silence for several long moments.

"Assuming you are right, why do you bring this information to me?"

"Because we have a common concern," he said softly. "Nyson is your son, and Elizerain was my wife."

"I see," Niola murmured.

"If I'm right, you can't afford to send elf warriors into the Butcherblock Mountains. But you can send me. There must be some sort of magic that will get me there before their ship arrives."

"Forgive me, but what can one man do to turn the tide of battle between ogres and dwarves?"

"Not much," he said forthrightly, "but I can rescue Nyson and Elizerain and get them clear of danger before the fighting starts."

To her shame, Niola found herself actually considering his proposal. This troubling self-knowledge made her answer more sharply than she otherwise might. "I doubt my son would agree to walk such a craven path."

"Even if he knows he's being used to lure elves away from the forest? Seems to me his duty is to get clear of a fight that doesn't concern him and get back to Faydark to join one that does."

Yes, most likely Nyson would heed that tale. If only, Niola thought ruefully, she could be sure it was true!

"You know where their ship will land?"

"Close enough," he assured her. "Can you send me? Now?"

The wizard considered him for a long moment, wondering what had been left untold. "You seem most eager to get on with this."

Davin's lips firmed into a thin line, and his twinkling eyes went flat and cold.

"Let's just say I'd like to find Elizerain before a certain necromancer does."

That, Niola could understand. The rage she'd felt upon discovering the final entry in her son's grimoire burned as brightly as it had when her eyes first fell upon the ugly spell.

"Perhaps," she said slowly, "we might be able to help each other after all."

22

The Dawnwalker

MAGICAL TRAVEL WAS NOT AT ALL WHAT Davin had expected. Not that he'd given the matter much thought, but he'd vaguely assumed it would involve swirling lights, a blast of wind moving impossibly fast, maybe a sensation of falling. The reality was far less dramatic—more like the slight jolt he felt when he awakened suddenly and wasn't quite sure where he was.

And his new elven allies seemed determined to keep him unenlightened as to the details of this particular magic. A dozen or so wood elf warriors crowded around him like a flock of buzzards dedicated to keeping a tasty-looking carcass from getting up and running off. Several of the elves kept hands near the hilts of their weapons, ensuring that Davin's attention was on the circle of warriors around him and not on anything resembling a landmark. The journey involved two stops, with some walking in between, but Davin wouldn't have been able to retrace the path if there'd been a mountain of gemstones at the end to beckon him onward.

He was therefore relieved when they emerged in a

dense forest, a light-filled, brilliantly green place quite unlike Davin's native Faydark. The elves hustled him along at a near-run, slowing only when they reached a hard-trodden footpath.

Davin shouldered his way out of the crowd and stomped over to Regren Steelforger, a captain of Kelethin's elite Emerald Warriors and the leader of this merry band.

"Why didn't you just have your boys blindfold me and be done with it?" he demanded.

The elf blinked in apparent surprise. "That would have been . . . impolite."

"My point exactly," Davin snapped, abandoning sarcasm for plain and heated speech. "In case you've forgotten, this is *my* party. You're just here to help."

"We are here," Regren said evenly, "as a personal favor to Lady Niola Impholder. Your presence is a regrettable necessity. Had you not threatened to raise a general hue and cry if you were *not* included, you would even now be sulking over a tankard in some tavern."

The elf's words confirmed a suspicion Davin had held since his audience with Niola Impholder.

"This isn't an officially sanctioned quest, is it? In fact, I'd wager my best dagger your king knows nothing of this little rescue!"

"That is none of your concern," Regren said sternly.

Davin smirked and folded his arms. "So, what story did you give your superiors? Scouting the outskirts of Faydark for orc activity? Going on pilgrimage to ask Tunare's blessing on the battle to come?"

The elf's only response was to point toward the west. "Follow this path. It will take you to the docks. Learn what you can about those who are holding the elves we seek and report back."

"What about you?"

"We will remain in the forest, of course. A dozen Feir'Dal warriors on the docks might draw attention, whereas a single scruffy human will not."

Davin lifted a hand to his chin and felt the undeniable rasp of a two-day stubble. He shrugged. "I resent that, but I suppose I can't argue with it. Where will I find you?"

"You won't. We'll find you."

It was on the tip of Davin's tongue to remind the elf that he'd spent most of the last four decades hiding from Faydark's elven authorities, thank you very much.

And that, he noted ruefully, was evidence of the bruising his pride had taken of late. Taunting elven law-keepers might provide a momentary salve, but the inglorious career of Davin the Dark was unlikely to continue for long if he flaunted it under the high-held noses of Kelethin's elite guardians.

So the bandit leader merely touched one forefinger to his brow in an ironic salute and set off down the path at an easy run.

After what seemed like hours, the tall, gray stone wall of the dock area loomed up before him. Davin stated his name and business—invented for the occasion, of course—to the pair of stern-faced dwarves at the gate, each of whom, Davin noted, wore a small fortune in chain mail and rune-carved weapons.

Once, he might have tried his light-fingered luck with that small silver mallet on the belt of the brown-bearded dwarf. An "accidental" stumble to distract, a deft flick of a knife against leather straps, an exchange of entertaining insults, and he'd be on his way. Of course, that was before he'd lifted a necromancer's coin purse. Odd, he concluded wryly, how a curse could change a man's outlook.

Davin resolutely pulled his thoughts back to the present and considered the scene spread out before him. The dock area was a strange mixture of marketplace and meadow. Merchants bustled here and there on the broad green expanse. Carts carried goods to and from the ships—two ships at the docks and another coming in. None of them resembled the battered trawler Davin had glimpsed in Grib's sea glass.

As Davin moved closer to the dock, he noted that the walled area was a large half-circle, with both ends of the stout wall extending well out into the sea. The wooden docks had the look of elf-craft—the broad, tightly fitted planks were nearly identical to the platforms of Kelethin—but the stone wall, simply by virtue of being stone, was probably the work of dwarves.

The stout folk were known to protect their interests vigorously: the wall was well patrolled, and Davin noted quite a few heavily armed dwarf guards sauntering through the market. It was just as well he'd resisted the temptation offered by that silver mallet.

Fortunately, he had other vices, and, at the moment, a surfeit of time and coin to devote to them.

The bandit found a rough tent-tavern near the docks where dried travel bread and tolerable ale were sold. He ordered a tankard and settled down on a keg-turned-chair to watch for the *Prawnbane*. According to the high elf sea captain Davin had consulted in Felwithe, the weather and tides were such that a one-masted ship should be coming into port today or possibly tomorrow. It could be a mite tricky keeping himself occupied until then without drawing suspicion.

Best drink slowly, Davin concluded as he lifted his empty tankard and beckoned for a refill.

He drained that tankard and was well into his third before another, far more challenging problem occurred to him: if Elizerain caught sight of him, he might as well charge in with drawn weapons and horns a-blazing, for all the difference it would make.

Oh, she wouldn't give him away deliberately or speak a careless word, but she'd give him away all the same. His Rain could spin a tall tale with the best of them, but her every thought and emotion was written on her face, clear enough for a blind man to read.

That, Davin supposed, represented a type of honesty, and was damned inconvenient from his point of view. For quite different reasons, it probably didn't suit that straight-arrow ranger running with Elizerain these days, either.

Which, come to think of it, suited Davin just fine.

He grew a slightly tipsy grin and raised his tankard in salute to the absent ranger. "Here's to impeccable morals."

The merchant, a gray-bearded dwarf whose face was seamed with years and battle scars, looked up from the tankard he'd been spit-polishing. "Eh? What's that you're wanting now?"

"Wanting? Hardly!" Davin's shudder was only half-feigned.

"Morality, good sir, cannot be poured from a bottle," the bandit said expansively, waving his tankard for emphasis. "It cannot be bought, bartered, or stolen—and may all the gods be praised for that, or I might have accidentally found myself in possession of some."

"Bought, bartered, or stolen," the dwarf repeated as he looked Davin up and down. "So which are you? A merchant or a thief?"

"At the prices you charge, there's a difference?"

"You're also paying for the view," his host informed him, "and for a place to watch without being watched. A safe place, and maybe a listening ear. That's worth far more than my ale, and that's a fact."

Davin lifted one brow, a task he found surprisingly difficult to coordinate. "Having partaken rather freely of your ale, I'm not inclined to argue with that assessment. But your offer of discreet conversation is appreciated," he added hastily, not wishing to give offense—never a wise approach when dealing with people who served food or drink.

"Suit yourself. Most people like to talk, is all," the dwarf said as he reached for a squat blue bottle. He poured a hearty portion of dark amber fluid into an equally squat pottery cup and pushed it toward Davin.

"This is on the tavern. You get one free for each half-keg you drain," he added dryly.

The bandit's eyes widened as the rich, complex aroma of dwarven spirits floated up to him. He reached for the cup and took a sip. The potent brew filled his mouth with a pleasant sort of fire and warmed him all the way down. In the face of this hospitality, his disinclination to share his story suddenly seemed churlish.

"Mine is a fine tale," he told the dwarf, "but I'm warning you, the telling of it will be thirsty work."

Davin's host shrugged and topped off his cup. "Bottle's full, and I've got nowhere better to be. Suppose you start with what ship you're waiting for, and why."

"I'll do better than that," someone said heartily.

For a moment Davin was puzzled. The voice was his own, but it seemed to be coming from a long ways off and through no will of his own.

"I'll tell you about the blood red harp," that voice went on, "and the fair elven lass who carries it. There's dark magic in the tale, battle, treachery, a hint of lost love, and more than a little regret. In short, something for everyone."

"Any dwarves in this tale of yours? Or would that be asking too much?"

Davin tossed back the contents of the cup. The keg chair beneath him tilted alarmingly. He braced his feet wide and waited for the makeshift tavern to stop spinning before replying.

"Something for everyone," he repeated grandly as he pushed the cup toward the barkeep. "Though I suspect the dwarf might be the villain of the piece."

"Wouldn't be the first time," his host said calmly, "and the notion don't offend me none. I like a good tale. As long as you're talking, I'm pouring."

That struck Davin as the best offer he'd had in years. So he mentally backhanded the tiny, frantic voice in the back of his mind that voted to the contrary and reached for his newly filled cup.

THERE WERE FEW PLACES IN FAYDARK WHERE A blue-eyed Koada'Dal enchanter and a Teir'Dal envoy with skin as black as his heart might meet with impunity. The palace of Emperor Crush was one such place. In a small backroom, the two elves sat together, Cyntharia Starflower's golden head bent confidingly close to Ambassador D'Vinn's moon-colored locks.

Although it was exceedingly difficult to guess what the dark elf might be thinking, Cyntharia thought he seemed pleased by her report.

"I am confident in everything the orc bandits told

me," she concluded, "for I have their leader, one Mangle Wolfskinner, under an unbreakable compulsion. He will do whatever I say and tell me anything I wish to know."

The dark elf leaned back and regarded the young necromancer with a calculating gaze. "A valuable spell, and not one that is familiar to me."

Was that doubt in his voice? Cyntharia quelled a twinge of panic and sent him what she hoped was a modest smile.

"I developed this spell myself and taught it only to a few. It is not widely known."

"A powerful enchantment indeed, if it could persuade a band of renegade orcs to enter the employ of an ogress," D'Vinn observed, lifting his wine goblet to salute this feat. He sipped, then added, "I am curious, though, how you came to know of Mirdit Smallplague and her ambitions."

With difficulty, Cyntharia kept her countenance pleasantly neutral. D'Vinn had heard this part of her story. She doubted very much that the ambassador's memory was faulty, so what was his purpose in asking? Was there some spell at work that would check the truth of her words or urge her to speak more freely than she otherwise might?

The elf chose her words carefully. "This knowledge came to me through the dwarf who was recently a slave here. This dwarf is known to the elves—at least," she clarified, "to those of us in positions of power and authority. It is considered courtesy for dwarves entering elf territory to make their presence and purpose known."

"And that would be?"

"The dwarf tracked Mirdit Smallplague eastward, for she had a certain axe taken from the field of battle."

Cyntharia shrugged. "Quests to reclaim a hero's weapon are common among dwarves."

"That explains the dwarf. What of the ogress?"

"What does any ogre want?" she countered. "The wretched creatures live to fight and plunder. The Mudtoe Clan was notorious for waylaying travelers and ambushing dwarf patrols. Mirdit Smallplague desires nothing more than to return to the life she knew. For that, she needed help."

"Which she did not receive," D'Vinn noted.

"Not from the orcs of Crushbone," she agreed, "but the dwarf followed her into this citadel and offered to show her a back way into a dwarf outpost in exchange for the axe."

The dark elf lifted a snow-white brow. "And she didn't suspect he might betray her?"

"Of course she did, and she retained her suspicions for quite some time. But no amount of torture could budge the dwarf from his story, and eventually the ogress came to believe that he was as committed to his quest as she to hers."

The dark elf nodded and reached for an obsidian decanter. "More wine?"

Cyntharia's glass was nearly untouched, but she held it out and allowed the ambassador to pour a bit more. She took a sip and managed, just barely, not to grimace. The Teir'Dal preferred a dark, smoky potion that was quite unlike the high elves' herb-scented meads and deceptively light, floral wines.

"Emperor Crush was a little vague on the subject of just how the dwarf and his three elven 'servants' escaped," D'Vinn observed.

Cyntharia kept her expression carefully neutral, for

that was the most delicate and dangerous issue the dark elf was likely to raise. No good could come of the Teir'-Dal knowing of the treasure trove, or the orcs learning of the elusive passage out of their fortress.

"I believe the official story is that they died in the slave pits. Mirdit smuggled them out, doubtlessly with the help of some of the soldiers."

D'Vinn accepted that explanation with a noncommittal nod. "So all seems to be going smoothly. I will admit that I had reservations, especially where Nyson Impholder was concerned."

"It was easy to convince Mirdit Smallplague to take a hostage. She is extremely intelligent, as ogres go, and she knows she can't engage the dwarves in open warfare unless she can unite the ogres of the Butcherblock Mountains under her banner. To do so, she will need a victory to boast about and treasure to offer. A captive from an important elven clan will be seen as both. She also knows that any large ogre army will draw the attention of Faydark's elves, and she believes an important elf hostage will keep the elves out of the fight."

The dark elf studied her over the rim of his goblet. "What if she is right?"

"She isn't," the necromancer stated. "I know Niola Impholder well. She believes the sun rises and sets merely to give variety to the length of her son's shadow. Niola has power, wealth, and influence. If anyone can convince King Thex to empty Felwithe of warriors and call out Kelethin's Emerald Guard to rescue her son—and, incidentally, to come to the aid of the dwarves—it is she."

Ambassador D'Vinn thought for several moments. "Does the dwarf know of your hand in this?"

In truth, Cyntharia was not sure how much Trobe

might have guessed. If he caught sight of her in Crushbone, he might well have wondered what business a high elf female could have in Emperor Crush's palace.

"He does not," she said, hoping that it was true. "Mangle Wolfskinner has been a surprisingly efficient envoy. He and Trobe have been trading goods and information for quite some time. And bringing together Trobe and Niola's son was easily done. Any important personage visiting Kelethin for the Songweavers' Feast is assigned a guard. And as I have already said, elves in positions of power know about Trobe."

"And what of the other elf with the Impholder boy and his guard?"

Cyntharia shrugged. "A fledgling bard. She is of no real consequence."

The dark elf nodded gravely. "Then you have answered all my questions but the most important one: why should I put my trust in someone who so readily betrays her own people?"

His tone was still pleasant, but Cyntharia marked the glint of malice in his eyes. Very well, if D'Vinn could speak bluntly, so would she.

"Because, as you well know, it is the service you required of me. It is the price I must pay to achieve my heart's desire."

"To study necromancy at the academies of Paineel," D'Vinn said, a delicate thread of disbelief weaving through his words. "An unusual ambition for a Koada'-Dal maiden."

Cyntharia's chin rose, and her gaze turned flinty. "I am accustomed to doing whatever I set my hand to, and doing it well. I not only succeed, I excel. It is unusual for an elf of my years to hold a position at Felwithe's Arcane School."

"So I am told. But that is not enough?"

"I wish to learn magic in *all* its aspects, the dark and hidden as well as the spells one casts in daylight. To this end, I sought admission to the schools of Paineel not once, but three times," she said softly. "Thanks to my study of old, forbidden tomes, I knew far more of necromancy than most of their scholars—more, perhaps, than some of the teachers! But they refused me. In an effort to raise enough coin to bribe my way into the schools, I took some students. One of them was accepted, while *I* was not! *This will not stand*."

D'Vinn studied her with wry amusement. "The Teir'-Dal are no strangers to pride and ambition, but I daresay you are unusually cursed by these virtues, even by our measure."

"So you will do as you promised? You will use your influence to get me a place in Paineel's school of necromancy?"

"If all goes well, you will be elbow deep in dusty old tomes and desiccated spider guts before the new moon."

She rewarded him with a brilliant smile. "If ever you need the aid of dark art, come to me first."

"You may count on it. So you will be setting sail at first opportunity, I imagine?"

"Very soon," she assured him.

"Because you understand, of course, that your future usefulness to the Teir'Dal on Faydwer will be limited if any of your fellow Koada'Dal learn of your, shall we say, divided alliance?"

Cyntharia's lips firmed with disapproval. Plain speaking

she appreciated, but veiled threats were insulting and poor manners besides.

"That goes without saying," she said politely, "and with all due respect, it *should* have."

For a moment Ambassador D'Vinn's expression wavered between stunned outrage and kindling wrath. Then an expression of wry amusement crossed his face, and he inclined his head in a slight bow.

"Your pardon—my words were less than subtle. It would seem that I have been dealing overlong with Crushbone sensibilities."

"That I understand only too well," she assured him. "I will be glad to have done with orcs and ogres—except, of course, as subjects of necromantic experiments. I find that what ogres lack in conversational graces, they make up in their tolerance for vivisection."

"A pleasant thought," D'Vinn said, with no discernable sarcasm. "Will you need assistance finding transport to Paineel?"

Cyntharia hesitated. The path toward her deepest desire lay out before her, straight and broad. But there was one small matter that might, if left untended, undo all her work:

According to one of her informers, the female wood elf with Trobe was under a compulsion curse.

Nyson knew of this spell, but Cyntharia wouldn't have thought him capable of casting it. He could muster enough dark magic to bend a lesser mind into answering a few short questions, but surely nothing approaching this!

But if Cyntharia was wrong about Nyson, if the young Koada'Dal was indeed capable of such magic, he could put an end to Mirdit Smallplague's plan before the ogress could satisfy the terms of Cyntharia's bargain with the dark elf ambassador. And if D'Vinn had reason to reconsider their deal, her dream of dark magic would never emerge from the confines of her entertaining nightmares.

And that, she simply could not allow.

Cyntharia smiled sweetly at D'Vinn. "I will find my own way to Paineel. There is a small personal matter I must attend, and then all shall be as you say."

ELIZERAIN WOKE TO DARKNESS AND A SENSATION of rocking, jolting movement. For a moment she thought she was back aboard the *Prawnbane*, but the rumbling that filled the air and reverberated through her bones was that of a cart moving swiftly over hard-packed ground. The air coming in the small knothole by her ear held not the tang of the sea but the deep green scent of a forest.

She shifted experimentally and began to slide her hands around her small prison. There wasn't much of it to explore. Her knees were drawn up to her chest, and a circle of tightly fitted planks surrounded her. Apparently she'd been packed into a large wooden barrel.

"Xander?" she whispered.

"Hush, lass," advised a deep, rumbling dwarf voice. "He's safe, and the lad as well. There was a sleeping draught in yer stew this morn. Sorry about the barrels, but it made it easier to move you elves off the ship this way, in case someone's keeping watch. Packed up Mirdit, too."

The thought of the ogress stuffed into a barrel or crate cheered Elizerain considerably but didn't change her own circumstances in the slightest.

"If Mirdit is boxed up, what's to stop you from letting

us go?" she asked, hating the pleading note that had crept into her voice.

A long moment of silence followed, broken only by the creak and rumble of the cart and the sullen clopping of mule hooves against hard-packed dirt.

"Can't do it," Trobe said at last.

"Why not?"

A vicious thump sent a shiver through Elizerain's barrel. "Hold your tongue, elf," snarled the ogress. "Your lid is fastened down. Mine is not."

Elizerain subsided, not seeing any other choice. Fortunately the cart slowed to a stop before too long, and her barrel was unceremoniously shoved off the back.

She hit hard and rolled several times before coming to rest on her hands and knees. Nails shrieked in protest as the lid of her prison was pried loose.

Sunlight flooded the barrel. Elizerain blinked away the sting of sudden brightness and crawled out on limbs stiff from disuse. Nyson had already emerged from his crate, looking quietly furious as he helped Trobe drag a still-sleeping Xander from a barrel. Mirdit slapped the wood elf awake and dragged him to his feet. She thrust a large bundle of weapons into his arms and gave him a shove in the direction of a nearly imperceptible forest trail.

While Mirdit loaded up the other elves, Trobe turned the wagon around and gave the lead mule a sharp smack on the flanks. The creature took off at a trot, as if eager to put some road between himself and the ogress.

The little band walked steadily until nearly twilight, finally emerging in a large rock-strewn clearing near the mouth of a cave.

A dozen or so ogres had set up camp in this forest

hideaway, and they all looked up when Mirdit and Trobe marched the prisoners into camp.

Elizerain wasn't sure what was worse: the acrid stench of their hulking, unwashed bodies or the coldly assessing expression in their red eyes. They might have been regarding a trio of cornered rabbits and considering whether to roast or boil them.

She swallowed a lump of fear and forced herself to take stock of this new foe. Though all were currently staring at the new arrivals, they'd been engaged in a variety of listless pursuits. Three of them had been tossing dice; a few more were idly poking at a campfire with sticks. They seemed a dispirited group, to say the least.

"Zarchoomi! Cornflunk!" called Mirdit. "What, no greeting for your sister?"

Two of the ogres rose from the fire and shambled over. The larger one gave Mirdit a companionable swat on the shoulder by way of greeting.

"Why you bring elfs?" he inquired.

His brother shrugged. "Why not bring? The meat's stringy, but elfs fill up a pot quicker than rabbits."

Mirdit waved this notion away with an impatient sweep of one hand. "All in due time. Zarchoomi, where are the rest? Surely you've recruited more ogres than this!"

The big ogre scuffed his toe in the dirt, looking oddly like a chastened child. "This all we got," he confessed, his eyes on the ground.

"Did you tell them we'd have weapons? Treasure?"

"We think you not come back," Cornflunk said bluntly.

"Unlike some, I do what I set out to do," she said

snidely. "Well, we can only start from where we stand. Why don't you help the dwarf unpack the weapons."

"What dwarf doing here?" inquired Zarchoomi.

Trobe paused in the act of cutting the bindings on a tarp-wrapped bundle.

"Since I'm standing right here, I can answer fer myself," he said grimly. "I got scores to settle and an axe to bloody, same as your sister. Take this."

He tossed a long-shafted pike at the ogre. Zarchoomi caught it handily, gave it a quick whirl to test the balance, and examined the keen, shining blade with obvious pleasure.

"More?" he demanded, pointing to the bundles Xander and Nyson had carried.

"Yeah, but those weapons still need oiling and cleaning. Did most of them on the ship. You'll have the rest soon enough," Trobe said curtly.

Zarchoomi ran one filthy green finger lightly over the blade and gave a grunt of approval as blood welled up. He turned an evil grin to his sister.

"Maybe we get more ogres after all."

DAVIN SLOWLY BECAME AWARE OF A DISTANT drumbeat, dull but insistent. Several moments passed before he realized the throbbing came from his own head and resonated through the rough plank table upon which he'd apparently fallen face down.

He pushed himself off the table and squinted toward the dock. Sunset hues of rose and gold and dusky purple were staining the sky and spilling into the harbor. He'd been sitting in this tavern for hours, few of which he remembered.

Puzzled, the bandit reached for his cup, which lay on

its side beside a sticky pool. A few dried leaves clung to the bottom of the cup. Davin crumbled one between his fingers and sniffed. Over the lingering scent of dwarf spirits was a sharp, telltale aroma. Davin knew this herb and used it himself when he wished to impose a swift, deep sleep upon someone who might prove troublesome awake.

He planted his boots firmly and surged to his feet, his hands lunging for the dwarf's throat. He slammed the treacherous merchant against the central tent post hard enough to set the entire structure swaying alarmingly.

"Why did you drug me?" he demanded as he dragged the dwarf up to eye level. "Why?"

The dwarf gurgled and gestured to the chokehold Davin had on his throat. The bandit relaxed his grip. His captive slid down the pole and dropped to his feet with a heavy *thunk*.

"The people you're looking for are long gone. Let 'em go," the dwarf advised.

For a moment Davin wondered what possible knowledge the merchant could have of his business. Memory returned in a sudden, sickening rush.

Oh, he'd been quite the storyteller, and now he would likely hang for it. Provided, of course, that this dwarf lived long enough to carry the tale.

His face must have revealed something of his thoughts, for the dwarf backed away and held up both hands like a groom trying to gentle a spooked horse.

"You've naught to fear from me," he said soothingly. "If I repeated every tale I heard over too many cups, I'd be out of business by the next high tide. I just like to know what's going on dockside, is all."

Davin swept up the coins he'd put on the table to pay

for the ale. The dwarf merely shrugged, as if to acknowledge that this was a fair enough price for a lost afternoon.

But Davin's foul mood could not be appeased until it was shared, so he snatched the blue bottle and stormed out of the tent tavern. The dwarf's yelp of protest brought a grimly satisfied smile to Davin's face.

He promptly forgot the dwarf and turned his thoughts to the task at hand. So he'd been delayed; what of it? He'd been raised and trained by a ranger. To his keen eye, a forest trail was as easily read as the invitation in a lady's smile. He could track Elizerain, no problem.

A gruff shout of warning brought him up short. Davin fell back a step as a heavily laden handcart trundled by. He studied the large wooden crate on it with growing consternation.

On second thought, there might be a problem.

What if Elizerain and her companions were moved out by wagon? There was no way Davin could know which set of tracks was hers. Even if she had gone on foot, he'd likely follow a dozen paths or more before he found the right one.

Davin turned his gaze to the docks. The *Prawnbane* was still in port. Finally, a bit of luck!

He regarded the blue bottle, and a small, hard smile curved his lips. He'd stolen it to annoy the treacherous ale merchant—a small act of vengeance and a most fortunate impulse.

The bandit strode purposefully toward the dock. Sailors were a notoriously thirsty lot, and Davin intended to separate one of them from his secrets before the moon rose.

IN THE CAPTAIN'S CABIN ABOARD THE *Prawnbane*,

Chanzoon Nexis paced the floor as he awaited the coming of night and the wondrous transformation it would bring.

Three days had passed since the wood elf bard had unwittingly unleashed the magic of her blood red harp upon him. From what the necromancer had pieced together, the Dawnwalker curse required three days to work its way through body and soul, to find the fine line between life and death and twist it into an ever-shifting, never-ending existence.

All his life Chanzoon Nexis had studied death; now he was about to defeat it!

The necromancer unlatched the porthole and stared out to sea, his eyes greedy for the signs of coming night. All that remained of the sun was a thin curve of crimson above the western horizon. It would not be long now.

He stood in rapt anticipation while the sunset colors faded to silver and the sky deepened into sapphire. Still he waited. Stars appeared, and to Chanzoon's eye they seemed to wink knowingly to each other. The drunken roars of laughter from the sailors' quarters rose in volume, as if to mock the still-human necromancer.

For human he undoubtedly was, and he showed no sign of transcending that state any time soon.

Hope dwindled, disappointment grew into fury, and at last Chanzoon whirled away from the porthole and stormed off the ship.

He hurried through the walled dockside area. Ignoring the warnings of the dwarven gate guards, he strode into the forest and immediately left the path. He had no fear of losing his way because even now he could feel the tiny, insistent pull of the enchanted string he had placed on the red harp. He would find Elizerain, but not just yet—and not as he was now.

The necromancer walked until he reached a small glade, not too far from the docks. There he stopped and began to cast a variation on the summoning spell Alisar had used to draw undead creatures to his forest tower. With it, he could compel illusionists whose magical abilities were less than his own.

The spell held risks, of course. Greater magic wielders might hear the call and come to investigate. Chanzoon would have to take the chance that there were none who surpassed his power within range of the spell.

But he was not overly concerned; in fact, in this dismal outpost he only hoped he could find someone equal to the task!

Once the spell was cast, Chanzoon settled down on a fallen tree to wait.

Luck was with him; before much more than an hour had passed, a small, weathered man stumbled into the clearing, clad in the dull brown and green garments of a forest dweller. He blinked at Chanzoon, looking rather like a sleepwalker who'd just awakened from a forgotten dream.

"What is this?" he mumbled. "Who are you?"

The necromancer rose to his feet. "Someone in need of your services and willing to pay well for them. I require a spell that will transform my appearance, one powerful enough to last until I dispel it."

The mention of money seemed to bring the newcomer out of his daze. He swept a thoughtful gaze over Chanzoon and pursed his lips. "What did you have in mind?"

Chanzoon described the form he wished to take, and they haggled briefly over the price of the necessary casting.

The illusionist promptly began a complicated chant. A faint mist of twinkling light settled over the necromancer, surrounding him with a hiss and fizzle pleasantly reminiscent of sparkling mead.

When it faded, Chanzoon gazed down at his hands. His long, tapered fingers were thrice their normal size and covered by tough, gray-green hide.

He lifted one of these massive paws to his face and explored the square, jutting jaw, the protruding fangs, the heavy brow ridge. His fine robes were gone, replaced by deerskin leggings and a rough tunic. A dark cloak and heavy boots completed the transformation.

"Quite satisfactory," he said, noting with pleasure that his voice was likewise transformed into something rough and uncouth.

He tossed a coin purse to the illusionist, much as one might toss a marrow bone to an obedient hound, and left the clearing with a swift, impatient stride.

Chanzoon set off toward the north, trusting the harp's magic to lead him to Mirdit Smallplague's captive bard. The ogress was building an army, that much Chanzoon had surmised during his time aboard the *Prawnbane*. No doubt the ogress would welcome the services of an "ogre shaman."

And since ogres were not known for their fondness for elves, no one would think it odd if he were to take a dark interest in one of Mirdit's elven captives.

A deep, grating chuckle rumbled from Chanzoon's lips. Before he was through with Elizerain, she would cast a defensive spell of sufficient strength to finish what they'd begun.

Back in the clearing, the illusionist stood in apparent bemusement until the crunch and rustle of Chanzoon's footsteps disappeared into the distance. Then one hand traced a swift, complicated gesture, and a haze of light surrounded the brown-clad man. From this halo stepped a high elf woman, clad in a sky-blue gown. In her true form, she was blond and beautiful.

And, at the moment, exceedingly troubled.

There were things at work here that she did not understand. What had brought Chanzoon Nexis to the Butcherblock Mountains, and what business did her former student have with ogres?

Moving with stealth and silence that a shadow might envy, Cyntharia Starflower slipped into the night-dark forest.

THE MOOD IN THE MUDTOE CLAN CAMP WAS FESTIVE that night. After a hearty meal of unspeakable stew washed down with ale that could melt scrap metal, Mirdit called on Elizerain to declaim the song about Trondle Ogrebane's treachery and his coming death.

The bard did as she was bid, but never before had she played with such reluctance. It was difficult to concentrate on the ogress's ballad with so many evil red eyes upon her. It was harder still when the story began to weave its spell over the ogres. Elizerain could see the tale take hold of them, inflaming their lust for slaughter.

After the ogres shooed her off and bent their hideous heads together over softly growled plotting, Elizerain went to the far side of the camp, as far as her ogre guards would allow. She settled down and began to play, needing to erase the memory of the strange ballad and the ogres' too enthusiastic response—and the sickening conviction that part of the responsibility for whatever happened tomorrow would be on her hands and head.

She started a familiar jig, but within a few measures the cadence changed, and the melody wandered off into a minor mode. A new song emerged from the strings, without thought or will on Elizerain's part, leaking from the harp like mead from a punctured wineskin. After a while she began to sing the verses that came to her unbidden:

One is the sun that rises
And one is the sun that sets.
One is the soul that dies at dusk,
Then death with each dawn forgets.

Great is the Dawnwalker's sorrow,
And blood is the Dawnwalker's wine
Once song-cast magic, for good or for ill,
Cause life and death to entwine.

Red is the color of longing,
And red is the color of song.
The Dawnwalker follows the blood red harp
And the bard who did him this wrong.

There was more, but Elizerain cast the harp away and scrambled to her feet, appalled and enlightened.

"Tunare have mercy," she whispered. "I used the harp to attack the necromancer!"

"And to heal me."

Nyson's resonant baritone was no more than a whisper at her shoulder, but his voice suddenly seemed deeper than usual, more compelling.

Elizerain turned slowly to face the young Koada'Dal. He lowered the hood of his cloak. In the flickering light of the campfire his golden skin looked unnaturally pale, and his eyes held an eerie luminescence. A cold stillness lingered about him, and his sad smile betrayed a flash of fang.

"*One is the soul who dies at dusk*," he recited. "Isn't that how the song goes?"

Elizerain nodded, certain that no words could find their way past the lump in her throat or the mingling of sorrow and terror in her heart.

"You've nothing to fear from me, Songmistress, and you have no need to fear the necromancer as long as I, you should pardon the expression, *live*," he said softly. "For if the ballad tells the truth, there can be only one Dawnwalker."

23

DIVERSION

AS ELIZERAIN STARED AT THE KOADA'DAL, much that had been odd or puzzling or downright disturbing fell suddenly into place: the little gnome in Kelethin, killed by Geminar Wolfsong, the half elf bard who'd claimed the gnome had been a vampire. Nyson's nightly disappearances from their shipboard sleeping quarters. Even her own strange dream of shipboard rats and terrible thirst.

Dear goddess! Was *that* what the young elf felt, how he lived?

She sank to the ground and buried her face in her hands. "Oh, Nyson, I am so terribly sorry!"

He knelt beside her. "It was not knowingly done. When you cast that healing spell during our sojourn in Crushbone, you saved my life." A fleeting smile touched his lips. "At least, during the daylight hours."

Even now, Elizerain's native curiosity could not be denied for long. She lowered her hands and peered at him. "What's it like?"

He was silent for a long moment. "Once you get past

the moment of death, it is not unbearable. There are even advantages. During the day I am much as I ever was, but after dark I am stronger, faster. My senses seem to be sharpening. I think in time there will be other powers, too."

All of this sounded familiar, yet Nyson was not acting like the vampires in any tales Elizerain had heard. "But aren't you . . . thirsty?"

"Oh, yes," he said without hesitation. "And the thirst grows even as my strength increases. But it's nothing I can't control. Perhaps that is a benefit of the Dawnwalker curse."

"So apart from being dead and thirsty, you're still *you.*"

But even as Elizerain spoke, she knew that to be untrue: little in Nyson's bleak expression recalled the naive and arrogant between-age elf she'd met only a few-score days earlier.

But Nyson considered her words seriously, and after a moment he nodded. "Yes, I would say so. That might not always be true, but it seems to describe what I feel at present."

"So what are you going to . . . eat?"

An expression of distaste crossed his face, which Elizerain found far preferable to the despair that haunted his eyes.

"I will manage," he said flatly.

She was about to press him for details when a trill of birdsong caught her attention—a faint, contented ripple, like the coo of a sleeping dove. It was not at all out of place amid the hum and chirp of the nighttime forest, but her eyes widened, and a brilliant smile lit her face.

Nyson seized her shoulders and spun her away from

the ogres before any of them could see her reaction. "What is it?"

"Davin," she whispered. "I just heard his night-bird call. I don't know how, but he's found us!"

The high elf glanced over at Xander, who was helping Trobe oil and polish the rest of the swords they'd brought from the treasure trove. His face darkened for a moment, but it was hard to fault Xander, considering the well-armed ogre standing over him. The ranger could hardly choose what tasks he would perform and which he would refuse. They might have left Crushbone behind, but they were still slaves.

"We should get word of this to Xander."

"And won't he be pleased," Elizerain said dryly. "At the moment, I'm more concerned about letting Davin know what's happening so he can take word to the dwarves Mirdit's about to attack."

"But will he do this?"

Elizerain considered the question. In truth, she was surprised that Davin had traveled across Faydwer to find her. After all, he'd been quick enough to leave her behind in Antonica. It was possible, of course, that he felt a debt of sorts toward her. When matters touched his pride, Davin could occasionally put his own best interests aside—and sometimes his common sense, as well. Assuming he had rescue in mind, would he expand his noble impulse to include a dwarf outpost?

"Let's find out," she said at last.

She gingerly picked up the discarded harp and settled down on the ground.

Her fingers poised over the strings for a long moment before she could bring herself to play. Seated beside her, no more animated than a statue of golden marble, was evidence of the havoc the little red harp could cause.

But if the ballad told the truth of the matter, the damage had already been done. As long as Nyson lived, as long as there was a Dawnwalker, the harp's strange magic would be content.

Elizerain took a steadying breath and struck a rippling chord. She began to sing of the coming battle, covering her purpose by telling the tale in a manner ogres would likely find appealing. Indeed, some of them wandered by to listen, grinning horribly as the bard sang of Trobe's treachery and the slaughter that was sure to come. And as she sang, she silently willed Davin to hear the words unspoken and to get the message to the dwarves.

And most importantly, to do the right thing—for no other reason than it *was* the right thing—just this one time.

GRIB OF THE GREENLEAVES STOOD AT THE RAIL OF the *Rusty Cutlass,* his head thrown back like a hound scenting the wind.

He was wet to the skin, his graying hair plastered to his skull, and the brisk, chill wind snapping at the sails went straight to the marrow of his old bones.

And he'd never been happier.

By Tunare, how he'd missed the feel of a ship's deck beneath his feet, the scent and sting of the sea on his face! Mayhap Davin could be persuaded to take to the sea after he had finished this foolishness involving the elf wench.

The bandit's contented gaze swept the horizon as he enjoyed the last few moments of his watch. A brief squall had blown past during the night, and dawn was making rosy promises of a fine day to come.

A thin black line arose from the northern horizon. Grib raised his glass and squinted toward the ship, and what he saw made his heart give a painful leap.

The ship was sailing south, and veering toward the sunrise. There was no port that way but for the pirate dock from which the *Rusty Cutlass* had set sail. Not that Grib and his mates were above relieving a ship or two of its cargo, but neither were pirate ships above robbing each other. Even at this distance, Grib could tell that the *Cutlass* was no match for the massive ship sailing swiftly into view.

As if it could sense his thoughts, the ship turned out of the wind and dropped its foremost sail. When a black sail began to rise in its stead, Grib seized the alarm bell and flapped it with such frantic vigor that he feared he might take flight.

Pirates boiled up from the hold, weapons in hand. The captain strode over to Grib's side and lifted his own sea glass. What he saw inspired a long, inventive string of curses.

The ship had changed course and was sailing straight toward them, with a speed that could only be magic-aided. On its death-promising black sail was emblazoned an emblem: a gigantic orc's skull with crimson eyes.

"That's Crushbone's mark," Grib said.

"A shipload of orcs?" muttered the captain. "With *magic*? What the bloody blazes is *that* about?"

"Reinforcements, most likely," the bandit said. "Looks like the Crushbone orcs have plans. Kelethin, I'm guessing, and judging by the size of that ship, perhaps on to Felwithe after."

The captain nodded, his eyes on the black sail. "Sounds reasonable. Don't see what they'd want with us, though."

Grib shrugged. "Mayhap they fear we'll turn about and carry a warning back to the elves."

This notion brought a bark of harsh laughter from the pirate. "Never have I been accused of harboring good intentions before, and I don't mind saying it's a damned inconvenient time for someone to start."

A thunderous boom parted the salt-laden air, as if clearing way for the enormous, fiery arrow streaking toward them. Grib instinctively ducked as the ballista bolt, its point wrapped in flaming, oil-soaked rags, tore through the sails.

The captain had already spun away, shouting orders to man the fire buckets.

The heavy thud of metal against the ship's side had Grib rolling away—not a moment too soon, for the next throw sent an anchor-sized grappling hook sailing over the rail. One spiked end bit into the deck. Old wood shrieked and splintered as the hook was wrenched back. It caught on the rail, and the *Cutlass* jolted sharply, sending sailors tumbling to the deck.

Grib struggled to his feet and gazed with dismay at the rapidly closing ship. Well-armed orcs crowded the deck, grinning in anticipation. Several score of the brutes were hauling at ropes attached to grappling hooks, reeling in the smaller ship like a securely hooked fish.

Risky, Grib thought, to pull in a burning ship, even with the wind blowing the flames away from the attackers. Even as the thought formed, orcs began to throw boarding ladders across the divide. They jostled each other at the rails, eager to be first to the slaughter. They roiled down the ladders like a swarm of gigantic rats, their taunting shouts rising above the snap and roar of the rapidly spreading flames.

Not much of a risk after all, Grib realized. In moments, the pirates would all be dead, and the orcs' ship would pull clear. By the time the *Rusty Cutlass* burned to the waterline, the orcs would be well on their way to the forests of Faydark.

Not much Grib could do about any of it, save make the best death he could.

The bandit set his feet wide and raised his dagger to catch the first sweep of an orc's heavy sword. Grib's thin steel blade snapped, and the sword swept in to dig a blazing furrow across Grib's chest. He heard the grate of sword against bone before the pain hit him. And then, in one terrible moment, he knew exactly what the burning ship must be feeling.

He staggered to the rail, falling once under a blow from a huge green fist. Dragging himself to his feet with frantic haste, he dove at the rail and tumbled into the sea.

Cold, soothing water enfolded him. For just a moment the pain ebbed, but then the burning sensation returned with renewed fervor. Grib looked down at his chest. Blood poured from the wound, which seemed to be growing wider, almost as if the flesh was burning away from either side of the sword cut.

A poisoned blade, then. There was no hope for him, but still he clutched at the gaping wound as if he could hold life inside his body with his hands. Even immersed in the sea, his flesh was hot to the touch and starting to blacken along the spreading edges of the sword wound.

Howls of agony escaped him, sending rifts of bubbles rising to mingle with the blood curling away through the water. Water rushed into his lungs to fill the void, and Grib began to sink deeper into the sea.

Drowning was said to be a painful death, but Grib wasn't in any position to judge. The poison was making its way into his blood, setting his flesh aflame. He tried to scream again, but could manage only a faint gurgle.

It was then that he saw the sharks. Two of them, closing in fast, oblivious to everything but the siren call of spilled blood.

Despite everything, a grim smile touched the old bandit's lips. The story of his death was one Davin the Dark would relish. The Greenleaf bandits were big on settling scores. Grib might not settle with the orc who'd poisoned him, but he was about to give these damned fish one hell of a bellyache.

MORNING BROUGHT THE OGRE CAMP TO BUSTLING life. Left to his own devices, Xander Fletcher set to work on a pair of long daggers, smoothing a sharpening stone along ancient edges and rubbing the blades with oil.

This choice of occupation earned him a cold glare from the young Koada'Dal and a puzzled look from Elizerain. And that pained the ranger more than he would have thought possible.

The wood elf ranger had spent a lifetime doing his duty and holding his own counsel, but it was difficult to bear the look in Elizerain's eyes. There were things he couldn't tell her, and she read in his reticence a lack of trust.

His own fault, partly. He'd been harsh with her over her relationship with Davin the Dark. It hadn't helped that the bandit leader kept turning up, but as far as Xander could tell, that was none of Elizerain's doing.

A sigh escaped him, and he reached for the last of the

swords they'd taken from the treasure trove. Just this one more, then they'd all be honed and polished in preparation for the battle to come.

Which led to yet another thing he couldn't tell Elizerain.

The need for secrecy weighed heavily on him. It was just as well that Elizerain and Nyson seemed content to keep their distance.

A shout of outraged protest rose above the early morning noise and shattered Xander's troubled musings. Cornflunk, one of Mirdit Smallplague's brothers, stormed toward the breakfast fire, brandishing the limp carcass of a small, brown goat.

"Someone kill!" he howled, shaking the goat.

The ogress shrugged. "So put it on a spit and sear it for breakfast."

"Blood gone. Makes good sausage," Cornflunk grumbled sullenly. His small eyes swept the campsite and locked gazes with Xander. "Maybe elfs take."

It was a ridiculous accusation, but Xander was not about to dismiss it. The ogre had been casting baleful glances at the elves since their arrival, and it was only a matter of time before he came up with an excuse to kill them.

Mirdit was scolding her brother when a shout went up from the perimeter guards. Zarchoomi strutted into camp, grinning broadly. Behind him walked a tall gray-green ogre, better dressed than most of the Mudtoe band in deerskin leggings, good boots, and a flowing dark cloak. Behind *him* shambled a dozen or so dead ogres, some in rather advanced states of decomposition. Xander thanked Tunare that the new recruits stood downwind of the camp.

Zarchoomi loudly extolled the power of the shaman who'd come for the chance to kill dwarves and turn their slain corpses against their living kin. He made a good story of it, but Xander's attention was seized by another small drama.

Cornflunk was creeping toward Elizerain and Nyson, murder in his red eyes and a rusted knife in his hands. Before Xander could call out a warning, the young high elf whirled toward the ogre and flung out one hand. A small ball of flame hurtled toward Cornflunk, hitting him squarely in the chest and knocking him back several steps.

The ogre let out a high-pitched yelp, almost a scream. Zarchoomi's storytelling abruptly halted, and the camp plunged into silence. For a long moment the ogres regarded Cornflunk's blackened, smoking leather tunic and the knife that lay at his feet.

Xander smirked. He'd heard that dropping a weapon was considered a major sign of weakness among ogres. Judging from the appalled expression on Mirdit's face and the speculation in a dozen other pairs of ogrish eyes, the tale was based in truth.

"Yellow-hair elf throw magic," Cornflunk whined, pointing an accusing finger at Nyson. "I say we kill."

"I agree," the ogre shaman put in quickly. "Elven magic might help the dwarves."

The ogres turned to Mirdit to decide the matter. Her scarred face mottled with anger and perhaps also with embarrassment over her brother's loss of face.

"No one is to harm the elves, any of them, until I say so," she decreed. She cast a scalding glare at her younger brother. "And when the time comes to kill them, I will do it myself."

DAVIN THE DARK HAD NEVER THOUGHT TO FIND himself discussing battle strategy with wood elves, but here he was, crouched in a circle beside no less a warrior than Regren Steelforger.

The news Elizerain had passed along created a bit of a dilemma: if the dwarves learned of the coming attack, the ogres might figure out where the leak came from and decide that an elven bard was too troublesome a hostage to keep alive. Fortunately the wood elves agreed with Davin's assessment. They tossed around various suggestions, but none of them seemed likely to get the three elves safely away.

"You need a diversion," suggested a musical female voice.

Davin looked up, impressed that someone could walk up without him hearing. When his gaze took in the newcomer, however, his next response was wary alarm. A surprising response, considering that the quiet-footed speaker was a high elf woman of unusual beauty, not to mention the possessor of a few nice pieces of jewelry that Davin wouldn't mind stealing.

But the elves didn't seem to share his reservations. Regren hailed her as Cyntharia Starflower and praised Tunare that their quest would be aided by so powerful an enchanter. Judging from the delighted expression on the faces of the other warriors, Regren wasn't just being polite.

The only one who didn't look happy was Cyntharia herself. "Where are the others?" she demanded.

Davin spread his arms wide in a gesture that encompassed the small band. "This is it."

"Thirteen elves and a human?" Cyntharia demanded. "This is the sum of all the forces Niola Impholder can muster? Is her only son, blood kin to King Tearis Thex, worth so little?"

"The king knows nothing of this," Regren cautioned. "We came here to rescue Nyson Impholder and his companions."

The necromancer lifted one golden brow. "I see. And I suppose you care nothing of the dwarves who will die at the hands of these ogres?"

An uncomfortable silence fell over the elves. Apparently Regren and his boys had been sworn to secrecy about the elves' larger plans, even where such luminaries as this pretty female were concerned.

Finally Davin came to their rescue. "The dwarves will manage just fine," he said dryly, echoing Niola Impholder's response to the same question. "My concern is the elven hostages. If we warn the dwarves, there will be a larger battle, and the chances of the hostages being killed go up. I say we get them out now."

"And then we send a messenger to Kaladim," one of the wood elves suggested.

"That's not our first concern," Davin said briskly. Nor, as far as he was concerned, was it their second or third concern. "If we can get a message to the dwarves later, fine. Let's concentrate on getting those elves out of there. Agreed?"

The elves nodded.

Davin turned to Cyntharia, who was eyeing him with an expression usually reserved for something you'd scrape off your boot. He gave her his most charming smile. "Now, about that diversion . . ."

THE OGRES WERE STAMPING THE BREAKFAST FIRE into ash when Elizerain heard the trill of a moss wren—a distinctive five-note melody that the birds invariably sang twice. This singer, however, flattened the high note just a little, and the break between song fragments was just a heartbeat too long. The difference was subtle, and no one was likely to recognize it except those who knew the day-bird call of Davin the Dark. And, of course, other moss wrens.

Elizerain looked around for Xander and noticed that one of the ogres was listening, too. It was the newcomer, the shaman. He glanced in her direction, and their eyes met and held in a moment of shared knowledge.

Before Elizerain could wonder what that meant, the ogre flung a hand toward her. A small ball of dark energy hurled toward her, too fast to dodge. It hit her like a blow from a giant's fist, lifting her off her feet. Her back slammed into a broad tree trunk, and she felt the wet warmth of blood soaking her hair.

She slid down the tree, her vision dancing with blue and white stars against a rapidly darkening field. Perhaps that was what made the ogre shaman's form waver. The last thing Elizerain saw before darkness claimed her was a pair of pale blue eyes—strangely familiar eyes—staring at her with naked hatred.

XANDER SAW THE ATTACK, AND HE LEAPED TO his feet as the ogre shaman closed on a helpless Elizerain. Risking discovery, risking everything he had come to do, Xander drew his daggers from their magically hidden sheaths and slashed both of them across the throat of his ogre guard.

He ran at the shaman, one dagger thrusting forward and the other lifted for a slashing blow. But he stopped short, several paces shy of his target, as suddenly as if a wall had sprung up between them.

A jolt of power made the dagger in his left hand flame like a candle, and for a moment he could see the bones gleaming through the flesh of his hand. Then that flesh was suddenly, inexplicably gone, and the dagger dropped from his skeletal fingers.

Agony such as Xander had never imagined possible seared up his arm and exploded in his chest. Unable to draw breath, he dropped to his knees.

The ogre turned to him and sneered. "Let us hope the bard has a more impressive defense."

It seemed to Xander that the shaman was about to say more when the ashes of the morning campfire exploded into a burst of wildfire.

CHAOS RULED THE OGRE CAMP AS THE MUDTOE clan worked frantically to douse the flames. Off to one side of the camp, Cornflunk and one of his cronies were beating a smaller ogre for the crime of throwing a fatty joint of meat into the flame, but Mirdit had other suspicions about the fire's origin.

She seized one of the undead ogres and hurled him toward the flames. The creature stumbled through, tripped on a log and fell face down, lost in a renewed surge of brilliant flame.

Her nostrils flared as she sought the stench of roasted, rotten meat. Nothing rode the wind but the usual scent associated with decomposing ogres.

Not even, she realized suddenly, the smell of smoke.

She whirled toward Zarchoomi. "Get the wheel!" she spat. "Ready the warriors."

Her brother's red eyes narrowed. "Elfs," he said in disgust, suddenly realizing the true nature of the flame.

Zarchoomi began to roar out orders. The ogres left off their battle with the illusionary fire and began to gather up weapons. Three of them darted into the cave and took out a large wheel, such as might be used on a river ship. It had been mounted on a wheeled platform.

Mirdit gestured to the pair of ogres guarding the young Koada'Dal. One of them promptly balled his fist and hit the high elf below the ribcage, hard enough to lift him off his feet. Before the youth could catch his breath, the other guard backhanded him. The elf sagged to the ground, senseless.

His guards dragged him toward the wheel and tied him to it, limbs spread out wide. They gave the thing a spin and formed ranks behind. Two ogre warriors began to push the device forward, bearing it into battle like a macabre standard—or, more to the point, a shield.

The ogre shaman trotted over to Mirdit, shouting something about the fire being an illusion. A little late, the ogress observed sourly.

The shaman pulled up short, staring in bemusement at the spread-eagled elf. "What foolishness is this?" he demanded.

It occurred to Mirdit that the shaman's speech was only intermittently rough. At times, he expressed himself as well as she could, and that, in her opinion, was a matter of some concern. Cunning ogres she knew in plenty, but never had she met one who spoke as she did.

"That'll keep the elves from using arrows."

As suddenly as if her words had conjured them, elves

erupted from the emerald underbrush, daring the ogres to leave the clearing and pursue them into the forest.

"Elves?" the shaman repeated. "How did elves find us?"

Zarchoomi, who trotted up with an armload of weapons, pulled up beside his sister. "Elfs know everything happens in forest," he grumbled as he thrust a javelin point into the ground. "They talk to trees, maybe."

Mirdit shrugged, unconcerned. "Let them come. They won't risk killing the young Koada'Dal."

But the elves did not come. They did not need to, for the ogres suddenly had their hands full with a foe in their very midst. The undead ogres had turned on their living comrades.

"Only a necromancer could do this," muttered the shaman. "The elves must have one in their ranks."

Zarchoomi hoisted a javelin and hurled it with all his strength at the animated corpse headed their way. The weapon slid easily through half-rotten flesh and pinned the undead ogre to a tree. The creature's arms and legs continued to move as if its charge had not been interrupted.

The Mudtoe ogre grunted with satisfaction and turned to the shaman. "Elfs don't like death magic."

"I knew one, once, who was inordinately fond of it," the shaman said thoughtfully.

IN THE BUSHES BEYOND THE EMBATTLED CLEARING, Davin turned an admiring gaze to Cyntharia. "That was quite a diversion."

But the high elf shook her head, and her beautiful face

was troubled. "That was none of my doing. There is a necromancer with the ogres."

"If so, he's not a very loyal sort," the bandit observed.

"You have no idea," she said dryly. Her eyes widened as a new possibility occurred to her.

"Or perhaps," she said softly, "there is more than one necromancer with the ogres."

24

If You Can't Steal, Trade

DAVIN LEFT CYNTHARIA STARFLOWER'S SIDE AND circled around the clearing. No doubt Regren Steelforger would flay him for leaving his post, but Davin figured the high elf female could fend for herself.

He slipped quietly through the forest, stopping only to slice the throat of an ogre who'd knelt to pull an arrow from his boot. But he could conceive of no way to rescue the elves.

Nyson Impholder was obviously beyond reach, and Davin couldn't get to Elizerain without charging through a small melee of undead ogres. Between Davin and the captives was Trobe, unfettered and unguarded.

The wretched dwarf was pacing, as if eager to join the fighting. Davin noted that, and his eyes narrowed as he remembered the ballad Elizerain had sung about the coming battle and the dwarf's treachery. An icy heat began to kindle in the bandit's breast, and to his surprise, he recognized it as wrath. It had been long years since he'd felt any emotion stronger than pleasure or self-preservation. But a dwarf, working with ogres? That just wasn't right.

Davin's fury gave birth to a new idea. He looked about for a stout stick and crept closer to the pacing dwarf. At just the right moment, he leaped from the bushes and whacked the treacherous little bastard right between the eyes.

Davin caught the dwarf as he fell and slung him over his shoulder with all the care he'd lavish on a sack of dung. He sent a loud, ringing raven-call soaring over the battle to signal retreat and set off at a trot for the meeting place he and the elves had decided upon.

If the orcs wanted their guide back, they'd damn well have to trade for him.

REGREN STEELFORGER GAZED DOWN IN DISMAY AT the bruised and bloodied dwarf lying at his feet.

"Why did you do this?" he demanded.

Davin the Dark folded his arms and glared. "He's selling out his own kind to the ogres."

"Trondle Ogrebane? That's absurd. His lifework is to rid the Butcherblock Mountains of ogres!"

Davin toed the dwarf. "Maybe so, but this one's name is Trobe."

The wood elf warrior threw up his hands in exasperation. "You can hardly expect him to announce himself and his intentions to all and sundry. His true identity and purpose are hidden, known to only a few of Faydark's elves."

Davin glanced at Cyntharia Starflower. She was sidling carefully away from the group, and the expression on her beautiful face confirmed his suspicions.

"Including her?" Davin demanded, pointing at the retreating enchanter.

The high elf stopped and met his gaze with a faint, superior smile. "Of course. The elves are not the only people concerned about rumors of an alliance between the dark elves of Neriak and the orcs of Crushbone."

"Teir'Dal allying with orcs? That's ridiculous."

"Not so," Regren said gravely. "Even as we speak, Ambassador D'Vinn, an envoy of Cristanos Thex, Queen of Neriak, resides in Crushbone. We have received confirmation of it from an agent of our own."

Davin glanced back to Cyntharia. "Since you know this dwarf, I'll bet you're eager to talk to him. He's been to Crushbone, and he might know a few things about evil alliances the elves might want to hear."

"I know of him," Cyntharia corrected. "We are not personally acquainted."

"About time to remedy that, wouldn't you say?"

The elf hesitated, and her gaze darted toward the stirring dwarf. "I see no real purpose in it."

"No reason to avoid it, though, is there?"

By now the wood elves were starting to look curious. Cyntharia's chin lifted, and her blue eyes met Davin's challenging gaze squarely.

"No reason at all."

A groan from the dwarf drew all eyes from the high elf enchanter. When Davin glanced back, she was gone.

FROM HIS ODD VANTAGE POINT ABOVE THE BATtle, Nyson listened with satisfaction to the sounds of chaos in the ogres' ranks. After the battle faded away, his captors left him on the wheel, apparently forgotten, for a long time as they tended their fallen. It was difficult to keep up the pretense of senseless stupor, especially while the ogre shaman went about animating the newly slain. The day was nearly spent when the ogres remembered Nyson. Rough hands cut the ropes tying him to the wheel and dropped him unceremoniously to the ground.

They hauled him to his feet and dragged him back toward the other prisoners. Nyson didn't have to pretend to stagger, because long hours tied in a highly uncomfortable position had left him stiff and awkward. His unsteady progress drew jeers and taunts from his captors.

Just as well. The ogres were ready to kill him for defending himself with a small spell. Dawnwalker or no, he'd be dead before nightfall if the ogres suspected that *he* had been the source of the confusion in their undead ranks.

The other elves had fared worse than he. Elizerain had cut her head where she struck the tree, and Xander's left hand had been reduced to bone. The ranger was obviously in terrible pain, but he refused to let Elizerain retrieve her healing spell, for doing so would reveal her singing sword.

Nyson glanced toward the patch of sky over the clearing. The sun had passed its zenith and disappeared into the western canopy. Before too much longer, other secrets would be revealed. When that happened, the three of them might have to fight their way out. Without Xander, they wouldn't have a chance.

"Let the Songmistress heal you," Nyson urged the ranger.

"That can wait," Xander said, speaking through pain-gritted teeth. "The elves captured Trobe. Mirdit wants him back, of course, and she has agreed to a trade. The three of us for him."

The high elf settled back on his heels, startled and pleased by this news. That would resolve everything except—

Except the reaction of his fellow elves when night fell and his new, dual nature was revealed.

Before the full impact of this thought could settle in, an ogress stumbled into camp. As she was the only female other than Mirdit, her arrival caused considerable stir.

The ogre sow spared not a glance to any of the males, but came directly to Mirdit. "I have a message for you from Ambassador D'Vinn," she said in clear, cultured tones.

Nyson's head snapped toward the speaker. Her voice was familiar and very, very dear. It was too cruel that he would hear his beloved's voice reflected in this monster.

Even as the thought formed, the ogress's shape began to melt away. In her place stood Cyntharia Starflower.

Cyntharia, alive!

Nyson's heart leaped with joy, and he started toward her in a glad rush. Then her eyes met his, and something in them stopped him cold. Only then did the full impact of her words strike him.

I have a message from Ambassador D'Vinn.

The world spun around him, and he went to his knees. He sensed Cyntharia's approach, heard the whisper of silk as she knelt beside him. Her arms slid around him, and her sweet breath brushed his cheek as she leaned close to his ear.

"Turning undead ogres—very impressive," she whispered. "It's a shame to waste such potential for dark magic, but if your mother will not rouse herself to rescue you, perhaps she can be goaded into taking revenge!"

Pain and grief and shame and fury raged through the young elf, yet in some corner of his mind he noted the setting sun and the familiar pain of his approaching death.

Cyntharia had not quite finished taunting him. She stroked his cheek as one might pet a favorite cat.

"I'm truly sorry, my pretty youngling, but I'm afraid you've grown too powerful to live."

Nyson felt the change come over him: a bone-chilling, soul-deep cold that thickened his blood and slowed it to a crawl. His breath stopped, and his air-starved lungs screamed in protest. He was dying, yet there was a paradoxical sense of coming alive. His senses sharpened, and his muscles hardened into something more than mortal flesh.

"Too powerful to live," he echoed softly. "You are more right about that than you could possibly know."

He slowly raised his eyes to hers, watching as the realization of what he had become washed over her face in shifting waves of shock, wonderment, and terror. Then he leaned into her mocking embrace, and his lips sought her throat for one final, deadly kiss.

ELIZERAIN WATCHED IN HORROR AS THE HIGH ELF female disentangled herself from Nyson's embrace and walked into the campfire. For many moments the camp was in an uproar as the ogres tried to pull her from the flames. But this time, the fire was no illusion.

Nyson came over to the other elven captives and sank down beside them. His shoulders slumped, and the hood of his cloak fell forward to shield his face.

The bard found herself at a most uncharacteristic loss for words. She cleared her throat. "Did you—"

"Yes, I compelled the traitor to go into the fire," he

said softly. "She was dead when she went into the flames. A mercy, perhaps, she did not deserve."

Xander's gaze flicked from Nyson to Elizerain. "Have I missed something?"

"That was Cyntharia Starflower," Nyson said softly. "I thought she could do no wrong. I thought her dead. Obviously I was mistaken on both counts."

The ranger leaned forward. "Was she with the rescue party?"

"I believe so, yes."

Xander slumped back. "If the elves know she betrayed them, they will also know that she could betray Trobe. They will never make the trade."

"She didn't say anything about Trobe to Mirdit," Elizerain pointed out.

"They cannot know this, and not knowing, they would not send Trobe to his death."

"They might not have a choice," Elizerain said hesitantly.

Xander frowned. "There is always a choice."

"Not if it's taken out of your hands." She drew a long breath. "Davin came after me. He's with the elves. If he wants me back, he'll find a way to make the trade."

Xander was silent for a long moment. "And you only see fit to tell me this now?"

She lifted her hand to the back of her head, where her thick hair was matted with blood. "What with one thing and another, the right moment never quite came up," she said. "And for that matter, you've no room to talk about keeping secrets."

"I have made vows," he reminded her. "And the secrets I keep are not likely to bring harm to others."

Xander's gaze dropped to her hip, where her sword

rested, still cloaked in Nyson's invisibility spell. "Only bards of great power can earn a singing sword. By carrying one, you made a promise you cannot keep, and you put young Nyson in great danger."

Elizerain's jaw dropped. "Who led whom into Crushbone?"

"Be that as it may," Xander said, "but his mother, thinking you were what you presented yourself to be, entrusted him to your care. She knew I would follow him, yes, but she also understands the implications of the sword you carry. She thought she was sending her son in the company and care of seasoned, powerful adventurers."

Elizerain turned away from the accusation in his eyes. "I didn't steal the sword, if that's what you're asking."

"However you acquired it, carrying a singing sword makes a statement your skills do not support." Xander fell silent for a long moment. "Is there anything else I should know?"

Elizerain glanced at Nyson. The young elf averted his eyes, but not before she saw what there was to see. He was too proud to ask this favor, even silently.

"I've told you all my secrets," she said at last.

"But I," Nyson said quietly, "have not. It was I who turned the undead ogres against each other. I have acquired some small skill in the art of necromancy. Cyntharia was my tutor, and she insisted that I inquire into all schools of magic. As you have no doubt surmised, it was she whom I followed to Crushbone."

"She lured you there," Xander said slowly. "She gave you into Mirdit Smallplague's hands. The ogress knew who you were all along, which is why she kept you as a hostage."

"While Cyntharia obviously thought my mother would empty Felwithe and Kelethin to rescue me." The young elf paused for a small, ironic smile. "I am strangely glad to discover that she was wrong."

"How broad was your training?" Elizerain asked abruptly. "Do you know much about shamanic magic?"

"A little," the elf admitted. "Why?"

"Can shamans command the undead?"

Nyson thought it over. "I'm not certain. Why do you ask?"

"Next time you can do so without drawing attention, look at the ogre shaman's eyes. Only once have I seen that particular shade of blue."

"The necromancer?" asked Xander.

"Chanzoon Nexis," Elizerain confirmed. "The necromancer who cursed me."

"The Songmistress no longer needs to fear the curse," Nyson said softly. "She knows the truth of the harp. And if you had heard the ballads she sings, so would you."

Xander's face, already haggard from pain, drained of color. "The Dawnwalker," he murmured. "A creature of two natures, awakened by the voice of the blood red harp."

Despite the gravity of their situation, a smile burst over Elizerain's face like a sunrise. "I didn't think you listened to my songs."

The ranger waved this aside. "Of course I do. I heard them all, every word, but only now do I understand. Chanzoon Nexis wishes to become the Dawnwalker."

"He is too late," Nyson said as he reached for the hood of his cloak.

But Xander's good hand shot out and seized the

young elf's wrist. "Don't," he said quietly. "Remember what I told you about the value of a hidden weapon."

After a moment's hesitation, Nyson nodded.

Xander knew, Elizerain realized with a jolt of surprise. He understood what Nyson had become and didn't condemn him for it—or her, for her part in it. Her gaze caught Xander's, and what she saw there made her forget their quarrel.

He glanced down at her hip and the singing sword hidden there. "I was wrong in chiding you," he admitted. "I have been wrong about many things, but why did I doubt that magic was yours to command, when I've always heard it in your songs and seen it in your smile?"

"If I didn't know better," Elizerain said slowly, "I'd think you were courting me."

"I'm not worthy of that honor, Songmistress. Whoever last wielded the sword you carry, I doubt they were half the bard you are."

Elizerain blinked away sudden tears. "But I still remember all those bawdy ballads," she promised him. "And since the necromancer *did* curse me to make sure my songs ring true. . . ."

The ranger's pain-twisted face managed a tiny smile. "Indeed. Perhaps I might let him live, after all."

She returned his smile with one of her own, one that was warm and sweet and full of promise. For once, Xander did not turn away from the silent invitation.

"YOU GOT TO SEND ME BACK!" ROARED TROBE.

"Are you so eager to die?" demanded Regren Steelforger. "We don't know what the Koada'Dal traitor told them. It's too big a chance."

Trobe folded his arms. "Maybe so, but it's mine to take. Do you want yer kin back, or not?"

"Of course we do, but we'll not sell your life in trade."

"What good is a life, if the life*work* goes undone?" Davin asked. "Let's consider this from the dwarf's view. If the ogres don't have Trobe to lead them to the dwarven outpost, they have no reason to gather their forces into one place. If there's a chance that Trobe could destroy the rest of the Mudtoe clan and most of their hired fighters in a single blow, he's got to take it."

"What he said," the dwarf said, eyeing Davin approvingly.

"Besides," the bandit went on, "you boys have a fight of your own ahead. Wouldn't you rather be in Faydark, protecting Kelethin from the orcs? The dwarves can take care of their own."

"Again, well said," Trobe said stoutly. "Send me back, and let's all of us get on with our affairs. And after, we'll all meet in halls of Kaladim to drink to our victories."

The thought of seeing with his own eyes that fabled dwarven stronghold, that hoard of gold and precious gems mined from the Butcherblock Mountains, brought a warm glow to Davin's heart and a smile to his face.

The dwarf snorted. "Smile like that around my kin, and they'll likely make you turn out your pockets before you go."

Davin burst out laughing, for what seemed the first time in years. "Get Elizerain back for me. That's all the treasure any man could want or need."

25

To Each His Own

As the long hours of night dragged on, Chanzoon Nexis stumbled along at the end of the ogre column, seething with frustration. He had been helpless to stop the trade of the bard and her blood red harp—and all the power they promised—for a worthless, treacherous dwarf.

The odious little fellow was setting a brisk pace through the forest, one that Chanzoon was hard-pressed to meet. His borrowed form might look long-legged and strong, but in truth he was a man, smaller in frame and strength than the ogre he appeared to be. He was more accustomed to books and scrolls than the rigors of a hard march, much less the battle that would come at march's end.

He waited for his chance, then ducked into the underbrush and all but held his breath as the sound of the ogre army faded into the north.

Then he followed the magic that would lead him to the blood red harp.

Closer and closer he came, the magic luring him like

an elusive melody. When he was certain he was almost upon her, the night shadows stirred, and a pale, golden figure stepped into a spill of moonlight.

The necromancer stopped dead, staring in horror at the silent high elf standing before him. He recognized the young Koada'Dal who traveled with the bard, the elf known as Nyson Impholder . . . and yet it was *not*.

Chanzoon knew the undead, and he immediately grasped the reality of the creature before him. And with that realization, his dream of dark glory shattered.

"There can be only one Dawnwalker at a time," the youth said, putting words to the necromancer's loss.

Chanzoon's whirling thoughts seized the possibilities in this statement and swept away the immobilizing sense of despair.

"So be it," he said. "Let us see who learned best from our sadly departed Cyntharia, for it would appear we had a teacher in common. And perhaps," he added slyly, "a lover as well?"

The young elf actually hissed at him, revealing the long, slender fangs that would disappear with the coming of day. "Whatever she might have been, you aren't fit to touch the dust from her footprints."

"And you are?" the necromancer taunted. "We are much alike, we two, but with one important difference: *I can command the undead.*"

Chanzoon began to intone the words to a terrible spell, one that would compel the elven Dawnwalker to tear out his own eyes.

But as the first syllable left his lips, a new surge of magic flared up around him, and the bright, sharp pain at his throat cut off his words and his breath.

A garrote, he realized, feeling the wire tighten and dig

into his flesh. The magic that poured from it left no doubt as to its nature.

"The string you added to Rain's harp," Davin the Dark's gloating voice confirmed at his ear. "I thought you'd come looking for it, and I've got to tell you, I'm a man who takes great satisfaction in being right."

Frantic for air, Chanzoon tried to dig his fingers under the wire. But it was drawn too tight, and his fingers came away wet with his own blood. He reached over his head and clawed wildly at the hands that held him, but Davin was a big man and powerful, even without the added strength that came of hatred and a lust for revenge.

Suddenly Chanzoon remembered the compulsion curse. Despite what he'd told Davin, the curse remained. All he needed to do was recall it.

He poured all his formidable will into the task. Slowly the pressure at his throat eased. The necromancer fell to his knees and rolled away, gasping for breath. The sound of Davin's sword dragging slowly, unwillingly from its sheath was sweet music to him.

Davin the Dark advanced on the young elf, slowly, as if he were walking through water and battling a strong current. The compulsion dragged him forward, but he fought mightily against it. His face was red with exertion and twisted with rage and denial. Tendons stood out on his neck like exposed tree roots. Chanzoon almost had to admire the man's tenacity.

A faint growl came from the bandit. A moment passed before Chanzoon realized that Davin had spoken a single word. It sounded suspiciously like, "Thirsty?"

"As a matter of fact," the Dawnwalker said coolly, "I am."

The elf advanced in a sudden flash of gold and blue.

Before Chanzoon could speak a single word of a spell, a new pain—sharp and exquisite—struck his ravaged throat.

Oddly, his next response was not terror, but exhilaration. The harp's distinctive hue came from the pure blood of Mayong Mistmoore, and those the Dawnwalker slew partook of the dark lord's lineage. Chanzoon might not become the Dawnwalker, but he would rise a vampire.

It was a death he could embrace.

Chanzoon waited for the fabled ecstasy to enfold him. Instead there was a sharp, savage tearing. The Dawnwalker darted back as quickly at he'd attacked, and Chanzoon sank to the ground, one hand clamped to his torn throat.

The young elf spat out an unspeakable mouthful and wiped the back of one hand across his lips. He accepted the flask the bandit handed him and tossed back a long draught. This he spat out as well, this time in the direction of the dying necromancer.

"On the whole," the elf said as he eyed Chanzoon with distaste, "I find shipboard rats rather more palatable."

Davin the Dark came to stand at the youth's side. He folded his arms and cocked his head as he regarded the man who had enslaved him and cursed his Elizerain. "I can't think of anything that would add much to that. You sure he won't come back long-fanged and thirsty?"

"Quite."

The bandit smiled and pulled a stout stake from his belt. "If it's all the same to you, I'd like to make sure.

"Besides," he said softly as he dropped to one knee beside the necromancer, "it's about time I started settling my own debts."

WHILE DAVIN AND NYSON HUNTED CHANZOON Nexis, the rest of the band gathered to tend their wounds. Apparently their rescue had released Xander from his vow of secrecy, for he and Regren Steelforger openly discussed the coming battle between the orcs and the elves of Faydark. And since their meeting place was also the site of a magical gate, as soon as Nyson and Davin rejoined them, they would be whisked across Faydwer and into yet another battle.

Elizerain was pleased to see Geminar Wolfsong, the half elf bard who'd helped her in Kelethin, among the warriors who'd come with Davin. Geminar brushed aside her thanks and offers of future favors.

"There are no debts between us," he said firmly. "I will long remember your kindness to me that night."

She gave his shoulder a quick squeeze and went to check on Xander. She'd cast the healing spell on his hand not once, but three times. It looked nearly as good as it had before the necromancer's attack, but it was still stiff. Try as he might, Xander couldn't move the fingers.

Finally Elizerain shook her head. "You can't fight this way."

"I can," he insisted. "Shape my hand into a fist. As long as I can hold a bow, I can fight."

His gaze shifted to the gate, where elven warriors were disappearing into a swirling halo of multicolored lights.

After a moment's hesitation, Elizerain did as he asked. Xander strung his bow and took an experimental pull, nodding with satisfaction when his left hand held tight.

"Time to go," Regren said, beckoning for them to enter the gate.

•

The two wood elves stepped in together and emerged into deep forest shadows. Dawn had not yet broken, but already Faydark resounded with the roar and clash of battle.

For just a beat or two, Elizerain stood frozen by the enormity of the conflict. She'd been told that the Emerald Warriors had been leaving Kelethin for days, letting any watching orc scouts believe they were headed westward, only to circle back and hide among the trees. And in Felwithe, the guard had done the same. She had no idea there were so many warriors in the elven cities. The clatter and clamor of swords, the trampled underbrush, suggested many hundreds of elves scattered about the forest.

And the orcs! There weren't half so many in Crushbone! Where had they all come from?

A hurled warhammer spun toward her, breaking her stunned reverie. Elizerain dived and rolled aside, coming up with her singing sword in her hand.

Orcs, at least eight or nine of them, began to close in on her and Xander from three sides.

The glint of flashing gemstones caught her eye. Nyson was fighting his way through to them, his jeweled sword moving with preternatural speed.

Xander launched the first of his arrows, taking one of the orcs through the throat. Elizerain took position at his back, sweeping up her sword to meet the downward slash of an orc's steel. A trail of faintly glowing blue notes marked her blade's passage.

As she caught the descending sword she spun on her back foot and kicked out hard, aiming for the orc's leather codpiece. The brute uttered a high-pitched shriek and dropped to the ground, where he curled up in agony.

"Elizerain, what are you doing?" demanded Xander.

She sputtered in exasperation and darted forward to hamstring the orc who was closing in on Geminar Wolfsong. The orc she'd felled started to rise, so she kicked him again for good measure.

"I'm no warrior. Dirty is the only way I know how to fight."

"Not that," the ranger said, "*this*."

To demonstrate his meaning, he fired off three arrows in quick succession—so rapidly that Elizerain's eye could hardly follow the movements. An orc centurion fell slowly forward, like a great tree toppling. Xander's three arrows had found their marks: one in each eye, the other transfixing his throat.

"Keep fighting," the ranger urged her. "Your sword is lending speed to the rest of us."

A sense of wonder filled Elizerain like soft, warm light. Chanzoon Nexis, whatever else he might have done, had spoken one truth: she was no fledgling bard, but a Songmistress of considerable power.

Later, she'd consider the implications of that.

Elizerain ducked under the sweep of a rusty axe and came up in a lunge. Her sword found a gap in her attacker's leather armor. Blue notes flowed down the sudden spill of blood, and winked out when the orc fell face-first into the puddle.

She palmed the ground with her free hand and found a fist-sized stone. As she rose, she flung it at one of the orcs fighting Nyson.

The stone caught the orc right on the bridge of his nose, just under the heavy ridge of bone. The orc's piglike eyes crossed, and he slashed out wildly, accidentally cutting one of his own comrades. The injured orc roared and whirled toward his fellow. Nyson left them to settle matters on their own and sprinted toward a new opponent. Elizerain noted with satisfaction that, thanks to her sword, the mortal Nyson moved just as fast in daylight as the Dawnwalker would after the sun set.

And so it went, throughout the long day, until no orc stood within sight. But the sound of muffled fighting drifted through the deepening shadows, and Regren Steelforger motioned for his Emerald Warriors to gather.

"Most of the orcs will be in retreat. We should hunt down as many as we can before they reach the safety of Crushbone."

"Let's get to it, then," Elizerain said. Xander and Nyson echoed the sentiment with firm nods—probably, she noted, because they were too weary to speak.

"No, your part in this is done," Regren said sternly, addressing himself to Xander. "If you are ever to regain use of that hand, you need rest. In fact, all three of you do. It did not escape my notice that you three fought twice as fast and hard as nature intended. The magic of the bard's sword is powerful indeed, but there's a price to be paid for such exertion, and none of you is immortal, even though young Nyson, like all between-age elves, might think he is."

Regren noted the wry, bitter smile on Nyson's face and thought he understood its source. "I suppose you've heard that said more than a few times. Most young elves have, and with good reason."

"Indeed," Nyson said softly. He drew himself up and gave the older elf a low, respectful bow. "I thank you for your counsel, Captain Steelforger. We will do as you suggest. Good hunting to you."

Regren clapped Nyson on the shoulder, then turned toward the east. He took off at an easy run, and the wood elf warriors fell into step behind him.

After the clatter of battle, the forest seemed unnaturally quiet. But only for a moment: Faydark could not long be denied. The chirp of bird and insect began anew, and the forest creatures began to stir as they prepared for the coming night.

Nyson covered his face with both hands and slumped against a tree.

"Go," he murmured. "It's coming upon me again, and I'll have to hunt soon."

"We can wait," Xander said softly.

The high elf dropped his hands, revealing a face twisted with despair and streaked by the blood red tears that spilled from his eyes.

"To what end?" he demanded. "What possible place can there be for me? I can't return to Felwithe, not as I am."

Silence hung between them, as heavy as the night mist that drifted down from the canopy.

"I, for one," said Elizerain slowly, "have always wanted to learn some dwarven ballads. Goddess knows, a single one could keep me occupied for days. And we could pick up songs along the way! You might find that enlightening, Nyson. According to tavern ballads, maidens are enthralled by dashing, tragic heroes."

A reluctant smile twitched one corner of Nyson's lips, and a spark of hope lit his blue eyes. "I heard we have an invitation to Kaladim. I think Trobe suspects my . . . dual nature. Perhaps he will help smooth the way."

"As will we," Xander promised.

The young elf sighed. "Still the bodyguard, I suppose."

"You need the harp," Xander said softly, his eyes on the bard. "While I, it would seem, need the harper."

Elizerain grinned. "I knew you'd come around, but I don't mind saying that it took you long enough!"

She was about to say more, but the ranger swept her into his arms and silenced her with a kiss.

"You won't be sorry," she promised, when at last they paused for breath. She cocked her head, considered, and then amended it to, "At least, not more than once or twice a day."

The wood elves did not notice Nyson slip off into the forest. The need to hunt was imperative and the thirst a burning, terrible thing, yet some of the despair had lifted from the young elf's heart.

There were worse fates, he supposed, than a life of travel, adventure, and music, and far worse companions. Elizerain would always be seeking new tunes and stories, and Nyson didn't doubt she would find plenty of trouble along the way.

His own path was far from certain, but such companions as these would make the journey worth taking. Perhaps, in time, he would be ready to face his family and friends and let them know what he had become. Perhaps there might yet be a place for him in the service of his people.

And according to Elizerain's tavern ballads, maidens were enthralled by dashing, tragic heroes.

Nyson's sad smile broadened into a grin, and suddenly his unbeating heart felt lighter.

Perhaps Elizerain, he mused, was not the only one who had reason to seek the truth of old tales.

Epilogue

For as long as he lived, no matter what other marvels his eyes beheld, Davin the Dark knew he would not forget the victory feast hosted by King Kazon Stormhammer of Kaladim.

The dwarf stronghold was not at all what Davin had expected. The tunnels of Kaladim were surprisingly comfortable—warm and dry, broad and tall enough to make Davin feel oddly at ease. The taverns were cozy, the shops plentiful and full of finely crafted items.

Kaladim's palace was a marvel of riches and workmanship. Beautiful mosaics graced the floors, and the long tables in the feasting hall gleamed with gold and silver plate and cunningly designed tankards. It was all Davin could do to keep from slipping pieces of cutlery into his boot. And the high-heaped platters of food held the most inviting fare he'd ever beheld. Dwarves, it would seem, took cookery as seriously as they did any of their other crafts.

His boys would have loved this, Davin thought, but alas, the Greenleaves were no more. The last anyone had seen of Grib, he'd set out to follow Davin westward.

Two of his men had been caught up in the fighting between the elves and orcs of Faydark. His own part in the battle had brought him to the keen attention of Kelethin's Emerald Warriors, and the search for Greenleaf hideaways had become a favorite elven occupation. All things considered, Davin thought it best to disband.

Wood elves, he noted sourly, had a lot to learn about gratitude.

His gaze shifted to the trio of elves seated at a place of honor. Gratitude indeed! After all the trouble he'd gone through to rescue Elizerain, she could barely spare a glance in his direction.

Someone began to thump a tankard on the table. Others took up the chorus, until the great stone hall reverberated with a sound like war drums. Several moments passed before Davin understood what that signified: Trobe—better known to his kin as Trondle—was making his way up the aisle that separated the two long tables, striding toward the small head table where the dwarf king and his high advisers sat. The rhythmic thumping, Davin surmised, was the dwarven equivalent of applause.

Apparently Trobe had not had an easy time of his battle with the ogres. A bandage swathed his left hand. One eye had swollen shut, and a new scar stretched across one lividly bruised cheek. He walked slowly, with a distinct limp, but there was a smile of great satisfaction on his face and a large hemp sack slung over his shoulder.

He made his way to the king's table and dumped the contents of the sack on the floor. The hall fell silent as three large heads rolled out.

King Kazon rose to his feet. "These would be the Mudtoe ogres you been hunting?"

"Zarchoomi and Cornflunk," Trobe confirmed. "Seems they've ambushed and roasted their last travelers. The third one was Mirdit Smallplague, the ogre sow who started this recent trouble."

"Well done." The dwarf king smiled and nodded toward one of his advisers. "Never thought the day would come that someone collected the reward Byzan Bloodforge keeps promising."

A tall, broad-shouldered dwarf wearing a gorgeous vest of fish-scale armor rose and looked Trobe up and down. "Looks like I'll have to cut the Bloodforge armor down a mite, you being so skinny and all, but I'll have it done for you by the time yer beard grows back, no worries."

"Don't bother," Trobe said stoutly. He swept one hand in a broad arc to indicate the feasting hall. "Now that I'm back to home, I'm feeling a mite peckish. Should be back to size in no time."

The king threw back his head and laughed, clearly pleased by the dwarf's comment. "Then set to, old friend."

Trobe settled down in the indicated seat of honor and began to pile his plate with great enthusiasm. His kinfolk followed suit. Apparently, Davin noted dryly, the severed heads on the floor had little effect on the collective dwarven appetite.

The feast went on for many hours, with much telling of tales and singing of songs. Elizerain shone at both, when she was not laughing and talking with her two elven companions. Davin noted the bonds between the three of them, especially between his Rain and the wood elf ranger.

His Rain no longer, the bandit noted wistfully.

A stubby forefinger prodded him in the shoulder. Davin turned to regard the hero of the day.

"Elves are heading off come morning," Trobe announced. "Suppose it's for the best."

Davin managed a smile and shrug. "You're probably right."

"This thing is far from over," the dwarf went on. "The orcs took a setback, but they're like rats—there's always more a-coming. And once dark elves get an idea in their head, they don't let go of it easy. We'll be hearing more from the Crushbone and Teir'Dal alliance."

Trobe paused, then added significantly, "Might be we Kaladim folk could use a few allies of our own."

"You're asking me to stay on?" the bandit asked incredulously.

"Hunt ogres, collect bounty." The dwarf shrugged. "There are worse ways to pass the time."

Davin lifted a hand to the stubble on his chin. "I suppose it would give me an excuse to grow a beard."

Trobe snorted. "More like an excuse for a beard."

The companionable insult brought a slow smile to Davin's face. "Anything I should know about dwarven attitudes toward stealing?"

"Yeah. Don't get caught."

The dwarf chuckled at the dumbfounded expression on Davin's face. "Why do you think we're wanting you to stay? The halls of Kaladim are full of right-thinking, law-following folk. If war's coming, you got skills we might be needing."

It made sense, and it felt right. Even so, Davin's gaze shifted to the elven bard for a long moment.

"I never heard of dwarves employing the likes of me. But not all tales find their way into a ballad, I suppose."

"True enough," Trobe agreed. A broad grin split his battered face. "But just to be on the safe side, I won't tell the elf lass you said so."